High Praise for **BROKEN MIRROR** by Cody Sisco

"Sisco has created an immersive cyberpunk world as the setting for an elaborate murder mystery and conspiracy thriller; the copious amount of worldbuilding detail is truly impressive. Victor is a relatable hero with eclectic friends in Ozie and Elena... The world and the characters work together to effectively form a cohesive story about how easy it is for society to classify a group of people as dangerous outsiders. A fantastic science fiction thriller with a sincere and important message."

—*Kirkus Reviews*

"An empathic, sensitive, and gripping alternate history, cassette future, bio-hacking techno-thriller that will keep you page-turning to the end."

—Matthew Kressel, Nebula Award-nominated author of *King of Shards* and *Queen of Static*

"Cody Sisco swings for the fences with this ambitious alt-history look at addiction and mental health in a world where all should be well but is most definitely not. If this is just the start, it will be a treat what comes next!"

—Sherri L. Smith, award-winning author of *Orleans* and *The Blossom and the Firefly*

"Victor Eastmore is an unlikely hero who we immediately root for. His constant struggle for some sort of normal existence is distressing, and his journey to find who murdered his grandfather is an intense roller coaster ride, but we gladly take the ride with him. Broken Mirror is an exciting and fascinating look at a society that fancies itself evolved almost to perfection but, in reality, is as broken as some of its inhabitants."

—Frank Castelluccio, author of short stories in *RFD Magazine*, *Made in L.A. Vol. 4*, and *Avalon Literary Review*

"Cody Sisco's *Broken Mirror* daringly plays with time, geography, science, and language with breathtaking results. Set in an imagined recent past, in a rear-ranged world with brilliant medical advances, equally brilliant new weapons, and recreational drugs, nothing is what it appears. In its unpredictability, it feels like negotiating an ominous funhouse filled with sunlit dread. *Broken Mirror* is a consistently absorbing thrill ride full of scary but satisfying twists and turns."

—Manuel Igrejas, author of *Imaginary Boyfriends: Short Stories*

"Cody Sisco crafts a world rich in adventure and intrigue, as *Broken Mirror* takes us to the future to confront corporate greed, tech regulation, and stigmas around neurodiversity, all while weaving a t̶ ̶ ̶ ̶ ̶ ̶ ̶ ̶ ̶ ̶ ̶ ̶ ̶ ̶ ̶ ̶ ̶ ̶d to know ourselves."

—Kate Maruyama, author of   ctive

D1736450

"Cody Sisco's *Broken Mirror* is a queer alternate history in which Victor Eastmore flees across a reimagined but recognizable America, determined to prove his grandfather had been poisoned. Victor is compelling and sympathetic, but he is hobbled by a potentially violent psychological condition he struggles to control, by allies whose true motivations are often at odds with his own, by a family who would rather see him institutionalized, and by the larger conspiracy targeting people like himself. The world of *Broken Mirror* is thoroughly realized, and as readers learn more about its history and where its timeline branched off from ours, the more they learn that Victor's paranoia is entirely justified. Sisco's novel is tightly plotted and wildly inventive, and it explores the ways stigmas against mental illness and addiction can be weaponized for profit and control."

—Michael Kiggins, author of *And the Train Kept Moving*

"With *Broken Mirror*, Cody Sisco questions our reflex to blame the human condition on those who are deemed as 'other.' This murder mystery set in an alternate history that feels all too close to home searches for truth amidst abuse of power and the silencing of unconventional minds. Rich with themes of mental health, racism, gender and sexual identity, this first installment of the Resonant Earth Series is a vibrant and sexy ride."

—Allison Rose, cofounder of Made in L.A. Writers, author of the Tick Series, and the upcoming memoir *Of Course I Love You*

"Cody Sisco's expansive worldbuilding presents a dystopic vision of a fractured America that feels all too depressingly real. Cryptic hackers, tangled loyalties, and family secrets make *Broken Mirror* a high-tension read."

—Cynthia Zhang, author of *After the Dragons*

"*Broken Mirror*, Cody Sisco's well-paced and entertaining debut novel, didn't show any first-book jitters. Drawing readers in with compelling, captivating, and well-thought-out characters like Victor Eastmore and Elena Morales, this thriller and murder mystery set in a sci-fi world centers on a mysterious mental illness. The book and plot rush through zigs and zags with sex, romance, death, and a notebook of wild dreams. Sisco proves a talented writer, leaving readers wanting to crack open the next book as well."

—David Fitzpatrick, author of *Sharp: A Memoir* and *Wolf-Boy*

"A poetic and often tragic narrative about social stigma, wealth, and a troubled young man looking for a future in a society that shuns him. Cody Sisco's *Broken Mirror* resonates with anyone who has ever felt lost and confused and yet resilient."

—Sara Chisolm, author of short stories in the Made in L.A. anthology series

"Cody Sisco has created an alternative reality in *Broken Mirror* that holds engaging characters, amazing action sequences, and a mystery that will have you reaching for the sequel as soon as you reach the last page. Highly recommend!"

—Gabi Lorino, author of *A Magical Time Called Later*

BROKEN MIRROR

BROKEN MIRROR

[signature]

CODY SISCO

RESONANT EARTH PUBLISHING
LOS ANGELES, CA

Resonant Earth Publishing
PO Box 50785, Los Angeles, CA 90050
resonantearthpublishing.com

Second edition: August 2024

Library of Congress Control Number: 2024906740
ISBN: 978-1-953954-07-7 (paperback)

Author photo by Nate Jensen

www.codysisco.com

FOR ALL THE GHOSTS' FAVORITES

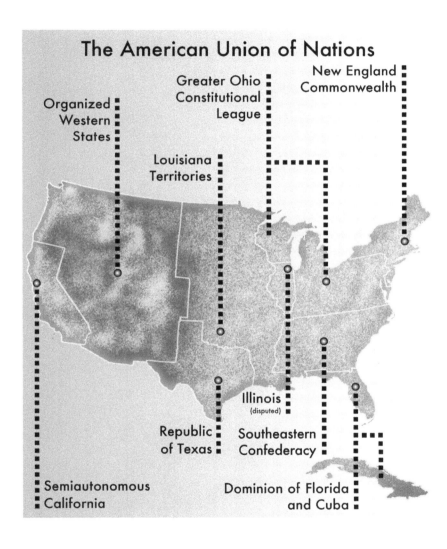

The American Union of Nations

Organized Western States

Greater Ohio Constitutional League

New England Commonwealth

Louisiana Territories

Illinois
(disputed)

Republic of Texas

Southeastern Confederacy

Semiautonomous California

Dominion of Florida and Cuba

1

A new universe called to me, and I answered, ignorant of the harm in crossing over.

—Victor Eastmore, *Apology to Resonant Earth*, (transmission date unknown)

Semiautonomous California
29 February 1991

It's one thing to die quietly with things left unsaid among family members. It's another thing to do what the great Jefferson Eastmore did with his secrecy and architecture of conspiracy: keep essential truths from Victor and put him on a collision course with an uncanny future.

Victor gazed across City Lake toward the tessellated foothills, where the elite families of Oakland and Bayshore kept their hedges trimmed and thorny. His grandfather's sarcophagus was up there, surrounded by marble pillars and gold-gilt fencing shaped like twisted strands of DNA. A tidy and neat brick gravemound would never have sufficed, since at the end of his life, Jefferson was as grandiose as his cancer-curing career. The stones were plucked from the canals of New Venice, and a plaque listed the man's many accomplishments. Not listed was his failed effort to cure Victor of mirror resonance syndrome.

Victor spun around to face the city skyline. The morning was bright and windy. The timefeed on his MeshBit indicated thirty minutes until his reclassification appointment. He could go and wait in the anteroom, but his anxious vibrations might shake the building to its foundations.

He took a breath. No going back. Before the sun reached its zenith that day, his path would materialize. If he were lucky, he could stay a Class Three: free but under close supervision. Or he could become a Class Two: under guard, imprisoned, at a rancho in the hinterlands. He whispered a cherished but inconsistently effective mantra to fight off brain blankness: *The wise owl listens before asking who.* Each episode of blanking out was one more step toward mirror resonance syndrome's inevitable tragic end: becoming a comatose Class One, insensate, a forgotten ward of the government. The only unknown factor was how quickly the future would crash against him.

He trudged along the shoreline, tensing and relaxing his jaw, trying to distract himself. Glittering towers rose exultantly city-side. Squally breezes swooped out of a cloudless, azure sky and assaulted bulrushes, sedges, and cattails in the shallows where a grid of waterplots penned them in.

Granfa Jefferson had been poisoned. Victor knew it. He had proof. But his family didn't believe him, and if he said any more about it, he would be locked away. Fair? No. Surprising? Not really. After all, his life was a farcical succession of tragedies. It wasn't time to give up, though. Not while he had unanswered questions.

The palm trees encircling the lake rustled like cheerleaders shaking their pom-poms. The water rippled, creating countless sun flashes on the lake's surface, and afterimages glowed and pulsed when he closed his eyes. The stench of goose shit turned his stomach.

He wedged the MeshBit's detachable sonobulb in his ear, then called Elena. She answered right away. This was not the first time her promptness was suspicious.

"See?" she said. "When a friend calls, you should answer. Right away. Not never."

"I know. I need your help," he said. "My appointment is here. I'm having trouble."

"Where are you?" she asked.

"City Lake. West shore."

"I can't get there in time."

You were there for Granfa Jeff's funeral. You showed up at my apartment whenever you wanted. Why can't you be here now?

"Then talk to me," Victor said. "Anything to keep my mind off my theories about Granfa Jeff."

At the time, Victor had nothing close to the truth about Jefferson's secret messages and plans for conspiracy and counter-conspiracy. He couldn't have guessed his role in the proliferating conflagration that would transform every person on Resonant

Earth and beyond. No one could have predicted the neuro-contagion that eventually radiated beyond the American Union of Nations, or the mind-machine hybridization that became humanity's destiny, or the fact that crossing over to another world would become a possibility rather than paranoia. If Victor had guessed any of it, he might have failed his reclassification deliberately and shown up at the gates of a rancho to check himself in. All this was a lot to have piled onto a mentally unstable young adult.

"But you found radiation on the data egg," Elena said. "I believe you. We're going to figure this out."

Her confidence gave Victor warm tingles, but the timing was all wrong. *Murder bird, murder bird—those aren't the words I need right now.* "Let's talk about anything else. Please, I'm desperate. As usual."

Elena's recent return to Semiautonomous California had helped him, even if something felt off with her sometimes. And right now, he was feeling supercharged, like his world hinged on every movement, every word, and the right shift in thinking could set him free, if only he could figure out what that might be.

She took a breath. "I think you should leave SeCa."

Although the bioconcrete path beneath his feet was firm, he was unsteady, as if balancing on a tightrope swaying in the wind.

"If I don't show up, they'll reclassify me in absentia. I could never come back."

"Why would you *want* to come back?" Elena asked. "They treat people with mirror resonance syndrome like criminals. You haven't done anything wrong."

Victor paced toward the lake's edge. Crowds of lotus leaves floated, looking sad without their blossoms. "Remember when we talked about moving to an island? I said we could stargaze all night."

"And I would make a pie out of real coconut flesh. Yeah, I remember. A wish is a lie, Victor."

Elena was right. He couldn't afford to dream. Until he found a cure, his blanking episodes made him a danger to everyone.

She went on, "Without mentioning the thing you don't want me to talk about"—he had no doubt she was rolling her eyes as she said this—"I will say that after what you told your family, I think you leaving SeCa isn't such a bad idea."

Static came through the sonobulb, like a cotton ball pressed too deeply into his ear. His parents, granma, aunt, and cousin all thought he was losing his mind. They might be right, but why couldn't they just *listen* for once? His stomach ached as he remembered the disbelief, disappointment, impatience, and the hint of fear on their faces—ugh, the memory was a knife twisting in his guts. It was good that the Personil was dulling his emotions; without it, he'd be lost in a storm.

He checked the screen on his MeshBit and tensed—only a few minutes until his appointment.

Leaving wasn't a solution. It wasn't. He cleared his throat and said thickly, "No matter where I go, I'm still, you know, *me*. If I go blank here, people know what to do. Out there … I don't know what would happen."

"No. The good people of Semiautonomous California aren't lining up to save you. SeCa is the problem. It's the good versus evil Cathar mindset. Other places are different. You can get away from discrimination. Away from surveillance. There's no future here for you."

Victor sat on a bench facing the lake, closed his eyes, and smashed his fists together. She was saying he could go somewhere the Carmichael laws couldn't reach him: the sandy beaches of the Southeastern Confederacy, an island within the Dominion of Florida and Cuba, or maybe a cabin in the mountains up north at the border between the Louisiana Territories and First Nations of Canada. But if what Ozie had said was true, that other nations were passing laws based on SeCa's, soon there would be no place truly free for people like him. Maybe leaving would buy him some time. Maybe that would be enough.

"It's that different elsewhere?" Victor asked.

Elena said, "People in Texas think a broken mirror is seven years' bad luck."

He barked a laugh. A nearby jogger did a double take at the sound. "I've never thought of myself as a bad-luck charm. At least seven years is better than a lifetime."

She sighed. "Texas is wild. Everyone is fighting all the time. The government is barely functional. It's chaos, but it's not oppressive. I don't know. I can't explain it. Maybe you should see it for yourself."

Cody Sisco

She was rambling, like old times. She was finally warming up to him again.

She wouldn't have killed Granfa Jeff. She had no reason to. She wasn't a killer. Oh yes, she'd returned carrying secrets, but an Eastmore murder wasn't one of them.

His MeshBit pinged, and his heart suddenly pounded. "I have to go."

Elena spoke rapidly. "Don't let them trick you. Not all the questions are going to be fair."

"How do you know?"

"I've been asking around. Try to keep calm and rational."

"As opposed to psychotic and homicidal? I'll do my best."

Victor discontinued the feed, took the sonobulb out of his ear, reconnected it to the MeshBit, and tucked it inside his pocket, where it bumped against the slightly radioactive data egg that was somehow supposed to save him from being locked up. He exhaled loudly, then walked toward his reclassification appointment.

2

The workers Victor passed on his way through the business district were the lucky ones. Employment came easy for SeCa union members, whereas he was reliant on the Classification Commission's Safe Places program and his family's influence. That hadn't stopped him from trying to join, of course, but the union recruiters hadn't even acknowledged receipt of his application. "It must have been lost," they told him when he confronted them about his third submission. It probably hadn't helped that his granfa and the unions had feuded for decades. And no one wanted to work with someone like him—unreliable, possibly dangerous, at risk of going blank on the job.

He was crossing the street when a horn blared and brakes screeched. The sounds hit him with the force of an explosion. He dropped to his hands and knees, heart thudding, his vision splotched by yellow haze. He covered his ears. The resonant effect faded marginally. He looked back and saw a woman clutching a small child. One meter away was a silver car, a new Erbeschlitten. Smoke billowed from its wheel wells.

A near miss. Nothing to do with Victor. No reason for his pulse to be thumping behind his eyes. Sensitivity was the most aggravating consequence of MRS; anything could set him off. He was a harp, his strings so tightly wound a breeze could play a chord and make him resonate.

The woman didn't dare cross in front of the car, whose driver was rocking in his seat like a jockey on a horse. He raged incoherently at her, and then the car sped away. Probably a stim addict—the only group vying with Broken Mirrors for the bottom level of the social hierarchy.

Victor took a few breaths to calm down. It would do no good to show up for his appointment ready to explode.

He entered a ten-story modern ziggurat that filled the entire block. An elevator took him to the sixth floor. Brass plaques lined an endless hallway of doors. He followed signs to Dr. Santos's office.

Victor wished this evaluation could be performed like all the previous ones: by Dr. Tammet at Oak Knoll Hospital, with Granfa Jeff nearby to encourage and calm him. But with Oak Knoll closed, Granfa dead, Dr. Tammet gone, and the Health Board calling the shots, there was no going back. No choice but to see this new doctor.

Victor stepped into the small reception room. Two faces turned toward him then snapped back to their reading material: other MRS patients, maybe. They shifted in their chairs and avoided eye contact. Victor was glad; there was enough anxiety bubbling inside him without adding their fear to the mix.

On the far side of the room, a young receptionist sat in a cabinet-sized alcove, separated from the room by a thick-glass window. She scrutinized Victor as he approached. A sonocircuit embedded in the glass allowed him to speak his name to her. In a flat, uncaring tone, she told him to take a seat and wait his turn.

The chairs and tables were made of hard plastic. A steel door with no handle led, presumably, to the doctors' offices. This setup was nothing like the cozy, familial atmosphere of Oak Knoll. He felt pinned down by all the precautions and suspicions. The men pretended not to notice him. Resonance, barely perceptible, like a low hum, tinged the air with anxiety and fear.

Victor sat and flipped through a magazine, stopping at a feature article about a dispute between Semiautonomous California and the New England Commonwealth. NEC-Automation, the biggest robotics company in the AU, wanted to build a factory in SeCa. Opponents accused them of establishing a beachhead to repeal SeCa's Carmichael-induced ban on autonomous vehicles. Members of the SeCa legislature called it an example of a "resurgent imperial mentality." They trotted out the Carmichael deaths as well. He wanted to care about these things, patterns in the world, the ebb and flow of history. But he felt insulated, maybe due to the Personil again. Or maybe he couldn't care about anything except the next hour of his life and the many dangerous mental pitfalls he had to carefully avoid if he wanted to pass the examination. It was sad how limited his emotional range was—sad but necessary.

The man with the crew cut coughed and wheezed, and the other man was still, his eyes closed in strained meditation, even when the sound of the Erbeschlitten's horn filled the room. Neither of the men flinched, though the horn sounded again and again. Of course, the resonant echo was only in his own messed-up brain.

Not now, please!

A low rumble reverberated in his chest. His vision started to blur and double as his heartbeat skipped and fluttered along with a rush of adrenaline. *It's starting. Oh, shocks, oh no …*

Two worlds resonating; lines going fuzzy, colors blending. Blankness scrambled his perceptions and put a lick of euphoria on the tip of his tongue. He tried to keep some perspective. *I'm lucky; if my brain was wired differently, going blank could feel like drowning or being lit on fire, like in my dreams.*

Elena had told him he had nothing to worry about, but the fumewort was wearing off, and he hadn't dared bring any vials of tincture with him. He ran his hands over his thighs, counting long breaths despite the galloping panic in his chest, but Dr. Tammet's motion and breath exercises weren't up to this challenge. This would be a routine exam, required by law, with the power to decide if he should be locked up forever. Victor gripped the data egg in his pocket. Before he died, Granfa Jeff insisted that Victor took the data egg to his next reclassification appointment and that it would help. *How?* Ozie had told him the same thing—that the data egg would help—and that Granfa Jeff had been assassinated, no question about it.

No—he couldn't think that. Not until the appointment was over.

Victor held up the magazine, trying to redirect his unsteady mind. It was futile. He doubled over and rested his chin on his fists, unable to hold back a tide of worries. He shouldn't have to contemplate exile. The American Union had rooted out racism through Reconstruction and the Permanent Enlightenment. A majority of people in SeCa and the other nations of the AU could trace their ancestry back through lineages that a century ago would have been called white, black, and red. Victor sometimes imagined having darker or lighter skin rather than his mid-tone brown, but there wouldn't be any real-world consequences to such a change. *Skin is* skin, everyone said, and racist institutions and systems had been overturned throughout the AU. Why couldn't they do the same with the stigma around mental illness? *No one is captaining the boat, that's why.* Reconstruction had led to Repartition, from USA to AU, and now the nations of the American Union were only a flotilla of loosely connected vessels, adrift in the doldrums. One day, they'd break free of each other and head in different directions.

It was a useless game imagining different histories, yet he couldn't stop himself. His dilemma was a historical peculiarity resulting from cascading bad decisions that landed on the backs of a small percentage of Semiautonomous California's citizens. Someone could have stopped Samuel Miller, the Man from Nightmareland, as four-year-old Victor had called him, and prevented him from destroying Carmichael. Or Mía Barrias might not have survived to demand that SeCa lock up as many people with MRS as could be diagnosed. What if the response to the syndrome had been entirely different? Maybe Alik wouldn't have picked the fight with Victor that ruined both their lives. Jefferson Eastmore might have cured MRS, instead of shutting down the project. He could have lived, instead of leaving this mystery at Victor's feet. The world didn't have to be the way it was. That was what was so frustrating—things could have turned out differently. Why, Victor often wondered, was he stuck in a world that hated and feared him?

He stared at the magazine, blinking back wetness in his eyes. He gave up trying to read it. Leaning forward, he asked the other patients, "How long have you been Class Threes?"

The man with a crew cut, who looked to be in his late twenties, looked up sharply. He glanced at the receptionist and said in a low, wavering voice, "One year."

They could have sampled him for an employment application, driver's license renewal, or child custody battle. More and more interactions with the SeCa bureaucracy included a DNA swab and screening for the MRS gene.

The other man, older and pudgy, eyes still closed, shook his head.

"How about you?" Crew Cut asked quietly.

"Eleven," Victor whispered.

The older man's eyelids flew open. Crew Cut's gaze was piercing. Their scrutiny and awe were unwelcome. Victor felt no pride in his longevity as Class Three. It was out of his control.

Cody Sisco

Crew Cut cleared his throat. "I recognize you now. The Eastmore."

"What about you?" Victor asked the older man.

The older man blinked and licked his lips, listening to their discussion. He'd said nothing. His meaty limbs and neck seemed to belong on a different torso, as if specific dimensions had been compressed and other parts inflated—a balloon made of flesh accustomed to being squeezed. They all were, in a way.

"Come on," Victor said encouragingly. "They can't stop us from talking."

The man returned a puzzled expression. "But I'm not. I'm not a Broken Mirror. They called me yesterday. Said I had to come here for an evaluation. It's all a misunderstanding."

Red wine-colored splotches formed on Crew Cut's face. "How do you think it works?" he asked. "You think they politely ask when you might check into the asylum? It starts as an appointment, and your life is never the same." He sat back, crossed his arms, and stared up at the light strips.

Victor's cheeks flared hot. The danger people with MRS posed couldn't possibly account for the indignities they were subjected to. Ozie could be right. Something else might be going on—something his granfa had been killed for.

Victor shoved the thought away. "It hasn't always been like this," he said, hating the whine that crept into his voice. He'd been protected and coddled, but now that he was alone, he shouldn't be surprised everything was more brutal. "It's like an ever-tightening snare."

"You're right," Crew Cut said with bitterness. "We'll all be taken to the ranches eventually. Even you."

Elena's warning echoed in his ears. *Not all the questions are going to be fair.* "You must have had a couple of appointments so far. Have they ever asked you about Carmichael?" Victor asked.

Crew Cut's mouth dropped open. He looked away.

The woman called the older man to the door. He rose jerkily and, with a hasty glance at the others, staggered forward. The door slid aside to allow him to pass and closed behind him. Victor saw nothing of the other side.

"I heard that they started asking us about Carmichael. Is it true? Do you know?"

Crew Cut folded his arms again, a pathetic gesture of self-protection. In another world, Victor would want to reassure him, get him to open up, gently take his hands, wrap him in his arms, and find better ways to spend an hour together. Choices like that were for people with less pressing problems. Perhaps the Carmichael questions were baseless dark-grid conjecture. There was no point in dragging anyone, even people with MRS, through that hell. Ozie may have got it wrong.

The woman called out Victor's name, and the door opened. He stood and stepped forward.

The young man asked, "How do you manage it?"

Victor paused and tried a reassuring smile that felt more like a grimace. How could he explain years of therapy and hanging on by a thread? "Never surrender," he said. The door slid shut behind him.

3

At the threshold of a door with a blue, blinking light above it, Victor braced himself for a barrage of questions. He had completed years of coaching and therapy. He would pass. *Be polite. Be brief. Be normal.* He repeated the mantra under his breath as the door sprang open.

Dr. Santos sat in a high-backed synthleather chair behind an enormous wooden desk. His baby face was smooth, round, gleaming in the lightstrips' glow, and topped by hairs as wispy as spiderwebs. A typepad and flatscreen monitor were positioned within reach. Victor's records, he presumed. Now that Oak Knoll's records were gone, erased in Granfa Jeff's annihilating data purge, the files possessed by Dr. Santos would be the most comprehensive documentation of Victor's physical and mental condition.

"Empty your pockets and sit down, please," Dr. Santos said in a high voice. He gestured toward a bowl on a small table by the door. His vowels sounded slightly twisted, as singers sometimes contorted their words to make an odd rhyme work.

Victor swallowed hard as he moved to the table, thinking about the data egg. With a shaky, desperate sleight-of-hand, he transferred the data egg from his pocket to his underwear while appearing to fish out his MeshBit and place it in the bowl. Hoping his pants didn't bulge at the crotch too much, he approached and sat. The chair was deep and tilting, forcing him into a semi-reclined position, and the synthleather gripped his body. He felt he was about to be swallowed whole, like an insect caught in the flower of a pitcher plant. A tall cone-shaped lamp threw a bright circle onto the ceiling.

After a full minute of silence, the doctor said, "Victor Eastmore."

It didn't sound like a question. Though maybe it was a test. "That's correct, sir."

Dr. Santos looked up. "You should call me 'Doctor.'"

"Yes, Doctor." Already, this was off to a bad start.

Dr. Santos opened a desk drawer and placed a pyramid-shaped device on the table, twisting its top until the apex lit up green.

He began speaking. "This is a formal psychiatric evaluation under the Carmichael edicts of Semiautonomous California. This recording will be shared with the Classification Commission of the SeCa Health Board, to be used as evidence in the event of any legal challenge. Victor Eastmore, you hereby waive any potential claims against me, including damages and harm that may result from my determination of your status. Say, 'I agree.'"

Polite. Brief. Normal. Don't forget to breathe.

Dr. Santos leaned forward and waved a hand at Victor.

"Uh, yes, I agree."

Dr. Santos rose from his chair and walked behind Victor. Suddenly, a low hum surrounded him, tingling his skin and blurring his vision. The chair was generating an electromagnetic field—another set of data to feed to the authorities.

"What is that?" Victor asked. "That feeling?"

"Hmm? Oh. This chair uses an array of Dirac-monopole active-resonance sensing units to sample your neurological activity."

"Sounds like shockstick tech," Victor said, suppressing the urge to jump from the chair.

"Nothing of the sort! Let's get started," the doctor said, returning to his seat. "I've reviewed your records. You were diagnosed in 1979. You have a history of violent behavior, lapses of judgment, and fugue states, the most notable being two years ago on the National University campus in the spring of 1989. To be honest, you're fortunate to be a Class Three. I probably wouldn't have made that call, but—let's see." He paused for a moment to read the file. "Dr. Tammet documents your progress in mood stability, impulse control, and interpersonal communication. However, her license to practice medicine in SeCa has lapsed. Her entries in your record are no longer valid."

Victor tensed. Could evidence supporting his continued Class Three status be swept aside so easily?

Dr. Santos said, "In any case, I'm not sure any progress in your outward behavior will impress me sufficiently if the underlying neurobiological condition has deteriorated. We'll see."

The hum of the chair surrounded Victor, oscillating and thrumming. It felt like bees swarming around him.

Cody Sisco

"Well?" Santos asked.

"Um, I'm not sure what the question is."

"Should you be a Class Three—"

"Yes," Victor answered. "I'm making progress—"

"Excuse me. I don't like being interrupted."

"But—"

"The question"—Dr. Santos paused, glaring—"is whether you should remain Class Three, meaning you are safe to be out among the public. Tell me about your medication."

"Personil," Victor said. He closed his eyes. When he opened them, bees were swirling around his head, humming loudly in his ears. The air started to fill with gray smoke, ebbing and flowing in concert with the scanning chair's fluctuations. The sensations were far more substantial than his usual synesthesia; they seemed tangible, palpable, real things in the real world rather than artifacts of his brain's processes.

"And? It says here Dr. Rularian prescribed one fifty-milligram pill twice per day."

Victor focused on Dr. Santos's words. Personil every day: that was the official story. "Personil was supposed to help me maintain emotional equilibrium."

"*Was?*"

Victor thought better of saying, *You know, before I threw the pills down the toilet.* He scratched his arm; the buzzing and smoke irritated his skin. He pictured scales forming in the cells of his epidermis, a noxious pus oozing from between them.

"That's what Dr. Rularian told me. That Personil would make me feel stable," Victor said, but he suspected that Dr. Rularian must have known it was a lie. Personil provided numbness, not stability. Was a lie told to counter another lie equal to the truth?

"Have you had any episodes or outbursts in the past ninety days?"

"No." He scratched his arm again, trying to relieve the itching. Could Dr. Santos have seen footage of the scene at the funeral? He could tell the doc that it wasn't an outburst; it was a vision, but that would get him locked up immediately. A trickle of laughter tickled his throat. He coughed it out.

"Loss of memory?"

"No."

Dr. Santos steepled his fingers and pressed them into his fleshy neck, creating dimples like the buttons constraining the fabric on the synthleather chair. "Irritability? Mania?" he asked.

Victor tried to determine whether his throat was as swollen as he perceived it to be. Swallowing with difficulty, he said, "No. To both questions."

"How does the medication make you feel?"

Victor blinked and breathed. "Calm." His voice hummed discordantly with the chair's buzzing. He interlaced his fingers and let his hands sit heavy on his crotch, pressing where the data egg was hidden. Physical sensations kept anxiety and delusions at bay—so Dr. Tammet had always said. She also noted that *imagining* being calm was the same as *being* calm, but her words seemed irrelevant in moments like this. He focused his gaze on the midpoint between his knees rather than the eyes peering at him from behind round lenses, still visible through thick gray smoke.

Dr. Santos picked up some papers and examined them. "Are you taking any other medication?"

All the saliva in Victor's mouth dried to paste. Did he forget to fill a prescription? Or did Dr. Santos suspect about the tinctures?

"Does my file say I am?" Victor asked.

Dr. Santos dropped the papers onto the desk. "I asked you a question."

"No, Doctor. I'm not taking any other medication." *I am your polite patient, your faultless apprentice, your very normal minion. Let me dance for you, Doctor!*

Dr. Santos rose, walked around his desk, and tried to perch on its edge, but it was too high. He settled for leaning against it. "You are working at a biotech firm. Part of the 'Safe Places' program. Tell me about your job."

"I manage computing resources to run DNA analysis for Gene-Us, Ent—I mean, BioScan, Inc. There was a merger. Recently."

"That sounds like a highly technical position."

I am an information wizard! Victor took a deep breath and tried to relax into the padded material of the chair. "I graduated university with high marks."

Dr. Santos cocked his head. "I'm asking about your work, not your education."

"What is the question?" Victor exerted pressure on his jaw to keep his teeth from grinding together.

Dr. Santos scowled. "Young man, it's in your interest to cooperate. Your future depends on it. I'm trying to help you. Tell me about your job. How is it working out?"

"I like it." What else could he say? *Think!* "I like the challenge. It's my job to make the computations as efficient as possible. I'm good at it."

"With whom do you interact? How many people are in your group? Do you get along with your coworkers?"

Victor tensed, trying to keep the questions ordered in his mind. It helped to physically imagine them floating in space, to his left, straight in front, and to the right. Unfortunately, smoke wafted distractingly past them. Left first: with whom did he interact? "My supervisor runs the sequencing operations. Her name is Karine. She's—" But the doctor hadn't asked about his supervisor per se. "I interact with her most often." He cleared his throat and moved on to the next question at the center. "There are eight sequencing data engineers, including me."

Finally, the question of how Victor got along with his coworkers hovered—he had to tell a delicate lie.

"I get along with most of them."

"Most?"

He couldn't tell the doctor that he'd almost gotten into a fight several times and that Sarita, in particular, had been the subject of numerous murderous fantasies—harmless stuff, if he wasn't suspected of harboring psychotic tendencies. "They tease me sometimes. They call me names. A few of them do."

"I don't care about their behavior. I care about yours. How do you respond?"

Dr. Santos should care about them. They were the ones who caused problems; he would do just fine if they left him alone.

"I ignore them. I try not to hear what they say."

"That's not a good response. Someone with your condition must always consider your surroundings, social cues, and speech. You can't hide from your problems; you must confront them."

That didn't make any sense. Victor's entire strategy for dealing with his condition was to cut himself off from the world and keep it from affecting him and, as importantly, to keep his confused inner life from seeping out. "You want me to tell them to stop calling me names?"

"I didn't say that! You need to confront your problems. Your coworkers can do whatever they like. But your entire brain has short circuited; it moves too quickly to anger and violence. You have to be honest with yourself. Notice how you react emotionally.

Experience the emotion, and then let it go. It's a matter of self-control."

That made a little more sense, but Victor still thought Dr. Santos didn't really understand him or his condition. "Dr. Tammet taught me to manage my emotions."

Dr. Santos laughed. "Advice from a discredited therapist is not going to help you." He moved behind the desk, sat, and took up Victor's file again. "Tell me about your dreams."

"What?" Victor gulped. They had never asked about his dreams before. He hadn't told any medical person about them. Not the doctors at Oak Knoll. Not Dr. Tammet. Not even Granfa Jeff. He'd only ever told Elena. Dr. Santos couldn't have known about them.

"Your dreams," the doctor repeated.

Was this a standard question now? He couldn't describe his dreams to Dr. Santos. He would be locked up for life.

The doctor continued, "Your sleep patterns. Any nightmares? Narcolepsy? Insomnia?"

"I used to have trouble falling asleep, but the Personil helps." This was somewhat true. The medication helped him fall asleep, usually during meals. He'd had nightmares of drowning in a bowl of soup more than once.

"So, nothing else about your sleep to report?"

Victor shook his head.

"Hmm." Clearly skeptical, the doctor pressed his lips together. "There's a new part of the procedure. Bear with me—it's not typical of most psychiatric evaluations. Listen to this statement, and then tell me how it makes you feel."

Dr. Santos read a detailed account of the events in Carmichael from when Victor was four. It started with the months Samuel Miller spent secretly setting fire traps and explosives throughout town, each one equipped with a quantum trigger. The account included Mía Barrias's testimony to the Classification Commission about what she saw the day he triggered them all, the day of her honeymoon: the fires, the autonomous vehicles programmed for murder, the bodies, including her husband Claudio's, who were victims of Samuel's modified shockstick. The sleeping smoke drifted through town so that Samuel could round up the stragglers and execute them. Victor listened with a sinking feeling in his gut. He'd lived through the carnage, surviving the day by being locked inside his house, alone and afraid: afraid the fires would burn him up, afraid his missing parents were already dead, afraid that the man he'd seen in his nightmares would find him and kill him. The account Dr. Santos read aloud wasn't merely words; they were tortured echoes, gateways to the past. Even the vidfeeds they played in school weren't this graphic.

Then Dr. Santos began to read the transcript of the semi-incoherent statement recorded by Samuel Miller explaining how his actions were meant to create a bridge between two universes.

Two! Victor shivered. The number occupied a strange territory in his brain. Sometimes the number seemed like a gateway to deeper meaning, a flavor of a strange mystery that begged to be tasted, savored, and investigated. Dr. Tammet said his feelings about the number two were another example of counterproductive pattern-seeking, a mirage to be ignored.

What was Dr. Santos saying about Samuel Miller and crossing over? Why tell him this? The bridge-between-worlds theory was as fanciful and speculative as trolls under bridges demanding tolls. No rational person would believe it.

Dr. Santos completed the Carmichael account. "What is your response to that?"

Victor said, "I don't have one." It had nothing to do with him. A memory best forgotten.

Dr. Santos frowned. "You feel nothing?"

His heart pounded. Blanking out right now would be sweet oblivion. "No. I mean that I'm not responsible. I'm not him."

"Victor, listen carefully. The Carmichael edicts ensure what happened there will never happen again. You—like Samuel Miller—have been diagnosed with mirror resonance syndrome. Unless you can prove that you are not a danger, it's in the public's best interest for you to be sequestered for a very long time, maybe forever."

Dr. Santos leaned back in his chair, breathed in, and let the air out slowly. "Now that you understand the question, please state your response."

Victor sensed the field surrounding him as a vibration, a little beyond the limits of his perception. All his words, expressions, gestures, and brain activity fed a data storage matrix somewhere, encoding him for classification. And the data egg—what was it doing?

The doctor was waiting for a response. What if he answered incorrectly? What if his brain had already answered for him?

He looked at the recording device. There had to be a reason to record his answer. The stupid question must mean more than he'd realized. And Dr. Santos was giving him a second chance to answer it.

Victor spoke each word carefully. "He should not have done what he did. It was wrong. He was ... he was wrong. I hate him."

Dr. Santos nodded. "I have to say, for someone with your pathology, I'm impressed you've been living unassisted this long. However, given your past behavior, I'm not inclined to agree with your present classification. Unless the statements from your employer or the brain scans convince me otherwise, I'm afraid you'll be downgraded to Class Two and moved to a ranch in Long Valley, where you'll receive proper care. My office will be in touch with our determination within the week. If it were up to me, my conclusion would be immediate, but the law requires us to be thorough. In any case, you may as well pack up your things. The enrollment process, once underway, can be quite ... brisk."

As Victor drew in a breath to object, the humming of bees returned and reached a crescendo. The world was blotted out by swirling gray dust that solidified in the air like quick-setting cement. Dr. Santos rose from his seat and turned off the brain scanner. A buzzing became silence. Victor got up stiffly, collected his items from the basket, and moved to the exit, his surroundings twisting back into normalcy.

Dr. Santos waited for Victor to pass through the door and directed him down the hall. Victor took swift steps toward the exit and into the elevator, where he transferred the data egg from his underwear to his pocket stealthily. Seconds passed like hours and vibrated in his chest. Finally, he passed into the sunshine and fresh air, but despite the warmth of the sun, he shook while he waited for the shuttle bus. Throughout the journey, people on the bus stared, but he couldn't stop the shaking, which continued long after he arrived home, rushed into the kitchen, and poured ten vials of fumewort tincture down his throat.

4

Victor and Elena drove along the Bayshore road and then cut inland to the expressway.

I'm doing it. I'm really leaving everything behind. And she's coming too.

Skyscrapers glittered in the moonlight. Forested hills formed silhouettes against the silvery sky. Ohlone Hill stood apart from the others like a duckling that had wandered away from the brood.

Oakland & Bayshore's northern border grew closer. Topped with razor wire and floodlights, the capital wall came into view.

Guard posts were situated along the wall, a structure which extended into the bay shallows for half a kilometer. On the other side of the wall, a tent city sprawled in the marsh flats, a chaotic jumble of narrow, jagged lanes and rickety shacks. Cooking fires flickered. This mess of humanity was unbroken from the shoreline to the wide viaduct of roads skirting the Bayshore hill—the elevated expressway.

Victor slowed the car in advance of the security checkpoint. The lanes narrowed, and dividers rose. He and Elena were waved through at once. The checkpoint was intended to prevent refugees from entering the Bayshore region, not leaving, but passing unquestioned was still a relief.

They crossed the arc of the Bayshore Narrows Bridge over the channel of water that marked the northern border of the Bayshore region. They could see the boats, which carried lumber, rock, and other materials west toward the open bay. Emerging onto a moonlit plain, Victor kept checking the rearview mirror to make sure they weren't being followed.

After about sixty kilometers, Victor took a turnoff that degraded to a gravel drive and then a dirt lane, a little-used route between one field of desiccated alfalfa and another. He pulled behind a tree and turned the car around so that he could speed back to the highway if necessary. No vehicle could approach them without being visible for at least a half mile.

They reclined their seats and shared a single thermal blanket.

Victor's sleep was fitful. When the sun rose, he started the car, jolting along the road. Elena woke up after the first few bumps.

In a thick, sleep-slurred voice, she said, "Let's find a town so I can get a few things. Toothpaste. Some clothes. An air freshener."

The SeCa Long Valley stretched around them. For a brief span in the seventies, the combination of good soil and a burgeoning workforce of impoverished refugees wrought a green miracle. It enabled SeCa to feed its own and export to other nations. Then, the eight-year drought came. The snowpack vanished from the mountains. Streams slipped beneath the gravel and clay. The Long Valley baked and hardened. Many starved. After eight years, the rains returned with a vengeance, though snow was still a rarity. On a clear day, it was possible to look across the plains and see the Sierras, but today, the gray haze hid everything except monotonous scrublands and dwindling Long Valley farms. It was flat, empty, and desolate—the dried-up core of Semiautonomous California.

Elena grimaced. "Reminds me of the Republic of Texas," she said.

"What's it like there?" Victor asked. "Besides looking like this, I mean."

"Rotten." She didn't elaborate.

They reached a small town where delicatessens, fruit stands, and bric-a-brac shops lined the street.

Elena pointed. "Stop there."

Victor parked along the main road. On either side, small shops leaned into their wood frames. Elena disappeared inside one, while Victor found a bakery that sold breakfast sandwiches and faux-café. He paid, waited a few uncomfortable minutes under the smiling gaze of the gray-haired proprietress, collected his order, and took it outside.

Egg and pork smells escaped the bag, and his stomach rumbled, but he resolved to wait for Elena to eat. It would be time for his morning dose of Personil on a typical day. He reminded himself to drink a tincture before they resumed driving.

He found a concrete plaza with shrubs and flowering orange poppies in planters, leading to a small grassy area. A few parents tried to corral their running, screaming children. Wearing large sun hats, an old couple sat on a bench and watched the world go by. Several people squatted next to blankets on which cheap devices, books, and kitchen supplies were laid out for sale. Buildings painted bright pink and green surrounded the plaza, but their metal downspouts were warped and blackened with soot and scorch marks.

A wave of dizziness came over Victor, and he closed his eyes. Someone bumped into him, and he lurched forward. The bag fell from his hands onto the ground. Grabbing the person to keep from falling, Victor came face-to-face with a middle-aged man with a pinched, weathered face. Wiry black hair ringed a large bald patch on the man's head.

"Watch where you're going!" the man said, pushing Victor away.

The world was spinning. Victor leaned forward, hands on his knees to steady himself. "You ran into *me*."

The man grabbed Victor by the shoulder. "What did you say?"

Pressure built in Victor's face. Blankness flowed into him. He couldn't tell left from right. "Leave me alone!" he said.

The man sneered. "You're a Broken Mirror, ain't ya?"

Victor began whispering Dr. Tammet's calming mantra. *The wise owl listens—*

Victor felt a shove in his chest and a sense of falling as blankness took him.

5

The situation stank, and Elena didn't see a clean way out.

Steps away, water lapped at the rocks protecting the shore of Alameda Island from being reclaimed by the tides. The sole bridge in sight, connecting Oakland and Little Asia, barely rose above the water, looking ramshackle, like rafts bolted together and in danger of drifting apart. It was a clear night with stars twinkling and Venus lowering herself between the Golden Gate headlands' knees slowly, ever so slowly, to eventually dip into the salty ocean.

Elena sighed. Bayshore was unlivable, yet it was so fucking beautiful.

A message was on her MeshBit from Lucky and Bandit; they demanded to meet with her. She returned to her apartment and, as she waited for them to arrive, noticed she was chewing on a thumbnail. She stopped herself and swore loudly all the shitass phrases she'd learned in the Republic of Texas, and then swooped through the small, stifling, basic rental unit into the tiny, poorly ventilated bathroom to file down the damage. So, now she had a smooth thumbnail again, but the situation still stank.

Bandit and Lucky had seemed normal the first time they came to her. They were very professional in sheer-and-shiny navy-blue skintight clothes that showed off their obsessively maintained physiques. They set up check-in times to coordinate their schedules and keep track of Victor's movements, and everything was crystal clear and smooth. They claimed the Eastmores were simply putting money on the table to make sure Victor didn't get into trouble. They spoke about his boss, Karine, with a familiarity that would be hard to counterfeit. Elena had agreed to keep an eye on Victor because she believed everyone had his best interests at heart.

Working with Lucky and Bandit was just part of the job, as she understood it.

However, a string of coincidences thereafter made Elena second-guess everything. Victor had flipped out at the funeral and found evidence of radiation exposure. He'd become best buddies with an herbalist, who then disappeared. His reclassification got moved up. Ozie was back in Victor's life, and that was really bad news. And now Lucky and Bandit were on their way over on short notice.

The apartment's overloud buzzer made her jump, and then it buzzed again, and again. It was pissing her off. She rushed to the door and flung it open, ready to give them a piece of her mind, but Lucky zoomed in, trailing a sweet, cloying smokiness. Bandit was close behind, his eyes red-rimmed and wild, seemingly leashed only by taut and straining optic nerves.

"Why aren't you with Victor?" Lucky demanded.

Time slowed as Elena evaluated exactly how forthright she should be. The two svelte animals bounded through the small apartment with energy to spare, sniffing out their quarry.

"He's not here. Shall we go find him?" Elena asked sweetly.

Bandit threw Lucky a look that said he wouldn't mind if things got violent. "Were you with him last night?" He leaned against the door frame leading to the kitchen, then straightened up and started pacing.

Elena clocked it then, the problem, a new development. *Laws, this is a stinky mess.* Lucky and Bandit must be using some jazzy, sharp-edged substance that was poking and prodding them into delirious agitation. Either they weren't the professionals they pretended to be, or they had as tenuous a relationship to sobriety as she did.

"Last night, he went *across the bay*," Lucky said, with the kind of outrage only appropriate if Victor had torn a child limb from limb. She jabbed her finger in a direction Elena was pretty sure was not west. "You weren't with him. You weren't tailing him. You didn't warn us."

Elena swallowed what she really wanted to say and played it dopey, wide-eyed, and clueless. "He went to Little Asia? Why?"

Both Lucky and Bandit stopped, poised, about to pounce.

Elena didn't wait. She smacked her forehead. "I told you about his herbalist friend, right? Didn't I? He probably went to go see her."

The tension in their stances seemed to soften. They looked at one another, and Elena could have sworn something passed between them, maybe shame or fear or guilt.

Doubts began to gnaw. With their ties to the Eastmores, the two of them might have had an opportunity to poison Jefferson. They didn't seem like the type who could access serious contraband, like radioactive materials, but maybe they had connections.

Still, Victor said two people had kidnapped his herbalist—that could have been these two. And Elena hadn't signed up for kidnapping. She was done with that forever. Too stinky.

"Okay, you're right. I screwed up," she said. "I see how maybe I've been cutting him too much slack. I'll keep on it." She mimed tapping her MeshBit. "You'll get updates more often than you want. You'll get tired of hearing from me."

"Come on," Lucky said, already approaching the front door.

Bandit hustled to follow, was out the door, turned back, and said, "We want to know when he's awake, when he's asleep, when he's eating, when he's shitting, when he's wanking—Everything!" He slammed the door on his way out.

Semiautonomous California
3 March 1991

Now, standing alone outside a pharmacy in the tiny farm town of Gaobeidan while Victor bought them breakfast down the block, Elena held up her MeshBit with a voice-only connection. "We're in Long Valley," she told Bandit. She assumed Lucky was also listening. Like her, they said they were only trying to help Victor; a justification starting to wear thin.

Bandit said, "You shouldn't have let him leave Oakland." He sounded annoyed and gruff. During their first encounter, he'd been all smooth talk and charm, haloed. Now his horns were showing. "Where are you? Stay there, and we'll meet you."

Her back stiffened. She wasn't going to take any orders. Besides, Victor had to leave SeCa to save what he could of his freedom ... and his sanity. She could see him unraveling by the hour. "No. We're heading—I mean, we stopped. I don't know the name of the town."

She wanted some distance, some time to figure out what was really going on. To figure out if it was all simply paranoid contagion. It would help to talk it through with Victor, but would talking relieve his paranoia or ramp it up? She couldn't afford to find out. Her steadiness, her trustworthiness—the threads he had once hanged by—had snapped long ago and now existed only in his memory of her.

"You don't know where you are?" Bandit sneered through the sonofeed.

She gnawed on her lower lip, deciding how much truth to feed him. "Some dusty town in Long Valley. Victor wants to leave SeCa."

"We'll catch up before then, don't you worry," Bandit said, now sounding unconcerned. "Just don't let him go alone."

Elena paced along a strip of grimy gravel at the side of the road, making an orbit around the two bags of supplies she'd bought. A manure smell wafted from a field nearby. She didn't look forward to seeing them again; she was starting to dread it. "Tell me again exactly what your goal is here."

"Same as yours. To keep him safe. That includes keeping him safe from himself, which is going to be difficult until we bring him back to Oakland. You need to help us do that."

Shouting erupted from the small plaza where she'd left Victor. "I've got to go," she said, terminating the feed.

Elena pushed into a buffer of onlookers and spotted Victor. Bad situations arose wherever he went, yet he never stopped fighting, never gave up. He was the toughest person she knew. That's why it crushed her to see him this way.

He stood at the center of a crowd while a salt-and-pepper-haired man strutted and crowed around him, poking his stomach, flicking his ear. Victor slowly shied away each time the man prodded him but made no effort to evade the abuse. When she saw Victor's eyes—glazed and empty—she knew he'd gone blank.

Elena dropped the two wax-paper bags that held clothes, water bottles, and snacks for the road and elbowed her way forward as the crowd jeered and laughed at something. The man asked, "Should I?" He held his hand against Victor's crotch, saying, "Anyone want to see what happens?"

Elena felt heat in her face and charged at the man. Her velocity was enough to knock him on his butt. She tumbled to the ground too but got to her feet quicker. She hesitated. No doubt the man deserved a throttling, but that could cause a lot of problems. They were already doing a terrible job of remaining inconspicuous. She turned back and knelt next to the man and, reaching into her pocket, quickly pulled out a wad of dollars, and held the bills in front of the man's eyes. "You get this if you stand up and quietly walk away. No harm, no alarm. Tell all your friends gathered here too. Deal?" she asked.

The man grabbed the money. As he slowly stood, she pulled Victor away from the man and the audience. She sat him down and whispered his silly owl-and-cuckoo mantra. He began to blink and look around.

"He your pet freak?" the man asked, approaching them. Elena pressed her lips together and stared him down, and the few remaining gawkers until they turned away. His jabs didn't matter. She and Victor were leaving to fight another round.

Victor sat a few paces away, conscious again, blinking. "Why'd you pay him?" he asked. "What did I do?"

Elena lifted him by the elbow. "Nothing. Let's go." She hoisted her shopping bags and led Victor toward the car.

He planted his feet. "Tell me, Ellie. That wasn't spare change."

"Forget about it. Come on. We're still in SeCa, remember? We've got to keep moving."

"When did you come into some money?"

Elena paused. He didn't need to know that his family was paying for her companionship. Besides, she would have done it for much less. She wished she could explain it to Victor, but this wasn't the right time.

"I found a MeshCash machine on the moon minting books of cash," she said. "Be glad I've got lots of bills. Some of the places we're going to pass through aren't exactly credit friendly."

An itching sensation spread from her elbow to her fingers. She scratched her forearm and pushed the thought of stimsmoke out of her mind.

Victor hung his head. "You don't have to come with me, you know."

Elena moved closer and intercepted his gaze. Snark was always their first shared language, but this moment needed directness. "You're not getting rid of me. I'm in this. All the way."

"I'm not sure anyone can help." His shoulders drooped.

"Well, I'm sure for both of us. Come on."

They loaded the bags in the car, got in, and said nothing more. She wanted to ease his mind, but what could she say except "Perk up" and other inanities? His troubles were real and not solvable through idle talk and false positivity. Her deception wasn't helping either, so she kept silent, mostly, except when she couldn't.

"I'd feel more comfortable driving," she said as he started the engine.

He gave her a pained look. "I'm good now. I'm back. My blank outs don't come on *that* fast. I can feel them brewing. I won't drive us off the road."

She leaned against the headrest and turned her face to him. "You have my complete trust," she said, softly.

Victor navigated through town to back roads leading to the foothills. They stopped in the middle of nowhere and ate the now-cold sandwiches—bacon, eggs, and cheese on country bread. She could tell by how he listlessly nibbled his sandwich that something was bothering him. Which of any dozen of his problems was he chewing on?

They drove on. An orchard flashed by.

Elena's itching returned. She rubbed her thumb down the length of her arm, not using her nail, not wanting to tear the skin, knowing she'd have to scratch again and again and wouldn't feel relief for days.

A vista of hills—the grass and oak tress still green from winter rains—greeted them when they rounded a bend.

"Hey, Ellie, I was talking to Ozie—"

"Fucking Ozie?" she snapped.

He gave her a knowing, amused look. She and Ozie got along like two cats in a bag. *Two again*, this time accompanied by complicated feelings of attraction and repulsion. "Want me to go on?"

She sighed. "Might as well hear it," she grumbled. "Since you trust him so much without him ever earning it."

"He says there's a place we can go. He can help us cross into the OWS, but we have to sit tight. I think I have enough herbs to wait it out."

She looked at him. What would Personil withdrawal feel like? Nothing like stims, she'd bet. It was making her skin crawl. She ran her nails down her arm. The momentary relief was worth the next round of itching it provoked. "Herbs, huh? Instead of pills? That explains why you lost it back there," she said.

Victor sat a little taller. "They're helping me."

"Are you sure? It doesn't look like it to me."

"If I could control it completely, it wouldn't be a disorder," he said wearily. "They *are* helping. In fact, that reminds me ..."

He slowed to a stop on the side of the road, although for all the traffic they'd seen, he could have taken up both lanes without a problem. He dug into his bag. His hand emerged with two glass vials, which he tipped into his mouth and swallowed, grimacing.

"Smells boozy," she said wistfully.

He resumed driving, his actions now stiff, like an automaton running a program. She'd always admired him for doing his best, despite being a second-class citizen. She would've eaten a bucket of pills long ago had she been in his shoes. But maybe SeCa society's restraints were finally wearing him down. And the benefits of being an Eastmore seemed less and less to balance the costs.

Victor said, "I wish I knew how people know that I have MRS. And why they react the way they do."

He your pet freak? She thought of the man in Gaobeidan and replied, "It's not you. Not entirely. People are wound tight here. Any little thing sets them off. It's funny, in Texas, even when their farms are being burned and their families held for ransom, people are more laid-back. They get mad and scared, and whenever they need to be, they're fast enough to catch you yesterday, but they don't let life grind them down. But here ..."

"But what is it about *me*?"

"I don't know," Elena admitted. "Something in the way you look at people, I guess. It feels—I don't know—charged somehow."

"Charged?"

"Forget I said anything."

There's a time when we'll talk about that, she thought, *but not now, not while you're on edge.*

She drew a nail down her arm again and felt a tingling shiver in its wake. Being near Victor again felt bittersweet, because watching him struggle made her feel more alive.

"So, what's the plan to get us across the border?" she asked.

"I don't know."

Victor's voice sounded flat and distant. She knew the battle for equilibrium was being waged inside him, even though there was no sign of it on his face. His mind was a minefield that never got swept. What happened in Gaobeidan could have been prevented. She had to tread more carefully if they were going to get through this. Warmth spread in her chest: they were on the road with nothing ahead but opportunity. It was a familiar feeling, from back when her troubles were limited to his troubles, a generosity marred only slightly by a sense of superiority. Maybe it was just nostalgia for simpler times.

Victor continued, "We're supposed to wait somewhere outside Truckee."

"How long?"

Victor shrugged. "A couple days maybe?"

"It's a house, right? I didn't buy any camping gear." She waved toward the bags at the rear of the car.

"I don't actually know. All I have is a location."

Morning sunlight had chased away the ground fog. Its beams streamed through the windows of the car. Heat rose from the dark plastic dashboard and the clipped velour fabric covering the car seats. She cracked the window. Dewy, cool, and grimy air rushed in.

Elena rubbed the numb spot on her upper ear. The stimsmoke damage was probably permanent. She should have asked the clinic staff in New Venice whether there was a treatment to restore the missing sensation. She wedged her thumbnail between her teeth, releasing a sliver of pork fat, the last remains of her breakfast sandwich.

"Who do you think those thugs were?" she asked. "Not the fools in town. The ones you said took your herbalist."

"I don't know. I didn't get a good look at them. It was dark. I think maybe they've been following me since my reclassification appointment." His voice had regained its vibrancy. "I thought they might be the ones who're supposed to take me to the ranch, but—"

"Maybe you're right," Elena said, relaxing in her seat. He didn't know about Lucky and Bandit. That was good. He wouldn't be happy to know she was keeping secrets. She watched Victor closely. His gaze moved in a cycle between the road and his mirrors.

Elena scratched her arm again, digging her nails in, feeling a tingle throughout her body, an aftereffect that hadn't faded days after her last high. "We need a word for what we're doing. What is it? An excursion? An exodus? An expulsion?" she asked.

"An exorcism. I'm leading the bad spirits out of SeCa."

Elena wrinkled her nose. "That doesn't sound like you."

"People can change," he said. "Something Pearl said ..."

The look he gave her was impossible to read. She felt like he was studying her, and a shiver ran across her arms. She shifted toward the open window, the wind buffeting her hair. She scraped the strands from her face and gathered her hair into a ponytail, held it, let it go, surrendered to the breeze for a moment, then tied it back tight again.

Victor said, "I was thinking about lives we might have lived. In a normal world, we could have worked together."

The image of a gleaming laboratory at the SeCa National University came to mind—a proper research facility with the latest instruments, a gleaming, polished MeshHub, and experts in the most advanced biological and medical techniques. Who wouldn't want to work in that kind of environment? Of course, it wouldn't be that simple: she had five years of going down the wrong track to make up for. And some mistakes couldn't be undone. Although, now she was clean, she had more options.

"You always said you wanted to be an astronomer," she said. "Do you like computational biology more now?"

He grinned and said, "Biology is fine, but if I was normal, I don't think I'd settle for it. The universe is almost big enough for me."

Oh, nice. She smiled to hear Victor bantering again. Her memories were full of his funky verbal serves and her quick returns before their lives drew them apart. "Are you in love with the stars?"

"Stars are sexy."

Elena giggled. "Stars are not sexy. *Cells* are sexy. Astronomers grow up to be sad old hermits. Biologists pump out loads of babies."

He snorted and nodded. Elena smiled. He was such a strange bird, so tricky to pin down. His epic mood swings could have traversed the solar system; much worse than when he was younger.

She looked out the window and saw a scorched orchard; the burnt trees like black figures lined up in rows. Her good feelings drained away. Devastation as meaningless and harmful as she'd inflicted in Texas. Would she ever descend to such savagery again? She hoped not. One murder was already one too many—although, murder wasn't as rare as she'd grown up believing, it turned out.

"Hey, can I ask you something?" she asked.

"Sure," he said, his eyes fixed on the road.

"How did you know Jefferson was poisoned?"

He paused before replying, and she wondered how far he trusted her. "He had a hidden lab room at Oak Knoll. There was an image, a kind of photograph, that showed he'd been exposed to alpha particles."

"Yes, but that was later. You said you knew he was murdered. I was there at the funeral, remember?" *Ask me why. Make me tell you the truth.*

His eyes flicked across the landscape. "I didn't *know* that he was murdered. It was just a feeling."

She shifted toward him. Somehow, despite his condition, he'd seen the truth when no one else had. How? Why couldn't he see through her lies, too? "But you—what's the word?—you *intuited* something. Strange, don't you think?"

Victor smirked. "I've been called worse."

"That's not what I meant. Like your dreams—"

Victor's hands tensed on the steering disk. "We're not going to talk about those. Or the fact that you told my parents about my dreambook."

Elena shifted back toward the window and crossed her arms. She'd get him to open up eventually.

6

"What about your family?" Elena asked.

Victor glanced her way. The passenger window framed and silhouetted her face. In the background, a dry creek bed ran parallel to the road, and desiccated oak trees stood barren.

She looked at him expectantly. "Are you going to call them? Do they know you're leaving?"

Victor leaned forward, adjusting the position of his butt on the seat. The car maintained a steady speed. "The more people who know where I am ..."

"The more they can help you," she said weakly. She sounded like she didn't really believe it.

He said, "Or the more the information could leak out, and whoever's following me can track me down. I know that sounds paranoid," he said, "but I trust what Ozie told me."

"I'm not so sure you *should* trust him." Elena smirked. "His leaving was a good thing. Wherever he went. The two of you were toxic together."

Victor almost laughed. *Two,* with a delicious and dangerous erotic frisson.

Elena and Ozie had never got along. The closest friends he'd ever had possessed the same charge, but despite both being drawn to Victor, they'd repelled each other strongly.

"Well, he's the one getting us out of SeCa, so we'll find out soon enough."

Looking back, Victor figured he was always going to leave Semiautonomous California. But it had taken a while for his false hopes to sink and dark currents to draw him away. Two weeks before he hit the road with Elena, he went to Little Asia and discovered that the herbalist, Ming Pearl, known simply as Pearl, was somehow already in Granfa Jefferson's orbit. That was the first sign that his control over his own life was an illusion.

"You're early to the party," Pearl said with her annoying way of using light and levity to disguise a dark and heavy situation. "Why not start dancing?" She smiled a cannabis-bright goofball grin. "I know a brainhacker with some music to make you really groove." She gave him the MeshID that put him back in touch with Ozie.

That was the second sign that his life was being manipulated, and it would have been clearer if Ozie wasn't playing his own games, hiding behind a digital mask.

Semiautonomous California
27 February 1991

Victor sat forward in his office chair and pinged the MeshID, not sure what to expect or how Pearl's mysterious brainhacker was supposed to help him. It was dark outside. The cypresses at the edge of BioScan's property were bending in a strong breeze like slender giants bowing to the rising moon. Eventually, the vidscreen filled with a shadowy figure, a dark smudge that hinted at being broad-shouldered and short-haired. A blurry filter covered the face and clothes. Why vidchat at all if the image was going to be obscured?

"Victor Eastmore," a tinny, distorted voice said. "Ahead of schedule. Hmm ... I know you got this MeshID from Ming Pearl in San Francisco. You're self-medicating now, she tells me."

Victor sat back in his chair, suddenly feeling exposed.

"Don't worry, our feed is masked," the figure said. "It won't register on any logs." The man's smugness was apparent even through the obscuring filter.

"She said you could help me."

"Correct," the figure said.

Victor asked, "Why would you want to?"

"To expose Jefferson Eastmore's assassination."

Victor blinked at the vidscreen. Until then, the word that bounced around his brain was *murder. Assassination?* Really?

"I assume you're not going to let your family's heroic patriarch go unavenged." The sonofeed rippled electronically, masking the figure's voice.

"Who are you?" Victor asked.

"Think of me as someone who likes to help people who need help from people like me."

The oblique non-answer, a familiar bantering style, tickled Victor's memory. He shrugged the thought aside and asked the more important question, "Why did you say Granfa Jefferson was *assassinated*?"

"'Granfa?' Until you cast off your family's linguistic fetishes, you will never achieve full autonomy."

Another memory tickled. Victor ignored it. "I told maybe five people I thought he was murdered. None of them believed me. You say *assassination*. Why? Tell me."

The figure maintained a frustrating silence. Victor heard the gurgling of the cooling circuits in the office computers nearby. The lightstrips above his head seemed to pulse; maybe the bioluminescent algae inside were going to sleep. Victor waited another few breaths, then lost his patience and shouted, "Tell me!"

Gruff gurgling came through the speakers. The figure reached out of the frame and put an object on its head that resembled a crown. He sounded out of breath when he spoke again, and an additional scratchy distortion came through the sonofeed. "If you're seeing the herbalist, I'm willing to bet you've stopped taking Personil. These next few weeks are going to be tough, and you have a reclassification appointment coming up."

Victor bristled. "You think you know so much about me, but you—"

"Hear me well!" boomed the voice. "Due to a series of traumatic events and your socially conditioned untouchable status, you carry more than a healthy share of guilt and shame within you. Beyond mitigating your MRS symptoms, you need some serious psychological and neurobiological reconditioning, which I would be happy to help you with."

Victor's breath caught in his throat. The arrogance! The naked condescension. If he could reach out and throttle the figure, he would. "You want to hack my brain. No, thank you." He hovered his finger over the "terminate feed" command.

"Control yourself. You know as well as I do the importance of cognitive equilibrium. Rest assured, I'm going to help you achieve it."

"Cognitive equilibrium?" Victor leaned forward, scrutinizing the figure's outline. The casual superiority, slippery deflection, intensely personal needling, and dramatic doom-ridden flair—they all clicked into place. "You just gave yourself away, Ozie."

The figure tore the crown-ish thing from its head, slammed a hand on the keyboard, and the feed went dark.

His friendship with Ozie had always been tempestuous, transactional, and, truth be told, slightly exploitative, too. So, his dramatic reappearance wasn't too shocking. It made sense that Ozie had become a brainhacker. He'd always loved computers and excelled at data analytics, engineering, and all the hard sciences—more so than Victor, who got top marks in those subjects without the innate conceptual brilliance that Ozie used to build bespoke gadgetry. Of course, Ozie would find ways to hack into the human brain: to him, everyone was a machine with varying sophistication in their programming. And just when they were drawing closer at the beginning of senior year, approaching the edge of something like a sexual-romantic relationship, Ozie had disappeared. Victor thought he'd been reclassified without leaving a trail of records. Apparently, he'd gone into hiding or maybe escaped SeCa completely.

Victor knew he should get up, walk away, and forget about any talk of murder and assassination. When he'd found polonium on the data egg, he thought it was probably due to a defect in the manufacturing process. Victor was no engineer, and knew next to nothing about radioactivity, but he understood that quantum storage devices were dangerous to make, as well as polluting. Victor had a reclassification appointment to worry about, and he couldn't afford to listen to Ozie's crazy theories. But maybe Ozie didn't know about the polonium? Victor drummed his fingers on the desk. Curiosity got the better of him, and he sent another feed request to Ozie.

This time, Ozie appeared unfiltered on the vidscreen, dressed in black, sitting on a high-backed, overstuffed chair, nearly invisible in the low-lit room. Through thick-rimmed glasses, his eyes blazed. A metal cap that resembled an overturned colander sat on his head.

"Greetings from the Organized Western States," Ozie said in a low, carefully controlled voice.

Victor smiled. He hadn't realized how much he'd missed Crazy Ozie, who was constantly chafing against an ordinary existence, inventing some unbelievable tech, and pushing his buttons—someone he could say anything to.

"Tell me about your magic hat," he said.

Ozie leaned toward the vidlens and bowed his head. The device wasn't metal but a painted-gray ceramic bowl with protruding nodes that Victor assumed were magnetic coils. Ozie said, "I do my best thinking when wearing this."

"Tell me what you're thinking now."

"I think that you have to come to terms with your monster-self complex. Our fight is bigger than your diagnosis. The Health Board bagged the big fish: if an Eastmore could be diagnosed ... well, now they're itching to move you into Class Two. And now they've got new reclassification protocols."

"Wait, you're not saying my original diagnosis was politically motivated, are you?" Victor and Ozie had spent many hours discussing their symptoms, trying to understand themselves better by understanding each other, but they'd never talked about anything so sinister.

"I'm saying your diagnosis fit into their plans; your reclassification will doubly so."

"*Their* plans?"

"The Health Board."

"This is classic conspiracy nonsense," Victor said. "I shouldn't be talking to you."

"Jefferson said you'd come looking for me when the data egg opened."

"But ... it hasn't opened."

"No, you—Ah ... Oh! I see." Ozie touched his throat and gently stroked it, a familiar nervous tic that Victor found both sensual and off-putting. "Um ... That's not what I was expecting."

"What were you expecting?" Victor asked.

Ozie had on his puzzling-through-a-mystery face. "I'm not sure I can be of much help yet. Jefferson was quite the planner. Now, I guess his timeline is all messed up. Even so, the unopened data egg may be enough to subvert the new reclassification protocol."

"What do you mean? How?"

"Quantum magic." Ozie flashed a broad smile, white teeth gleaming bright, blotting out every other part of the feed.

"You're a dick, Ozie. Tell me about this new reclassification protocol."

"It's all kinds of messy. Jefferson opposed the latest revision. Unfortunately, with him out of the way, everything will go forward.

More diagnoses. More ranchos. More facilities. We're talking doubling or tripling our numbers. And SeCans will welcome the thousands of new jobs along with the expansion."

"You think there are that many undiagnosed Broken Mirrors?"

"I don't use that term of oppression." Ozie sighed. "SeCa is just the first phase. Next is the New England Commonwealth, the Southeastern Confederacy, the Northern League, Europe, and on, and on. Draft bills are already circulating. SeCa incubated the system. Now, it's going to send its nasty fascist laws around the world like a virus. You seriously didn't suspect that's why they got rid of him, *assassinated* him? He was a man standing against the flood, and because he was Jefferson Eastmore, he was successful at it. While he lived."

"Do you have any proof?" Victor asked.

"You mean like the vidfeed showing him being poisoned?"

Victor froze. Recovered his breath. Blinked.

Ozie smiled cruelly. "Got you. Unfortunately, no, not yet."

"And somehow, I'm supposed to take you seriously," Victor grumbled.

"As death." Ozie leaned toward the camera. His hound dog eyes filled the screen. "I care very much about you. Together, we'll get to the bottom of this messy mess. The Classification Commission is the target. We need information. We start with mapping our enemies' relationships, testing their communication channels. Their narrative consistency. Ask questions. Probe their answers. A conspiracy is like a body. Yes, they've got hands and limbs, but we're really looking for the brains."

"How does any of this help me with my reclassification? I won't be any use to you on a rancho."

Ozie leaned back, his whole face once again in the frame. "I was serious about the data egg. Bring it to your appointment. It'll help. Watch what you say. And stay cool. The dark grid says the doctors started asking about Carmichael."

"Why would they do that?" Victor asked.

But Ozie terminated the feed and vanished from the vidscreen before Victor had finished his question.

Victor rose from his chair and paced in front of the windows. The wind had died down. The trees were now nodding at each other, confiding, gossiping. Ozie had once explained the dark grid to Victor, something about a parallel hidden computing system that lived within the Mesh, but he hadn't understood the tech speak. To Victor, the dark grid was a source of the rumors and untrustworthy conspiracy theories that Ozie was always a sucker for. However, what if, this time, he was right?

He took the data egg and held it up. His breath passed over it to no effect. He gathered some spit and let it drip onto the egg. Nothing happened. "Open," he whispered. Nothing happened.

Beyond the dark window and his own reflection, wetlands stretched toward the bay. Grasses rippled in the wind, lit by a nearly full moon. It was a clear night. "Granfa, what did you do?" he whispered into the blackness.

Victor had lived most of his life knowing he was different, dangerous, and a problem to be solved, or at least managed. But if the diagnostic protocols were being manipulated now, couldn't they have been manipulated back then, too?

Shame and guilt, blame and self-doubt. Beneath it all, somewhere at his core, he had always believed there was a tiny spark of goodness, of rightness, deep inside, even when it couldn't be seen or felt. His true self—an infinitesimal mote, a fact of nature, as inevitable as the entire universe—couldn't be denigrated by such small things as diagnostic protocols and human folly. Could that part of him unfurl and blossom?

Pearl and Ozie had both urged caution, saying he should move carefully and keep information to himself. Yet he'd already shared his suspicions with his family and Elena. Perhaps it was too late to sneak around. The problem, as it had been all along, was that he lacked proof. He would need to get a sample from his granfa's body, but the thought made him sick to his stomach. With his reclassification coming up, he couldn't afford to break into an abandoned hospital or exhume his granfa's body. But if he didn't pass the test, he would never get another chance. Victor stared at the dark Bayshore wetlands, feeling stuck at a crossroads where the only road he wanted to take was the impossible one. He wished he'd never been born.

7

Driving east, Victor was humming to himself while Elena napped in the passenger seat, believing he was truly leaving all bad vibes behind and that his growing sense of liberation wasn't a trick his mind was playing on him.

He stopped in a small town in the foothills. It was their last chance to refuel before heading into the mountains. Elena fidgeted as he pulled into a parking space and awoke. He could tell she was worried about his symptoms because she pointed out the gas station's Freshly, asking if a juice would help him. While she was around the back of the shop, using the restroom, he waited in line. There was a Freshly practically on every corner back in Oakland, and the shop was comforting and familiar. The young woman in front of him smoothed a stray wisp of her copper-colored hair as she glanced back. He pretended not to notice. Flirtation wasn't on his agenda. He had a country to leave, a mind to salve, a sanity to preserve.

Slyly, he dug into his pocket and, with a magician's misdirection, yawned, tilting his head back and masking that he was swallowing a dose of fumewort. It would take a while for the effects to kick in. His skin tingled, as if the overhead lightstrips, and the microscopic animals powering them, were stroking him with gentle radiative pressure, and he tilted his head back to enjoy the sensation. The benefits of having a hyper-reactive, synesthetic brain were few and far between. He enjoyed what he could.

The queue didn't move quickly, and Victor began worrying that they shouldn't have stopped here. But he'd started to feel the resonance coming and thought a Freshly juice bioenhancer might be the best thing. As in all Freshly stores, behind the counter were displayed berries, stone fruits, and citrus bathing in a chiller cabinet's cool mists. Vegetables, still actively photosynthesizing, stewed in irrigation baths. These were another form of medicine— a subtle, possibly ineffective self-prescribed tonic—but he needed all the help he could get.

The holographic menu listed cognitive enhancers, mood-altering compounds, and metabolic calibrators. His gaze lingered on hormone adjusters that allowed customers to mix and match bioactive additives to shift aspects of their gender expression. Maybe someday he'd feel stable enough to play with those. In addition to equal portions of fruits and vegetables, he would ask for two doses of languor—*two* with comfort and ease—and a triple shot of equilibrium. He rehearsed his order quietly to himself.

As the line moved forward, he spotted something else familiar. He knew one of the workers, Ric, who was chatting up each customer like they were old friends. Ric was handsome, almost painfully so, often causing customers to fumble for words and blush, Victor included. It wasn't simply natural attraction: when Victor observed Ric's face, he saw electric blue filaments dancing on a rosy background, gauzy good humor overlaid by cascading chaotic excitement. He wanted to press their lips together and ride the wave of their combined giddy energy.

The young woman waiting in front of Victor turned again. Reddish-brown hair was gathered in a black synthleather band at her neckline.

She looked him up and down. "Did you say something?"

Victor held his breath and looked away. Out of the corner of his eye, he could see orange filaments glistening on her anxious face. Her long, slender arms and fingers were rigid, pinned to her sides.

"Hello? Did you hear me?" she asked. The collar of her shirt was unbuttoned, revealing a freckled, sunburned neck.

He kept his silence. He only wanted to buy his juice bulb and get back on the road. And maybe have a quick chat with Ric. Alone. In the dark. A boy could dream.

In a quiet hiss, she asked, "Are you a Broken Mirror?"

Victor swallowed a curse, shifted his gaze to the menu, and pretended not to have heard the commonplace slur for people with MRS. He'd been called it a thousand times since his diagnosis; he used it on himself sometimes. But her name-calling was nothing next to his sweat-soaking nightmares, or the threat of being reclassified and sent to a ranch.

"Why won't you answer?" she demanded.

He glanced into her narrowed hazel eyes. Filaments of her confusion, shame, and anger flowed into his brain. Sounds from the shop faded, replaced by waves of hostile pressure. Her emotions had infected him.

Victor wrenched his gaze back to the menu board. He said in a quiet, strained voice, "I don't want to talk to you."

Her face drew closer, reddening. She shouted, "I am not ashamed."

Ashamed of what?

The other customers turned and stared. The employees stopped what they were doing, trying to judge the need to intervene and which one of the pair was bad and who was good—a classic Cathar pastime. Victor was bad. He'd been told so often enough. In Semiautonomous California, having MRS made you the worst possible kind of person.

As his symptoms spiraled, everything in his field of vision undulated. Bile boiled in his throat. Fumewort wasn't calming this storm. His heart pounded the way it had in Carmichael when he was four years old, locked in his house, crying at the sounds of explosions and screams outside, wondering if his parents would ever come home. Sometimes danger was in his head, and sometimes danger was real; it was difficult to know the difference.

The juice shop's interior blazed sun-white, and blankspace surrounded him like steaming rain, slick on the skin ... except there was no skin, no touch, no sound in blankspace. There was only the infinite possibility of peace and silence and calm, a lightness and buoyancy so seductive that it could take over and he would be gone.

The young woman looked around. "I won't be insulted!"

Victor's fingers curled into claws, eager to gouge out her eyes. He mouthed his calming refrain. *The wise owl listens before asking who. The dark forest hides the loudest cuckoo.* He tried picturing the birds he'd sketched with charcoal pencil to help dissipate episodes, layers of shaded feathers, delicate and textured. But in his mind's eye, the owl clutched the cuckoo and flapped away.

The young woman loomed closer. "What are you saying?"

One of the workers approached and asked her what was wrong.

"What is he saying?" she cried.

Blood pulsed in Victor's ears, blotting out her voice. His consciousness slipped toward blankspace, a seductive, cool nothingness that would leave his body vulnerable and witless. *Fuck—not now.*

Someone hissed Victor's name, jolting him. Ric jerked his head toward the exit and mouthed, "Go!"

Victor turned toward the door and ran.

"You need help!" the young woman yelled at his back.

Outside, the blaring of fire-truck sirens made him duck his head and whimper. People on the sidewalks, unbothered by the sirens but wary enough of him, stepped aside to let him pass. Of course, the sirens were only in his head, echoes of Carmichael.

He stopped and turned to see Ric burst out of the juice shop, carrying a bulb of pink liquid. He waited, rooted to the spot.

"Are you okay?" Ric asked as he handed over the drink.

Victor snatched the juice bulb and emptied half of it in panicked gulps. He wiped his mouth with the back of his hand, thinking that Ric deserved a hug, at least. "Why'd she have to get up in my face?" he said, panting.

"Who knows? Maybe she's on stims. Or off her meds. Try to shake it off," Ric said.

"Thank you," Victor said, still feeling flustered. He sucked the bulb until the last pulse of sweet, tangy liquid was gone. Every drop of calm it could provide was necessary. Maybe she *was* off her medication. Victor had lost control of himself often: at dinner with his parents, at work at Gene-Us, alone at home.

"You work here now?" Victor asked.

"I moved, yeah. To be closer to my brother. There's a double dose of languor in there. I wasn't sure what else you needed."

Victor extended his MeshBit to pay.

Ric smiled. "No, don't worry about it." He wiped his hands down his silver synthsilk apron. "Vic, you've been a Class Three for a while, right?"

Victor nodded, feeling his cheeks flush. He'd been a Class Three longer than most. He was lucky. And he'd had more help managing his condition than all the Broken Mirrors in Semiautonomous California.

Ric said, "My brother's Class Two, and he's not doing great."

Was any Broken Mirror doing great? Victor didn't think so.

Ric said, "Do you think someone you know could check on him?"

Victor shook his head. "I'm not in touch with my family right now."

It was no surprise that people assumed the Eastmores could make miracles happen. Ric probably believed that Victor enjoyed all the privileges that came with wealth and power rather than being an embarrassment and a disappointment to his family.

Ric eyed Victor, looking him up and down. His lips were parted, moist.

Victor hesitated. What passed between them was an exquisite, erotic energy that pulled and teased and thoroughly confused him. What was it exactly that others saw when they looked at him? How could some people fear him, some crave him, and some do both simultaneously?

Victor spotted Elena getting into his car's driver's seat. "I'll see what I can do. I've got to go. Thanks again." He turned to leave, but Ric grabbed his arm. Victor didn't know if he wanted to shrug away or pull Ric close.

Ric asked, "He's okay out there on the ranchos, right? They say they're like summer camp."

The Class Two rancho Victor had visited in Carmichael was once a pleasant few acres of farmland on the outskirts of the famed and blighted town. Now, it was surrounded by electrified fences. It was most definitely *not* like summer camp. But it wasn't as bad as the concrete bunker on a nearby hill that held the catatonic Class Ones.

"Sure. Yeah," Victor said. "Be happy he's still a Two."

"It's not right," Ric whispered. "They caught him protesting. One cheek swab later ... I'm hoping they'll let me see him, that's why I moved. I send him packages of black cardamom seeds every month. You know about them?"

Elena was watching him through the windshield, miming turning the steering wheel. Her message was clear. *Let's go!* She was right. But Ric was looking at him with a sheen of hope atop bleak desperation.

"I don't," Victor said. "Why black cardamom?" He imagined the bitter black seeds in his cheeks, like a chipmunk with eccentric tastes.

Ric said, "He had a dream about them. It's the only thing he asks for. What are they really like? The ranchos."

Granfa Jeff had pointed out all the innovations that made one of the ranchos a kinder, gentler prison. Class Twos could access a library (but not the Mesh), and they farmed or fished their own food, and cooked it. It wouldn't be such a bad place if someone could be happy in confinement. But they could never leave, and they never got better.

"Not horrible, mostly. The worst part is the Mesh transmitter they fuse to their bones."

Ric winced.

"I'm sure it doesn't hurt. Sorry I said that."

Ric's shoulders slumped. "I hope you're right." He ambled back to the shop.

Victor flopped himself into the passenger seat, thinking about all the families torn apart by fear of MRS. He thought then of his own family and the assumptions Ric, and others, would make about the wealth and power of the Eastmores, as descendants of both enslaved and slave-owning families, who had benefited from reparations and rose to power during the decades-long period of post-Civil War Reconstruction, serving as the nation's most prominent example of reconciliation. In time, they became a symbol of the Permanent Enlightenment, amassing business interests as varied as energy and healthcare and brokering political favors to ease the Repartition of the United States into the nine nations of the American Union. The Holistic Healing Network, founded by Jefferson Eastmore, touched the lives of every American through its free cancer screenings and highly subsidized medical care. Only the very wealthy ever saw a hospital bill, and every American had seen the inside of an HHN clinic many times. Jefferson Eastmore's steady care, connections, and HHN clinicians, more than anything else, had kept Victor a Class Three for more than a decade—a miracle, without a doubt.

"Looks like you know him," Elena said. Victor nodded. "He's cute."

He nodded again. "Very."

"Let's hope he doesn't tell anyone you were here."

Cody Sisco

8

Semiautonomous California
3 March 1991

The smack of a juicy insect exploding on the windshield startled them, and Elena was brought back to the present. Victor was probably swimming in remembrances as well. Road trips had that effect.

She wished she could be honest and tell Victor how her life changed when she moved to the Republic of Texas, how unhinged she felt, careening between depression and anxiety, and how stimsmoke took her away from all that, for a short time, repeatedly and often. How the Puros had saved her, how she'd relapsed, and then how his family had saved her again.

She wished her life hadn't taken the turns it had. She'd been changed; the ground never felt solid under her feet, and the whirling between her ears continuously made her feel unbalanced. But her actions had consequences, and she had to live with them, no matter how dark and shameful.

She glanced over at Victor. She should tell him about Lucky and Bandit. He deserved to know the truth. How would he take the news? Would he forgive her for lying? His hair needed combing. He probably hadn't showered in days. His hands gripped the steering disk as if he were holding onto a life ring on the ocean. She couldn't blame him for the mess she had become. But if he'd been there for her, even a little, maybe she wouldn't have needed the Puros. Unbidden but not unwelcome oraciones, prayers, repeated themselves in Portuguese-influenced Spanish in her head. Los Puros sonao limpios, salvos, amadaos. Unidos, hastao lo ultimo. *The Puros are clean, saved, loved. Together, until the end.* She pressed a palm to her heart and breathed in calmness. The Puros were rebels turned social justice crusaders, frugal egalitarian farmers with a fondness for fighting and freedom. They were exactly what she'd needed to turn her life around. Even if some of them took things too far.

Still, it could have been different. If Victor's family hadn't rescued her, she would never have been to the clinic in New Venice. She wouldn't have rejoined the Puros and learned about the arms embargo. And she wouldn't have tortured the young Corp—that was the tipping point when she lost control of stims again, when her habit became a full-blown addiction. She pictured two dancers spinning, only the grip of their hands preventing them from centrifugal disaster.

"Are you still not taking your medication?" she asked.

He glared at her.

"I'm not criticizing. I'm asking. How do you feel?"

"It's hard to describe. I'm me again. I'm in my body, feeling like me, feeling …" He paused, breathed deeply, then began again, "When I was on Personil, it was like a layer between me and the world, between me and myself. Mostly, I felt numb, except when an episode came and broke through, and I could finally feel *something* again. It's different every time. Colors, sounds, or feelings take over, and I don't … I'm not myself anymore, in a new way. That's when the blankness comes. It swallows me up."

"And then?" There was a similarity to her experience with stims, but he made it sound like she'd experienced only a fraction of what it was like for him.

"Most of the time, it's nothing. Nothing at all. I'm gone. But sometimes, right before the blankness hits, the universe opens up. Dr. Tammet called it euphoria, but it's more than that. It's like I'm going somewhere beautiful and dazzling, and that's okay because it's all the same. Everything is part of the same stuff: me, the world, all the stars and galaxies, we're all one."

Elena relaxed into her seat. Blankness didn't sound all that bad. It sounded like a release from a world that required so much to keep going.

They were nearing the foothills. The flat valley floor had given way to gently undulating land, and the road rose and dipped, continuing due east. Trains heading to the resorts of Lake Tahoe, carrying SeCa elites to their vacation homes, sped past every minute or so.

She looked at Victor. His eyes scanned the contours of the road as he drove. He didn't need to know about her past. He

Cody Sisco

wouldn't understand. Although, if she confessed to him about using stims, she could tell him about the good parts of being a Puro: the community, the farms, how they had tried to help her get clean and succeeded, for a time. How being with them felt real and grounding. He needed a refuge like that, a place to start again. But he wouldn't be able to see past the violence. Maybe she could prepare the way by describing the violence spreading across the Texas prairie. He should know it was the Corps' fault; she'd tell everyone if she could. The Puros were only defending themselves. And maybe she could ask him why a street drug spreading through the Republic of Texas produced his syndrome's exact symptoms.

"What's it like in the ROT?" Victor asked.

Elena sucked in her breath. She'd often contemplated the possibility that Victor was indeed psychic but always dismissed the fantasy. Still, it was uncanny the way his question tracked her thoughts. Maybe she had dropped too many hints about how much the Republic of Texas changed her.

"It's simpler," she said. "People are more normal. More normal than here, I mean. They want to be left alone. Their attitude is 'screw everyone else, we've got our own problems.' In SeCa, someone is always in your business, trying to fix things but messing them up worse instead. People in Texas believe in autonomy. It's not just a political thing. It's a way of life. Except ..."

"Except what?"

Elena watched dirt fields pass by. The ghost tang of stimsmoke lolled in her mouth. She couldn't tell him yet.

She said, "The ROT is missing something. It's like a blank canvas. In SeCa, you've got a lot of people with competing ideas—lifestyle designers, techies, Old Cathars, New Catholics, deep ecologists, sex cultists. The list goes on and on, you know? But in the ROT, there's no ideology. Maybe there was before the Repartition, but now people don't even believe MeshNews reports, like all that stuff is from another planet. You see a lot of strange things creep up."

"What do you mean, 'strange things'?" He looked at her, his expression that of a curious little boy. She confused him. He knew nothing about everyday violence and poverty and the blind faith that grows in such fertile soil. How could she explain the things she had seen? It was like the two of them were living in different universes. With enough time, if she told him bit by bit, maybe she could enlighten him. Maybe he would understand when she told him she was spying on him. Until then, she'd have to live with the aching feeling in her gut that she was betraying him. "People need to believe in something bigger than themselves," she said. "There's always someone selling a dream, so you get cults rising up. People start believing in supernatural stuff. Not like, 'Wouldn't it be cool if we could talk to ghosts?' They truly believe it. Other stuff, too."

"What other stuff?"

How could she explain the Corps to him? A mercenary force controlled by the Diamond King, a shadowy mafia figure operating out of Las Vegas and seemingly bent on making addicts out of the entire Texan population. She could tell him about the flood of stims the Corps had unleashed to hook as many people as possible and their enticing lies about the effects: unlimited energy, visceral fantasies, and the feeling that everything was as it should be. They never talked about synesthesia, mood imbalances, addiction, and nauseatingly powerful déjà vu.

Tomorrow, she would tell him everything. First, she needed time to figure out what to say.

"Never mind," she said.

9

Victor paced in front of the entrance to Oak Knoll Hospital, which stood vacant when it should have been bustling. His burned, like it was about to catch fire. He tried to pry the doors open, but they wouldn't budge.

Cognitive behavior therapy was the mortar to Personil's bricks. He was waiting to see Dr. Tammet, who helped Victor stay in control by giving him techniques to process and integrate his perceptions, ride the waves of emotional hyperactivity, and know when to seek out quiet darkness where his brain's wild gyrations could flare up and subside without causing harm. Medication and therapy weren't enough to cure MRS, but they made for a livable life.

A tsunami was building. A resonant episode grew more likely every second. He fought desperately against its pull as acid climbed his throat.

Remember the good things in your life, Dr. Tammet told him. *Gratitude heals*.

He was living a mostly normal life—if one considered taking daily medication and going to therapy sessions normal. He held a data analytics job at Gene-Us, the company that kept genetic analysis running smoothly at computing nodes throughout Semiautonomous California. His job proved that his intellect was exceptional, and his family provided him with resources and as much affection as they could spare. But someday, he knew he would become a drooling, insentient husk. Every resonant episode brought him closer to that fate.

Through blurry vision, he pounded on the hospital doors and, straining to see inside, shielded his eyes with his hands. The large atrium was bereft of people, an unlit gloom. Vidscreens above the information desk were dark.

Something in the darkened hospital atrium caught his eye. A figure moved closer. It was Granfa Jeff, alone. He was never by himself. Assistants and members of his executive team traveled with him, flitting around, and hanging on his every word. White and gray hair floated in wisps above his brow. His dark-freckled brown cheeks sagged as if he hadn't slept well.

The doors opened. Granfa stepped out and rested his palms heavily on Victor's shoulders. "Victor. I have some news that may upset you."

MRS helped him read his granfa's guarded expression. Deep blue sadness dimpled the skin around his eyes, and something else, a suppressed emotion, struggled below the surface.

In a low voice, Granfa said, "It's about the research into your cure. It can't continue."

Victor's mouth felt dry. He blinked, not believing what he'd heard, waiting for Granfa to correct himself. They couldn't do that, could they? Victor peered into the hospital's gloomy atrium. "Where's Dr. Tammet?"

"She moved away. She's gone to the Organized Western States. I made a huge mistake. Opened too many doors that should have remained shut. Oak Knoll is closing down. It has to be done."

After years of therapy, hundreds of appointments, and who knew how many ounces of Victor's blood drawn for tests, Granfa was shutting down the research program that was his only hope to prevent permanent catatonia.

"What's going to happen to me?" Victor asked.

Granfa's expression darkened, and Victor felt blankness rise.

Semiautonomous California
3 March 1991

"You okay there?"

Victor blinked. Oak Knoll was only a memory. He was in the passenger seat, feeling tugs of momentum as Elena gunned the car along winding curves in the road. They were surrounded by a thick pine forest.

"Was that an episode?" she asked.

He held out a hand. His fingers were mostly steady. "No. More like a memory of one."

"I think it's better if I drive us the rest of the way," Elena said. "I'm good for now, but I'll need directions in an hour or so."

"That's fine. Keep on keepin' on."

Victor crossed his arms and twisted in his seat, wedging himself deep to keep steady, remembering the last conversation he'd had with Jefferson.

Semiautonomous California
14 September 1990

Victor's blank outs sometimes ended with a shuddering, jarring return to his body, like waking by falling out of bed. This one was a jolt on his feet. The hospital loomed above, white, mute, sturdy, and impenetrable while his mind reeled. Windows above reflected patches of brightness onto the concrete in a checkerboard pattern. He had one foot in darkness, one foot crossing a border.

Granfa Jeff reached out as Victor backed away unsteadily. This couldn't be happening. He was better off blank, all his problems evaporating into mist.

"You said you would find a cure," Victor said. "You promised me."

"I wish …" Granfa's chest labored with every breath. "You knew our research was quasi-legal at best. We made—we took a very wrong turn. But this isn't the end for you."

Victor felt as if he were in free fall. Blankness rushed back, eager to consume forever the morsel it had so recently tasted. He whispered Dr. Tammet's refrain. *The wise owl listens before asking, "Who?"*

"I think we've been mistaken. Mirror resonance syndrome isn't as universally debilitating as we believed. We gain nothing by pathologizing it. I see that now. I've tried to tell the other members of the Commission, but—"

"I don't care about the Commission."

Granfa sighed and hung his head. "Things may seem bleak now. But I'm making contingencies. In time, under the right conditions, it will be possible for you to live a normal life."

In that moment, the trust between them crumbled. Granfa had saved him from the consequences of MRS, but only for a time. Victor was never really going to have a normal life; it was a mirage that Granfa was complicit in imagining, promising a miracle around the next corner. If Victor's fate had been pushed into the future, it was now springing back to smack him in the face.

"I'm going to end up *insensate*. *Comatose*. As dead as a living body can be. A cure was the only thing I could hope for. And now it's gone, so you can save money on staff and property taxes?"

Granfa reached out a hand to him. "There are other options. You must be patient. You can control your destiny."

Victor withdrew from the touch. "Oh, I know *all* about destiny. Read my dreambook sometime. Chronicles of the future as told by a perfectly *normal* Broken Mirror."

Normal meant medicated. Even now, the drugs were beginning to haze his vision and thicken his thoughts. He hated his slow-thinking self. But there was no alternative. Normal wasn't an option he understood to be possible.

"Remember what we've learned," Granfa said. "MRS is merely a biochemical phenomenon. It's simply a pattern, one you can change. Your mirror neurons work differently than most other people's, more excitable and less easily inhibited, true. That's your condition. That's not your being."

Granfa moved nearer and Victor allowed him to lean close and kiss his brow. Victor's stomach, tight and heavy with panic, softened a little. The love in Granfa's touch pulled him back from the abyss. Softly, he said, "Everyone thinks I'm going to become a killer. One day, I might." Victor looked into the darkened atrium. "How can you close the entire hospital? What's really going on?"

As Granfa glanced over his shoulder toward the building, a shadow passed over his features. The hidden coming to the fore, a surge of fear. What could scare him so badly?

"I wish there were some other way. I wish I could tell you everything now." Granfa's lips trembled. "I'm making preparations ... there's much to safeguard and time is so short."

"Preparations for what? Never mind. I don't care what you're hiding in there. Just, please, fix me," Victor whispered.

Granfa avoided Victor's gaze and stared into the hospital, seeming to weigh a decision. He placed an unsteady hand on Victor's shoulder and led him around the corner of the building into the shade of oak trees. It was a private spot, yet they were already alone. Still, Granfa whispered as he took a smooth black data egg from his coat pocket and gave it to Victor. "You are the master of your destiny. This is for you and you alone. It's locked for now. It has an uncommon key. One day, it will be important to remember. Keep it secret, Victor. You mustn't tell anyone."

The data egg weighed heavily in Victor's palm. It reminded him of holiday gifts. The family had a tradition of attending opera, ballet, and theatrical performances every Saturday in December. Data eggs recorded the shows and were shared only with the attendees—mementos and souvenirs for a privileged few. A strange calm settled on him as he stared at the data egg's ebony surface.

"Keep it with you, and you'll be fine. You can rewrite the pattern of your mind. Remember that. And remember, Victor: never surrender." Granfa tried to smile, a ghastly false grin. "Never surrender. Remember, never surrender."

Victor started to wonder if he was the only one with a mental disorder.

Never surrender to what?

He asked, "What are you so afraid of?"

"One day, you'll understand. I mustn't say more than that."

Semiautonomous California
3 March 1991

Elena wondered how many things a person could worry about simultaneously. She'd muted her MeshBit to stop its incessant pinging with messages from Lucky and Bandit and then turned it off completely. Victor had been mumbling something that sounded dramatic for the past half hour, and she was honestly considering slapping him back to his senses so she could get some quiet. And maybe most disturbing of all, a drone was following their car, keeping pace maybe ten meters or so above them.

She drove them into a pull-out and stopped the car. Trucks passed by, their engines whining from the steep climb. The drone hovered overhead. She poked Victor in the ribs, and he stirred, looking around, blinking.

"What's 'never surrender' mean?" she asked.

He looked confused momentarily. "Was I sleep-talking?"

"Yep," Elena said. "So?"

"Something Granfa Jeff told me not to forget. Why are we stopped?"

She pointed upward. "Drone."

He frowned, opened his door, and leaned out. When he spotted the drone, he quickly shut the door. "That's not good."

"Could be a coincidence, but I'm not going to bet on it."

"We can shake it off in the tunnel, I hope." The expression on his face darkened. "But if someone's following, they're probably expecting us on the other end."

"We don't have a choice," Elena said.

Victor nodded. "Let's go."

They resumed the drive and reached the Trans-SeCa Highway, an eighty-kilometer tunnel and the main route through the mountains by traveling underneath the Tahoe Forest ridgeline. The tunnel terminated at the border with the Organized Western States. Few other cars traveled the road with them, even though it was midday on a Friday.

Elena drove them into the shadows before the tunnel divided east- and westbound traffic and beyond where the drone could follow. Then she stopped, half-blocking the right lane. The minutes were agonizing as she waited, counting off the seconds, using Victor's heavy breaths as her metronome. The drone had to piss off; it couldn't just wait there, right?

Eventually, she ran out of patience and flipped a U-turn, and they exited and turned off the highway, free of their little spy drone friend. They continued along an old surface route through the wreckage of Truckee. When Victor was distracted by the scenery, she reached into her bag for a shockstick, which she slipped into her pocket where she could get to it more easily if needed.

They stopped to refill the car's biofuel tank at a service station on the edge of town. An attendant bumbled out of his kiosk and unspooled the hose. Victor held up his MeshBit to pay, but the attendant laughed. Elena paid the man with some of her cash.

Sunlight filtered through treetops, and the air had the coolness of late afternoon in the mountains. She wandered across a broad expanse of asphalt, followed by Victor's gaze, worrying her. She looked down the road at the town's remains. Few shops welcomed customers anymore. The Sierra Nevada Tunnel that ran underneath them provided a more convenient east-west connection between SeCa and the OWS and a better connection to North Tahoe City through a southern spur of the tunnel. Without through traffic, the town of Truckee had withered.

The Corps had an outpost around here, Elena knew. The Puros

were obsessive compilers of their enemies' activities. Most of the residents abandoned the town following the tunnel's construction. Only investment by a few adventurous and bargain-seeking union pension funds had saved the town from collapse. Then some Corp-affiliated dickies took up residence in abandoned homes and cabins, cultivating off-permit marijuana in the summer months and cooking stims in labs throughout the year, which started several forest fires, one of which had ravaged most of the main street. It was never rebuilt. Elena shifted uncomfortably at the thought of stims nearby.

When they returned to the car, Elena considered telling Victor about her shockstick. *No, better wait. I'll tell him everything, eventually, when he's ready.*

10

Semiautonomous California
3 March 1991

Now that they were in the mountains, alone, free for the moment from the people chasing him, Victor felt grief swoop down and grab him. He was rag-dolling in its clutches.

The car was creeping forward on a dusty single-lane unpaved track. Elena was concentrating on every dip and rock, trying to keep the sway and bounce to a minimum. And the only thing he felt was a big, gnarly, gaping loss.

Semiautonomous California
23 February 1991

Six members of the Eastmore family gathered at the hillside grave-yard overlooking City Lake. Only the near shore could be seen through heavy morning fog. Victor stood under a redwood tree that dripped onto his suit jacket as he stared at the grass, maintaining a precarious calm. The feelings swirling around him were treacherous and tidal. Better to concentrate on the landscape and draw comfort from its stillness.

A few clusters of headstones dotted the hill. They were outnumbered by burial mounds, a tradition resurrected after the Communion Crisis, the fall of the Catholic Church, and the Cathar ascendency in SeCa. Many of the mounds were simple, unadorned grassy lumps. The wealthier families had commissioned elaborate arrangements of paving stones, some polished to a fine patina that glowed faintly under weak, fog-blighted sunlight on this gloomy morning.

Ma said, "I hope the journey wasn't too rough." She glanced between Auntie Circe, who groomed the black collar poking out of her navy blazer, and Robbie, who looked slim and fashionable in his suit. He was all polish—round head, slicked hair, and shaved face—compared to Victor's frumpiness, wayward curls, and two-day scruff.

"Jets are very safe, Linda," Circe said, "and smooth. You should visit us sometime. See Europe."

Ma only smiled weakly in response. Fa grunted. They weren't the traveling type, preferring to spend time with severe and self-important society types attracted to the Eastmores' glamour. Their interests were limited to discussing the world, not living in it. There was no room for tourism, adventure, or exploration in Linda and Linus Eastmore's cloistered existence; fortunately, they could afford to bring the world to their door. Victor wondered often how much their preference for regimented cosmopolitanism was due to what they experienced in Carmichael.

Robbie took a long pull from a pipe and exhaled a sweet-smelling vapor. Circe lay a hand on Granma Cynthia's shoulder. Her other hand held an overstuffed bouquet of violets and white roses.

Victor wished he had his auntie's darker skin tone rather than a touch of his ma's paleness. People said skin is skin, which was true when it came to law and society, thanks to reparations, reconstruction, and the Permanent Enlightenment. Still, he sometimes felt closer to Auntie than Ma and craved a stronger resemblance between them.

Mourners were filing through the doorway of the mausoleum. The building's stone archway reminded Victor of Carmichael's Southern, Reconstruction-style homes. It was funny how the American obsession with turning a page on the Civil War continued more than one hundred years later. Under the rubric of the Permanent Enlightenment, righting the wrongs of slavery and white supremacy required every possible remedy, no matter how seemingly disconnected or absurd—in architecture, for instance, pillars were out and archways were in. But it was better to do too much than not enough. Victor shivered in the cold mist.

"It's time to go in," Ma said, pointing toward the last group slipping inside the doors.

Granma fiddled with a pair of gloves. Victor's parents hugged each other.

Circe brushed the shoulder of his cousin's suit, lifted her chin, and said, "All right, everyone, line up, youngest to oldest. Victor, you're in front. Then Robbie. Linda, Linus, follow behind them. Mother, you'll want to follow me."

"You make everything such a chore," Granma quietly scolded, but she took her assigned place.

Circe waved the bouquet. "You know the burdens we carry. We have to do this correctly. People are here to view us as much as him." She nodded for Victor to begin the procession.

He trudged ahead. They were a family of ducks, preening and waddling forward, following the breadcrumbs of tradition and decorum. Only he was the odd duck lurking among the raft, and they all knew it. He sidestepped off the walkway just outside the doors, wetting his black dress shoes on the dewy grass.

The other family members continued into the mausoleum and down the aisle, but Circe remained with Victor. He turned away from the open door and studied the arrangement of burial mounds, clustered to fit the contours of the terrain, trying to spot where the first Eastmore to be buried outside of New Venice would be laid to rest.

"There goes doing this correctly, huh?" he said.

"I know this is difficult for you," Auntie Circe said.

Victor looked at his wet shoes. "We fought the last time I saw him. He said I could live a normal life as he was closing the clinic. Ridiculous."

"Father wasn't well in the end. You have to try to see past his failings."

Victor barely heard her. "It's like he sabotaged me. The research could have continued. It's like he didn't want anyone taking credit for a cure after he was gone."

"I wouldn't blame him. It was his dementia."

"I don't see the distinction," Victor said.

"You don't? Really?" Circe asked, arching an exquisitely sculpted eyebrow.

Victor grunted. Clever Circe always managed to find the hole in any argument, but this time, she got it wrong. "Who would I be if I didn't have MRS, hmm? Every thought in my brain would be different. I can't *pretend* my way into equality. He was going to cure me, and now it's too late. It would have been better to have never had hope than to have it snatched away." He was almost spitting by the end of his little speech. *I'm so pathetic. And ungrateful. And hopeless.* At least in silence, no one knew how much resentment he carried.

Auntie Circe frowned and said, "What matters is that you remember your love for each other."

"I do wish I had seen him again."

"I'm sure he forgave you."

"You don't get it," Victor said. "I would have told him *I'm* still mad at *him*."

"I'm not going to tell you what to feel," she said. Her voice was stern, but a slight smile, visible by the barest lift in her cheeks, softened her expression. "It can take a lifetime to heal. But today's the only day you can say goodbye. Remember, death is simply a new start." She entered the mausoleum.

He shivered. Strange words. What kind of new start? Aunt Circe didn't hold to anything as banal as religion or believe in the afterlife. Maybe she meant the Eastmores would start anew, freed from their overbearing patriarch.

Victor felt in his pocket. For a short, panicked moment, he thought the data egg must have fallen out and rolled down the hill until he remembered he had left it on his bedside table. Mostly, he'd followed Granfa's command to always keep it close, but today wasn't a normal day. He took a breath and stepped through the doorway to the mausoleum. The benches on either side of the aisle were full. As he walked down the aisle behind Auntie Circe, nervous buzzing in his legs threatened to overtake his whole body. He didn't dare meet anyone's gaze. His footfalls seemed to echo more loudly than was possible, reverberating through the pews and up into the rafters. Each step seemed weighted, and his thighs began to shake. The coffin was high-lipped. He couldn't see the body yet. A flower arrangement bloomed with vibrant hues, vibrating reds, and resonant blues. Behind them, death. Two colorful bird-of-paradise flowers poked from a bunch of carnations—*always two, sometimes blue*.

His parents, cousin, granma, and auntie viewed the body and took their seats in the first row. The moment came when there was no one between Victor and the coffin. He stepped onto the dais and looked down at the corpse.

A familiar face, long, lean, and intelligent, even in death. The skin seemed lighter than Victor remembered, the brown not as dark, his freckles more pronounced. He also noticed dark circles the color of rotten plums around closed eyes and skin marred by splotches— irregular reddish-brown stains on otherwise immaculate makeup.

Cody Sisco

Only a few dull wisps of hair peeked from a white wool death cap. He looked wasted away. An illness would have to act fast to do so much damage in a short amount of time.

As Victor stared down at the body, bass notes sounded, intensifying, rumbling, vibrating in his chest. Darkness swirled before his eyes like black ash dancing in a breeze. Sounds of wings flapping and a raven's sharp screech ricocheted off the marble, piercing and buffeting.

Caw! Caw! Caw!

Echoes as loud as thunder.

People in the pews should have panicked. They didn't react.

His eyelids fluttered. Consciousness leaked into blank space.

Causal paradox swirling in a temporal hurricane. Vast knocking to open a door and shift orbits' traceries.

Victor gripped the coffin's rim as the wind blew forcefully; his every hair stood on end, and the cawing became a monstrous song, screeching its message like steel dragged across concrete.

A dusty, feathery presence enveloped Victor, smothering and choking. He went blank.

When Victor returned to his senses, he was bending over the coffin, hands clenching Granfa Jeff's lapels. The corpse's ribs flexed under the pressure, and a breath of foul air rose, smelling of gas and smoke. Like Carmichael. He'd returned with a horrible intuition.

Mourners' muttering filtered through the quiet mausoleum.

Victor had blanked out. With so many people watching! It couldn't have been for very long, though, because the numbness that accompanied a more prolonged absence wasn't there.

The strange calls of distant birds were gone, leaving something far worse in its place, a singsong whispering he couldn't tune out. *Murder bird, murder bird, did him in. Who let the murder bird in?*

His family members were gesturing for him to come down off the dais. Robbie waved a hand at the crowd—*look who's watching!*—as if Victor wasn't aware of the spectacle he was making. He could feel their stares. But rather than take his seat, he fled.

Standing a short distance from the mausoleum, Victor took a lungful of air. The Oakland & Bayshore skyline peeked through the fog. Dogs were barking, somewhere out of sight. Had he heard the barking as the ravens' calls? Was it all in his head?

He looked back at the mausoleum but knew he could not return, so he waited for the congregation to emerge.

Victor approached Granma Cynthia, the first out of the mausoleum. Wind fluttered the feathers on her hat. Black feathers. She smoothed a stray hair beneath her black scarf and gave him a chilling look. "I'm going home now, Victor. I'll see you this afternoon."

It was a command, not a question. Victor nodded. "Granma, what happened to Granfa Jeff wasn't natural."

She scowled at him. "What?"

"The way his hair fell out. And those splotches ..."

Her mouth twitched, and she gave him a harsh look. "You haven't seen him for months, and this is how you show concern?"

"I just think that maybe he—"

Granma Cynthia glared at him with disdain. "I won't be drawn into one of your speculations." She spoke quietly now that other mourners were milling around nearby.

The bile in his stomach rose and words tumbled out of him. "When I looked at Granfa's body, all I could think was that he'd been murdered."

Granma Cynthia's mouth dropped open for a moment. "Jefferson was 'murdered'?" she whispered. She glanced around. "That's entirely inappropriate, and at a funeral, no less. How can you say such a thing?"

Victor stared down at the grass. If he had a tail, it would be curling between his legs.

"His face looked ..." He tried his best to shape a complete sentence. His mind wasn't sluggish; it was racing at breakneck speed. "Did he say anything before he died? Anything suspicious?"

Granma Cynthia shook her head. "We've done so much for you over the years. Jeff was sure he could help you. It's such a shame when you get like this. I know it's not your fault; it's your condition. But sometimes it's too much." Tears welled in her eyes.

Victor said, "But—"

Granma Cynthia cut him off with a wave of her hand. "Jeff would know how to snap you out of this delusion, but I don't."

She marched to the parking lot and disappeared behind a row of cars.

Victor was pinned to the spot. The weight of what he'd just said sank him. Why couldn't he keep his mouth shut? He wanted to bury himself in one of the nearby mounds, inhaling raw dirt until his lungs bled—preferable to listening to the shrapnel of meaninglessness: *Murder, the murder bird murmured. Murky monster in a mirthless meander. Mortar meter, marbled mender. Murder bird, murder bird.*

Blankspace would be a relief.

He flexed his fingers and breathed, holding at the end of each inhale and exhale, determined not to slip away again, watching columns of mist that wandered like ghosts over the mounds, soon to evaporate and vanish. Samuel Miller would think the mist crossed over from this world to the next. That lunatic would murder fog if he could.

Victor told himself to snap out of it. But it was useless. It wouldn't be a mental illness if he could control it, would it?

People in hell want a glacier, Granfa used to say.

Semiautonomous California
23 February 1991

Jefferson Eastmore was known for creating teachable moments. So much so that Victor's fa and aunt had made an inside joke they didn't mind sharing with other family members. "Learn anything useful lately?" they would ask each other. This was usually followed by a sardonic grunt or eye roll.

The funeral was a low point for Victor. No question about that. Victor had let his condition steer his mind in a dark direction—what the fuck was a *murder bird*?—and he had to regain control. The drive from the cemetery, alone in his car, helped push dangerous thoughts away, as did the Personil dose he picked up from his apartment on the way, where he also retrieved the data egg, stuffing it inside a pocket. He pondered the situation as he drove and concluded it was possible to simultaneously miss Granfa Jeff *and* resent his failure to find a cure. Grief was complicated.

At the gate of the Eastmore mansion, sensors registered his approach and opened automatically. He parked in a garage separated from the main building by a narrow pergola covered in grape vines. Hieu met him at the front door. His white servant's hat nearly hid his salt-and-pepper hair.

"I hope you're feeling better," Hieu said, meeting Victor's gaze. He'd been at the funeral and witnessed Victor's difficulties before returning to the estate. He wasn't the type to gloss over or ignore Victor's condition, always asking how he was feeling and looking for ways to show that his position as head of the staff was much more than a job to him—it was a duty he undertook with genuine devotion to the business and the family.

Victor said, "I'll be glad when this day's over."

They walked together up switchback pathways and through a terraced garden of shrubs and small, tidy citrus trees with little flowers like fragrant white stars. After a steep climb, they came upon the Eastmores on a large patio, arranged in high-backed lounge chairs, covered in blankets to keep warm until the fog burned off. Victor joined them. Throughout the afternoon, they received close friends and a few notable officials. They discussed science, politics, the weather, and, at intervals and always tactfully, their memories of Jefferson Eastmore, the man who cured cancer and loomed large in the imagination of the American Union's citizenry and Victor's life.

Their recollections were a poor substitute for the man himself, who had constantly regaled the family with stories of his travels, insights from his research, and explanations of the intricacies of political machinations. Always lessons, always wisdom to pass on. The man couldn't help it; not even death could stop him. Victor's anger was fading, lifting, and being replaced by a slow, leaden grief. He sat with his family and said nothing, keeping his memories to himself.

The sun broke through intermittently as the fog thinned above the Eastmore estate, and finally, all trace of it was banished. The last of the visitors departed. Hieu brought a round of drinks: cocktails for his parents and lemonade for Circe, Cynthia, and Victor.

Victor had come a long way thanks to Granfa Jeff and Dr. Tammet. He had more skills and tools at his disposal. He had Personil. He did his best to maintain equilibrium. But without hope for a cure, that wasn't enough. He couldn't think any more about overcoming MRS; he had to accept it and live with it. MRS was a fact of life he couldn't resent or hide from. *Take it one day at a time*, Victor thought. *If other people have a problem with it, well, that is on them.*

Circe mentioned a new European astronomy project to observe patterns in cosmic microwave background radiation. Victor perked up. The telescope would generate massive amounts of data that would need special software to be analyzed, similar to the kind he wrote and managed for Gene-Us. He explained the challenges of working with large amounts of data, how to store it, process it efficiently, and produce an output that people could make sense of. His ma responded, "How interesting," and the conversation moved on. He tuned them out, thinking about how nice it would be to return to work the next day. He sat silently, smiling to himself, thinking how nice it would be to get launched in a rocket and to leave the solar system behind.

Semiautonomous California
3 March 1991

"Okay, trance time is over. We're here."

"What?" The cawing of murder birds was only in his head, he knew. Still, it made Elena difficult to understand.

"The end of the road. Literally. There's nothing here except a run-down cabin. Ozie knows your family is made of money, so I suspect this is his idea of a prank. He's not hiding us here until he can get us across the border. He's flexing his power over you. I know it turns you on." She smirked, looking down at him, holding the passenger door open and extending her other hand to him. "Sir, may I assist?"

He gripped her hand and got out of the car, then bowed his thanks. She curtsied back, and they both grinned.

They looked around. A cabin made from logs. A few stumps of the trees that became the logs. Nothing but wilderness and the single track they'd followed. He noticed tufts of grass by the stairs to the front door. He sniffed the air. The ground was dry, but there might be irrigation or a spring to feed thirsty plants. As he searched around the cabin for any sign of herbs that could supplement his treatment, he left a trail of disturbed dry pine needles and dust that rose and glittered in the rays filtering through the trees. Elena followed him for a minute, then cleared her throat with dramatic flair. "Excuse me, sir. May I be of assistance? Also, what the shocks are you doing?"

"If Ozie and Pearl are connected—" Victor shook his head as if to clear it. "I need more herbs. What I took from Pearl's shop will only last me a week." He paced over a thick layer of pine needles, looking around. "Maybe she had a garden here."

11

On the day after Granfa's funeral, a compulsion was at Victor's back, thrusting him forward. The atmosphere inside his apartment was stuffy and stale. He opened the windows, saw cargo ships waiting off Alameda Island, and breathed in a cool, moist breeze that smelled faintly of diesel and the ocean. A fresh start, maybe? Was he ready to move on from his nagging doubts about murder and conspiracy? Not quite yet.

He picked up the medical records he'd removed from Granfa's office and placed them on a side table next to his couch. Those were for later, for a time when he was free from Personil's haze. He took the herbalism book he'd borrowed—*it's only stealing if you don't put it back*—into the kitchen and flipped through it. Each turn of the page revealed dense descriptions of growing seasons, harvesting methods, and possible health effects. He'd never heard of most of the herbs in the book.

He flipped through the pages one more time and imagined tossing the book out the window, but then he saw the name printed in tiny handwritten letters at the top of the title page: Ming Pearl. Who was Ming Pearl?

Too intriguing to ignore. Too dangerous to investigate. Victor paced in his living room, clutching the book in both hands. Was the herbalism book a clue or a distraction?

The doorbell chimed. He put the book down, moved to the door, and opened it a crack. Elena pushed through, agitated and restless: lighter fuel for his current mood. His heart thudded in quick, clustered beats as he closed the door behind her. She scanned the room, looking for opportunities and threats. "Not quite Eastmore-class. Better than your dorm room, I guess."

His furniture had been selected randomly from Mesh catalogs to shortcut what would otherwise have been many hours of deliberation, and he was glad when she moved to the few colorful abstract paintings he used for meditation. Let her try to puzzle out what those were for.

She sniffed and turned away from the paintings. As she walked past, she ran her hands over the back of his dun-colored sofa as if it were a large, docile pet. She moved on, disappearing down the hall into the bathroom and reemerging a moment later, returning to the living room, eyes flicking around.

"When was the last time you had anyone over?" she asked. She had a look on her face that implied an unasked question, *"and fucked them?"*

Never. Sex was complicated. With so much sensory overload, it was nearly impossible not to go blank, as she knew well.

She sat on the sofa and fidgeted with the couch pillows, not meeting his gaze. He could tell her question was meant as a distraction.

"That's none of your business. What's going on?"

"I'm worried about you. Are you still on your medication?"

"Of course," he answered, more loudly than he'd intended. "It's mandatory."

"You can't hide anything from me. Your eyes go blank when you lie."

"They do *not*. Not *blank* blank, anyway."

She looked at him with skepticism.

He sighed. "I'm adjusting my dosing schedule. In fact, I was just about to take the next one. You can watch if you want. And if we're doing honesty, you have to answer one of my questions."

A flicker of embarrassment moved across her face—a creased brow, a twitch in her lips. "Fine."

"Why are you back in SeCa? Why really?"

"It seemed like the right thing to do," she said, not meeting his eyes.

"Vague. Not quite truthful. You're not very good at hiding things from me, either. How long are you here?"

Her fingers slid into the gaps on either side of her, between the couch's seat cushions, a gesture he found strange and oddly erotic. "I haven't decided." The anxiety and falsehood knotting her brow were apparent.

"Something's going on with you."

Elena pressed her lips together. "I'm here to help you, Victor—that's all. You look like you're hanging by a thread."

He snorted. "What's new about that?"

"They're going to lock you up one day for no good reason."

"I can think of a few excellent reasons."

She frowned. "Alik was an accident."

He glanced down at his feet. "You don't need to make excuses for me. Carmichael wasn't an accident."

"And you're not Samuel Miller. Don't get it twisted. They don't get to tell you who you are."

"I wish that was true."

"Then be happy someone is on your side." She took a step closer.

Victor felt backed into a corner even though he stood in the middle of the room.

A feeling passed back and forth between them, a desperate longing—not anything sexual; that feeling had died months before she left for Texas, though maybe it was time to test that assumption ... no, the pull was more of a desire to be acknowledged, to be valued, to be surprised by someone's capacity to love unconditionally. They'd been crucial partners during difficult times, and a bond like that could withstand years apart and mountains of resentment. If only they could each admit it. If only they could be truthful with one another.

"It's time for my meditation," he said, looking at the door.

Elena stiffened. "You're pushing me away again."

Victor felt her disapproval like a punch in the gut. The word that best described her attitude toward him was loyal, and he was underserving. But she wasn't being honest either. "I don't know what you want, but I can't handle it now. Granfa Jeff is dead, suspiciously, and everyone is pressuring me to take my stupid pills and forget about him. I'm barely holding it together; it's all jumbled in my head, and *you're not helping*. 'They don't get to tell you who you are.' That's true for you, Elena. For me, here, who I am is very much up to them."

Elena's eyes softened, but there was also something cold in them. "I'll go. But you're going to need me."

He said nothing.

"Take your pill. You promised."

Victor made a show of retrieving a pill from the bottle, filling a glass of water, popping it in his mouth, and washing it down.

He led her back through the living room, stopping at the threshold of the foyer. "Satisfied?"

She shrugged. "Yes, for now."

"Really?"

"Your family is worried. I don't blame them."

"One thing you've never done is side with them against me. Don't start now."

His jab landed hard. She stared at him, eyes blazing. But she held back a fiery retort. "Fine" was all she said, before she was out the door, closing it with a bang.

Victor bounded to the kitchen, leaned over the sink, and spat out the softening pill. Everyone kept telling him what to do. He was tired of it. His suspicions—about Granfa Jeff, about Elena, and his own decline—scratched at the insides of his skull, trying to get out. He'd let them out once, with Granma, but wouldn't make that mistake again.

In the living room, he looked at the herbalism book again. Ming Pearl. Whoever she was, she knew something about Granfa's illness. He had to find her and speak with her soon.

Semiautonomous California
3 March 1991

Elena followed Victor through the pine trees on his hunt for whatever he was looking for. Herbs? Sanity? She thought about the Puros oraciones. What would they say? *May you find the peace you're standing on.*

May we all.

She was helping Victor. And he needed it—that much she was clear on.

It was good to be moving after so long sitting in the car. The air was so dry it tickled her throat. She spotted a Jeffrey pine, tall, a soothing red-brown, with bark pieces interlocking like a three-dimensional puzzle. They completely surrounded the cabin, she realized. She went over to the nearest tree, leaned in, and sniffed its butterscotch aroma.

"Check this out," she called.

No answer. She looked around. Victor had moved behind a tree or beyond a ridge.

She knew he was struggling, wound tight and thrumming with the energy required to keep his wild brain in check. He needed her, even if he wouldn't admit it. But she was siding with his family against him, taking their money, feeding them information. Meanwhile, the family were refusing to see that *something* was going on. If Victor ever found out about the surveillance, how her methods were muddled, and her motives were less than pure, well ... who knows what would happen?

She sighed and began to search for him. It was easier back in Oakland, where she could simply listen to the sonofeed from the device she'd hidden in his couch cushions. Now, each step across a carpet of pine needles was heavy. Sometimes, the right thing to do *for* a friend was also the wrong thing to do *to* a friend.

I'm not used to being the asshole in this relationship. It's time to come clean.

She would find him and tell him everything, she owed him that much, and the rift between them could finally begin to heal. She could save him from doubting himself. And he could bring her back to her old, fearless self.

Semiautonomous California
16 May 1983

After Victor was diagnosed, most students didn't want to be seen with the kid who had put one of them in a coma, never mind that Alik was the real bully, refusing to acknowledge Elena's transition and dead-naming her every chance he got. Plenty of other kids had reasons to resent being made his target for humiliation, too. Still, people talked, and the social hierarchy in SeCa put people with MRS at the bottom. The facts of what Victor had done metastasized into gory rumors, comparing him to a cold-hearted, wild-minded demon like Samuel Miller. Elena acted as his protector, confidant, and publicist. It was a losing battle.

The pressure started to get to him, and her. They managed, wearily, slogging through a childhood interrupted by adult-sized worries. One May, when the tension got too horrible, she begged their parents to do something special for him, and after much pleading, they let both of them skip school for a day at the beach. The Eastmore and Morales families took a yacht—the Eastmores', of course—out in the early morning. Under a ceiling of fog that gradually dispersed, they carved a route north in choppy waters that calmed when they reached Tomales Bay. After oysters, caviar, and an unhealthy heap of fried taters, they were chauffeured south in a dune buggy caravan to a vast expanse of beach that separated a marsh from the tumultuous blue-gray Pacific.

While Eastmore staff erected tents and made the sandy expanse into an outpost for the families' relaxation, Elena led Victor toward rocks exposed by low tide. Their feet and ankles were chilled by a foamy inch of seawater, ice-shocking, and Victor made a show of going further, squealing as the deepening water rose above his knees. Elena, however, saw no use in numbing herself any more than was needed.

In the tide pools, they found starfish, tiny black crabs, and several much larger ones using their chitinous claws to ascend the rocks. Victor gently prodded a sea anemone with his finger to see it hide in a quick implosion and then slowly unfurl again. He and Elena jumped between rocks onto patches of sand, splashing when the waves came in, looking for stranded fish in the rock pools. The troubles of school, wary grownups, and opportunistically cruel kids faded away. They shivered in the cold spray then were warmed by the sun as they crawled across a rocky landscape that teemed with strange life. Victor seemed elated, shouting at her to, "Look! Look quick! An octopus!"

Sometimes, change comes on slowly and then arrives all at once. As the afternoon wore on, they didn't notice the tide turning. They were in a tiny cove, surrounded by tall rock walls like the ruined remains of an ancient temple. A heavy spray caught them in the face, and they laughed. But a moment later, they were pushed over by a wave that rolled right over them, followed by another and another. The water kept rising and surging until their feet no longer touched the sand. The water receded briefly and then returned, stronger than before. Elena saw Victor's panicked glance. They weren't so familiar with the concept of emotional contagion back then, and she didn't realize he'd picked up on her fear and internalized it.

He took a few gasping breaths and looked around frantically.

She gripped his shoulder. "We'll be okay."

He nodded and gulped. "Can we climb?"

They looked up at the meters of rock that loomed above them. Plenty of handholds but each one slippery and many sharp. The path around the rocks was mostly waist deep now; knee high only when the waves receded. Further out and back toward the curve of the beach, where their family had set up, she could see breakers, some two meters tall. Here, though, the odd angles of the cove churned the waves into frothy, foamy water.

Backwash tugged at the sand beneath her feet. "Step lively!" she shouted over the roar of water surging across uneven surfaces. It sounded like the rumble of drums.

Victor, meanwhile, had found footholds on the side of a boulder. Gripping with one hand, he reached out to her. "Up here." He made room, and they grasped the wall as the next large wave surged, rising as high as her thighs.

"What's down there?" She pointed to the other side of the boulder they stood on. A swirl of turbulent water rushed out and revealed sand. Maybe a way out.

"Help me down," he said.

She was adjusting her grip when a wave hit. She toppled, slamming onto one side, and the pull started to drag her out. Victor jumped down into the swirl, grabbed her by her arm and ankle, and when the next wave lifted her, he pulled her close, scraping across barnacles and other cruel life that scabbed the rock walls. She steadied herself on her feet again as Victor braced against the force of the oncoming wave and kept her stable. At the next ebb, they lurched up the slope. Another set of rocks blocked their view, but now, even when the waves came full force, there was only knee-deep water to trudge through. They hobbled onto dry sand, scorching under the midday sun, a welcome heat. She was chilled to the bone, although some scrapes on her arm and back felt like hot flames.

Victor stood immobile, staring back at the rocks and the waves that crashed and pushed and pulled.

"You're okay," she said, moving closer to wrap her arm around him.

"I'm still there. Stuck on that rock. In the panic. I'm there right now in my head, in the suck. It's what I feel like all the time."

She followed his gaze to the horizon, a misty haze obscuring the line between sky and sea.

"Well, you saved my butt. Though I'm a bit roughed up." She tried to wipe bloody sand off her arm but only managed to make her skin more raw. "You know, the first day I came to school as Elena, my transition day, it felt as cold as that water."

He looked at her, drawn out from whatever blankness had eaten at him. She could always tell exactly how far away he was mentally.

She continued, "Everyone was *fine*. The way the school handled it was fine. The teachers were fine. The other students, when they said anything, it was all exactly how we're taught a transition should go. Fine, proper, and cold, and ..." What was the word she was looking for? Insincere? Aloof? Soulless? "Everyone did the right thing. And it felt wrong. Except for you."

"Me?"

"You asked if I wanted a ride to school. No offense, but you're not usually that thoughtful. You made an effort. You asked how I wanted to spend lunchtime. You asked how I felt but said I didn't have to say if I didn't want to. You knew I was going through something, and you tried to help. Your heart was in the right place. I felt it. Everyone else just did what they thought they had to do. It felt like they resented that I could finally be myself."

"I can't take too much credit. Most of those kids haven't been through what I've been through. I see things maybe a little more clearly. Some things. Sometimes."

"They could have tried to see it my way or shown a little curiosity. They pretended everything was all right, which was somehow worse. Their acceptance was a murmur through a closed door. That's what I was worried about, and I was disappointed to be proven right."

"About what? I'm not following."

"Eli had a lot of friends. But I was afraid that Elena would have to start over. Part of it was me, my insecurities, I know that. I wanted a fresh start and pushed some people away because they would remind me of the past. I didn't want the past. I wanted the future. I'm saying that you're the only person who walked through that door with me."

Victor smiled. It was a knowing, sad but wise smile under a windswept and unkempt mess of hair, wet with sea foam and sand-speckled, and she loved him and told him so by squeezing his hand. Of course, he knew how she felt. When he smiled, she knew he felt the same.

"Well, I guess I'm two ahead then, huh?" he said. "If we're keeping score."

"We aren't keeping score, and we're dead even, considering all the times I shook your ass out of blankness, don't you think?"

"Okay." He shrugged. "We can be dead even—though it'd be better if we're *alive* even."

She didn't groan at his attempt at a joke, and he smiled to see her so annoyed. She said, "And that's how it works. We save each other's asses on the daily, and we stay dead even. Agreed?"

"Dead right."

And they had. Time after time. Until she moved to Texas, and he had cut ties. Now that she'd returned, something had shifted on the field. The tallying of points didn't work the way it used to.

12

A warm breeze shook tree limbs and wafted a sweet butterscotch scent. *We're lucky*, Elena thought, *that this dried-out part of the Sierra Nevada hasn't burned down.*

She found Victor staring at a non-descript patch of ground back toward the road. He seemed to be rousing himself from a trip to blank space.

"Come on," she said. "Let's check this place out."

The cabin was not impressive, just a small hut with a peaked roof, though the materials— smooth wood-composite and flawless gray trim—looked new. And it had some surprises, like plumbing and power; the sources of both were unclear. The interior consisted of an entryway, a living room with a wood-burning stove with its metal chimney shooting through the roof, a sliver of a kitchen, and a bedroom with a single bed and a wardrobe. Elena sighed. No toilet. There must be an outhouse nearby. Although it was heating up outside, the interior was cool. The walls were well-insulated, and the cabin would keep them warm at night.

"Welcome home," Elena said. "Let's hope the well hasn't run dry."

Victor said, "It beats sleeping outside or in the car. Bears are hungry for human flesh out here."

Elena sat on the couch, sending a cloud of dust into the air. "And bobcats," she said. "And the wandering women. And mountain Corps who call this place home."

"There are no Corps in SeCa," Victor said.

"Of course, there are—just not in the Bayshore. They run in all the abandoned places from here to the border with the Louisiana Territories. And don't forget Las Vegas, where they cash their paychecks. Where the Diamond King lives." She noticed his skeptical look. "Everyone knows the Corps' chief is the Diamond King of Las Vegas."

"I didn't know," Victor said.

"He runs the OWS, too, if you ask me, but that's more of a debate."

Elena got up and searched the cupboards for food. She found cans of vegetables, hard pasta, and other long-life foods crowding the shelves. "It's fully stocked," she told him. "I'll give Ozie credit for that." She ran the tap and drank a glass of cool water that tasted of earth and then a second one. "Who's he running with these days?"

Victor said, "A group of brain hackers. He can't enter SeCa without being arrested for being a Class Two."

She could see a storm brewing in Victor's eyes. He wasn't doing well. Damn, she'd been looking forward to getting everything off her chest, but now she couldn't risk saying anything to upset him.

Maybe he needed a distraction.

"Let's go see the lake. Please?" Elena asked.

Victor looked up, met her gaze, seemed to realize he was spiraling, and nodded.

Semiautonomous California
3 March 1991

On his way out, Victor saw the herb book sitting on the couch, opened to the inscription written by Ming Pearl. He flipped through pages to the entry on cardamom—the run-of-the-mill kind—which was disappointingly brief and said nothing about a black variety. The scientific name, *Elettaria cardamomum*, appeared in ornate script at the top of the page, and the line beneath indicated in smaller block letters that the plant was part of Zingiberaceae, the ginger family. A drawing showed a stalk composed of round pods and flanking leaves. Under the heading "Uses," only two words were written: "digestion" and "exorcism."

Semiautonomous California
25 February 1991

Around eight a.m., as he drove up the spiraling ramp of the Trans-Bayshore Rail Depot parking structure, he reminded himself that he wasn't investigating a murder. He was simply going to find an herbal replacement for Personil; although if he were asked, he'd have to call it a complement, not a replacement. An innocent excursion.

Trade with Asia and Oceania had fueled Oakland & Bayshore's growth. It was the main port for Semiautonomous California, its capital, and its largest city. Two million souls were packed into dense neighborhoods running up and down the flatlands and hills on the east side of the bay. And many of them transited through the dozens of rail lines that threaded through a labyrinthine complex of train platforms, plazas, pedestrian bridges, and a tangle of food markets, restaurants, and shops. No one looked twice at Victor as he made his way to the westbound platform.

The train was not the sleek European-built model he'd expected but an older one, perhaps transferred from the Southeastern Confederacy many decades ago and continually refurbished. Its metal looked rusted and almost worn through in places. He pressed himself into the last compartment. The train shuddered to life.

Victor peered out the window at the Golden Gate Strait as the train mounted the Bayshore Bridge. A few yachts were headed to sea through a narrow gap in the steep hills along the coast. Barely seaworthy fishing boats with an early morning catch were entering the bay and tacking south toward the San Francisco peninsula's decrepit waterfront, while larger cargo ships headed for Oakland & Bayshore's ever-expanding port facilities. Two steamers were being towed to immigrant processing centers on Angel Island, named for those unfortunate enough to arrive in poor health and never made it to the mainland. The island gave Victor the creeps, but he supposed it represented salvation to the refugees fleeing war and the drowned lands across the Pacific. On the San Francisco–Little Asia peninsula, wrecked buildings served as a reminder of the earthquake that had struck the growing town two decades after the 1829 Gold Rush. A few crumbling mansions, perched on the city's hills, overlooked refugee slums.

The train pulled into the terminal, which was, as usual, crowded with beggars, buskers, and corrupt police looking to shake down unsuspecting travelers. He moved quickly, never slackening his pace. Beyond the frontage road, a tall red-and-gold wood gate marked the entrance to Little Asia, which, in fact, occupied the entire peninsula. Victor passed beneath the gate as hawkers called out their wares:

stims, tailored euphorics, and other drugs. One man, his face a mass of sagging wrinkles and a wispy beard, shouted, "Aura" repeatedly, stringing the words together in an unbroken wail.

Victor turned at the sound of shouting behind him. Across the street, a few thugs took turns punching a middle-aged man in the gut, holding him by his ripped suit jacket. One of the thugs noticed Victor, signaled his friends to ease up and pointed at him. Victor froze, hoping that he'd only imagined them taking an interest in him. His mind could be misinterpreting, projecting his fears onto the situation. But his gut told him to move.

He walked quickly. Then, hearing the shouts of the thugs behind him, he started to run. He reached a corner and almost knocked over a short old lady as he pushed past her. A cyclist yelled and swerved as Victor darted across the street. He chanced a look behind him. The thugs turned the corner and spotted him again. He bolted inside a small grocery packed with racks of vegetables and bulk grains. Down the aisle, he found a door, and bumped into a teenage girl who pressed herself against the wall of goods to let him pass. He emerged into an alley and ran smack into someone who grabbed him and shoved him against the wall.

Two people, a man and a woman, barred his way. *Two*, a taste of fear and dread. The man who had grabbed him had spiky black hair. The woman's hair was tied in a taut bun. Both appeared to be around Victor's age or a little older. They had the muscles and skin tone of people who sweat often.

The gang of thugs rounded the corner and hesitated when they saw Victor wasn't alone. The spiky-haired man pulled a black shockstick with a red glowing tip from a waist holster and pointed. The thugs quickly retreated the way they'd come.

"Thanks," Victor said.

The woman sighed and said to her companion, "This was not our fault." She sounded foreign, European, maybe.

"Who are you?" Victor asked, breathing heavily.

"Don't matter. What now?" the man said, looking at his partner.

"Shhh," she said. "Let's just go."

They jogged to the alley's entrance. After a moment, Victor followed, but when he turned the corner, they were gone.

The street was filled with honking vehicles and some kind of demonstration between two groups of people. Victor paused, trying to recover his breath and get his bearings.

He spotted a young woman with smart-looking glasses and a book bag standing by herself. He approached her slowly. "Excuse me. I'm looking for Ming Pearl's shop on Front Street."

She frowned. "You're not a cop, are you?"

Victor laughed. "No one's asked me that before."

The young woman smiled. "Of course I know Pearl. She's legendary."

"Where can I find her?"

She looked him up and down and smiled slyly. "The door with the lotus flower halfway down the block. Good luck, handsome."

Victor followed the young woman's directions to Front Street and came across a heavy door. Its large, engraved lotus flower looked beaten, like someone had taken an axe to it. He entered. Inside the shop, the noise from the street was muffled. Crisp, bright lightstrips were spaced along the ceiling with obsessive precision. Boxes were stowed in racks, neatly aligned to brightly colored rectangles of tape on the floor.

He shuffled deeper into the shop and approached a low desk, where a small middle-aged woman sat using a typepad with more dexterity and focus than he'd ever seen. She wore a forest-green blazer, spotless and unwrinkled, and a white, collared shirt dotted with a bright red poinsettia pattern. Black wiry hair like burnt steel wool haloed her head. A pair of reading glasses threatened to fall from the tip of her nose.

She said a few words in Chinese.

"Are you Ming Pearl?"

She glanced up and then returned her attention to her typepad. "You want traditional medicine?" she asked.

"Yes, and I have a few questions," Victor said.

"Desperate. Always so desperate."

"I want to stop taking Personil."

She looked up and studied him. Her lips twitched, and something like a snort came out. She was hard to age, Victor thought. She could have been anywhere between forty and seventy years old. Lowering her head again, she continued typing. It looked like she was tallying numbers in the high tens of thousands.

"I can pay you," he said.

"You want something, you wait," she said, then ignored him again.

Victor explored the shop for several minutes and then returned to the desk. The woman wasn't moving. Her eyes were closed as if meditating.

"What are you doing?" he asked with a nervous glance around.

"Asking a question." She opened her eyes and stood. "They tell me I may help you," she said.

"Who?"

The herbalist leaned forward and looked at him with wide, bulging eyes and hands held up like claws. "My ancestor ghosts."

"I—"

She leaned back, cackling loudly. Her lungs rattled from the strength of her hooting. "I got you good, didn't I? Look, don't come at me with that mystical lady and her magical herbs nonsense. No, thank you. I like to keep every channel open, of course, sales and spiritual, and who knows how much wisdom a hallucination of ghosts might impart to me, but this time, considering who you are, I was consulting my conscience, and seeing how much of a sucker you might be." She stood up. "Call me, Pearl. It's nice to put a face to the name."

"You know … my name?"

"Yes, I know who you are. Jefferson made it sound like you would take your sweet time." Pearl cleared her throat. "What I mean is, I didn't expect you so soon. It's been a bad week. The last person with MRS I tried to help was reclassified. In a single day, she went from Three to One. I think she's in the Humboldt facility—not a nice one, I hear. I'm not sure I can help you, but I'll try."

Victor blinked. All the questions he'd prepared fled to the unreachable shadows. "I'm looking for black cardamom," he said at last.

"Useless! The dark grid is all wrong about that one. Good only for cooking. I have something else for you."

Her hand swiped across wooden cubbies lining the wall behind her desk. Each was neatly labeled in precise lettering. She plucked something out, turned, and revealed a sealed plastic container from which she removed a sachet of pink silk that fit in her palm. She emptied brown, twisted leaves into a shallow ceramic bowl. "Fumewort. Don't burn it. The combustion byproducts cause cancer—not that we need to worry about that anymore. Still, burning's no good. I'll show you how to make a tincture."

She came out from behind the desk, grabbed the bowl with one smooth gesture, and moved past him in short, pattering steps, her wispy hair nearly brushing his chin. She left behind a charred, woodsy smell. He followed her to several tables loaded with all kinds of envelopes, pouches, and boxes.

Along one wall stood a counter arranged with brown glass bottles. From a tray, Pearl plucked a pipette. She used it to suck a clear liquid from a jar and squirt it into a small glass vial. She pinched a few brown and flaky pieces of fumewort into a mortar and pestle, ground them up with quick and efficient violence, and scraped the powder into the liquid. She added water from the tap.

"Twenty milliliters pure alcohol and one hundred milliliters water, roughly. Add one gram of the herb. Wait at least one hour. Stable at room temperature. Drink the whole thing, though you might want to mix it with fruit juice. Some say it's like puke going down."

"What does it do?"

"Calms the mind. Anytime you feel panic, drink."

"This is all I brought." Victor held out the black coins.

Pearl looked at the coins but didn't take them. "I've already been paid. You'll want these." She pulled a dozen vials down from a shelf and arranged them in a box with a lattice to keep them secure. She put the box in a cloth tote, added the sachet, and handed the tote to him. "Let's see how this works, and if you need more, no problem."

He hung the tote off his shoulder. Could a few flaky herbs really help him? "How did you know Jefferson?"

Pearl said, "That's personal. I'll see you again soon."

"You seem sure that I'll come back."

Pearl smiled. "Won't you?"

"What you said earlier: you didn't expect to see me so soon."

"Jefferson told me you'd be skeptical. That you needed time."

Victor crossed his arms. He was sure she knew more than she was telling him. "What *exactly* did he say?"

Pearl waved her hands dismissively. "The fumewort should keep you out of trouble. You're not the only one seeking answers. Come back later, like next week or maybe next month," Pearl said.

"What aren't you telling me?"

She seemed resolved not to speak. Victor wanted to grab her blazer lapels and shake the truth out of her. Before his hands could reach out, she took him by the arm with a surprising force, spun him around, and escorted him to the door.

Why would Granfa Jeff ask an herbalist to help? When Dr. Tammet's treatments veered toward the experimental and holistic, Jefferson had steered her back to the mainstream. Did he have a change of heart about alternative therapies? And, really, what could herbs do for someone with such powerful symptoms?

The mystery pulled at Victor—the same pull he recognized from previous slides into blankspace: a precarious, cloying feeling. He couldn't trust himself. He needed to stay on the narrow path of sanity. He wasn't going to see Pearl again. He might not even take the fumewort tinctures. Okay, maybe one or two. To supplement the Personil. Like Circe had said, Granfa's death was his chance to start afresh.

He nearly bumped into a table on the sidewalk crammed full of little trinkets, pieces of jewelry, and slips of paper rolled into tiny scrolls. One jade figure caught his eye. It looked like a wolf and lion and bird, all wrapped up in the same body. A perfect present for Elena. She was right. He had pushed her away. He would try not to fuck it up again.

13

Semiautonomous California
25 February 1991

Victor returned without incident to the safer side of the bay, retrieved his car from the parking structure, and drove home. Back in his neighborhood, with robins chirping and flitting around in search of mates, twigs, and perches, he walked to the Freshly Juice Shop and bought a simple carrot-based concoction rich in beta-carotene and antioxidants. Ric wasn't there—another person who disappeared from Victor's life without warning—and the mood inside the shop was dull and dreary. Afterward, Victor stopped at a general store for a bottle of the purest alcohol. His purchase was logged, another indignity for Class Threes.

At home, he ground up all the fumewort, made a batch of twelve tinctures, and waited, sitting on his living room floor, meditating to regain calm after a tumultuous couple of days. With his eyes unfocused, he fixed his gaze on a painting, an impressionistic rendering of a galaxy of colorful stars. The image undulated and flexed. But whenever the vaguest hint of blankspace intruded, he found to his surprise that he could push it out of consciousness. For a moment, he missed the wave of euphoria that sometimes accompanied the run-up to a blank episode, that soothing, warm swell before the cooling splash and immersion into blankness. Did he miss it enough to induce it? Should an arsonist play with matches?

His MeshBit timer pinged. Victor got up, went to the kitchen, poured one fumewort tincture into the bulb with carrot juice, and held his thumb over the opening while he sloshed the mixture. He drank it down in three gulps. Hints of earth and alcohol cut through the familiar taste of the thin, silky carrot juice. Not like puke at all. It tasted like a fresh start.

Victor mentally scanned his body and then laughed at himself. He shouldn't expect instant results. He paced the room, trying to be patient and to push away a groundless suspicion that Pearl had scammed him. Though why had she been so cagey and dodged all his questions? When his gaze fell on the file of medical records on his coffee table, his breath caught in his throat. *Too soon. Give it time. Or not at all.* He retreated to the kitchen and heated a serving of leftover pork stew, eating too quickly and burning the roof of his mouth.

It was past noon. He couldn't stay in his apartment, freaking out over nothing. The medical records would be there when he returned if he chose to look at them. So, he drove to the Gene-Us campus, hurried inside, and sat at his desk. The brightness on the vidscreens in front of him needed adjusting, and he could hear footfalls in the hallway despite the carpeting. Mounds of work had piled up in his queue. He started with a large batch of proto-cancer gene screenings.

On the analysis tab, a jagged red line traced the usage of computing resources, a close-to-useless metric, too general. He applied a filter to show subcomponents of the gene sequencers' performance individually, including error rates in the sequencing flow and bottlenecks in the transfer of data from the sequencing machines to the Boze-Drive storage devices. He'd seen outputs like this hundreds of times before, but it felt like he was seeing the data for the first time. He pulled up another log containing thousands of lines of code and looked for anomalies. In a flash, he found where a subunit of the algorithm was looping, getting stuck on itself as it churned through millions of sequenced base pairs, filling the buffer with junk data interspersed with the good that had to go through secondary processing before being written to the Boze-Drives.

Sweat formed in his armpits, and he wiped his forehead. He wrote edits to the code and committed them, breaking the department protocol of cross-checking changes with another analyst. He reran the test. One minute passed. Another. The loops didn't come back. His new code had unkinked them. The updated algorithm resulted in a 23 percent efficiency gain. Most fixes topped out at one or two percent. *Laws, what a rush!*

The fair-haired, pink-skinned male analyst next to him wheeled his chair over and asked, "What are you hooting about?"

Victor pointed to the screen. "This took me less than five minutes."

The analyst cocked his head, reading. Then his lips parted agog, showing yellowed front teeth. "You're kidding me. Send me your log."

Victor swiped the records into the analyst's queue. A minute or so later, his colleague whistled. "That's incredible. Can I get you to look at something I've been working on?"

Victor wheeled over and watched a coding matrix rise on the vidscreen.

The analyst said, "I know there's a mismatch in here, but I—"

"There," Victor said, gently moving the analyst's hand off the touchpad and zooming in with his fingers. "I'll bet it's keyed off the wrong reference sequence. Check the library files from the Human Genome Initiative's feed. They might have updated them without telling us."

The analyst grabbed Victor's arm as if to verify he was really there. "What's got into you?"

Victor shrugged and smiled. "I just see it."

"You got laid or something, didn't you?"

Victor blushed. "That's my secret," he said, glancing at his desk drawer where he'd hidden a handful of fumewort vials. He didn't credit the herb for his new efficiency, not entirely. The Personil was also clearing from his system, allowing his thoughts to speed up to their natural potential.

That night at home, he looked at the Personil pill bottle. *Take your pills, they said. We're worried about you. We want what's best: an easy-to-control, hazed-out dope.* Blankspace in one direction and Personil vagueness in the other. One or the other, that's what he believed. But what if that was a mistake? What if he could balance in the middle? Rather than take a pill, he opted instead to take a fumewort dose. He gulped the liquid down at the kitchen counter, then returned to the living room to review Granfa Jeff's medical records.

He immediately noticed something odd, something he'd missed before when his mind had been caught in Personil's gluey grip. The papers from the first three months listed symptoms in detail and included multiple results from over a dozen tests. But after that, the paper trail thinned out. From September onward, there were no new prescriptions, only a few neatly typed notes, and barely any tests—all at a time when his granfa's condition must have been progressively worsening. It was as if both his grandfather and the doctor had given up.

Victor sat back on his sofa and tried to imagine a scenario to explain the records. The only treatment Jefferson had received during his final months was a prescription for Vasistatin. Surely, there were more invasive treatments available as well. Why hadn't he turned to those?

Maybe he had decided to stop fighting the disease. But that wasn't like him. He was the definition of tenacity and stubbornness—never surrender was his motto—but maybe his illness had taken such a toll on him that he'd welcomed the end. Or maybe dementia had taken hold, and he wasn't able to plan his treatment. But if either were the case, the doctors would have pushed treatment on him, or at least the records would show that they tried to.

Victor rifled through each of the papers again. Before Oak Knoll Hospital closed, a broad battery of tests for Jefferson had been ordered, and the results were thoroughly documented, some coming back with values well outside normal ranges, including hair loss, mouth ulceration, and kidney ailments.

After Oak Knoll closed, the number of tests diminished, and all came back within normal ranges, except blood tests for electrolytes and creatinine and electrocardiogram and angiogram measurements, which were all related to heart failure. Pre- and post-closure of the hospital, the results were staggeringly different. If not for the patient's name, Victor would have said the records were for different patients. He looked again at the post-closure results. They told an unmistakable story, but compared with the messy initial tests, they seemed too perfect, too spot-on. Something was wrong with the official explanation, the one his family and BioScan kept pushing. A truth was being buried.

A cold, hard knot formed in his guts. The records pointing toward heart failure were lies. He would keep digging until it was exposed and stay off Personil until the truth came out.

14

Elena retrieved Victor from where he got stuck in the pages of his herb book, and they were soon back in the car, heading south toward Lake Tahoe, jostling along a mountain road that hadn't been maintained for years. It took an hour to reach the pass.

"Where else have you been in SeCa besides Oakland? And the C-town, of course." She wouldn't say "Carmichael" aloud while he was on edge.

He said his parents rarely took him on vacations when he was young, perhaps because they thought he needed a strict routine. Elena's parents had always been too busy to take her on vacations. He listed aquariums, farms, and vineyards on the north and central coasts and small farming communities throughout Long Valley before they became too dangerous. She smiled; he was so cautious and naïve at the same time. She'd made the right decision to help him. And it was the right decision not to tell him about her past, yet.

They parked, and when they got out, Elena spotted an old, fading sign for a trailhead marked Deer Creek Lookout. After a short walk, they crested a ridge, and she gasped at the sight of a vast terrain, like an entire cosmos. Hotel towers and tourist businesses clustered near the shore and climbed the mountainsides, but they were high above it all, alone and unwatched. A seamless blue sky soothed her. They could finally breathe.

Victor asked, "What do you think this used to look like?"

"When? In winter?"

"No, before we were born. Before all these people, the towns."

She made a square frame with her fingers and panned across the view. "I'd love to see realpics from back then. It would have been beautiful." Before they were felled by decades of fervent construction, redwoods proliferated along ridges and filled the valleys. The blue, clear lake of years ago that sparkled in the sun was now green and clouded by algal blooms; too many nutrients had destroyed the delicate balance of the lake.

Dozens of rafts, decorated with giant helium balloons in the shapes of animals, dotted the lake's surface. Victor was eager to explain the science behind the restoration efforts, that the rafts trolled the lake to absorb waste materials and pollutants. She thought the crafts were about as attractive as such human-made additions could be. Without them, the lake would have long become another unnatural wonder of the West.

She widened her stance, thrusting one hand forward and the other toward the heavens, and proclaimed, "An ancient scene: sun and sky, terrain and trees, the clear crystal depths of a mountain lake." She let her arms fall. "It's porn for poets up here."

"Hmm, that was … *original*." Victor smiled, and his boyish expression charmed her.

She slipped her hand inside his and squeezed. She took a few deep breaths. "Try it," she commanded. "Do you feel it? The altitude?"

He breathed deeply, puffing his chest like a bird. Then he exhaled. He shook his head and tried again. After the sixth breath, he claimed he still hadn't induced an oxygen high. Around the tenth time, he teetered on his feet, and she wrapped an arm around him. He relaxed a bit, but there was a tension there too.

Together, they looked out onto the lake. They couldn't pick up where they had left off—more than friends, less than lovers—but maybe they could start someplace new.

As she turned toward the car, Victor reached out, gently grabbing Elena's shoulder. "Wait." He took a small item from his pocket and presented it to her: a red jewelry box with a Chinese character pressed into it in gold foil. He gently lifted the lid.

Inside, a glossy green pendant rested on a bed of cotton. Some combination of animals, parts fused like a mad creator's dream. She picked it up. The jade's contours were smooth and oily in her palm.

"This is something," she said, smiling.

"We used to watch all those movies of the Great Asian War, and you were always rooting for the Chinese."

She laughed. "And the Koreans. And the Filipinos. Anyone except the emperor."

"You made me watch *The Burning Shore* at least a hundred times."

"Because it's a masterpiece!" She rubbed the pendant. "This feels lucky. Where did you get it?"

"Little Asia."

She smacked him in the arm. "You know how dangerous that is."

"It's nothing compared to what you say about Texas. Anyway, I survived. See, I can take care of myself. And I thought of you, and ... well, how we used to be. Anyway, doesn't going to extremes for you show how amazing I am?" He smiled and almost looked like a different person, someone carefree and zany.

"You're in a mood," she teased.

"I know! I hope it lasts! Anyway, I got this to say thank you."

"Thank me for what?"

"All those years together. You taught me how to keep going. And now, you believed in me this time when my family didn't. You're probably why I'm not locked in an asylum."

"Don't say that word."

"You like 'Class One supportive living facility' better?" Victor asked, still smiling, but bitterness had crept into his voice.

"No." She sighed. They were only getting along now because she continued to lie to him.

"It doesn't matter. All I wanted was to say thank you. Will you let me?" He pointed to her neck.

Elena pulled back her hair. He clasped the chain around her neck and hugged her. Something was wrong, though; when he pulled away, he stared at the ground.

"What is it?" Elena asked.

Without looking up, he said, "I've been meaning to tell you. To explain. I didn't contact you after you moved because I thought you would be better off without me. I was holding you back."

She put a hand on his shoulder. "That's the stupidest thing I've ever heard," she said as she felt warmth rising in her cheeks. He might have thought it was affection, but it was shame. And as long as she kept deceiving him, it would grow until it consumed her.

Back at the cabin, Elena lay on the sofa while Victor made a meal of pasta with canned tomato sauce. She glanced through his dreambook. "What's this about you and Robbie and bombs falling all around you?"

"Explosions," he said from the kitchen. "Like world-shaking, fireballs from the sky, skin-melting explosions. And he kept saying, 'You know how to escape,' which was weird because he's never shown an ounce of confidence in me in his life."

"Skin-melting," she repeated back. The only feeling she could muster was relief her sleep wasn't so troubled.

15

Victor carefully stirred the pasta sauce, watching the swirls left in the wake of the spoon fade before his hand circled the pot again. He could almost forget that people were out to get him.

"Your dreams are incredible," Elena said from the living room.

His neck stiffened. "I told you about them before."

"It's different reading them. And there's so many. Where do they come from?"

The question was dangerously close to Nightmareland territory, where young Victor had thought Samuel Miller lived. Like Samuel, Victor, too, had believed his dreams were prescient. Victor, on good days, knew that they were just dreams.

"Have you been reading horror stories? Those could be inspiring your—"

"I don't read books."

He looked up from the pasta sauce and almost laughed at the puzzled expression on her face.

"I can't," he said. "The images stay with me. They're too real. I've got enough junk in my brain as it is."

He almost said, "Carmichael," but that was too obvious and painful. How could one traumatic event produce a lifetime of nights containing so many different scenarios, themes, and tortured dreams?

Elena was quiet throughout dinner. The wind rushing around the cabin sounded like a low-hooting owl, and the occasional crack of a breaking branch made them both jump. He watched her wrap spaghetti noodles around her fork, twisting them into a ball, but instead of taking a bite, she would twirl her wrist to unwind the noodles and return them to the bowl. And then she'd do it again.

The repetition was making his stomach flip and his skin crawl. Something was working its way out of her slowly like a splinter that was too deep to catch with tweezers, so the only thing for it was wait till it finally poked out of the flesh and could be grasped.

Semiautonomous California
23 February 1991

At dinner on the eve of Granfa Jeff's funeral, Victor sat opposite Auntie Circe, who directed servants with a glance or a graceful gesture. Beside her, Granma Cynthia seemed lost in her thoughts while dabbing at red-rimmed eyes with a black lace handkerchief. Fa and Ma held a quiet conversation, and Robbie fiddled with the silverware, rearranging it to suit his European sensibilities. Low-watt bulbs behind old-fashioned sconces and the dark, wood-paneled walls did nothing to lighten the mood.

The silence without Jefferson was heavy and dull, like a body soon after the heart had stopped beating, stiffening, growing cold, losing color. His guests livened the mansion with raised voices, laughter, and the occasional heated argument about the American Union's destiny in a world that seemed satisfied to ignore it. Tales of his travels provided glimpses of far-off places where no one had heard of Broken Mirrors. Victor admitted he missed Granfa's stories and conversations, which in their small ways, shined through cracks in the towering barricade of Victor's resentment that he hadn't known were there.

The bell for first courses chimed, and plates arrived heaped with delicate lettuces, roasted beets, and a firm cheese with a brackish smell that turned Victor's stomach. He moved the cheese to the far side of his plate and picked at the greens and beets.

"I actually detest Semiautonomous California," Robbie announced, unprompted. "Europe is wasting its money here."

Something about Robbie's self-satisfied, confident tone pressed Victor's buttons. "I think you're confusing propaganda with history."

Robbie smirked. The expression twisted his otherwise handsome face into something ugly and rodent-like. "Dear cousin, confusion is *your* area of expertise."

Victor bit his tongue.

"After Repartition," Robbie began in a pedantic drone that sounded more like a stuffy professor than someone who was, at twenty-five, less than a year older than Victor, "Europe generously helped the fledgling nations of the American Union find their legs. All of them, including SeCa, depend on European debt financing. It was a brilliant strategy. Now it's time for the AU to pay up and return that money home."

"Enough, Robbie," Circe said. "There'll be no talk of politics around this table today."

Chastened, he slumped and pouted.

Fa cleared his throat. "I suppose there will be questions about the company's future." He glanced at Circe, then pronged his salad with an affected nonchalance. He was nervous; anyone could see it. Circe had always been the favored sibling and was expected to take over HHN, so that couldn't be what was bothering him.

"It's a delicate balance," Circe responded. She sat with rigid spine, yet her narrow form was still diminutive. Granfa had been the only tall Eastmore. "I have to show that Father's actions over the past few months did no harm, yet at the same time, steer the company in a direction that puts all the rumors behind us. And I must do all this without—how did you put it, Mother?—without dragging the Eastmore name through a manure pond."

Fa said, "So, can we at least agree that we're *not* going to make a buck off the stim addicts filling our streets?"

Victor looked up, surprised. Were they planning to treat stim addicts in SeCa? As recently as a few months ago, there was talk of expelling the hopeless cases to other AU nations. SeCa excelled in carving off undesirable slices of the body politic and making them disappear. But he didn't think HHN would be complicit. He stayed quiet. He knew little of the family business. It was probably time for him to pay closer attention.

Circe raised an eyebrow. "We're a health care company. We respond to the needs around us. Here and elsewhere."

Granma forked a half globe of a small yellow tomato. "Could we leave business until after dinner?" She looked at her daughter. "Or perhaps you'd like to go over his will during dessert?"

Victor didn't sense any discomfort at the table beyond inter-personal prickliness and heavy grief. The great Jefferson Eastmore had died of heart failure. There was no mystery about it. The only mystery was in Victor's head.

Murder bird, murder bird, did him in. Don't let the murder bird win.

Black feathers narrowed his field of vision, gauze muffled sounds at the table, and weightlessness expanded in his chest.

Victor gripped the data egg in his pocket. He'd taken a pill after the funeral; he was sure of it. He shouldn't be having so many issues. Should his dosage be upped? Was this how the slide happened—steady for a while and then a sudden change?

Murder bird.

Fantasy or not, the incantation filled him up and blotted out all other thoughts. It wouldn't subside on its own. He had to expel it somehow. He excused himself, saying he wanted to rest, and shuffled out of the room. His parents let him go. For him, nothing was surprising about a nap during dinner.

Granfa wasn't murdered. The cause of death was heart failure. Medical records would prove it indisputably. Victor would murder the murder-bird rhyme with facts, evidence, and science.

He climbed the wide, carpeted staircase to the second floor and padded down the hall to Granfa's office. He gripped the knob, turned, and pushed. The door swung open with a loud, protesting creak. In the center of the room was a couch and two high-backed chairs with a low table between them. Off to the side was a reading nook with an overstuffed chair and ottoman. Bookcases flanked the bay windows overlooking the mansion's grounds. Against one wall, more bookcases rose above a large oak desk: Granfa's workplace when he wasn't touring the world.

He found a floor lamp, turned it to half-power, and looked around. *Knowledge comes to those bold enough to seek it.* A Jeffersonism. One of many.

Victor stepped to the desk and sat in the sizeable synthleather chair, absently sliding a book on the desk to the side. However, the book's texture caught his attention—slick and supple real leather. He looked more closely and recognized it as the handwritten compendium of herbal medicine Granfa had shown Victor on a foggy summer day just a few months before Oak Knoll had closed.

He tugged at the file drawer—locked. He stepped back. Something about the desk was wrong. He breathed deeply, relaxed, and looked again. A MeshTerminal with its vidscreen and type-pad dominated one side. The bust of Admiral Eastmore, his great-granfa, sat at the other corner. The sculpture sat oddly on the desk, tilting slightly. Victor lifted the heavy marble head, cradling it. Beneath lay a single brass key.

When he tried the key in the lock on the file drawer, it turned and opened smoothly, revealing folders labeled in neat block letters. Most were bank account statements and invoices relating to the running of the estate. But, in the back, a folder without a label held a dozen sheets of paper filled with checkboxes and unruly handwriting.

Medical reports from Oak Knoll Hospital, Victor realized with an adrenaline rush. Doctors' notes, test results, and prescriptions from the past six months. He pored over them. Only three months ago, after Oak Knoll had closed, the papers began to contain the words "heart failure." Three months seemed an excessive amount of time to obtain a diagnosis, especially when all the best doctors in the nation worked for Granfa Jeff.

Nothing else stood out in the notes. There must be some clue or connection he couldn't see clearly. Perhaps there were more electronic records. He tried the MeshTerminal, but he could only access his own cache, not Granfa's.

Victor sat back and cupped his hand around the data egg in his pocket. It probably held nothing, a silly greeting like those they exchanged for the holidays, only with added sentiment now that its author had returned to the earth. Someday, the data egg would open. That wasn't much help today. He wished he'd gotten the truth from Granfa Jeff rather than a vague non-explanation. "Never surrender," he'd said.

Never surrender to the murder bird.

Victor groaned aloud. The medical records hadn't helped. It was stupid to think facts could settle his brain's hyperactivity. Maybe it was time for an extra Personil. Or perhaps he could delicately ask a few more questions without arousing suspicions.

He went downstairs, hoping to find Granma Cynthia in her reading room, but it was empty, the lights off. Instead, he encountered Auntie Circe in the kitchen. She stood at a large island fitted with a sink, a marble countertop, and electric induction burners. She poured hot water into a carafe containing fragrant lemon slices and chopped ginger.

"Hey. I thought you left with your parents," she said, giving him a wary smile.

"I wanted to stay. Auntie, I—I messed up at the funeral."

Circe nodded, a silent agreement with his assessment. She poured some tea into her mug and took a small sip. "Victor, we all understand. Everyone handles grief their own way, and yours happens to be a bit more ... dramatic."

Victor shook his head. "I forgot my dose this morning."

"Are you caught up now?"

"Yes, and I'm taking an extra one before bed." He ran his hands through his hair and was surprised when they came away wrapped in several strands.

"Days like today are difficult for everyone," she said.

"The problem is I'm still thinking about it." He scratched along his jawline. "It keeps repeating in my head. How could I think for one second that Granfa was murdered?"

Circe filled her mug and inhaled. She nodded, seemingly satisfied. "We've come a long way since the start of the twentieth century and that kind of corruption." She took in another breath. "It's something we've left behind for the most part. Carmichael excepted."

Victor shook his head. "Even if there's something fishy about his illness or the timing of it, I shouldn't be blanking out this much."

"You might need to increase your dose. It's okay to ask for help. Personil is for—"

"Protection," he said, finishing the jingle. "Yes, I know. Protecting me from myself. Protecting everyone else from me." *Protection from the murder bird?* "I'll get over this hump," he said. "I'm trying. I looked through Granfa's medical records—"

Her eyes narrowed. "Don't tell Mother that."

Victor grimaced. "I thought it would help me stay grounded." A new thought occurred to him. "Was there an autopsy?" he asked. "Maybe if I read the report—"

Circe reached out and placed her hand gently on Victor's shoulder. "I know it helps to talk about your fantasies. But you can't indulge them. Your reclassification appointment is coming up. You need to show you're in command of your senses. We can't let you go the way of Samuel Miller."

Victor felt a chill climbing his spine. "Of course not. I'm trying. I am. I'm going to pull my life together. My job—"

"Karine speaks highly of you, and believe me, she can be a powerful ally. Gene-Us will continue to be a useful outlet for your intellect. Focus on that."

"I don't think she likes me."

"That's just her personality. Besides your job, though, don't forget to nurture your social connections. I saw Elena at the funeral.

I'm sure you're glad she's back." Circe smiled and drank her tea in several gulps. "Don't miss any more doses, okay?"

Victor nodded. "It would be easier if Granfa hadn't been acting so strangely. He was trying to tell me something."

Circe raised an eyebrow. "Tell you what?"

"I don't know, but he gave me this." Victor held up the data egg.

Her eyes focused on the black round shape. "A data egg? What's inside?"

"It's locked. He said it had an uncommon key. He said a bunch of stuff the day he closed Oak Knoll."

She placed the mug on the counter. Her movements were careful, precise. "Oak Knoll was a loss above all others. If only he'd consulted me." She smiled, but it didn't reach her eyes. "Hold onto that, Victor. Keep it with you. Tell me when it opens. Our mementos are precious, none so precious as those given by the departed." She hugged him firmly, then walked away.

Victor lingered in the kitchen after she left. A thought swam just outside the limits of his consciousness. Something about the medical records? He tried to reel it in but couldn't. He would take an extra dose of Personil as soon as he got home, but he wasn't looking forward to the dopey, gray, and lethargic feelings that accompanied the medication. One more glance through Granfa's papers, while he was relatively alert, might do the trick.

In the study, the medical records continued to whisper to him. There was something he wasn't seeing—if he could clear his mind of its fog. Rather than digging in his bag for a dose, he lay on the couch and settled his gaze on the herb book with its illustrations of leaves, stems, and roots. Then he closed his eyes, and as he fell asleep, delicate tendrils wormed themselves into the folds of his unconscious brain.

16

Victor put down his fork. The noodles in his bowl were cold, slimy. The wind had died down. Elena was scratching her arm, raising red welts, staring at her utensils.

"Ellie. You're not telling me something. What is it?"

She looked up at him. "You remember the day I left?"

Some ruptures are gentle, teasing apart like soap bubbles blown into the air lightly. Nothing had been that easy for a long time.

On the day before Elena left for the Republic of Texas, in the middle of their junior year of high school, every minute was a slow-motion rending of flesh, a heart pulled in two. She was grateful that Victor stopped by to help her pack up her things, but she wasn't sure they could get through it without crying. She greeted him at the door with a long hug and led him upstairs, hearing each step, every creak, counting down to an unknown future. Everything from the closet was strewn on the floor: catch-and-carry jerseys from her three seasons playing rear guard, knee and elbow pads, dresses from a phase when she'd amped up the estrogen, boots, and waders for fishing. There were shockingly few items that she wanted to bring with her. She started pushing the discards pile into a corner of the room, where she continued to add to it with mixed feelings—freedom spawned euphoria and a dangerous sense of letting go, like cottonwood puffs swirling in the wind.

Victor sat on the bed. "I can't believe you leave tomorrow."

"I know."

The papers in her hand were dusty and yellowing. She flipped through them as memories flashed by. If she didn't save these, would she forget them completely? She found a flyer for a school play in kindergarten. The cast list included Eli Morales—a relic from a past that didn't matter.

"What's this?" Victor asked. He held a binder, its pages sheathed in transparent film.

"Realpics mostly. Old ones." She sat next to him on the bed. "I used them for a school project. Careful. They're ancient."

She watched him blink, a furrow between his brows. The binder was open to a set of thin painted-metal plates. Printed across the top, in bright orange, was "The Purity Caucus." The plates depicted scenes of protest outside cathedrals. The people wore their Sunday best: elaborate hats, suits and ties, ankle-length dresses with bustles and corsets.

"These are from the late eighteen hundreds," Elena said. "They stopped taking communion and started documenting the withdrawal symptoms. They published *A Microbial God*; the rest is history."

"The Communion Crisis," Victor murmured. "These belong in a museum."

"I'm sure they already have copies. The Puros are a big deal in the ROT. My abuela complains about them all the time. I'm sure I'll see for myself."

"I'll bet she is secretly Catholic."

Elena laughed, took the binder, closed it, and added it to a box on the floor. "This is a keeper," she said. Then she pointed to the heap. "Help me with the pile," she said, pointing to the heap of useless life accretions.

"Box it up?"

"Trash it," Elena said. "What do they say? 'Make room for good things to come into your life'? It must be nice to be an optimist."

The boxes had been sealed and stacked in the living room where the movers could take them out when they arrived in the morning. It was already dark outside; Elena's parents had gone to a goodbye soiree thrown by their union friends, and she and Victor were dusty, sweaty, and famished.

"Honestly, I think Alicante would be perfect." She reached up to her ponytail, released her hair, massaged her scalp, then regretfully pulled it back and up and wrapped it again. "We can get a back booth so no one can see how grimy we are."

Twenty minutes later, they toasted glasses of cinnamon- and cardamom-spiced horchata while a Latin jazz band played in the other room. "You have to visit me." She looked him in the eye. "You know I won't be able to afford the ticket, so it's your responsibility to come visit me."

"Of course I will. To alleviate the crushing boredom. What are you going to *do*, Ellie?"

"I'm going to eat, drink, and screw a different swaggering Puro every night."

His face was a puzzle of confusion. "Puro?" he asked.

"It's what the dickies are called in Texas." She noticed the blank look on his face. "Dickie is short for syndicalist. The Purity Caucus metastasized into organized criminals—or freedom fighters, depending on your perspective—the ones who pushed for the Repartition. I did my research this morning. Abuela Julia sent me local MeshNews articles. I'm not moving somewhere without knowing what I'm getting into."

"I wish you could stay." Victor clasped her hand across the table.

She decided to give some unsolicited, brutally honest advice since she wouldn't be around to steer him gently. "Listen, screw the Classification Commission. You're not broken—you're stronger than anyone I know. You've got Dr. Tammet and your family. You'll be fine."

"You taught me, Elena. You showed me how to create the person you want to be."

He looked down. At first, she thought he was embarrassed. He fussed with his jacket on the booth bench next to him and then presented a lumpy parcel wrapped in the cartoon section of the *Bayshore Ledger*.

"You and your presents," she said, smiling. She unwrapped it and held it up, a white V-neck T-shirt with the "California United!" slogan written in golden cursive letters across the top and below it, the state seal printed in faded and blotchy black, like an ink stamp. Lady Victory sat on the crest of the Oakland & Bayshore hills, drapery hanging from one shoulder and one breast bared to the Golden Gate Strait.

"I should hate this, but I love it," Elena said. "It won't make me any friends in Texas, though."

Victor sipped his horchata. "It's so you don't forget to come back to us someday."

"Try to visit," she told him when she got up to leave.

"I will."

Semiautonomous California
3 March 1991

"I remember," Victor said. His eyes had a glazed quality, not quite focusing.

The cabin was so quiet Elena could hear her pulse thudding and the creak of the floorboards as her body swayed.

"We're exhausted," she said, feeling it in her bones. "Tomorrow, we'll talk. I promise."

He didn't object as he steadied one hand on the sofa and then kind of tumbled into it. She dragged herself to bed, amazed that exhaustion could sneak up like a thief and steal consciousness.

17

Victor woke on the couch in his granfa's office, tangled in a knitted blanket. Lê Quang Hieu, the house butler and Victor's favorite by far among its staff, probably covered him in the night and let him sleep. The man worshipped Jefferson and must have absorbed some of his fondness for Victor over the years. There were three kinds of people in the world: those who hated Victor, those who put up with him—he included his parents in this set—and a small group who genuinely seemed to like him: Granfa Jeff, Auntie Circe, Hieu, and Elena. Ozie was a wildcard in that classification system; he never could be pinned down.

Victor paged through his granfa's medical records again, some critical insight still escaping him. He also flipped through the pages of the herbalism book, ignoring a dizzying sensation that he'd seen these plants in his dreams. The title page came unstuck—he hadn't noticed it before—and he saw a name, Ming Pearl, and a message written by an unfamiliar hand in fine, black charcoal lines.

Jefferson,
A crisis is emerging. Will the same curiosity that served you so well throughout your career lead you to someplace darker than you can imagine? I presume we'll find out together.
Here's the book you've been so hot for. I'm sure you, me, and Metalhead can put together a better treatment alternative than what your other friends have in mind. Anything is better than the status quo.
Your mentor, advisor, and altogether superior colleague,
M.P.

An address in Little Asia was stamped in faded violet ink at the bottom of the page.

What did "a better treatment alternative" mean? Was that a reference to Personil, or was it wishful thinking on his part? As far as he knew, there weren't any treatment alternatives for MRS.

A gasp from the doorway set Victor's skin tingling. Granma Cynthia stood there in a padded silk robe, shivering … no, shaking with rage.

"Get out," she commanded in a whisper. Her tone chilled his skin. "How dare you? Jefferson's office is …"

Victor gathered the medical records into a folder. The book of herbal cures rested nearby. He picked it up and walked to the door.

Granma Cynthia stood tall as he approached. She pointed and said, "Are those Jefferson's? Leave them."

Victor dodged past her and hurried down the hall. He'd never been a "good" grandchild, unlike Robbie, who always won awards and excelled at touting his accomplishments. The herbalism book felt heavy in his hands as he hurried down the hall and descended two stairs at a time.

Granma Cynthia called to him from the railing. "You've lost control again!"

From the access road along the rock-strewn waterfront, the Gene-Us headquarters glinted like a glass and steel centipede curving around a parking lot that intermingled with the remnants of an orchard. The boughs of orange trees hung heavy with unpicked fruit, and a few sad globes had been mashed into the asphalt. Victor hid the herb book and medical records under the passenger seat. They would only distract him if they were within arm's reach.

When he entered the building, he found chaos. Instead of the usual nose-down calm he needed, his fellow employees scampered and shouted, their giddy voices echoing against tile and glass. Some enterprising coworkers stood on furniture and hung golden paper lanterns, signs of good fortune. A pack of administrative assistants stood by a water fountain. Victor heard the words "titles," "reorganization," and "quarterly," and when they saw him, they ducked their heads and spoke to each other more quietly.

On the reception desk, he saw a printed MeshNews article.

Holistic Healing Network Buys Controlling Stake in Gene-Us Enterprises

OAKLAND & BAYSHORE, 24 February 1991—The Holistic Healing Network (HHN), owned by the Eastmore family, will buy a controlling stake in Gene-Us Enterprises for AUD 2.2 billion, taking the gene-sequencing company private, according to a filing with the AU Corporate Registry. Circe Eastmore, daughter of HHN's late founder Jefferson Eastmore, will serve as acting chair and chief of the merged concern, which will be renamed BioScan Inc.

Ms. Eastmore is quoted by a local MeshNews agent as saying, "BioScan Inc. will use the latest genetic sequencing and medical treatment technologies to provide comprehensive health services while also exploring how these technologies can be used in the enhancement and addiction treatment markets. Our efforts fall under the umbrella of a new initiative we call 'Evolving Together' that will see us make a multibillion-AUD investment in new and promising research."

Victor felt a stab of resentment. The family company was buying his current employer, and no one had said anything to him. Maybe Karine could tell him what was going on. But her office was deserted. Empty drawers poked from their enclosures. Her framed certificates no longer hung on the wall. Exotic paperweights from far-off places she liked to show off—volcanic glass from the Kingdom of Hawaii, wooden idols carved by African tribes, beaded animals from South America—were missing from her desk.

A few seconds later, his MeshBit buzzed. The message from "BioScan Operations" ordered him to report to the sample preparation room on the second floor for a temporary work assignment.

Victor trudged to a room crowded with bins holding packages mailed in from all over the American Union that contained samples from cheek swabs. The procedures for preparing samples for DNA sequencing were straightforward. It was basic manual labor that anyone who could follow a checklist could do. It got a little fiddly with vials and pipettes, but Victor was smooth with his hands when he was focused. Eventually, he found a rhythm and had worked through half of the backlog by lunch.

As he entered sequencing commands on a typepad, his colleague Sarita walked into the room. She flitted in several directions at once—frizzy hair, nervous hands, luminous eyes, and lips painted the deep red of poison berries—all vibrating at asynchronous frequencies.

Sarita eyed him gleefully and laughed. "Is this your new role? Filling machines with spit?"

Victor refused to meet her gaze. "It's temporary."

"Sure it is." She sidled closer. "Did you hear? Karine got a promotion. Second chief!" Sarita smirked. "You know what that means?"

Victor pulled off a set of sterile gloves he'd been wearing to avoid contaminating the DNA sequencing machine and tossed them in the recycle bin. "She reports to Circe now," he said, stating the obvious.

"*And* she'll pass you off like a hot potato. She's meeting with each of her reports this afternoon." Her breathiness implied something sinister.

"Okay," he said, shaking his head to himself. Sarita could have been sucking up to gain favor with the nephew of the new chief, but scorn for a Broken Mirror prevented her.

She clucked at him. "Did you know about this? The acquisition?"

Apart from Oak Knoll Hospital, which he'd visited devoutly, the Holistic Healing Network was a vague, nebulous entity he'd heard about in pieces and never really understood. No one could see the shape of the whole cancer-curing elephant from just one of its parts. Perhaps Victor should have paid more attention to Granfa Jeff's stories. His parents cared little about the business, only the lifestyle it afforded them, and they couldn't be counted on for anything in a professional capacity. Circe could have kept him informed, yet she hadn't. He'd have to ask her about that. She said she trusted him. Was that true, or was it only something she thought he needed to hear?

Sarita was laughing at him. "That's what I thought. Left out of the loop, I see."

"Of course I knew," he lied.

"I would wager that Karine fires you today, and no one would bet against me." Sarita flounced away to infect someone else with her gossip.

Victor told himself not to be concerned with her insinuations and continued working through the day's batch of samples for the next hour. When he was between two batches of samples, his MeshBit chimed. It was time for his meeting with Karine.

The tang of facial cream and floral perfume greeted him at the threshold of Karine's office. She stood and waved him in. Taller than Victor by several centimeters, Karine had a moon face and a stiff, wispy corona of auburn hair. She lined her eyes with black pencil. The image of a frill-necked lizard popped into Victor's mind.

They sat down. "You probably heard that, as of today, I am second chief of the company," Karine said.

Victor exhaled slowly. "Congratulations."

"What do you like about your current role, Victor?"

He was at a loss. What was this about?

"You wouldn't have to leave everything behind. You'll continue to oversee our analytics division and plan our investments in computational resources."

"I'm not following you. That *is* my job." Was this a test? Did she want him to describe his job to reassure her of his competence? "I make sure we've got the computing power to analyze all the genomes that come through. I make sure we have the necessary hardware and that the software is as efficient as possible. I write code. I analyze data. I fill out requisition forms and budget requests. There's more, of course, but—"

"Of course. I know, Victor, but that *was* your job at Gene-Us. But as BioScan, we plan to go bigger and bolder. There's a special project I want you to lead."

Victor leaned forward. "What kind of project?"

"A gene-to-pathology mapping initiative."

He waited for her to explain in more detail.

She rested her forearms on the desk. "We want to correlate clinical data with the genomes of our patients—all of them. We are talking about sequencing millions of patients' genetic codes and tying that to detailed information about their medical histories. We need new clinical procedures, better sequencers, enhanced data management, storage, and analytical capabilities, and a new operations and marketing organization to sell the data to research groups. You would lead the operational capacity team of the Evolving Together initiative, and you would report jointly to me and Circe."

A promotion? That was the last thing he'd expected.

Karine tilted her head in confusion. "Well, what do you say?"

How did Karine already know so much about the company's future direction? She knew more than he did and had a plan ready. He was playing catch-up badly, and his mute confusion was obvious.

"I've known you a long time, Victor. I've seen your capabilities. We're underutilizing your talents. And you are singularly suited for this role."

"How so?"

"Evolving Together will have several focus clusters. The most important will be neurological disorders, including mirror resonance syndrome and stim addiction."

"The two of those? Together? That's ridiculous."

"Do you think so? Your priority should be to get up to speed with the research." Karine leaned forward, holding up her index fingers. "Both stim addiction and your condition have related neurological mechanisms: a heightened susceptibility to positive feedback loops and above-average cognitive inertia. Yours happens to have a genetic origin. We're finding that stims can change how genes are expressed in the brain, possibly due to prions that act like a cellular contagion—we have some evidence of this, but it's not yet definitive. The prions (or whatever change the stims are catalyzing) alter the shape of proteins throughout stim addicts' neural networks. In pathological terms, the resonance in a stim addict's brain is similar to mirror resonance in yours."

Victor understood what she was saying. But the idea that stims could rewire brain chemistry? It was revolting. He felt bile rise in his throat. If it were true, and he'd never heard of it, then Mesh editors must not want word to get out. It was one more sign of questionable healthcare politics in SeCa. Or maybe the relationship between the MRS and stims was a statistical illusion that would be proved false with enough data. He wouldn't mind being the person to shatter that illusion.

"In addition to your project leadership responsibilities," she continued, "there will also be a ceremonial role. You'll need to hone your public speaking skills and work with some pretty senior people in the organization and in government, so that will be a challenge, obviously. You have the face for it, though, and dissonant micro-expressions aren't a problem when speaking to a crowd of people."

He was unsure what to make of her newfound confidence in him. "I don't know—"

"Victor, this project is going to revolutionize biomedical research. Researchers will use this data for decades to understand why some people get sick and others don't, how genetic defects arise and get passed on, how to create targeted medical treatments. This is the future of health care, and you'll get to be a part of it."

Karine looked at him with focused intensity. Could she really have that much faith in his abilities? He couldn't shake the suspicion that she was setting him up for failure. Or, more likely, that all this was a direct consequence of him being related to the chief, an inheritor of company shares, and a high-profile mirror resonance patient.

He wanted to hear her say it out loud, or he wanted her to deny it so he might see the lie on her face. "Why me?" he asked.

She took a moment to respond. "You are a unique asset, and I would be a terrible manager if I didn't take advantage of it."

Victor imagined her jaw unhinging to swallow him like a giant python devouring a flightless bird. He remained silent. The scope of the project impressed and intimidated him. A large-scale comparison of genomics and pathology could change medicine as completely as the sequencing of the human genome and the cure for cancer. His natural intellectual curiosity, long slumbering, seemed to be awakening, and the world around him, which had seemed so orderly and understandable, was becoming somewhere he no longer recognized. A metal vent in the ceiling rattled. He considered his options. Karine was describing a great opportunity, but he didn't like being manipulated.

She cleared her throat. "You need to decide quickly. Nevertheless, I can't see that you have much of a choice. Things are changing, Victor. You need to keep up."

She rose and brushed her hands over the arms of her aquamarine synthsilk suit as if some odious substance had settled on her in the past few minutes. "I've spoken to Circe, and we agree on several points. You need to take your medication, drop this silly fantasy about Jefferson's death, and start seeing a therapist again. Agreed? We can't afford to take any chances with your mental health."

A lump formed in Victor's throat. She'd been discussing him with his family. Losing his grip on reality, they must have said, poor thing, needs to get back on his pills. How disappointed Dr. Tammet would be if she knew how foolishly he'd acted, indulging in dark fantasies and scandalizing his family. Karine was right. This was his opportunity to put the past behind him, and he had to take it.

She was waiting for him to answer. Victor closed his eyes and visualized Granfa Jeff's casket, imagining the click the lid made as he shut it tight.

"I'll do it. The pills. The job. Therapy. All of it. I'm in," he said.

"Good." Karine's boots clicked on the floor as she walked to the door. "There's one more thing." He opened his eyes. She said, "Circe wants to speak with you right away. She's expecting a vidfeed. You can use mine."

When she left, the air in the room smelled less sickly sweet, and he breathed easier.

Victor put his MeshBit on Karine's ident-pad. His aunt's face appeared on the vidscreen.

"About the merger," Circe said and then paused. She laid a hand on her neck as if in pain. "I am sorry we couldn't chat about it before."

"Karine told me about the promotion."

"Yes. She's got everything well in hand." Circe pushed a stray curling rope of dark hair further up her mound of ringlets. "Victor, patients around the world will thank you. We may even be able to find a cure for you."

Victor uttered a silent prayer that he'd be able to live up to her expectations and put his fantasies to rest—no more dreaming of magic plants and seeds that could solve all his problems. The hard path was the only path, a tightrope across a chasm. He'd walk it as long as he could.

18

Victor hurried through the open plaza at the heart of the Semiautonomous California National University's campus. It was a good day; not so many symptoms aside from the conspiracy theory swirling in his imagination. Above him, eight statues stood on tall plinths, celebrating the primary architects of the Repartition process that created SeCa along with eight other nations of the American Union.

He found Elena where they'd agreed to meet, at the base of the Admiral Eastmore statue, Jefferson's father. The Admiral's white marble face bore blank, polished eyes but their gaze looked beyond the narrow water of the Golden Gate Strait to a wide ocean of possibility for SeCa.

"I'm glad you're here. This is important."

She examined him and wrinkled her nose. "When was the last time you showered?"

"Doesn't matter. Come on." He started toward the Medical Sciences Building. "The lab isn't as busy during lunch hour."

"Wait," Elena said.

Victor turned. She hadn't moved.

"I'll help you with whatever you have planned," she said, "but we need to talk first."

"I know you think I'm obsessing. But the whole thing stinks. The hospital closure. How he looked in the casket. And the records don't add up."

Elena shook her head and held up a hand. "We can talk about that later. I'll help you. I promise. First, we need to talk about what happened with us."

Victor felt the blood drain from his face. Back then, they'd negotiated safeguards to protect themselves from the obvious risks of a teenage friendship veering into relationship territory: no dopey romantic gestures, no *sex* sex, and no talk of love. But it was the other direction—dissolution, decay, disappointment—that they should have been worried about.

Victor nodded mutely.

"Thanks. Until I get this off my chest ... Anyway, do you remember the day I left for Texas? I've been thinking about what you promised." Elena's gaze shifted toward the port and train terminals to the west. "You promised to visit."

Victor cleared his throat. "I promised to try to visit."

He studied the square of burgundy paving stone on which they stood. Flecks of mica sparkled, enticing, offering escape.

"Did you try?" Elena knew that he felt he'd betrayed her, first with his lie, then with his silence. She examined her nails. "If I hadn't counted on it ..."

Victor placed his head against the cool stone of the pillar, but it did nothing to calm the pulsing in his temples.

She looked up and whispered, "You know what it feels like to be burned."

His face stung as if he'd been scalded—she'd never used his nightmares against him before. He wanted to climb the pillar to the Admiral's great height and dive head-first into the concrete below. "Love" was too slippery a concept to describe what they had; "companionship" was too flippant.

"I thought of you every day," Victor said quietly. It felt pitiful when spoken aloud. *I thought of you, but what good is a thought unspoken?*

"You have no idea how much a few words or a fucking vidchat would have meant to me. A word might have saved me."

"From what?" he asked.

Elena didn't answer, only stared at him. It was as if she were counting the ways he'd failed to live up to her expectations. Her eyes—the off-green color of dry summer grass—were flinty, full of irrepressible will. She could be shocking stubborn, and he usually loved that about her, but being on the receiving end was like being impaled.

After a moment, she sighed and expelled a long breath. Her eyes were still hard.

Victor gulped. "I am *sorry*, Ellie," he said.

She looked at him with pleading eyes now. "I don't want to resent you. I want to move past this, and I ... I *can't*."

He looked at her again, seeing her not through the lens of his memories but truly, clearly, for the first time since she'd returned. Her brown hair had lost some of its shine. Her face had sagged a little, like it was losing its grip on the cheekbones beneath. Eyes bloodshot. She looked ten years older than her age of twenty-five.

Silent sufferers. Stubborn. Walls so high the tops are out of sight. No doubt, we are made for each other, Victor thought.

"Tell me what happened to you in Texas."

She looked at him with steel and sadness in her gaze. "Forget it."

Victor opened his arms, lifting them hesitantly, his palms up, pleading. She stepped towards him and into a hug. "I'm sorry," he said again.

They held each other for a minute, heart to heart, then stepped back.

Elena drew in a full breath and seemed to shed her skin of sadness before smiling. "Okay. Just tell me: what are we here for?"

Relieved Elena had let him off the hook, at least for now, Victor said, "The truth. That's all."

He led her across campus to the medical sciences building.

They entered the building, descended a set of stairs to the medical library, a space crowded with desks, computer stations within semiprivate cubbyholes, and a maze of bookshelves. It was busy with students murmuring to each other or hunched over textbooks. "There," Victor said, pointing to a terminal. He patted his bag. "I have my granfa's records. We're going to recreate his diagnosis and test its accuracy."

"That's what this is about? I thought you wanted help preparing for your Classification."

"That's not for a couple of months. No, I want us to look at the records in more detail. Do you remember how to run a predictive diagnosis?"

Elena frowned. "I haven't done that in years."

"Just make sure you privacy box the session. And don't use his real name. We can log in as me, but this is sensitive."

She sighed as they sat down together, he logged in, and she started tapping on the typepad, picking through command menus. Victor held up the sheet of the first set of test results so she could enter each measurement by date without lowering her head.

"Just like old times," she said.

Going through the doctors' notes was a tedious process. For each observation, they had to query a medical database to find the correct code and enter it into their model. Once they'd compiled all the data, Elena summoned one of the library techs, a pale young man with a thick blond mustache and a bald head. He double-checked the version number of the diagnostic model. He changed a few parameters related to reference patients (education and socioeconomic background) and the patient's early childhood (born and raised in New Venice in the Louisiana Territories and thus likely fully vaccinated and not subject to hunger or excessive stress).

"Mind if I stay to validate the results?" the tech asked.

Victor hesitated. Was the tech acting overly curious?

Elena shrugged and watched Victor with a sideways glance. To impress her with his nonchalance, he said, "Why not?" A corner of her mouth ticked up, and she moved to press the validate key to start the analysis.

"Wait," Victor said, "I want to restrict the input. Only data from before September."

Elena added a filter to the analysis and ran the program. A sundial icon spun on the vidscreen.

The tech asked, "Do you have a gut feeling about the result?"

"Congestive heart failure," Elena said. "High confidence." Her tone sounded like an accusation to Victor, but he let it slide.

"How about you?" the tech asked. "You look skeptical."

Victor sat back in his chair. "I am. That will show up, but with much lower confidence, between a third and a half."

The tech smiled at him. "You sound pretty certain. I wouldn't bet against you."

Victor studied the play of expressions across the library tech's face and found him surprisingly easy to read—a dose of curiosity, a desire to be helpful, and a hint of sexual attraction to both Victor and Elena, which was a bit unprofessional. They were in a library, not a bar. Still, Victor was glad to see the tech had harmless ulterior motives. If only Elena was as easy to read.

The sundial icon burst and vanished. The result came back as a list of probable diagnoses, the highest of which was congestive heart failure at 40 percent. The library tech clapped Victor on the back and didn't take his hand away. "You were spot on, doc. Can I get you to look at my elbow? It's been aching lately."

"Too much time on your own?" Elena snarked, miming a masturbatory gesture.

The tech laughed. His hand was a warm weight, an unwelcome distraction. Victor shrugged away. "Time alone is all I ever had," he said. "I'm more interested in the alternate diagnoses," he said.

Elena pointed to the vidscreen. "It's just a long tail of junk. Five percent chance of kidney disease. Three percent leukemia. Less than half a percent for Gilchrist-Ebbers syndrome, whatever that is. I'd say these results are conclusive."

"Hmm, you might be right," the library tech said, tapping the screen. "Look at this one. Radiation exposure? This says the likelihood is two percent, but I bet it's more like a million to one. You'd have to go into orbit for a few years to get a dosage high enough to cause these symptoms, and by then, you'd have all sorts of other problems related to low gravity. I'm guessing the subject isn't an astronaut?"

Victor barely heard the tech's babbling. Something about the idea of radiation set his skin tingling, and he could have sworn he heard the sound of wings and the grating cawing of a murder bird. *Two*, irradiated. He was pulled into blankness for a moment, then he was back, unsettled.

"Victor! Snap out of it!" Elena was leaning over him, gripping his shoulders and shaking him. She turned to the tech and said, "We've got it from here."

"Sure," the tech said, deflated. "Let me know if you need more help. Or anything."

Victor watched the tech walk away. He tried running a hand through his hair, but it got tangled, and hair came out with his hand.

What had they been talking about?

Radiation.

His granfa had lost his hair and had blotches on his skin. Victor looked around for a mirror, but there wasn't one nearby. What if he'd been exposed along with Granfa Jeff? Perhaps that was the reason Oak Knoll had been closed.

He should re-run the model focused on the symptoms and removing the lifestyle factors.

Elena shook Victor's shoulder. "Are you back? That came on so quick, I was scared. What triggered you this time?"

"Never mind that. I think there's something to the idea of radiation poisoning."

"No way! Radiation is at the bottom of the list. How can you refuse to see what's in front of you?"

"What if something bad happened at Oak Knoll?"

Elena rolled her eyes.

"Maybe it was something he was exposed to at the hospital. Maybe he didn't want to cause a panic, so he closed it down without explanation. And when he got sick, he said it was heart failure."

"Look at the evidence." Elena changed the filter to look at data from September onward. She pressed "Validate," and the sundial icon returned.

Within ten seconds, they had a result: "Congestive heart failure probability, 98.5 percent."

Victor squinted at the screen. *Too high. I'd expect 80 percent for a sure thing. This is beyond belief.*

"See?" Elena said. "Proof positive."

"It certainly is, but I don't think it means what you think it means."

"Oh, come on!" Elena slapped the vidscreen hard enough to cause the library tech to look their way. "You can't argue with a figure like that."

"It proves that these records—from September onward—point toward heart failure. I'll tell you why. Because all the tests from then on are focused on proving that condition. They're spinning a story, and you're falling for it. Every bit of evidence in these pages"—he flapped the papers against the vidscreen—"are *meant* to confirm the diagnosis. If you go looking for a rock, you'll find one."

Elena huffed and crossed her arms. "I've always hated that saying."

"Just hear me out." He held up a hand to stop her from interrupting. "I think, at first, the doctors couldn't figure out what was wrong, so they ordered all sorts of tests and exams. They came up with a pretty weak case for diagnosing him with heart failure. Then, suddenly, all their attention was put in that direction, and, big surprise, they found what they were looking for."

Her voice was soft and confident when she said, "But that would also be the case if he *had* heart failure."

"Here's what I think. Granfa Jeff starts experiencing symptoms of something. He gets checked out. The results are inconclusive. Then he figures out what's happening. But for some reason, he can't say it. He has to keep it secret. The last time I saw him, he gave me a data egg and said it would open when it's *safe*—he knew something, something he couldn't tell me."

Elena snapped her fingers. "Smarten up. You're a scientist. Look for the simplest, most logical explanation. He had a heart condition. Your suspicions are a part of your illness—"

"Condition," Victor said flatly. She should know better. "No, not this time."

"Don't you see—"

"Please go."

Elena reared back. "What?"

"Go," he said, raising his voice.

A few students in the library looked up from their work. The tech held up a finger, a warning.

Elena whispered, "You asked me to be here."

She looked at him pityingly. Or was it contempt? Was she simply humoring him? Why had she come back? She didn't care about him. She just wanted to watch him fail. To rub his condition in his face.

Victor whispered, "Why can't you help me for once instead of putting me down and making me feel like a lunatic?" Victor looked down, avoiding seeing the hurt he caused. "None of this should have happened. I should be working in a lab to better understand the biology behind my condition. I should be researching neuroscience and finding a way to help people with MRS. I should be working at Oak Knoll." People in the library turned and looked at him, but he couldn't lower his volume. "If I hadn't been diagnosed, I could've been an astronomer. I should be solving the problem of the Macro Void in the cosmic electromagnetic background. It all went sideways." He slammed a hand on the table. "It's not *right!*"

Elena pointed at his face and spoke to him with steely calm. "I've seen that look on you before, and from here, it's a short walk to crazy town. You know it. You feel it."

He shook his head violently. "I'm not imagining this."

Elena stood up and folded her arms across her chest. "I can't. I'm sorry. I can't do this with you. It's like you're not even trying. You need to up your dosage or talk to a therapist or something. They'll lock you up if you keep going down this path, and I'm starting to think that might be best."

Victor watched her go, seething, until she was out of sight. Then, calming his breath, he turned back to the vidscreen. Why would Granfa Jeff cover up the true cause of his own death?

19

After a morning spent in a roiling, complicated silence, Victor finally got a nod from Elena. He opened the cabin's front door and then followed her outside. They sat on a bench around the back of the cabin, listening to birdcalls and the occasional pinecone dropping through tree limbs to the forest floor.

She rested a hand on his knee. It wasn't a romantic grip, more like a sailor's hand clenching the rail of a boat in rough waters. "I want to tell you something," she said.

"I'm here," he replied. *Finally, she's ready to talk.*

After a long breath in, she began to unload. "When I moved to Texas, I didn't have any friends. You know what it's like. I was working and going to school. My parents were always asking me to help, too. Every minute of the day was busy but depressing, existentially so. I needed something good in my life when everything was bad. I tried to tell you earlier, but ..."

She gripped his knee more firmly and raised her gaze to the treetops. He recognized her urge to maintain control. He waited, letting her take her time.

Elena continued, "It was stupid. I mean, I knew better, but I didn't care. It started when I couldn't—I was out of control. I knew better, but I did it anyway."

"I'm not sure what you're talking about," he said as gently as he could.

With her other hand, she wiped away a tear. She caught her breath and leveled her gaze at him. "I started smoking stims."

Stims! She wouldn't do *that.* She'd always hated the thought of it. She would chop off an arm before she used stims. His expression must have communicated all that to her, and she withdrew her hand, sensing his disdain.

Victor put on a more neutral expression. From the moment she'd found him at the funeral, he'd sensed that she was different, harder, and crueler. He was finally getting the truth. "Sorry," he said. "Go on."

Elena wiped the moisture from her cheeks with her knuckles. She breathed in harshly, perhaps trying to trick her body out of its emotions, as he often did.

"Nobody told me how it would change me."

He struggled to find something to say. He didn't want to rub salt in her wounds. But, Laws, a stim addiction? "But you stopped?" he asked.

"Yes, I stopped. But the cravings are stronger than strong, especially when I think about ..."

Victor could see a hard-to-pin-down emotion leaking from her eyes and mouth. She felt relief after telling him, yes, that was coming through clearly, but there was something else, something greenish-yellow, shame or disgust, that she was holding back.

Quietly, he said, "There's something else, right?"

She nodded slowly, her eyes lowered to the ground. "There's a faction of dickies in Texas. They're called Los Puros. They helped me get clean for a while. They tried, at least."

She rubbed the jade pendant hanging from her neck. "They're good people. They're trying to provide a haven. As they tell it, during the Repartition, Puros fought for independence. Autonomy wasn't enough for them. The ROT government kept trying to shut them down, but they always bounced back. Then, Corps drug runners moved in." Her eyes narrowed. Yellow bitterness colored her expression. "It's a kind of war. And I'm in it. Or was. Will be, I guess, when I go back."

Elena rubbed her palms against her thighs. Victor didn't know what to say. This wasn't the Elena he knew. Some stranger had taken over her life.

"The thing is, a new kind of stim showed up a year ago. Aurora. Or sometimes just Aura. It's everywhere. I got hooked again. Everything looks, sounds, and smells so vibrant. Like how you've described your episodes." She glanced at him quickly, then looked away. "When I'm on Aura, I feel like I'm supercharged. All my senses fire up. It's hard to go back to normal again after you've felt resonance like that. Everything else seems muted, pointless."

For a moment, Victor was too stunned to breathe, then he lurched to his feet and reeled to the side of the cabin, resting an arm against it and steadying himself. People were using street drugs that mimicked mirror resonance syndrome. He'd dismissed Karine's suggestion that there was a relationship between MRS and stims as a statistical fluke. Had his reaction been based on undue skepticism? Maybe he hadn't wanted to hear what she had been telling him. Well, he was listening now.

Elena said, "I couldn't stay clean. The Puros kicked me out. It got awful."

Her voice cracked. Victor examined her face and saw a greenish-yellow blur move across it. She met his gaze briefly, then looked away. "I went to a clinic. There's one in the Louisiana Territories in New Venice. One of your family's. The program helped me. I'm sober now, and I'm glad to be sober. I'm going to stay this way. And ..."

He moved toward her and wrapped an arm around her shoulders. "It's okay," he said. Her resolve to stay clean silenced his questions and selfish concerns. "Let me know how I can help."

They had been through so much, always ready with a strong grip to pull each other through the tightest scrapes. Now that the lies between them had been swept away, nothing could stop them.

She wiped her eyes. "You are. Being here. It's so peaceful. All that feels like another life." She squeezed his knee. "We're good for each other, don't you think?"

20

The laboratory's worktable had a lip to catch fluids from spilling onto the floor. Victor's elbows lodged there as he slumped over the table. Alone and naked, locked in a room he'd reserved. He had covered the window in the door with metal foil for privacy.

He pressed his palms onto the cool nano-silver laminate surface of the table, blinked rapidly, and tried not to go blank. The sight of the data egg on the table seemed to help. A radiation detector that he'd scavenged from the university storeroom rested nearby. It was the shape and size of a finger. His skin still tingled, an entirely imaginary sensation, he was sure, from passing the probe along his naked body, starting at his feet and working his way up.

He looked at the test results again: positive for alpha particle exposure.

It was only meant to be a test run for when he could get a sample from his granfa's possessions. Now, he was finding evidence on his own body.

Was it possible to both believe and disbelieve something at the same time? He was caught in unreality, unwilling to trust his own eyes, unable to unsee the proof he'd been seeking. His paranoia, proven true, would mean a shift in every aspect of his life. Safety pillaged. Peace of mind erased—not that he'd ever had much of that. How much easier it would be to doubt his sanity and live untroubled by the conspiracy surrounding him, invading him, tainting him, body and mind.

The irradiation was the worst on his hands and face, though not enough to cause more than very mild symptoms: a loosening of hair roots in their follicles and a barely visible, patchy rash, signs he wouldn't have seen—that he *hadn't* seen—until he knew what to look for. The dose was small enough that he didn't have to worry about death or even moderate illness. Of course, cancer wouldn't be a problem, so that was something.

What didn't come as much relief was the radiation exposure's likely source—particles on the data egg—nor that the compound responsible for the contamination, an isotope of polonium, was extremely rare and human-made. Could it have been an accident?

Victor tried to raise Elena on his MeshBit, but she didn't answer. He didn't leave a message. She'd been so skeptical. He wanted to see her face—after he put some clothes on. She couldn't argue with his evidence. And she'd have to acknowledge that he was doing fine without the Personil—better, in fact, since stopping the medication had allowed him to see the truth more clearly.

The data egg, Granfa Jeff's final gift, held answers locked inside. He spoke to it, coaxing, pleading. "My name is Victor Eastmore, and I command this data egg to open and present its contents to me. Please? Access files. Accept command function 'open.' Initiate. Do something!" The data egg might as well have been a very slightly radioactive rock.

He dressed, trying not to think about how his shirts, slacks, and underwear were probably all contaminated. His apartment. His car. Where did the polonium come from? What was it doing on the data egg? And what did any of it have to do with his granfa's death?

He was tired. He was all used up. He sent Elena the test results, then dictated a message to his MeshBit, saying he had an important announcement and sent it to his family. He would make them listen and understand, and then they would have to decide what to do about it.

Victor drove to the main gate of the Eastmore mansion. It didn't open. He parked and exited the car, approached the sonofeed panel mounted on the wall, and activated it.

Lê Quang Hieu answered: "Eastmore residence."

"It's me, Hieu. Victor."

"I see, uh, that you're parked outside the gate. As you may be aware—"

"I get it, Hieu. Granma doesn't want me inside. But you have to let me in."

The sonofeed was silent. Victor imagined Hieu wavering, trying to determine the correct distance to hold the handset from his ear and mouth as he debated how to respond to Victor's request.

"I have something to announce. It's about Granfa Jeff's death. Please, Hieu, I'm trying to put things right."

There was a pause. "Put things right in your head, you mean?"

"No, it's more than that. I have proof."

Another pause, longer. "I'm sure you're doing your best. I just don't see how I can—"

"Is that Victor?" Granma Cynthia's voice came through the sonofeed. "Tell him I've had enough. Keep him out."

"Mother," Auntie Circe's voice intoned, "it will be better if we can resolve this. Lê Quang, it's okay, let him in."

"Not in my house!" Granma Cynthia sounded on the verge of tears.

"Very well, Mother. We'll all meet in the garden," Auntie Circe said. "Lê Quang, will you fetch Victor and take him to the gazebo?"

"Young sir—"

"I heard them, Hieu. I'll be here."

The sonofeed cut off. In the past, Victor had spewed outlandish theories about how the number two had magical properties, how China and Japan were planning an invasion of the American Union of Nations, and how MeshTowers controlled his mood swings. Still, all those were from before Dr. Tammet taught him how to sort fact from fiction. Now, things were different. Now, he held a truth too monstrous to believe and evidence no one could argue with. They would struggle with it, as he had, and eventually, the truth would win them over.

The gate slid open slowly, revealing Hieu.

"Come with me, young sir. We'll take the garden path. I'm sure this will all come to an agreeable conclusion."

When they reached the pavilion, Victor felt he was at the center of a violent storm rather than standing in his granma's garden under a blue sky while hummingbirds and bees buzzed and flitted, enjoying the warm spring day. His fa slumped against a pillar. A rotten egg smell—the scent of shame—wafted toward Victor. Ma kept trying to touch his face and stroke his hand, but Victor wanted none of her weak reassurance. This was serious, adult business, the most serious kind, and his parents should be rising to the occasion. They ought to listen and believe.

Granma Cynthia stood stiffly and wouldn't acknowledge a word Victor said. Hieu had retreated quickly. The only other person with them was Auntie Circe, who seemed to be listening but with a stony face.

"I'm trying to tell you," Victor said. "The evidence is clear. There's polonium on the data egg and on me. It must have come from Granfa Jeff. I think it's what killed him."

Auntie Circe shook her head doubtfully. "Victor, polonium is extremely rare. I seriously doubt—"

"I tested it. I tested myself. Look at the printout."

Granma Cynthia sniffed, but Victor could tell by her posture that it was a disdainful gesture, not one of mourning.

Ma said, "Sweetie, if you'll just calm down, I'm sure you'll see—"

"I *am* seeing. It's all of you who are refusing to look past your prejudices."

Fa looked up, frowning. He pointed at Victor, and it felt like a jolt of electricity. "You will not speak to your family this way. We raised you as best we could—"

Whatever lecture Fa was about to launch into was cut short by Hieu's return, accompanied by an urgent-sounding throat-clearing. He went to Granma Cynthia and whispered in her ear.

"Why don't we just open the gates to any piece of trash that wanders by?" She stalked toward the mansion.

"Who is it, Lê Quang?" Auntie Circe asked.

"Ms. Elena."

Victor whirled to look down the hill, but the gate was hidden behind bushes, trees, and statuary. He caught Ma and Auntie exchanging a look.

"What's she doing here?" he asked.

"You said you had an announcement, so I invited her," Ma said. "Please bring her up." She turned to Victor. "I know you feel this time is different, but I thought maybe if she was here, she could help."

Victor gripped the data egg in his pocket, regretting that he'd tried to explain anything to them. *They'll never believe me. I'm only a problem to be managed.*

Auntie Circe wore an expression of curiosity and concern. An ornate gold band held back her dark ringlets. She said, "When we spoke before, you agreed to give this fantasy a rest."

If he told her he still wasn't taking Personil, she'd just assume that was the reason for his behavior. "I know, but I found a supplement for my medication, and my mind started to clear. Now I see clearly."

"What kind of supplement?"

"Herbs."

She raised an eyebrow. "Interesting."

"It's not interesting," Fa said, "it's delusional."

Ma added, "He can't help it."

Fa said, "We all need to understand how serious this is. I've never seen Victor this ... this rebellious! None of you have. We're not going to get over this by pussyfooting around."

Elena strode up the path, leaving Hieu behind. Victor caught sight of her hands, what they held, and his breath caught in his throat. He felt his knees give way and fall on the grass, but his gaze never wavered. She was holding his dreambook.

His ma rushed over and asked him if he was hurt. Victor shrugged away and lurched to his feet, advancing on Elena.

"What are you doing with that?" he demanded.

She said, "You needed to see it."

"How did you—"

"I broke into your apartment, genius. After what you said at the university, I couldn't let you keep going. You need a reality check. This book proves your fantasies are dangerous."

The journal had been a gift from his granfa many years ago; everyone at the 1981 Eastmore reunion had received one. It was an old Eastmore tradition, his granfa had explained. Other family members probably used them as day planners, as scratch books, and for other innocuous reasons, but the red real-leather-bound book that Elena held had served an essential, almost holy purpose for Victor. Within its pages, he recorded dreams shattered by violence and soaked in blood.

How could Elena do this to him? He should never have told her about the dreambook. If his family read it, they would immediately try to place him in a Class One facility with the other extreme cases: the deranged, ultraviolent, mind-numb, and catatonic.

"We can't pretend you're okay," Elena said. "But we're going to get over this. Maybe it would help to write your ideas down here and let them go."

"I'm not writing anything down. I'm not going to copy these test results down and pretend they came from some fucked-up delusion."

"What test results?" Elena asked.

"Don't," Fa warned. "We can't indulge him anymore."

"The ones I sent you! They're right here." Victor waved the sheet of biopaper at her. "I tested myself for radiation. Positive on me and the data egg Granfa Jeff gave me. Here. You explain to them. I'm not getting through."

Elena took the sheet, looking at it skeptically, and began to read. As she did so, Victor grabbed the dreambook from her and tucked it under his arm.

Auntie Circe spoke softly. "I think we need to consider whether the Carmichael ranch might be a good place for you, temporarily, until—"

"Until what?" Victor snapped. They all knew his condition was degenerative.

Part of him wondered if he belonged at a ranch. It would be simpler. A life of so-called freedom that Class Threes enjoyed wasn't all that great anyway. And maybe he'd be safer there, less likely to hurt himself or others.

For as long as he could remember, he lived in fear that the events chronicled during fitful snatches of sleep would come true. After Carmichael, he'd started writing his dreams down on slips of paper and tearing them to shreds. Then he'd received the journal, and, gripped by a compulsion, he'd poured his dreams onto its pages. He never read through what he'd written, however. The details were too gruesome, too vivid; more than that, he didn't want to confront the truth of his mental illness as depicted in those pages. Every horrible fantasy, every fortune-telling dream only symbolized the ways his mind was broken.

Victor said, "No one comes out. You say you love me, but you'd rather send me away so you can get on with your lives, right? Admit it!"

Elena held up the biopaper. There was a look on her face like she'd eaten a bad apple and bit through a worm. "This is real?"

"Yes."

"But if this is right ..." She trailed off with a concerned look at his mother.

Ma snapped at her, "I didn't invite you here to encourage him!"

Auntie Circe said, "Victor, there is a way forward. Think about your future, your promotion. You don't want to walk away from an opportunity like that. Unless you—I hate to say it this way—but unless you snap out of this, we won't be able to use you as a spokesperson. You won't pass your reclassification. This is your last chance. You have to choose the life you want."

Granma Cynthia trudged down the path and interrupted: "I've had enough of this. I won't be made to feel helpless in my own home. The police are on their way. If Victor is here when they arrive, I'm going to insist they arrest him—if not for slander, then for theft, and whatever else I can think of. I gave the Health Board a call, too."

"Mother!" Auntie Circe advanced on her as swift as a tiger. "This is not the way to handle him." Granma Cynthia stood her ground.

Elena tugged at Victor's hand. "Come on."

"I'm not giving up."

"They're not listening. Come on."

"What's the point? I might as well just check myself into a facility."

Elena whispered, "If this is what you say it is, you might be onto something. Now come on, you win nothing by getting arrested."

His limbs loosened. As Elena led him down the path, he could barely form a coherent thought; her reversal was so unexpected. His parents called to him as he retreated down the hill.

At a twist in the switch-backing path, he hesitated.

"We need to go." Elena pulled at his hand.

"You believe me? About the radiation?"

"Maybe. I assume you didn't dose yourself. If this is true, then you're right; something doesn't add up."

Victor stood up straighter. "I'm right."

"You might be right. There's hope."

She was right. There was hope. He could find the truth, and he wouldn't have to do it alone. A warmth spread in his chest as they hurried to their cars. Someone finally believed him.

He and Elena passed through the gate and paused when they reached his car.

She asked, "So, Mr. Sleuth. What's the plan?"

Victor said, "We need to retrace his steps. Where he went, what he did in those last months."

His MeshBit chimed, and he squeezed it reflexively. The message started to play aloud.

"The Classification Commission hereby orders you to submit to a reevaluation with Dr. Santos at nine in the morning on February twenty-ninth, 1991. Location details are encoded in this message."

Victor's jaw hung open. Three days. There was nothing he could do to prepare in just three days. He was screwed.

Elena said, "I think you need a new plan. A fresh start."

21

We can help you.

Elena read the MeshBit message transcript from Linda Eastmore while she was sitting on the sofa and Victor wandered somewhere outside, probably in circles. She remembered seeing the message for the first time as she was lying on a stained and bare mattress pad, staring at the ceiling and resting between stim-fueled manic phases. The abandoned house she was sharing with other stimheads could have blown apart in a strong wind. Dirt caked the floors, except where her frenzied drug mates wore the wood planks clean with their pacing.

When she'd returned the call, Linda's voice had come through the sonobulb, sounding like a not-quite-human MeshNews reader. "I want you to come to SeCa. Victor needs you."

Victor was somewhere in the forest outside, maybe hunting for herbs again. Maybe he was getting space to stretch his crazy. Elena rubbed her face, trying to remember the last time she'd spoken to Victor's ma. She'd be expecting an update. The news from Lucky and Bandit was bound to be unsatisfying. How long would Linda keep sending her money after the updates stopped?

It hadn't been an easy sell. "He doesn't need *my* help," Elena had said.

"He's never had another friend like you. He's withdrawing from us, regressing. He's shutting out everyone, Linus and myself included, not to mention Jefferson, whom he adores, or did. I'm afraid of the consequences. You might be able to reach him," Linda said.

Elena's heart cracked open to hear that. She hadn't heard from Victor for five years, and she didn't like the past returning in this way. It should have been Victor on the phone apologizing for ignoring her, not his wishy-washy mother.

How far she'd come since then, from the Republic of Texas to New Venice in the Louisiana Territories. Those hazy weeks of withdrawal and treatment, every hour distilled to a simple question of whether she could endure and keep going. The sweat. The chills. The utter banality of her self-inflicted turmoil. The fear she would fall to pieces again.

She grew hard and brittle on her return to a SeCa because it didn't feel like a long-lost home. The ridiculous Eastmores: rich, privileged yet wrapped in layers of trauma, and deeply, habitually cruel to one another.

If Elena had done one good, important thing in her life, it was extracting Victor from that mess. Maybe good and honest was too much to ask. Or maybe she would get there with time, one step after the next.

Linda had asked in a tentative voice, "Do you think we failed him?"

Elena told her no. They'd arranged the best care for Victor while navigating their own traumas. But, in private, she wondered why they hadn't saved him from the Classification Commission's relentless policing of Broken Mirrors. Elena would save him instead. She had to keep fighting. She would succeed where his family had failed.

"We left SeCa," she wrote to Linda. The message would be sent the next time she connected to the Mesh. And it would be too late for anyone to stop them.

22

Victor drove home shakily after the news about his reclassification appointment being moved up. He refused Elena's offer of company. He needed quiet. He needed soft lights and clear thinking.

A few takeout bags from Johnny's Wok ensured he wouldn't need to leave home again, so he picked up ginger chicken, steamed greens topped with crunchy fried garlic, and hot bean curd with jellied lemon slices, but every bite roiled his stomach. After he opened a window, the chiller buzzed, as if offended to be asked to work harder, and the sound of the traffic was grating. Everything was raw and hot and sticky. He stripped off his clothes and lay on top of his bed, uncovered. Imagining his brain tissue blistered and swelling with pus, he stared at the lightstrips on his bedroom ceiling, throbbing in time with his heartbeat, and despaired.

Victor replayed the message from the Classification Commission. They'd moved up his date without explanation. The most paranoid part of his brain wondered if Granma Cynthia's phone call to the police had triggered some algorithm. Or perhaps she had influence with the Commission to expedite his appointment. He'd never considered anyone in his family vindictive, but he'd crossed a line with her, maybe with all of them.

Even with his eyes closed and his breathing steady as a metronome, his mind buzzed and crackled. Swirls of color eddied behind his eyelids in the close, hot darkness. He tried every exercise Dr. Tammet taught him: repetitive hand motions, visualization exercises, and humming sing-song mantras. Nothing helped. The hours oozed along.

At three a.m., Victor went to the kitchen and began pulling glasses and measuring cups from the cupboards, placing them next to bottles of alcohol on the counter. He formulated as many tinctures as possible without skimping on dosage, exhausting every scrap of fumewort. He set his MeshBit timer for one hour, then sat on the living room floor and stared at the glass bead mosaic on the wall. A mess of blue-green patterns piled on top of each other, it depicted some mathematical theorem that Ozie had recognized and called "seductive" while they were searching for apartment decorations at a scrap market beyond the Bayshore Wall. Victor programmed a timer on his MeshBit and counted breaths. When a ping sounded, he took a dose of the tincture, swallowing it in one fiery gulp. He continued methodically, one dose every ten minutes. By five a.m., with most of the vials emptied, his vision began to blur. Mercifully, his brain had ceased chattering. He staggered to bed, fell on it, and drifted to sleep.

He woke up two hours later to the sound of his screams. In the dream, he'd been drawn and quartered for a crime he couldn't remember committing. He trudged to the kitchen again, uncorked a vial of fumewort, and drank, letting the stinging liquid run down his throat while he made his way to the living room. He sat at his writing desk with the dreambook open to a blank page and wrote. When he was finished, he closed the book. It thrummed, seeming to emit a sound like a distant engine coming closer. When Victor looked away, the sound faded.

He raked his face with his fingers. There were only two days until his reclassification appointment; still time for his family to have him committed. His nightmares made sleep a terrible prospect, but insomnia would erode his self-control.

It was time to take some risks.

Pearl had said she could help him, and he knew she was holding something back. Even if she couldn't help him get rid of his dreams, get some real sleep, and pass his reclassification, he wanted her advice, her revelations, before he was locked up forever. Mist obscured the view from the train as it chugged across the bridge. While the Mesh signal was still strong, Victor left Karine a message saying he would be in the office by noon.

The fog thickened as the train continued. In Little Asia, the busy streets smelled of wet asphalt and decaying vegetables. The people disappeared into the grayness. Buildings dripped, awnings sagged, and few people noticed him with his dark trench coat cinched tight and hood pulled forward, matting his curls. He arrived at Pearl's shop and pounded on the front door. When it finally opened, she looked beyond him and down the block. Her face softened when she recognized him, and she beckoned for him to follow her into the shop.

The store was as quiet and neat as before. A box of shiny metal parts and pieces of gray-brown bioplastic sat on the floor next to her desk. She noticed him looking at the box and slid it out of view with her foot.

"Back so soon?" she asked.

"My reclassification is in two days." *Two to go. Count the letters. G. O. Two. Two means go.*

"You look like you're not sleeping."

"I'm not. The fumewort helps, but not enough. And when I can sleep …"

"You dream?"

His answer was instant, instinctual, protective, and false. "No."

"So, here you are, coming to me with a problem, expecting my assistance. And lying."

Victor bowed his head.

"Why do you think I help people like you?" she asked.

"I don't know. You like hopeless cases?"

Pearl rolled her eyes. "Do you know anything about Little Asia?"

Victor shifted on his feet. He didn't need a lecture, but maybe listening was part of the price for her assistance.

"Refugees from all over Asia, crammed together, crossing the Pacific to flee a war with deep, deep roots. I doubt they teach you about the Buddhist schism." The *m* in her *schism* lodged in Victor's ears.

"Not really. In history class, we spent one week combined on the Communion Crisis, the War of the Atlantic, and the Great Asian War."

Pearl sighed and then spoke crisply. "The assassination of the Empress Dowager started a fire that burns to this day. Resentments, factions, intrigue—all that traveled far across the Pacific. More fighting, a blight spreading. Then!" She smiled a false, toothy, bitter grimace. "The benevolent social engineers of Europe encouraged Semiautonomous California to pass the Refugee Act." Her voice moved from sarcastic to mournful. "Riots, segregation, rural allotments. The invisible legacy we inhabit. Why Oakland shines and the rest of Bayshore stinks and sinks. So, people keep moving here and elsewhere."

Her dried-up hands flitted, waving eastward, like flags in a breeze. She ran through a litany of difficult-to-pronounce towns dotting Semiautonomous California's Long Valley foothills: Jian'ou, Huizhou, Gaobeidian.

"The lucky ones avoid SeCa entirely. They make their way along the Cold Nile through the OWS or sail directly to the Democratic Republic of Mexico. Plenty of work. None of this Cathar colony nonsense. Here we have—"

"Pearl, can you help me get to sleep or not?"

"Am I boring you?" Her nostrils flared.

"No. I'm sorry. I am interested."

"Good liars get what they want. Bad liars get into trouble."

Victor bristled. "It's just ... my reclassification appointment got moved up, and you want to tell me stories and ... and ... wind me up for ... who knows why."

"You think I'm 'winding you up'?" she asked with an air of light innocence and heavy irony. The woman, with her changeling voice, was making fun of him, using every opportunity to tease him and draw out his troubles.

"You're telling stories. It's manipulative."

She smiled, revealing two rows of teeth that looked so white and perfectly aligned that they had to be fake. "One more chance, Victor, without lying: what are you dreaming of?"

His throat felt dry, and he reached for a tincture in his pocket.

Pearl grabbed his hand. "Come, come," she said. "I speak to many Broken Mirrors. They don't appear as haunted as you do." She raised his trembling hand, and he snatched it back.

"They're horrible." He swallowed thickly. Years of night sweats and thudding heartbeats. "I'm being chased, or I die. In pain. Burnt. Bloodied. Drowned. Falling from a cliff. Every worst thing you can imagine."

"When I speak to people escaping from across the Pacific, I hear many similar things." Her expression was kind now. She wasn't laughing or teasing.

May as well jump all the way in. Victor continued, "The dreams are strange in another way." He breathed with great effort. "I think sometimes I dream about things before they happen. Like in Carmichael."

Pearl's eyes lit up. "You poor Eastmores."

Victor felt his stomach knot. "What do you mean by that?"

"I might know your family history better than you do. You have, well, the Dowager Empress tale can wait another day." She gestured to a low chair and advanced on him sweepingly until he complied and sat. From a chiller, she withdrew a metal flask, poured milky streams into two small black ceramic cups, and sat across from him. He took a sip while she watched—anything to keep on her good side at this point—but he gasped when he tasted the delicious brew. It was sweet and sour, pleasant notes of cedar, fresh soil. He took another sip greedily. She smiled, though she still watched him with an expression of concern. "Your dreams come true, you say?"

He put the cup down empty and said, "When a refugee boat sank off the coast—it was two years ago—I'd already seen it happen. I was dead certain. And the fires in the camps north of Oakland, I saw that too."

"So much death," Pearl said, looking beyond him into the gloomy recesses of her store.

"Dr. Tammet says cause and effect get muddled in my head. That my memories form bad connections. She put it more eloquently than that."

"She may be right, in a way." Her voice took on a soft, faraway quality. "Memories help us make sense of time's hallucinations. But—" Her gaze locked onto him like a vice. "More refugees died in Carmichael than any other group. Samuel started at the nursery. Part of his experiment. When does consciousness start? How young can someone *cross over*?"

A wave of warmth rushed over him and Victor looked away. Even while he was sitting, the room began to spin. He wanted to pack himself away, like the contents of the glass jars tucked into their cubbyholes on shelves all around him. Vacuum sealed. Safe in silence.

"My sister's family lived in Carmichael," she said, eyes cold, watching him, interested yet merciless.

Victor got to his feet unsteadily, vision blurring. He picked up a glass jar, pulled the cork out, and inhaled the smell of dried leaves, spices, fungus, and dirt. He tried to stuff his mind full of the strange scents and leave no room for anything else.

"Is that why you need herbs, to save us from another Carmichael? From you?" she asked.

Violent thoughts invaded Victor's mind. He imagined braining her with the glass jar. Blood and shattered glass. A store full of medicine, his to pilfer. Such fantasies, however fleeting, were too dangerous to let simmer. He visualized sealing his urge inside the jar and then replaced it in the proper cubbyhole.

Facing her, he said, "I would never do ... what Samuel did."

She was shaking as she stared at the ceiling or, maybe, past it. A long, wheezing breath deflated her body. "What that demon accomplished should not have been possible. The signs were there to be read—the equipment he stockpiled, the way he went poking around people's yards. He showed up to every community event, every single one, and always, always had something bizarre to say. But he convinced everyone he wasn't a threat. That he was harmless. A harmless oddball who wouldn't swat a fly. Then, after, when his evil was revealed, he said he communed with ghosts and helped his victims cross over to a better world, one he saw in his dreams."

"I'm not like him."

"You're not the only Broken Mirror to say that."

"No, of course not, but—"

Her voice lowered to a seething whisper. "You want advice? I'll prophesize for you. You will never know peace until Samuel Miller is dead. He's a living ghost, haunting us all. You wonder why he let you live? Make peace with it. You didn't make this world, but you have to live in it. We all do."

She lit a small, rolled cigarette. Not tobacco or cannabis—the scent was more complex. "We say the Classification Commission is there to protect, but it's a punishment. We feel guilty that we let the massacre happen. To absolve that sin, we make the weakest among us suffer. The human problem: we're full of desires we seldom understand. Moved by forces unseen. Some dreams are better forgotten." She waved the joint in his face, urging him to smell the curling smoke, but she didn't offer it to him or explain what it was.

She looked at him with her head cocked and her lips pressed together. "Some people would say you have a mad ghost inside you." She waved her hand next to his face as if to dispel angry spirits around him.

"You believe in ghosts?" he asked.

"Not really. But if you asked me what possession looks like, I'd say, 'Look in the mirror.'"

"Thanks, that's a huge help."

She smiled a big, wide, toothy grin. She took another hit from the joint and seemed to drift away for a minute. She returned more somber.

"It's too bad about your grandfather, Victor. I'm sorry for your loss. Very sorry."

He picked up an abalone shell and watched the iridescent colors of the enamel shimmer, feeling his patience nearing its limit. His voice wobbled as he said, "If you have secrets, now is the time."

"How badly do you want to know the truth? It could be dangerous." Her voice had changed again, becoming softer, clearer.

Victor could tell she was deadly serious. "I'd do anything. I would. If you can help me, I'll—"

She held up her forefinger to silence him. "Don't make promises. The future is listening."

She smiled in that condescending way that he now recognized was and expression of her twisted sense of humor. "There's not much I can tell you. Jefferson said my data egg would open when yours did. Right now, it's just a lump." She opened a drawer in her desk and took out a data egg, matte black. Victor went lightheaded. Had his granfa given out data eggs filled with secrets like some beyond-the-grave hybrid of St. Nicolas and Guy Fawkes? To how many people? He patted the one in his pocket to make sure she hadn't done some magician's switcheroo on him. It was safe, inert, just like hers.

She continued, "So, until then, I guess I can only help you in two ways. Three if we're keeping score and you're feeling desperate."

"I'm obviously desperate," he said.

"Yes." She gathered two jars and set them on a black lacquered side table. Using a scratched plastic scooper, she filled a pink silk pouch with one jar's contents, tied it with ribbon, and held it under his nose. It smelled moldy, sweet, and slightly spicy. Familiar.

"I recognize that. Fumewort."

"That's one. Now, number two." She filled another pouch with the other herb and held it out.

He inhaled its scent through the silk. "Nice," he said. "Tangy. Sweet. Almost like jasmine."

"Calea ternifolia. 'Bitter grass,' you can call it. A lucid-dreaming herb. Allows you to take command of the dreams."

"That's delusional."

"You've heard the saying, 'Fight fire with fire'? Bitter grass will put you in control. Twist the threads of fate in your fingers. In dreams, in life. One is a reflection of the other. Bitter grass is the bridge."

"Tell me how I take it."

"Same as the fumewort. Tea or tincture works. A dose at bedtime."

"How much do I owe you?"

She shook her head. "Jefferson already paid me."

Victor put the two pouches in his pocket. "You said three ways you can help me."

"Two is terrific, but three is theatrical." She laughed when he shook his head in rueful disgust. "Here." She unspooled a roll of butcher paper and carefully ripped a small piece the size of two fingers, scribbling something with a charcoal pencil.

Victor took the slip of paper from her and saw a MeshID written in squarish numbers. "Whose is this?"

"Someone who can help you."

"How?"

She nodded at the paper. "Ask him. He can be trusted as much as anyone, which is not a lot. Even a lie can be revealing. You'll like him. He's a brainhacker." She winked knowingly.

"That's illegal."

"In SeCa, maybe. Talk to him. Then come see me again. Maybe we can crack these open together." She tossed her data egg into her desk drawer, which landed with a thunk.

Victor held up the slip of paper. "Is this some sort of trap the Health Board made to—"

Her laugh, hawk-like, cut him off. "Best to keep suspicions to yourself until you can prove them." She shook her head. "I should move to Europe, open a new-age herbal paradise serving everyone poison tea." She cackled, and shivers crawled up Victor's back. "But only the sick need medicine. The rest need a reason to believe they're sick."

Victor grimaced. He was starting to understand her sense of humor. He grabbed the sachets, ignored her crooked smile, and turned toward the door.

She called out behind him, "I know you, Victor. You're the ghosts' favorite! Come back soon." Her laugh hooted behind him as he ran for the door.

Outside, he uncorked a vial of fumewort tincture and drank every drop. His gullet bristled and his brain ached. He hurried to the train station, making sure not to stumble over people squatting in front of shopfronts cooking their morning meals of soup and dumplings on portable stoves. The scents were intoxicating and pungent, yet, strangely, they didn't induce his synesthesia. Perhaps the fumewort was suppressing it.

The strip of paper she had given him crinkled in his pocket. Whoever Pearl wanted him to contact probably wouldn't even respond to his ping, but he would at least try.

23

On their second day of purgatory, morning came with sunrays blasting through fire-scarred trunks and patches of surviving pines. They sat outside, drinking faux-café and listening to the trees rustle and creak around them. Reading more of Victor's dreambook, Elena didn't envy his dark imagination.

Every once in a while, he would glance over, a question seemingly pressing against his closed lips, but he never said a word. They spent the day in silence, waiting for Ozie to tell them it was safe to cross the border. She tried to tell him about Lucky and Bandit, but the words wouldn't come. It was as if she'd used up her last confession and had to wait for more to grow in the soil of her betrayal.

Around six o'clock, with the sun descending into the Long Valley, Elena couldn't take it anymore and started pacing. "This is a pretty sweet cabin. It could be a real homestead. Are we going to stay here forever?"

Victor ran a palm across the wall's wood siding. "I can afford better than this."

"Me too," she said. "That's not the point."

He narrowed his eyes. "Where does your money come from? I can't imagine you holding down a job while stims-impaired."

Elena turned away. He'd been stewing on the question for at least a day and had tricked her into admitting it. "The thing about the Puros is—"

"I don't care about the Puros!"

She whirled on him. "What's wrong with you? Did you take your herbs?" To fight like this was like a scene in a tragicomic, melodramatic film. A pure case of cabin fever ... if only the stakes weren't so high.

Victor reached into his bag and pulled out a vial. She watched him drink, wanting to tell him to stop, not knowing why. Maybe he was doing exactly what he needed to do to calm down. She just wished she knew how she'd triggered his anger and suspicion and how not to do it again.

"Happy?" he asked. "This isn't about my condition. I'm asking about you, how you can show up with a bag full of cash. How you can swear never to use drugs and then decide maybe it's not so bad to get addicted to stims—"

"This is why I didn't want to tell you. You have no idea."

"I don't know what it's like to lose control? Please. We uncovered Granfa Jeff's burial mound. We just left him there exposed!"

"Who's we?"

"It's going to be all over the Mesh by now! Everyone's going to think—"

A chime shut him up quick. He looked at his MeshBit, and then like the sun breaking through a fog bank, he smiled. If only her moods were as swiftly changing. Maybe she should try whatever he was dosing himself with.

Victor said, "It's Ozie. He sent us a route." He relayed Ozie's instructions to follow a mountain road to a border station. They needed to cross during a two-hour window when Ozie had somehow arranged for it to be unguarded. They had to leave now.

When they got in the car, Elena sighed with relief. She would have gone insane with nothing to do if they'd stayed any longer, and Victor *was* insane, so it helped that both of them were now temporarily pretending to be sane together in fragile synchronicity.

Beyond Truckee, they followed a winding, pitted road for several kilometers, lit only by the car's headlights and star-speckled dusk, skirting the well-maintained avenues linking ski resorts to North Tahoe City.

"What is that?" Elena asked, pointing to something white off the side of the road, partially hidden behind a stand of trees. A trail of crushed shrubbery led into the forest.

Victor slowed and leaned his head out the window. "It's a Bountiful van." He parked on the shoulder. "Like the one I saw in Little Asia. Looks like an accident."

Elena said, "It could be a trap." She put her hand in her pocket and gripped the shockstick.

"Pearl could be stuck in there."

Cody Sisco

"Who?"

"The herbalist. Where I got all the tinctures keeping me stable. Stable-ish."

"Yeah, I can see that. But why would she be all the way out here?"

Victor got out.

"No! Stop!" Elena called.

Victor ignored her and approached the accident. The van had been stopped by a tall, double-trunked redwood. He opened the rear door of the van and shined his lightstick inside. It was empty. No blood. No body. No restraints. Likewise, the glass-strewn cab was empty.

Elena had joined him, and she circled the van, scanning with her own agenda. If this was Lucky and Bandit's vehicle, they must have run off the road and hiked to safety. But how could they be this close? She hadn't told them anything since Long Valley. Was this a failed ambush? Elena wondered if Ozie could be trusted. Perhaps he'd made a deal with them and offered a ransom for Victor. But why abandon the van?

"Whoever was driving was hit from behind," Victor said. "Look at the rear bumper. They must have hiked down to the city. Maybe it was Tosh …"

"Who?" She had the sense that his secrets would come back to bite her in the ass.

"Never mind."

"Whatever. Let's get out of here. We have a deadline, remember?" Elena turned and started back to the car. He followed, sweeping his lightstick in front of them.

24

The day after the reclassification appointment, Victor tumbled onto a bus to the office. There was no way he would drive after everything that happened yesterday. Stumbling, dazed, he contemplated his last week of freedom. Only a week, maybe less, until they sent him to a ranch to be chipped and locatable by MeshTowers and MeshSats that bathed every square kilometer of the American Union in microwave radiation. A week until he was banished to a farm somewhere in SeCa's hinterlands. A week until the end of his life as he knew it. And then how long before he would descend into catatonia?

Goodbye, Victor. Hello, mute husk.

The passing streetscape of buildings, trees, and people barely registered. He looked at his MeshBit. He should call someone—his parents or maybe Circe. But he couldn't do it. After the scene he'd made in the garden, he was sure the news of his early appointment would be greeted with relief. Only one person could help him. Karine. Get her to intervene in his reclassification.

Victor stalked through the Gene-Us—now BioScan—reception area. The first hints of swelling outrage tingled on his skin. He was good at his job—more than good, he excelled. What would he do on a ranch? He knew nothing about cattle or growing crops. It would be a waste of his education and talents. This is where he should be, at the forefront of genomics, making a contribution to science, technology, and progress. He was an Eastmore, after all.

Walking past the floor of sequencing analysts, with the threat of internment hanging closer than ever, Victor saw his surroundings in a different light: full of sharp edges, harsh chemicals, and heartless people. If Ozie was right, the genetic tests that helped diagnose MRS were run through sequencers here. The company didn't want to help people like Victor. The company needed to diagnose people like Victor to turn a profit. He must have resented the company at some point, but he couldn't remember when. How thick had the fog of Personil been for him to not see what was so clear now? He'd been toiling in the machine that would crush him.

Victor marched to Karine's office. He found her reviewing a data table on her vidscreen, and he sat down across from her desk. Karine sat back silently.

"There's been a problem with my reclassification, and I need your help," he said.

He tried to read her expression using the color technique. Purplish pride and rust-colored disdain showed in the crooked way she set her lips and the lines around her slightly narrowed eyes.

"The doctor said I might be downgraded to Class Two in less than a week. No, it's worse than that. He sounded almost certain."

"I'm sorry to hear that," she said.

"He said a positive report from my employer might sway his decision."

She crossed her arms. Her bracelets jangled like wind chimes in an earthquake. "Surely you see that I'm in a difficult position with the merger."

Victor wasn't sure what she meant.

"Now that I report to your aunt, it would be an obvious case of nepotism if we intervened directly." She drummed her fingers on the desk.

"It was different yesterday," he said. "The doctor used a new device, and the questions were different. He told me details about Carmichael."

She looked at him with impatience written on her pursed, downturned mouth.

"Have the MRS diagnostic protocols been updated?" he asked.

Her frown deepened. She said, "I can't discuss that aspect of the Health Board's business with you."

"I have a right to know! The records must be public—"

"They are not. Not in this matter. I'm sorry, but I can't discuss it."

"But something's changed. My reclassification—"

"Look, Victor, I have to walk a meticulous line. I have BioScan responsibilities, and I have Health Board responsibilities, and I need to keep them separate. And you need to uphold your end of the deal. No more crazy talk."

"I'm asking you as a friend of the family."

Karine blinked.

"Please," he said. "I need to know what's going on."

She sighed and bit her lip. Then she straightened her shoulders, seeming to come to a decision, and said, "After Carmichael, they pursued every possible line of inquiry to understand why Samuel Miller did what he did. They looked at his genes, brain, body chemistry, and microbiome—he was run through every psychological test that had ever been used and many that were still experimental. We continue to study him. We're always learning more."

"What does that have to do with me? Or any other person with MRS? He's a freak. A once-in-a-lifetime oddity."

"An oddity who killed hundreds of people."

"He did that. Not me. I deserve a normal life."

Karine looked at him sadly. "Whether you deserve one or not, how can you believe that's possible here, now?"

"Do you want us all locked up for one man's crime?" Victor asked hoarsely. "Am I nothing more than my condition?"

Karine flinched, a hurt look on her face. In a steel-cold voice, she said, "I've said enough."

They stared each other down for several seconds. Then, with a growl of frustration, Victor left the room. He'd made a mess of it. He should have found a way to ask the right questions and keep her talking. However, he didn't feel panic, only a deep sense of resignation. He'd worried for so many years about losing control and being tossed into a Class One facility that the Class Two ranch would be a relief. He wouldn't have to worry about fucking up anymore. He could be himself.

Later, Victor didn't even try to begin his daily tasks at his workstation. He pinged Ozie but got no response. He pinged Auntie Circe, and she initiated a vidfeed session.

"What's wrong?" she asked.

"My reclassification didn't go well. It's like the whole system is rigged against me."

"Victor, you know better than—"

"Did you know about the change in the diagnostic protocols?"

Circe sat up and leaned toward the screen. "Victor, remember your therapy. Are you still taking your medication? You have to give up this obsession about Father being murdered."

"No. Not if this is my last week of freedom. I will spend every second I have figuring out what really happened to Granfa."

Circe said, "We've talked about this."

Victor said, "But I found traces of radiation on the data egg."

"I'm so sorry he gave you that egg. At least he didn't manage to do you permanent harm."

What was she saying? That Granfa Jeff had tried to poison him? Victor gripped the data egg in his pocket. Bile rose in his throat. Was the data egg poison or an answer to his questions? Was Ozie right about there being a conspiracy, or did they share a paranoid delusion?

"Did Father ever explain why he canceled the research at Oak Knoll?"

Victor squirmed in his seat. "No."

Circe nodded. "He behaved erratically, almost paranoid, over the past year or so. He almost lost the company in a takeover." Circe's face now filled the screen. "A lot of what he did is unexplained."

Victor's throat tightened. "You said it was dementia." The words tasted sour in Victor's mouth.

"It was more than that. I know that he was hiding something from me. *He* was never diagnosed with mirror resonance syndrome, but..."

Wait. Could Granfa Jeff have been a Broken Mirror?

Victor couldn't speak past the lump in his throat. He looked up at the ceiling, his mind churning with the implications. Granfa Jeff had had an ideal family life. He was a medical hero known all over the world. A large proportion of humanity had been inside one of the Eastmore clinics for treatment to prevent cancer. If he had MRS, it must have been a far milder, non-degenerative case than Victor's. If it had been known that Jefferson Eastmore was a Broken Mirror, it could have changed how people felt about them all. Was it possible?

Circe continued, "Before his delusions overcame him, we think he came close to a cure."

Victor's attention snapped back to Circe, and he hung on her words like a lifeline. "A cure?"

"We don't have a lot to go on, Victor. His self-destruction was well-crafted and nuanced. I've looked through the records left on our network, so I know there was a compound called XSCT, but he had a head start destroying his work, deleting files, and moving people around. I'm not sure we can ever reconstruct all of it. But some things were saved. Victor, we might be able to get *your* cure back on track. I'm going to need your help, though. Can I count on you?"

The blood drained out of his head in one beat, then came rushing back the next. He nodded, weakly.

"I'll need you to take your Personil."

"I'll take my Personil," Victor said. "After I— "

"After what?"

After I go take a look around Oak Knoll. "Nothing. I'm just tired. I promise I'll go back on Personil."

His auntie's eyes lit up with compassion and relief. "You're a strong and brave young man, Victor. I'm very impressed. It'll be a new start."

She terminated the feed.

That afternoon, he was unable to concentrate and watched the clock till it was a reasonable time to leave. He ran from the office to the parking lot, before he remembered that he'd taken the bus that morning. The journey home seemed interminable, but finally, he was home. He jumped into his car, consumed three vials of fumewort tincture, and drove to the shuttered Oak Knoll Hospital. Standing before the hastily erected mesh-wire fence, he scanned it for a weak spot. He squeezed through a gap, pleased there seemed to be no security around. Clearly the company didn't consider the old building worth protecting.

He walked past a vacant security checkpoint and a few low-slung concrete buildings. After a few minutes, he arrived at the main hospital building: four wings, ten stories high. For all the hospital meant to him, this had been a leading genetics research facility in the American Union and a place of healing. Now, it was a husk, emptied of people and purpose. Disused. Abandoned. A waste.

The entrance was covered by aluminum sheeting affixed to the facade by metal pins the size of large fingers. He couldn't go in there. Images from his time in the building haunted him. The echoing hallways, the small square rooms where he gave blood and submitted to countless psychological tests, the waiting areas with glass windows looking out toward the bay.

Victor looked for another way to get inside. He walked next to the southern wall. More than a meter beyond his reach, the windows were too high to be used unless he could find something to stack underneath them. Around the corner, he found a narrow concrete stairwell leading down. At the bottom was a metal-banded door that swung open when he tugged it, surprisingly smoothly at first and then with a painful metal-on-cement shriek, sticking a third of the way open. He squeezed through.

Glittering dust cascaded through the narrow shaft of light at the threshold, illuminating a thin slice of the interior. A low-ceilinged corridor stretched ahead between ductwork, pipes, and machinery: water heaters, chillers, electrical cabinets, and racks stacked with boxes.

Victor took a few steps and allowed his eyes to adjust to the dim light, looking for a way into the main building where he knew the layout well. A lump formed in Victor's throat. His career, his life's ambition, his destiny—to help people through science and medicine, to continue the Eastmore legacy of healing and progress—should all be playing out in the rooms above him. Instead, he was searching around the dark basement. He explored the perimeter of the room by touch. A lightstrip activation panel did nothing when he pressed it. A pair of double doors in one corner seemed promising; each had a porthole at eye level.

A high-pitched scream shot through the dark.

Victor jumped and fell against the wall, breathing heavily. That sound—what was it? He strained to see in the blackness. His heartbeat reverberated in his limbs.

Another scream ripped through the room, painfully loud. Victor realized it was metal screeching on the concrete floor. The begrudging outer door was being pushed open. He straightened and listened. He edged backward along the wall as a beam of light flashed on, sweeping the room. Victor ducked to a crouch behind a large storage cabinet on wheels. The beam moved toward him. He was trapped.

"I know someone's here," a man's voice said. "The perimeter sensor was tripped, and I got a bunch of sensors inside this place." The voice waited a few breaths in silence. The man sighed. "I know you're still in here. Show yourself!"

Who was he? Probably not a police officer, Victor reasoned. Whoever the man was, he must have been monitoring the property from nearby to get here so quickly.

Clip. Clop. Clip. The man walked further into the room. "I don't like hide-and-seek, so why don't you come out? What are you doing down here anyway? There's nothing left."

Victor weighed his chances of escape if the man became hostile. He might be able to knock him out with a pipe or a wrench if he could find one. But not if the man was armed. Victor wasn't trained for knife fighting, and in the dark, there was too much to bump into and trip over. Or the man might have a sonic grenade, deafening in such close quarters, or a shockstick, sleep jabber, fire grenades, or any number of other exotic weapons. Victor's skin burned, remembering the people who died when their houses in Carmichael exploded.

The man took a few steps closer. "Come out where I can see you," he said.

He kicked away some bits of metal. Each skittering clinking sound made Victor's chest shudder. He crawled on his elbows, trying to remain quiet, like a mouse hiding from an owl.

The light beam moved toward other parts of the room. Victor got up and took a few crouched steps. The beam of light flashed back. A bright glare in his face blinded him, and he jerked back into hiding. Time to try something different.

"Just checking things out," Victor said in a deep voice, trying to sound authoritative. Then he slunk to the ground and used his elbows to pull himself forward. His only clear path was deeper inside.

"I could gas you," the man called out. "My guess is you don't have a mask."

Adrenaline flooded through Victor. He sprinted to the double doors and blew through them as the man's light found him. He stumbled forward into a hallway that was empty and lined with closed doors on either side. The man's lightstick beam followed Victor as he ran. He found a stairwell door unlocked and flew up the stairs.

He climbed three floors, hoping to exhaust his pursuer, and whirled down a hallway on the floor designated for long-term patients. He had been here many times to visit Alik.

Victor sprinted toward the end of the corridor. He could take the other stairwell down and escape from a first-floor window. Something caught his foot. He almost fell. Arms spinning wildly, he regained his balance.

Hissing surrounded him, and a fog cloud arose. Fatigue sapped his muscles. He slumped to the floor and drifted into unconsciousness.

Victor woke confused, groggy, hanging by his armpits. A man was holding him up with ease.

The man said, "Tell me what you're doing here, or I'm not responsible for what happens; you are."

Victor struggled. The man lowered Victor to his feet and moved a hand to his throat. Through his fear, Victor got a proper look at the guy. In his late thirties or early forties, he had honey-colored skin, a jutting jaw, and wide-spaced eyes on a narrow face. A black knit cap sat snugly on his head.

"Let me go," Victor said, hating how pathetic his squeezed voice sounded.

"No."

"Please, I'm allowed to be here. My grandfather built this place."

The man released Victor. "Huh. Didn't recognize you. If you try anything, you're in for more pain than you can handle."

Victor shuddered and balled his fists. "Who are you?"

"Name's Táshah."

Victor backed away, holding his throat. "Tasha? That's a girl's name."

"I go by Tosh," he said. He smiled and showed his teeth. "*Táshah* is Kaddo for 'wolf.' I worked for Jeff."

Victor took another good look. Black hair poked from under Tosh's knit cap like greasy porcupine quills. He looked weather-beaten, like an old chair left on the porch, but there was a hardness to him, a way his eyes glared that hit Victor in the stomach and twisted. And he had muscles bulging everywhere.

"You don't look like a doctor."

"I worked for him *personally*."

Victor tried Dr. Tammet's color technique. Tosh's face was a jumble of hues, too many to make sense of. But his musculature, how he'd handled Victor like a straw doll, marked him as a thug or an extremely vain muscle worshipper. Or both.

"Death doesn't cancel the kind of debt I owe him."

"Why are you spying on me?"

Tosh chuckled. "Don't flatter yourself. Jeff asked me to keep an eye on things here after it closed, among other things. I've got cameras and sensors all over the place." Tosh's open manner changed. "Has the data egg opened?"

Victor took a step back. "You know about that?"

Tosh raised his hands, palms forward, but Victor didn't believe for a second he had nonaggressive intentions.

"Has it opened?" Tosh asked.

"No, it hasn't."

"Huh. Tell me what you're really doing here."

Victor started to take another step back, but Tosh gripped his arm. Suddenly, he was behind Victor, who found himself kneeling with his arms pinned painfully behind him and Tosh pulling on them every time he moved.

"What are you doing here? The truth, and maybe I'll let you go without popping your arms out of their sockets."

Victor tried to throw his head back to connect with Tosh's face. He missed. Tosh's grip tightened and pulled Victor backward, sending searing pain through his shoulders and making him scream.

"No point screaming. It's just you and me."

Victor sagged onto his heels, breathing hard. "I'm looking for something," he said.

"Looking for what?"

Victor hated telling him, but he had no choice. "The research for a cure. He might have been close before he was …"

"Before what?"

A week to go and nothing to lose, Victor thought. *Might as well say it.*

"Before he was murdered."

"*Murdered?*" Tosh released him. Victor almost fell forward, but Tosh caught his shirt and helped him to his feet.

Victor sighed and leaned against a bulletin board. "I found something on the data egg. Traces of a rare, human-made radioactive element. It could explain his health problems. But I don't know what to believe."

Tosh looked thoughtful. "I know about your disease. The Broken Mirror thing."

Victor wondered how well Tosh knew Granfa.

"You think he was poisoned?" Tosh asked.

"Maybe," Victor said.

"Let me show you something."

Tosh walked to the stairwell. Victor followed him up six flights. His legs ached, and he couldn't stop yawning from the residual effects of the sleeping gas.

"Come on," Tosh called out from half a floor above. "You're going to want to see this."

The top floor was sunnier than the rest, thanks to long skylights that repeated along the ceiling like the dashed dividing lines of a highway. Tosh paused in front of an open door. Inside, wire mesh racks held cleaning supplies, jugs of bleach, and other cleaning products. A mop, buckets, and plastic cones that said, "Wet Floor" stood to one side. There was nothing there to see. Then Tosh stepped forward, reached behind the supplies rack, and pressed a control pad on the back wall that looked like a standard lightstrip panel. The wall and rack both swung backward, revealing another room. Victor breathed shallowly and followed Tosh inside.

A few books were piled on otherwise empty bookshelves. The windows were covered with sections of black plastic. Chem lab equipment sat on a worktable, still plugged in as if the technician had just stepped out for lunch. Victor picked up a silver lightstick from the table and turned it over. An inscription on the butt read, "J. E."

"What is this place?" Victor looked around the room, which connected to others on either side that were empty. There were no doors back to the hallway except for the secret one he'd come through.

Tosh took off his cap and ran his fingers through his black hair. "It's mostly junk. Some equipment. The valuable stuff is gone."

"Explain."

"After he closed the hospital, Jeff had me set this up using solar power from the roof. Anybody wandering through the building wouldn't even know this was here, and I made sure no one got in. You found one of my gas traps downstairs. Jeff knew where they were and came and went as he pleased. Until ... well, he wasn't able to move around so well toward the end."

"But why is this place so secret?"

"Don't know. He told me that after he passed, I should destroy everything. I'm nearly done. These books and this equipment are the last to go."

Victor paced the small room. What had his granfa been doing here? There were no logbooks, nothing like a journal or research notes. He felt an ache in his chest, picturing Granfa Jeff alone, spending his last days here. The man deserved better than that.

Tosh watched him as if Victor's expression would reveal a clue as to the purpose of the secret room.

Victor waved a hand at an empty desk. "Was there paperwork? Files? Computers?"

"He wiped the computers and destroyed the files."

Victor massaged his arms and shoulders where Tosh's hands had dug in. The books on the shelves covered a hodgepodge of topics. Renal function. Cell cycles. *The Mineralogical Handbook.* Victor thought briefly about the herbalism book he'd found in his granfa's home office. He might have been referencing that, too, looking for something. A sick man looking at minerals and herbs, holed up in a hospital, playing with lab equipment.

Aloud, Victor murmured, "I looked through his medical records. He must have known he was being poisoned. But he kept it quiet. Maybe he tried to find a cure-all by himself."

Tosh swung his gaze over the room, nodding. "He was crafty."

Victor was glad he finally met someone who didn't greet everything he said with skepticism. "You don't think I'm crazy?"

Tosh gestured to the workbench. "Jeff always played a long game. I knew something was wrong. I guess poison makes a lot of sense."

Victor looked around the room. "Are you sure there's nothing left of his data stores?"

A lump formed in Victor's throat. His eyes felt warm and moist.

Tosh rubbed his jawline. "There's one thing."

Victor looked up. "What is it?"

"He told me to save one thing for you. For when the data egg opened, and you came to find me. But your data egg hasn't opened, so—"

"*What*? Why didn't you say so sooner?"

Tosh smiled, a hard, cruel twist of his lips. "I was Jeff's friend, not yours. It doesn't look like much, a kind of photograph, just black and white blotches. I thought it looked … artful. I had it framed."

"Artful," Victor repeated. Tosh seemed as cultured as a bag of bricks.

Tosh glowered, reading Victor's tone. "You're the last person who should be making assumptions about people."

"I want to see it," Victor said.

"Then we'll go to my place."

They retraced their steps down the stairs and through the dark basement. With each step, Victor felt more wary. He didn't know anything about Tosh. But Tosh believed Granfa Jeff was murdered, that's why, and that should be enough to trust him. But Victor's uneasiness didn't fade. Maybe Tosh hadn't been a friend to Jefferson.

When they were back outside, Victor tripped over a tree branch and cursed.

Tosh shushed him and then froze. "We're not alone," Tosh whispered.

Victor looked around. The wind lifted the moist air from the bay, cold enough to give Victor chills. The light was fading by the minute.

"Keep quiet and follow me."

Tosh crept toward the gap in the fence, and Victor followed on legs still wobbly from the sleeping gas. Tosh scanned the hillside, grumbling. "You're being followed: two people. We'll lose them on the way to my place. Come on."

Victor looked around but only saw trees, bushes, and shadows. *Two* skulking around. He'd run into that man and woman in Little Asia. Had they been following him since then? No, that was paranoid thinking. Tosh was merely trying to scare Victor into trusting him. As soon as he saw what Tosh had to show him, they would part ways, and Victor would watch his back the whole time.

They drove separately, Victor following Tosh and looking in his rearview mirror for headlights, but he didn't spot any. Twenty minutes later, they arrived at an oversized spray-and-set fabricated home in South Bayshore, where new, ostensibly utopian neighborhoods had chewed up marshland and orchards to accommodate vacation homes for European elites.

Inside Tosh's house, the walls curved seamlessly into the ceiling—contours of sprayed mycelium-based composite that could withstand and dissipate seismic waves stronger than any previously recorded earthquake had produced. Tosh wasn't much of a homemaker. The same sand-colored paint covered every visible wall, and a few chairs and couches were the only furniture. The man popped into a small room and returned with a picture frame.

"We're looking for the same thing, Victor. Together, we'll find it." He squeezed Victor's shoulder and looked at him with a wily smile.

Victor's skin tingled—from either fear, arousal, or both. Then Tosh handed him the frame. It contained what looked like an old, blurry photonegative of a nebula. In the center, was roughly circular black haze, with another smaller black blob extending below it. If Victor narrowed his eyes, the image almost looked like a face. Of course, it could be anything. People were likely to see faces anywhere: in rock formations, on toast, in soap suds. It was how the human mind worked.

Victor took the plastic film from the frame and held it up to a lightstrip hanging from the ceiling. He noticed a square dark patch in one corner. He turned the film over and saw a small label: "J.E. alpha exposure, 1990-Aug-25."

The hair on his arms rose. Alpha exposure. Signs of radiation, again.

Victor lowered himself slowly onto Tosh's black synthleather couch trying to process the image's meaning. His granfa had tried to find a cure for radiation poisoning, and he'd failed. He said, more to himself than Tosh, "Ionizing radiation from polonium would do this. Enough of that, and there'd be internal scarring. DNA damage. His organs, maybe his heart. His skin, his hair. The blotches."

Tosh held up the film and squinted at it. "You could be right."

Victor said, "We need better evidence."

"Such as?" Tosh asked.

"A radioactive corpse."

25

In Victor's apartment, he and Tosh waited for full dark to descend to take the radiation detector they'd purloined from the university to the graveyard. Sunlight through the window from low above the horizon cast strange, bright shapes on the living room wall.

Tosh made jokes about how great sex among the burial mounds would be. Victor imagined hands scraping against stones, the smells of dirt and flowers, cold wind on warm skin, and shivers up his back. He told Tosh to stop, but Tosh seemed too amused by Victor's discomfort to let up.

Victor's MeshBit chimed. A message from Ozie read, "Dark grid blowing up. MRS crackdown? Check on plant lady. Urgent. Seconds ticking."

"We need to get to Little Asia." Victor approached Tosh, who was staring through the window at the sun glinting off the bay.

"You know, the view is so nice from here. I could get used to it." Tosh wrapped his arm around Victor's shoulders.

"Did you hear me?" Victor asked. He tried to squirm away, but Tosh held him tight. "Get off!"

Tosh said, "Slumming over there isn't my idea of a good date night."

Warmth radiated from Tosh's body. It made Victor's stomach queasy. "Would you stop with the jokes?" Victor said. "They're creepy."

Tosh released Victor and nudged his side with his elbow. "Don't worry, sourpuss, you're not my type."

Victor brushed his clothes where the man had touched him. "Good. I'm not interested."

Tosh wore a shocked expression. "Not interested at all? You're a puzzle, aren't you?"

"Not interested in *all that*." Victor waved a hand at Tosh. "It's too much."

"Your loss. I lean androphile myself, if you're wondering. Helps keep me focused."

"Wonderful," Victor deadpanned. "Can we just go?" He strode to the front door and opened it.

"Suit yourself." Tosh stepped toward the door, stopping at the threshold. "Why Little Asia?"

"I need to check on Pearl, the woman I get my herbs from—my medicine, I mean. She knew Jefferson, and I think she's in trouble. And I need to stock up."

"I see. And if you don't get your medicine?" Tosh mimed his head exploding with hands launching sideways from his ears.

"Let's not find out," Victor said.

"Why do you think Ming Pearl is in trouble?" Tosh's voice was all innocence and kittens, and his eyes blinked coquettishly.

Victor suppressed a groan. He hadn't said her full name, but Tosh already knew it. "You know her too, I guess?"

Tosh answered Victor's question with only a sly grin.

"My friend Ozie is a brainhacker. He says something is wrong with Pearl." Victor massaged his aching forehead. "I don't know why I'm telling you all of this."

"Because I've charmed you." Tosh held up a warning finger. "This is your one freebie. We check on your lady, and then we go to the graveyard. No other detours."

At the Trans-Bayshore Rail Depot's westbound platform, a clattering, old-timey, condensed-ethanol-fueled train pulled into the station while a real human voice announced the boarding. Tosh and Victor rode over the bridge just as the sun dipped behind a fog bank. The other passengers sat staring blankly at each other across the central aisle. No one consulted a MeshBit. There were no juice bulbs, no glossy magazines. Even books were likely too expensive for the people who lived on the other side of the bay. But several guarded gray synthsilk bags of produce lay at their feet, and Victor smelled something like a barnyard, maybe a chicken or a small mammal. His foot tapped a beat on the bioceramic tiles covering the train car's floor. At least he wouldn't be venturing alone this time, and Tosh was as muscled as they came.

The train descended from the bridge to the peninsula coastline. They disembarked and hustled through the teeming, soot-covered

Cody Sisco

corridors of the transit center, exited to the street, and stayed close to the waterfront, where everyone was pushing to reach their destinations before the twilight faded completely. Heading west and then south, they rounded the base of a steep hill and entered slums lining the shore. The stink of mud and sewage wafted through the air, and his ears filled with the sounds of dogs barking, men's coarse laughter, and the night women's shrill calls.

They arrived at the herbalist's shop without incident. Testing and finding the door unlocked, Tosh entered first. Victor followed, and his heart jumped into his throat.

Lightstrips illuminated a complete mess. Towers of bins and boxes had crashed to the floor, spilling dried herbs everywhere, raising a confusing mix of smells. Victor and Tosh pushed past the debris and found that Pearl's desk had been cleared of its papers, ledgers, and knickknacks, and the mess lay scattered all around.

"I assume it doesn't always look like this," Tosh said, taking a stun stick from his jacket pocket as he advanced deeper into the shop.

Victor carefully stepped over the shattered remains of glass jars. His heartbeat thudded from his chest down to his fingertips. He found fumewort and bitter grass in their cubby holes, stuffed the herbs inside paper envelopes, and stowed them in his pockets.

They moved further in, but Pearl was nowhere to be found. A few metal measuring cups lay scattered on the floor.

"This is her work area. I think she lives upstairs." Victor pointed toward a door.

Victor's MeshBit vibrated. There were three messages from Elena in his feed, each asking, "Where are you? Call me!" He deleted them. An unknown MeshID appeared next to a blank message. Victor requested a connection and seconds later heard Ozie say, "Did you find her?"

Victor heard urgency and fear in Ozie's question. His heart thudded faster. "No. I'm at the shop. There are some overturned boxes and broken glass."

"No, no, no," Ozie moaned.

Tosh walked into the room, jerking a thumb over his shoulder. "I found a bunch of electronics back there." He noticed Victor's MeshBit and pointed. "Who is that?" he mouthed.

"Is someone with you?" Ozie asked, panic running through his voice.

Tosh heard the question and shook his head at Victor.

"No," Victor said, looking at Tosh, who nodded his approval. "I said, 'I found some electronics here.'"

"Of course you did. If Pearl's gone, we need to accelerate our plans. You're going to steal BioScan's data and bring it to me."

"What? Why?"

"I want to expose the MRS gene sequence. The world needs to have access. I need you for this."

Victor's eyes unfocused as he pictured genome records stored in BioScan's data vaults, each one containing billions of bits encoding DNA base pair sequences. The MRS gene sequence was encrypted, a trade secret that gave Gene-Us a monopoly on testing services. What Ozie wanted was impossible. Victor would need more processing power than existed on Earth to reverse engineer the black-boxed sequence. Unless ...

Victor told Ozie, "It's not possible."

"Why?"

"Cracking the encryption is beyond what any computer, any thousand computers, could do in a reasonable amount of time," Victor said. "Maybe if we had eternity. Or ..."

Theoretically, he could compare patients' sequences and the encrypted sequence against full unencrypted genomes. He would have to create a data crawler to filter out known genes and perform head-crunchingly complex calculations on what remained. It was worse than finding a needle in a haystack. It was finding a specific grain of sand in a desert using a microscope to search through it. But it might be possible.

"Look, what I'm saying is probably fully in goofball territory, but I could test BioScan's data against the gray zone sequences from full human genomes. Although it would be a nasty algorithm. I'm not even sure it would work."

Victor heard Ozie inhaling with acute desperation, though when he spoke, his voice was soft like a child's. "Imagine you had a computer with enough processing to do it. What else would you need?"

"A copy of the Human Genome Initiative's gene libraries. And permission, of course."

"Forget permission, we're doing this. Grab BioScan's encrypted data and bring it to me. That's the first step."

"No. It's a crazy idea." It was also illegal and not something Victor should do while his reclassification was pending.

"While you're at it, I need you to plant a back door on their network. I've got a few scores to settle."

"No! Look, Ozie, I said I would help you if it helped me figure out what happened to my granfa. This has nothing to do with him."

"It does. Trust me. He wanted to reform the Classification Commission or, barring that, destroy it. Vic, here's the truth: you can't stay in SeCa. Your time there is almost up."

Victor spun around. Tosh was digging through boxes, making a lot of noise. He plugged his ear and pressed the MeshBit closer to the other. "What do you mean? Circe was going to try to take care of it."

"It's not that simple. People are watching you."

Cold fear gripped Victor's body. He went to the window and looked at a few passing pedestrians. A small group huddled at the entrance to an alley, passing something between them that gave off clouds of smoke. A Bountiful van with its creepy-cheery smiling flower logo and some cars were parked along the street. "I don't believe you," Victor said softly.

"I've been monitoring Mesh traffic. They're using semi-sophisticated masking software, but I can say with confidence that two people are following you, and they know you've been to see Pearl."

Victor reeled away from the window. "You're the one who told me to come here! And you thought it would be a good idea for me to return? Who are they? Are they from the Commission?"

"Yes," Ozie said, but he didn't sound confident. "Do as I say, or they will take you to a ranch. It's that simple. I can help you leave SeCa if you get the data for me. Otherwise, you're on your own."

"Leave SeCa?" That's what Elena had said he should do. But his family was here, his life. Where would he go? "I can't—"

Ozie yelled, "There isn't time for your indecisiveness. You're not in control here. If you want my help, you do what I say. Are we clear?"

Tosh grabbed the MeshBit and terminated the feed. "He's playing you."

"What?" Victor blinked.

Tosh took Victor by the shoulders and shook him. "Wake up. He's messing with you, telling you what you want to hear to make you run errands for him. Fetch this. Steal that. Guy's got his own agenda and was clearly high. Let's get out of here."

Victor sighed. Ozie sounded normal, for Ozie. "He's not high. He's like me. But that doesn't mean he's wrong."

The MeshBit chimed. Victor answered.

"Sorry I yelled," Ozie said. "You need to look around for where Pearl keeps her electronics."

Victor remembered Tosh saying something about a box of stuff. "Why would she—"

"Pearl was my brainhacker distributor for Oakland & Bayshore. You need to find a data leech. It'll look like a thick metal bracelet with a Hexagon logo. It clamps around a MeshLine and lets me read and write traffic remotely. But I can't transfer BioScan's sequences—those are too big—so you'll need to grab them and put them on a Boze-Drive. It looks like—"

"I know what a Boze-Drive looks like," Victor said. "BioScan has a ton of them."

Tosh tossed a box at Victor's feet. Black plastic and chrome peeked through the flaps. "I'm done with this bullshit. If you really care about what happened to Jeff, then meet me at the graveyard." He brushed past Victor and left through the front door.

Ozie said, "Was that Tosh? Good riddance."

"You know each other?" Victor was tired of being in the last car of the clue train.

"Too well," Ozie said.

Victor found a small oval clamp in the box, the data leech, which he put around his wrist. "Got the leech," he said.

"Good. Now, get BioScan's data, get proof of what killed your grandfather, and then get out of town. Try to shake your tail. I'm sending you an address in the mountains. Don't try to cross the border until you hear from me. It's going to—Oh, no!"

"What?"

"They're there."

"Who's where?"

"The people following you. They're there. Get out!"

Victor rushed to the front door, opened it, and stepped outside. Movement caught his attention. The rear door opened on a Bountiful van down the street, and a man dressed in black got out. Victor caught sight of someone inside the van, also in black, leaning over another figure seated on the floor underneath a bright lightstrip. The seated figure wore a pink synthsilk sweater and navy pants. A blindfold constrained frizzy black hair. Pearl!

Victor's lungs seized.

"Victor?" The sound came through the MeshBit far too loud. The man who'd descended from the van looked straight at Victor.

He turned, closed the door, and locked it. He rushed toward the back of the shop as he heard the front door being bashed in. He clambered up the stairs into Pearl's apartment, which consisted of a living room with floral-patterned, synthsilk-covered furniture, a tiny kitchen that smelled like jasmine rice, and a small bedroom and bathroom crowded with bottles of ointments and oils.

Sounds moved underneath him from the front of the store toward the back. He would never make it past them. He shuffled to the window, trying not to make any noise, but they must know he was upstairs. Outside, it was a sheer drop to the sidewalk below. There must be a fire exit somewhere. He moved through the apartment, trying not to make a sound, but the floorboards creaked with every step.

A tiny window in Pearl's bedroom opened onto a narrow alley with only a meter-wide gap between her building and the next. He pictured wedging himself against the adjacent building and worming his way down. Or he might fall.

The stairs creaked.

He hobbled to the kitchen and spotted a window next to the chiller cabinet.

He opened the window. There was no fire escape, but there was a small flat ledge with no railing, big enough for two potted plants. An old, aluminum-bodied car was parked below, cutting the distance for the fall.

Victor's vision blurred as he swung one leg over the sill, kicked off the plants, and climbed out, shutting the window behind him. The ledge sagged underneath his weight.

He heard voices coming from Pearl's bedroom as he scooted to the edge of the ledge. Attempting to lower himself, he lost his grip midway. Falling felt like slipping into blankspace, time stretching loose, weightless, expansive, with adrenaline-spiked euphoria.

The return trip was more abrupt.

His back slammed into the car's roof, and the wind was knocked out of him. A few passersby watched as he rolled off the car and limped down the street, doubled over. He took a few gasping breaths when his diaphragm cooperated. His two pursuers would catch up to him any minute, and he was sure no one in the street would help him. The Bountiful van was steps away. He hobbled over and tried the handle, but it was locked.

He staggered away down an alley. Heaps of trash blocked his way. Trudging through them, clambering and clomping as if through snow drifts, slowed him down. He considered diving into one and hiding. Then he spotted an open door and recognized the restaurant he'd fled through on his first trip to Little Asia. He ducked inside and shut the door behind him. Steam wafted through the restaurant's storeroom, carrying the scents of frying meat and noodles. He shuffled inside and hid behind a stack of buckets.

His back throbbed, and sharp pains shot through his ankle. He couldn't run anymore. He sent a message to Ozie telling him about the Bountiful van holding Pearl and asking if he could send help. *On it*, came back quickly.

A canvas bag of onions lay on the floor near his feet. A mason jar full of tiny black seeds caught his eye. For a moment, he thought he might have found black cardamom—funny, the things his brain fixated on. He dumped the seeds on the floor and shoved the jar into the onion bag. He would need the jar in the cemetery.

Victor took a deep breath and walked through the kitchen, ignoring the confused looks of the cook and busboy. The manager looked surprised when he passed her, stepping into the main seating area. He shuffled forward, never wavering from his goal, the front door, even as shouts in Mandarin beat against his back. A hand gripped Victor's arm. He bared his teeth, and the restaurant manager cowered.

He exited to the street and shuffled onward, carrying his sack, determined to get to the graveyard. Victor was afraid of authorities, madmen, rude people, wild animals, strangers either following him or kidnapping people he knew, his shifting and unpredictable moods, going blank, and not much else. Certainly not graveyards. Ghosts held no sway over him. Still, a graveyard at night shrouded in fog and shadows wasn't something he expected to enjoy.

As he approached the gatehouse door, it opened, and Tosh poked his head out. "Glad you made it. Shall we get started?"

"Could have used your help back there. You missed a chance to knock some heads together. How did you get in?" Victor asked.

"I'm good with locks. And prioritizing." He handed the radiation detector to Victor.

They moved through the gatehouse and hiked up the drive, which curved up the hill to the mausoleum before splitting into several footpaths leading among the grave mounds. On the way, they stopped at the groundskeeper's warehouse. Tosh fiddled with the door and opened it. Inside, they found motorized carts, machines for transporting sarcophagi, and gardening tools, including ceremonial shovels. Tosh picked out a metal bar and one of the sturdier garden shovels.

They reached Granfa Jeff's mound, easily identifiable with its fence of DNA-shaped metalwork. A large bust of Jefferson Eastmore glowed in the moonlight atop the rear wall. Stones had been piled around the sarcophagus, burying it.

Victor stared at the bust's face. Anger and hurt at Granfa's possible betrayal lingered, but Victor had misunderstood. Everything Granfa had done—the hospital closure, the data egg, shady plans that somehow linked Pearl to Ozie to Tosh, the foundation's change in direction, the layoffs—had been his way of fighting a common enemy, an enemy currently grasping for Victor.

"I'm sorry, Granfa," he whispered.

His vision blurred, and he wiped his eyes. This was no time for sentiment. He was so close to the truth.

"Hurry up," Tosh said.

Victor knelt, placed the radiation detector's case on the ground, and unfastened the clasps. With a press of a button, the machine clicked on and issued a static hiss. He held the device by a handle, gripping the detector rod in his other hand. Standing next to the piled stones, Victor waved the detector rod back and forth. The hiss did not change.

Tosh said, "Will that work through the mound?"

"It shouldn't. That's what I'm checking for. If we got a reading, we would know the machine wasn't working."

Tosh scratched his head. "But if we do get a reading, we still can't be sure that means that it's working."

Victor showed Tosh how the detector clicked when he brought it near the data egg. *I'll need a lead sheath before too long, should have got one when I first learned about the polonium.* "I'm willing to accept any signal it picks up as solid evidence."

Tosh loosened stones from the mound, and Victor carried each one to the dirt outside the walls, laying them down so he could correctly replace them when they were done. Twenty minutes later, the lid of the coffin was disinterred. Victor ran the detector rod along the coffin. There were no perceptible blips.

The coffin holding Jefferson Eastmore was designed to stay sealed for eternity. Tosh twisted the shovel tip into the seam between the lid and the coffin. The shovel bent. He tried again, ramming the thin edge of the crowbar in. The lid creaked. Tosh threw his weight on the crowbar, levering it up and down while Victor held the shovel handle and pushed. The crack opened wider until, finally, the lid broke open. Tosh and Victor lifted it off.

Victor looked inside.

"Damn," Tosh said, sniffing and turning away.

Victor stood transfixed, frozen; his breath was locked in his lungs. There was a body, and it was his granfa's. Though it had been weeks, there was no sign of decomposition. Whatever preservatives they'd pumped in seemed to be working. The corpse lay in a fancy suit, looking just like it had during the funeral, except then there had been daylight, and now the pale glow of the moon struck the dead flesh, illuminating it like a paper lantern.

Victor hated seeing him like this again.

He waved the detector rod over the torso, head, and along every limb. There were no readings. Victor set the radiation detection device down and gestured to his granfa's face. "We have to get his jaw open."

Tosh's eyes darkened. "There are degrees of desecration, and that goes over a line."

"Please, Tosh. I've got a hunch," Victor said. This was worse than awful. He'd take ten episodes of blankness not to have to do this, but he had no choice. "We need to open his jaw. But I can't do it."

"I'm not sure I can either," Tosh said, shaking his head. "I've done some shit in my time, but this is ..."

"I know it's a lot to ask, but don't you want to know the truth?"

Tosh sighed and pulled a folding knife from his pocket. "This won't be the worst thing I've done for Jefferson, but it's close."

He extended the blade of the knife and locked it into place. Leaning over the coffin, he shuddered as he wedged the knife between the corpse's teeth and worked it back and forth. He was careful not to let the gray-brown lips touch his hands, Victor noted before he averted his eyes. Tosh grunted, and Victor caught a glimpse of his muscles straining. Then Tosh twisted with his whole body. There was a cracking, tearing sound. Victor looked and saw the corpse's open mouth, the tendons stretched, the jaw unhinged from its resting place, not by much, but the gap was big enough for the detector-rod.

Tosh was looking somewhat green—a genuine color, not the illusion of synesthesia.

"Thanks, Tosh," Victor said. Then he inserted the end of the device, hands shaking and vision blurred by tears. The speaker buzzed and hissed, emitting rapid, popping blips. Victor maneuvered the detector rod as much as the narrow opening allowed. The counter registered levels of radiation unmistakably higher than the background rate. They had a signal. Granfa Jeff's body, notably the soft tissues inside his mouth, was still emitting alpha particles weeks after death.

Victor's chest tightened, and he held back a cry. He blinked. He felt the panic and despair his granfa must have felt when he discovered he was poisoned. Why hadn't he told his family? Why had he lived a lie and died by it, too? Although he *had* given Victor the data egg. Locked and full of secrets.

An icy wave of sadness crashed over him. His granfa had never given up on him. Granfa Jeff tried to warn him and to prepare him for what was to come. Victor shivered and tightened his grip on the radiation detector. He withdrew the rod from the corpse's mouth.

"What now?" Tosh asked.

Victor's limbs felt stiff and his mouth dry. He looked at the dirt and the stones. They had a long night ahead to rebuild the burial mound, but first, they had to desecrate the corpse even more. "We need a sample. His tongue. A few teeth ..." He couldn't finish his sentence but took the small mason jar from his jacket pocket and handed it to Tosh.

"Fine." Tosh didn't look fine. He looked enraged. He gestured at the coffin. "Choose your cut. Tongue, you said?"

Victor clenched his fists. "You don't have to be an asshole about it." He thought for a moment. "I guess robbing a grave isn't the worst thing a Broken Mirror has ever done."

"You said it," Tosh agreed, then froze. He pointed down the hill.

A car's headlights shone through the bars of the entrance gate. They dimmed, and in the moon's glow, Victor watched as two figures passed through the gatehouse and started running toward them.

26

Elena lowered the car window and leaned her head out. Down the slopes were the bright, glitzy lights of Tahoe City. They climbed the eastern ridge in looping switchbacks that made her queasy.

She knew she should tell Victor about Lucky and Bandit. But now that they'd started acting so weird, she couldn't explain what she didn't understand.

The border checkpoint was a set of shacks and scanners on the desert plain with a nearby MeshTower, blotting out stars with its dark silhouette. As Ozie had promised, no staff were on duty, and the barriers were all raised. Elena wondered how he'd arranged it and whether they could trust someone with that kind of power.

Victor drove across the border to the Organized Western States without incident. The checkpoint was quiet. If any officials were present, they were out of sight. Across the border, they passed Bartley New Town—gated communities, luxury commerce clubs, and other exclusive retreats of the OWS elites—and continued into the desert.

"Are you going to tell me where we're going?" Elena asked.

"A diner where the brainhackers hang out. Close to SeCa but beyond the reach of its police. Ozie's there."

She could see the diner's corona long before the building came into sight: it lit up this part of the desert like a neon nightmare. Huge, coiling solar-cell ropes were strung in loops, towering over the structure, spelling out "The Springboard Café." Multicolored lasers blasted radiation into the desert on every side. A rotating vidscreen cube displayed ultrashort films that featured various human organs, including giant genitals, showing how nerve patterns were activated by brainhacking scripts.

They parked in a gravel lot and walked to the entrance. Elena followed Victor inside, wondering what had happened to Bandit and Lucky, but more importantly, how she was going to help Victor now that he was calling the shots.

Semiautonomous California
2 March 1991

"Hurry," Victor said.

Tosh reached into the corpse's mouth, cut out Jefferson Eastmore's tongue, and sealed it inside the mason jar. He handed the jar to Victor, then tugged him by the elbow, leading him behind the grave mound's surrounding wall and hissing in his ear, "I'm going to draw them away. I'll catch up with you." Tosh sprinted away.

Swaths of light played over the hillside. The figures climbed closer.

A tinkling of metal-on-stone rang out from where Tosh had gone, and the lights swiveled after him.

Victor crouched low and crept to an oak tree a few meters down the hill, favoring his injured foot and carrying the jar containing Granfa Jeff's tongue.

When Victor looked back, he froze.

Granfa Jeff's body lay exposed to the air, defaced, a violation nearly as taboo as murder. Victor's eyes watered. He alone couldn't lift the coffin lid to replace it.

"Sorry, Granfa," Victor said quietly.

Glancing back to ensure the figures were still following Tosh, Victor limped down the hill and through the gatehouse as quickly as he could. He jumped in his car and drove home, knowing it was risky: that was the first place anyone would look for him. But if he was leaving SeCa, he had to collect his things and hope Tosh would lead his pursuers on a long, circuitous chase.

Walking to his front door, he wondered if he should follow Ozie's plan. It was one thing to rob a grave at night, but people would be working overnight at BioScan. Going there, as Ozie had wanted, was surely asking for trouble. Maybe he should pack a bag and leave SeCa now.

On his front step, Victor pinged Ozie, "BioScan too risky. Let's talk."

Ozie replied with a text message. "Bring BS data to exchange for info about what JE was up to."

It was pure manipulation. Ozie couldn't be trusted. But he hadn't told Victor the whole story yet—but he would; Victor would make him. He would get the data from BioScan, his leverage, and then head to the mountains.

He opened the front door and reached for the light panel. Something moved in his living room. His heart pumped adrenaline. He gripped the glass jar tightly. A figure jumped up from the couch.

The lightstrips popped on. Elena stood there, startled, and gave an embarrassed half-wave. Victor slammed the door behind him, setting the glass jar down on the entry table. "What are you doing here?"

Elena's hair was pulled into a tight bun, which her hands smoothed repeatedly. "You wouldn't respond to my messages."

"So you broke into my house?"

"I just want to help."

"The more you keep saying that, the less I believe you." He wiped the sweat off his brow. "Sorry, it's been the worst kind of day."

Elena blinked at him, and the whites of her eyes glowed orange—a sign of anxiety.

He asked, "What is it? What's wrong?"

She gulped. "I have to tell you—"

"What?"

Elena sighed, seemed to stand taller, and then said, "Some people came to ask me some questions. A man and a woman. They're watching you."

Victor felt his gut convulse. The couple from Little Asia and the graveyard. "Why?"

"They said they want to keep you safe."

And zebras are horses in jazzy attire. No way. Keeping me safe isn't high on their priority list, whoever those people are. He said, "They were lying. Must have been."

"They left me a MeshID and told me to contact them when you got home." Her hands fretted with the hem of her shirt. She looked nervous. Could she be lying?

"Don't do it. If they come to you again," Victor warned, "don't tell them anything. They're dangerous, Ellie. They kidnapped Pearl."

She flinched. "Kidnapped who?"

"Someone Granfa Jeff knew. If they're the same ones that came to you, you are lucky. They took Pearl; they had her tied up in a van. Ozie's trying to track them down." Victor rushed to the kitchen and started collecting vials of tincture and bottles of alcohol and distilled water.

Elena followed him, gaping as he shoved everything into a backpack. "What is all that? Victor? Talk to me."

"I have to get out of here." He brushed past her into the living room, unsure whether he could trust anyone.

"Why?"

"Listen. Before, I only suspected his body was irradiated. Now I have proof." He pointed to the glass jar holding a lump of tongue.

Her gaze fixed on it. "What is that?"

"His tongue. It was all I could get. His body belongs in a lab. Elena, I think his death is connected to my condition. To the way people like me are diagnosed."

She took a deep breath. "Why would you think that?"

"The Health Board changed the diagnostic protocol for mirror resonance syndrome. There are going to be a lot more people like me in the near future. Maybe Granfa Jeff stood in the way, and so someone took him out. I need to get out of here."

Victor went to his bedroom closet and arranged underwear, pants, and socks in a backpack to cradle the glass vials. He took a small box from under his bed, where he'd been hiding the little jade figure that he had wanted to give Elena.

He retrieved the herbal book, his dreambook, and the glass jar, then swept into the bathroom to grab a few toiletries and the lightstick he'd picked up at Oak Knoll. He kept the data egg in his pocket, along with his MeshBit and wallet.

"I think that's it," he muttered to himself.

Elena asked, "Where are you going?"

"BioScan."

"You packed all that to go to work? Nope, I don't buy it."

"I *am* going there."

"Hey," Elena said, rubbing his shoulder. "Let me help. What can I do?"

Could he trust her? She was so erratic in her attentions, insistent about certain things but absent when he needed her. He never knew when her mood would change. But who was *he* to turn *her* away? He needed help, even if it meant simply accepting a few small gestures of friendship. If Elena was willing to help, he wanted her nearby. His doubts were merely paranoia; she deserved better than that.

The decision to let her come along lifted a weight off his shoulders. Victor smiled. "Okay. Come with me as far as the office."

They walked outside to his car. He looked around, but there was no sign of anyone following them. Victor pulled open the driver-side passenger door and put his things in the back seat. Elena got in the front seat.

Victor drove to the BioScan campus. He left the keys with her and took his bag. "I'll be right back. If anyone comes ..."

"I'll think of something," Elena said. "You have your MeshBit, right? So I can contact you?"

"Yeah." He patted his pants pocket and felt the metal cylinder.

He lumbered to the entrance; his ankle throbbing every time he put weight on it. His MeshBit unlocked the front doors. His presence would be registered in the after-hours log, but he could see no alternative. He retrieved a Boze-Drive from the storeroom, leaving another trace in the logs. This was so dumb. But it was less dumb than the other things he'd done in the past few hours.

The marketing office was dark. He turned on the lights, found the input cable to Sarita's MeshTerminal, and wrapped the data leech around it. If Ozie was as good at hacking as he claimed, preloaded spyware would keep the theft from being logged. Eventually, maybe, Sarita would have to answer some questions. He returned to his office, booted up his terminal and vidscreen, and navigated BioScan's systems until he reached the sequencing database. He put the Boze-Drive next to the spectrum relay and paired them.

Victor found the encrypted MRS reference sequence and started transferring it and as many individual records as possible. The process would take ten minutes. As each second ticked by, Victor grew more anxious. Would he be able to get away? The strangers might show up at any moment. Ozie would figure everything out. Victor just had to make it to the Organized Western States in one piece.

The Boze-Drive reached half its capacity. The office was quiet except for the whirring sounds of liquid heat sinks. Victor tried to raise Ozie on his MeshBit again, but there was no answer. He looked up the address he'd received. The road outside Truckee in the Sierra Nevada Mountains didn't have a name, only a number: twenty-two. Victor twitched. *Two twos.* Some twos registered; some didn't. This one carried a sour foreboding. He didn't trust himself to drive serpentine roads in the dark and would have to stop somewhere on the way for the night.

What to do about Elena? She said she wanted to help him. By her own admission, nothing was keeping her in SeCa. But wouldn't he be putting her in danger by bringing her along?

The Boze-Drive completed copying the data, and Victor stuffed it in his bag. His MeshBit chimed. It was Auntie Circe. He activated the sonofeed only. "Auntie?"

"Victor, I'm on my way to the mansion. I convinced Mother to let you in again. If you went to Oak Knoll, I want to hear about it."

Victor felt split in two. He wanted to see her, beg his family's forgiveness, and return to his semi-normal life. But he'd seen the evidence. He couldn't let Granfa Jeff's death go unresolved. And when his family learned what he'd done to the corpse, they'd probably send him to a Class One facility.

"Victor, are you there?"

"Yes, I'm here. I did go to Oak Knoll. There's—there's nothing left. What's so special about the XSCT compound again? You said it might be related to a cure?"

There was a long pause. Victor felt the weight of the Boze-Drive in his arms. What would Auntie Circe do if she knew he was stealing? How much more could he disappoint his family before they disowned him?

Auntie Circe cleared her throat. "XSCT was a gene therapy delivery system. We were running animal trials to measure whether we could suppress the MRS gene when we lost everything. At least a year of work is gone." She sighed.

"Why didn't you tell me this before?" he asked.

Jefferson Eastmore had perfected a technique using viruses to deliver self-destruct codes to cancer cells. However, it depended on a detailed understanding of cancer genes. As far as Victor knew, the mirror resonance syndrome gene wasn't fully understood. If researchers had found a way to suppress the gene, that might mean a cure was possible.

She said, "I didn't want to raise your expectations unnecessarily. You've seemed volatile lately. And the merger has been demanding my time. I'll see you this evening?"

Victor gulped. "I don't think so. Elena and I ..."

"A date? How sweet! Victor, that's wonderful. Of course, I'll be around for the next few days. Come find me."

A lump rose in Victor's throat. It hurt to lie to her when she'd always believed in him. "I love you, Auntie."

"I love you, Victor."

He terminated the feed and limped down the hall. Whenever he thought of it, the prospect of a cure sent his pulse racing. Why had Granfa Jeff destroyed it? Victor rubbed the data egg in his pocket. The answer must be there. There must be a way to open it. Maybe Ozie could help with that, too.

"Hey!" someone shouted. It came from a conference room where several employees sat amid remnants of an Italian takeout.

Victor kept walking.

"Victor! What are you doing here?"

He recognized the voice as belonging to Sarita. He turned and said, "This is a late night for you."

She rolled her eyes. "This merger is killing me. None of the systems are talking to each other, and Karine's riding me to—well, you know how she is." She winked at him.

Victor saw a chance to cover his tracks, at least temporarily. "That reminds me. I'll be working remotely for the next few days. Would you remind Karine if you see her? She asked me to work on a special project, and I need to focus on it without distractions. I came by for one of these." Victor held up the Boze-Drive.

"Oh, I get it. You got a fancy new title, and now you're going to Bermuda to celebrate. Must be nice to be an Eastmore."

He bit back a retort. As long as she passed on the lie for him, he would be grateful. "Thanks, Sarita. You're the best."

She snorted, smiled wryly, and returned to the conference room.

Victor continued to the exit. The moon shone down on the near-empty parking lot, casting shadows and creating places for strangers to hide and watch. Where were Pearl and Tosh? He wished he could do something to help them, but the only thing he could do was save himself.

He reached his car and knocked on the driver's side window. "I'm driving."

Elena smiled and scooted over. "Sure, boss. Where are we going?"

Victor sat in the driver's seat and shut the door. "Back to your lodge to drop you off."

"No way." Elena crossed her arms and slumped in her seat. "You're not going anywhere without me. Tell me what you have planned."

The moonlight from across the marshlands lit her face in eerie blue tones. "I think it's better if I don't," he said.

"Victor—"

"Those people might come back." He hooked a thumb behind him toward the towers of Oakland, its hills topped by brightly lit mansions, and the dark-shadowed cemetery where Jefferson Eastmore's body lay exposed. "Better if you don't know anything."

"It's not better. It's a terrible idea. What if you get into trouble and no one knows where to go looking for you? Are you headed back to Little Asia?" Across the bay, the fog layer hovering over the peninsula glowed a dull red.

He shook his head. "I'm leaving."

"*Leaving* leaving? As in, leaving SeCa?" A goofy smile spread across her face. "That's wonderful."

Victor looked around at the BioScan parking lot. Everything he knew was in SeCa—his family, his job. "How is that wonderful?"

"It's what I've been saying all along. You're better off somewhere else—anywhere else. I'm coming with you."

"You're not."

"Come on, we can leave from here. I'll pick up whatever I need somewhere along the way. I travel light."

"But you don't even know where we're going!"

"I'm not worried. You can't keep a secret for more than a few minutes. Not from me." The corner of her mouth formed a smirk. "I'm not getting out of the car. You might as well drive." A look of alarm crossed her face. "Unless you're going to go blank."

"No," he said. "I'm good right now."

Should she come with him? She knew him better than anyone. Maybe a friend was the best thing he could hope for now since everything else was topsy-turvy. He'd always been able to hold himself together much better when she was around. He hoped he could trust her.

He said, "All right, we leave now, but I don't think we should drive all night."

Elena shrugged. "You're driving. You choose the turns."

27

Victor regretted stepping inside the Springboard Café right away. It felt designed to trigger an MRS episode. How did it not drive Ozie right out of his mind?

The entryway was festooned with lightstrips, vidscreens, and mechanical sculptures that flexed and hinged in resonance with patrons' voices and movements. A MeshTravel bulletin posted next to the door reported that the atmosphere inside the restaurant was so mentally exhausting that the owners had built an annex to the cafe where candles, drapery, and soft-droning music made it a popular and relaxing place for those digital respite-seeking souls who could get past the automated doorman.

Victor and Elena had their MeshBits confiscated and locked in silencing boxes. They stowed their bags in the vestibule's automated cubbies except for one that held the Boze-Drive and a very important sealed glass jar. The mix of vidscreens and neon motion signs resembled the chaotic jumbles of Victor's dreams. They moved further inside, stopping when the floor buzzed, and an array of red flaming *X*s, like a one-sided tic-tac-toe game, appeared beneath their feet. He studied the blazing letters roasting underfoot while they waited for a table, being careful not to lose himself altogether in blankness. A few minutes later, the *X*s disappeared and were replaced by a rushing blue ribbon of photonic water that directed Victor and Elena to a semicircular, overstuffed booth where they sat down.

A young, tattooed woman, ornamented with several large hunks of silver covering parts of her neck, ears, and forehead, approached and touched the table. Images of food and drink swam across it.

"Place your order here, and the bots will bring your food. This button allows you to vidchat with the cook if you want. He gets lonely. Tell him about any special dietary requirements before he starts preparing the meal; otherwise, we don't guarantee not to poison you. Click here if you want to speak to a human, and I'll come back and yell at you." She winked at Victor and swished away.

A few other tables were occupied by gritty road-dusted loners and small groups, talking and reviewing Mesh feeds together. The music, which had no distinguishing features other than being loud, rhythmic, and artificial, masked the conversations around them.

Elena chose meatloaf and mashed potatoes. Victor ordered a cheese sandwich and Caesar salad with a half-liter of local beer.

"You're drinking?" Her eyebrows arched.

"Yes."

"Should you?"

The hair on his neck bristled. She was the one addicted to drugs, not him. "Yes. There's no reason I can't drink a little like everyone else."

"I thought—"

"I'll be fine. I go to bars all the time now. It's how I practice being social."

Elena's eyebrows arched even higher, but she didn't say more.

While they waited for their food, Victor used the table's interface to scan SeCa MeshNews headlines. He couldn't see any mention of his granfa's grave being defiled, the theft at BioScan, a missing herbalist, nor an AWOL heir to the Eastmore fortune. It might be just a matter of time before those things became big stories, but somehow, he doubted they would get covered at all. As that thought sank in, it scared him. How powerful were the people behind his granfa's death?

Nonetheless, as he scanned through global headlines of diplomatic gaffes and delays in mega-construction projects, it was comforting to know that the world continued in its mixed-up way.

"What are we doing here? What does Ozie know?" Elena asked.

Victor leaned back in the booth. Ozie would no doubt try to enlist Victor in some scheme. He also knew much more about Jefferson's plans than Victor did, and now that he was here in the flesh, Ozie couldn't hide behind a screen anymore. He would have to fess up. "I guess we'll find out soon enough."

Elena's attention seemed to wander. She looked around, eyeing their fellow diners and glancing toward the entrance. It made

Victor uneasy. Was there something else she wasn't telling him? He watched her drumming her fingers on the table.

She looked down and shrieked. Other diners turned to stare.

"What?" he asked.

Elena cackled and looked at him with tears in her eyes. "I accidentally ordered four plates of fries, two roast chickens, a beer, and a piece of chocolate cake. Where's the cancel button?"

Victor squirmed, unamused. She seemed on edge, crazed, more volatile than usual. Or was this normal, and he was just now noticing it? He pressed a few fingers to the table to cancel the order.

"Wait!" she yelled. "I want the cake. And the beer."

He canceled everything else. "We can split it," he said.

She frowned. "Maybe."

Their food arrived five minutes later, on a platter held aloft by a robot with a tuxedo painted on its chassis and a tiny top hat above its boxy camera face. The robot deposited the plates precisely and gently, placing Victor's beer on a cooling pad. A speaker mounted on the thing's shoulder emitted a mechanical squawk. "Enjoy your meal!" It rolled away with a quiet whirr of motors.

Victor shook his head. "NEC-Automation can build robots a thousand times more advanced than that. But SeCa bans them, so they show up here as retro kitsch. Do you ever wonder what life would be like somewhere unafraid of the future?"

Elena took one bite of the meatloaf, grimaced, and pressed an icon on the table to order a beer. "Texas uses them to farm, but only on the best plots of land. They're expensive. And targets for thieves. I assume Europe has more robots than people by now."

Victor took small bites of his sandwich. Bread and cheese and lettuce for contrasting crunch. He heard her sigh twice and then a third time. She was looking away from her food, eyeing his plate slyly. He had ordered more than he wanted because she was always picking at his plate.

"What's wrong?" he asked as if he didn't already know.

"The meatloaf—it's dry and mealy," she said.

"Have some sandwich." He passed her a portion and started on his salad, enjoying the juicy crunch of the hearts of Romaine.

Her beer arrived, and she took three big gulps and sighed. "So, is Ozie going to show up or what?" she asked, but her gaze wandered.

"He said he'd meet us here." Victor shrugged. "This place is very much his vibe. Brainhacker central."

"Does he have implants? I hear they can fry you good." She chewed the meatloaf, forked some potatoes into her mouth, and took a sip of beer.

"Just a headset, I think. The magnetic kind."

"He must be crazy, though, messing with his brain."

Victor blinked at her. Noninvasive neuromodulation of the central nervous system, or brainhacking, used electromagnetism or ultrasound to affect brain functions. The technologies had been available for twenty years. Therapists were still arguing about what treatments were appropriate for different conditions. But they weren't at all dangerous when used carefully.

He took a bite of his sandwich. "He's like me with the herbs. Or like you with stims."

She pushed her food to the edge of her plate. "Have you ever tried it?"

"Brainhacking? Yes. A little."

She looked up at him. "Did it work?"

"Not really, maybe a little bit. My sleep got better. During the day, I was calmer. Not a whole lot. It was Dr. Tammet's idea. She decided against it after a few weeks of no results." No results that he'd told the doctor about. His dreams had been less horrific, but he hadn't wanted to open that can of worms.

Elena looked skeptical. "Wasn't that risky, though? I mean, especially for you?"

"I came to the conclusion that it was riskier *not* to try *anything* that might help."

"I'm sorry. I didn't mean—"

"It's fine."

They continued eating in silence.

As they finished their meal, a young man with dark skin and darker, close-buzzed hair walked to their booth and sat down. He stared at Victor through black, square-rimmed eyeglasses. "You made it. Good. Your MeshBits are compromised. I'm melting them down. And your car is being examined for bugs."

Before Victor or Elena could react, Ozie continued, "What is she doing here? I told you not to bring anyone."

"She's helping me." Victor kept his voice level, hoping Ozie wouldn't make it a bigger deal than it was or latch onto his doubts about her. "Look, Ozie, I've had enough of running around in the dark. I want to know what you know."

"Oh, sure. No problem. I have the answer you're looking for. Let me put it in the form of a question. What would have happened if Abraham Lincoln was killed that night in the theater instead of his wife?"

Victor rolled his eyes and noticed Elena did the same. Ozie hadn't changed. Victor had fallen asleep to his elliptical musings and the humming of brainhacking equipment all through their first year before Ozie vanished. "Could we not do this right now?"

"Or anytime," Elena muttered.

Ozie smiled wearily. Behind his black-rimmed glasses, his eyelids drooped; the lower lids were deep red, like a hound dog's. Billowing around his thin frame, his plaid shirt looked tired and faded. "I'm going to make a point. Humor me. What if Abe Lincoln was killed instead of Mary?"

Victor shrugged. "Probably the same stuff. The Union would have used that as an excuse to crush the South even more."

Ozie held up a finger. "But maybe not. Abe went batshit over Mary. It wasn't politics that led him to destroy what was left of Southern culture. It was a vendetta. He persecuted the Confederate leaders. He provided restitution to the enslaved people from the lands confiscated from white elites. He gave Yankee politicians and companies free rein to remake the South. Which earned him major blowback."

"Which he steamrolled too. Ozie, this is irrelevant," Victor said.

"Agreed," Elena said. "Irrelevant and creepily obsessed with the long-dead past."

"It's not! Reconstruction led directly to the Permanent Enlightenment—civil rights and anti-imperialism—which led to Repartition. Without Repartition, SeCa would be nothing, another neglected territory of the United States. The OWS would be a disorganized wilderness. You Eastmores would probably still be mucking around some Mississippi River tributary. It didn't have to be this way." Ozie leaned forward, eyes wide. "Or take the Archduke of Austria. The continental war that unified Europe started because of another failed assassination attempt. Do you think that's a coincidence?"

"I'll humor you for two more minutes." Avoiding Ozie's crazy eyes, Victor gulped his beer and said, "It's insane to argue that the attempted assassinations of the Archduke of Wherever in the nineteen tens and President Lincoln decades earlier are related."

Ozie puffed out his chest and lifted his chin. "Insanity is a matter of perspective. I'm not saying they're directly related, but they are part of a pattern. History is not just policies and demographics. Sure, those matter. After the War of the Atlantic, Europe demanded reparations, which drained the United States' treasury and paved the way for the Repartition. We all know that. But sometimes the individuals can make a difference: Lincoln, the archduke, Jefferson."

Victor stiffened. Ozie had always liked to press Victor's buttons by making up stories. Once, he'd told Victor that Samuel Miller had broken out of a Class One facility. Victor had nearly fallen out of his chair in the university cafeteria, and Ozie had laughed and hooted until tears streamed down his cheeks. Victor sat back and crossed his arms. "You promised me information if I brought you the BioScan data. This is all just speculation." It sounded like Granma Cynthia said it, tinged with sourness and disappointment.

"Fine. I'll tell you what you need to hear, but she can't stay," Ozie said.

Elena's jaw dropped, and she gripped the table's edge as if to overturn it.

"Ellie," Victor pleaded.

Giving up easier than he expected, she said, "Yeah, I got it," and slid out of the booth with her beer mug. "I'll be in the chill room, racking up a tab for you. Save the cake for me when it comes. All of it." Her glare slipped off Ozie without any perceptible effect.

Ozie smiled, showing his canines. He leaned forward when she was out of sight and said, "Give me the Boze-Drive."

Victor replied, "Tell me what's going on first."

"Okay, I'll start with the good stuff. I fucked with the Mesh feeds for the SeCa-OWS border crossing and bought you some time. A digital trail will show you headed back into SeCa and bouncing around Long Valley towns for the next week. Also, I heard from Pearl."

Victor placed his hands on the table to keep them from shaking. "And? Is she okay?" he asked.

"They let her go. *After* I paid them five thousand. But we don't think it's safe for her in SeCa anymore. She'll be here in a week."

Victor relaxed against the synthleather seat. "Do you know who they are? There was a drone following us before we turned off the road for the cabin. Was it theirs?"

"I'm still figuring that out. I'll look into it" Ozie fidgeted in his seat. He'd always been the type to resent a question he couldn't answer.

Victor looked at Ozie more closely. He hadn't changed much in five years. A little less hair at his temples. Fuller in the face, maybe not as slim around his waist. He looked anxious as always, though, eyes flicking around the cafe. Still, Victor believed he could trust him. Or, more to the truth of the matter, he had woefully few people he could trust and no better option than to put himself in Ozie's orbit. "Do you think they killed my granfa?"

Ozie stared at Victor and shook his head. "No. They're thugs. Different problem."

"How do you know?"

"Because five grand is a ridiculously insignificant sum of money. They're small time. Killing Jefferson Eastmore—that's huge."

Victor waited for him to elaborate.

"Our opponent is much craftier than those two. Here's what I know." Ozie leaned forward on his elbows. "Something is going on between Semiautonomous California and the Organized Western States, something bad. I think Jefferson got mixed up in it, and people with MRS are caught in the crossfire."

"Go on," Victor said, glad that Ozie was at least on topic, but he worried this was the beginning of another ridiculous conspiracy from a mind as fractured as his own.

"Near as I can tell, the diagnostic protocols for mirror resonance syndrome will be standard throughout the American Union within five years. Throughout the civilized world within ten. Globally within twenty."

"Why does that matter?"

"Motive," Ozie said. "Jefferson was holding everything up, trying to change the course of history, the way he did with his cancer cure. He had a couple of things going. His pilot projects for Class Two ranches raised questions about the effectiveness of Personil. He advocated cognitive-behavioral therapies, herbalism, and brain-hacking as alternatives—that's how Pearl and I got dragged in. He also had side projects in the OWS researching MRS genetics that would have been illegal in SeCa. He wanted to do away with the Classification Commission's ass-backward system. His ideas weren't popular—too radical, some said. Now that he's gone, no one else has the means and stature to question the system."

Ozie paused and looked around to see that they weren't being watched. The lights of the café blinked all around them. Loud, clanging music filled the dining hall. Diners appeared preoccupied with conversations and playing with bits of tech lying around. Victor watched his old friend and wondered if he'd lost his grip on sanity or if he'd lose his own by believing him.

Ozie continued, "Jefferson was special. He made a difference. Some people are like that. Mía Barrias, for instance, made a difference after Carmichael. If Mía had died, if she hadn't lived to tell everyone how horrible Samuel Miller's acts were, spreading the word like gospel, maybe we wouldn't have the Classification system at all. She wouldn't have made it her life's mission to get us locked up. We'd be running free, and Samuel Miller would have been an anomaly. MRS would be treated like any other health problem rather than an existential threat to society. Individuals make a difference. That's my point. Jefferson Eastmore would have made a difference. That's why he had to die, so he couldn't stop whatever they had planned. I know it."

I know it—that single phrase activated all Victor's doubt. How often had he said those exact words while referring to a blatant fantasy?

Victor rubbed his face and sighed, saying, "You're speculating again. The feeling I had that he was murdered, your conspiracy, the people following me—maybe they don't fit together. Maybe this is life simply being messy. Maybe the radiation was an accident."

Ozie raised an eyebrow. "You don't seriously believe that. Do you? You brought the tongue, right?"

Victor pushed back his shoulders. "Yes. But whatever is going on, we need facts to figure this out. Hard evidence. Not your theories of history." He took the mason jar holding a piece of his granfa's tongue from his bag and put it on the table. "We need to get this to a lab. Run some tests to find polonium and sequence the DNA to prove it's his."

28

Ozie looked at the jar with wide eyes and licked his lips. "Can do. It's safe with me." He placed the mason jar on the seat, looked at Victor, and grinned. "I'm glad you're here. You know how it is. You and I can stretch a line of reasoning to the breaking point, but together, we can keep each other honest. I know I can't do this alone. I tried feeding information to the police, the SeCa attorney-in-chief, the governor-general's office—none of them responded. They don't take me seriously. The stuff I found on the Mesh isn't court admissible. I'm trying to feed them enough to start their own investigation, but there's no sign of them taking the bait. I don't dare try the authorities here. We're on our own. That's where the Boze-Drive comes in."

"How so?"

"It's about patterns. I have a suspicion that can only be confirmed by getting the MRS gene sequence. Gene-Us was—and now BioScan is—the only company that can run the genetic test for MRS. So, the solution runs through BioScan."

"How?"

"I'm going to prove the whole thing is built on a lie."

Semiautonomous California
21 June 1979

Victor stared at husks of houses destroyed by fire, smoldering unchecked. In the street, bodies that had been crushed under the tires of self-driving vehicles had yet to be taken away. The asphalt was darkened by smears of commingled blood and soot, drying quickly under the onslaught of fervent winds.

Was this memory or blankness? Or some blend of both?

Smoke swirling, rising, spiraling away in ribbons. He wished he was up there, too, escaping into the sky.

It took hours for the police and firefighters to arrive from towns down in Long Valley. Meanwhile, Carmichael burned, urged on by deliberate sparks. His parents were gone when they should have been at home, comforting him and keeping him safe.

From Victor's second-story bedroom window, he saw the tech aide from school, Samuel Miller, turn down his street, searching for a target. Before he could move, those dark, haunted eyes found him. He held his breath until it felt like his ribs would break. An explosion somewhere broke the stare, and Samuel moved on to help more people "cross over," stalking Carmichael's citizens and killing with a shockstick, with automated cars, with explosive traps.

Later, people asked why, of course. How could a good person turn bad? Was it something to do with the Mesh? Such things didn't happen in Semiautonomous California, which was an oasis, a beacon, an example for the world.

Samuel said he was following instructions that came to him in a dream. We lived in a world of ghosts, and he was helping people attain higher states of being. Assisted quantum suicide—murder, actually—reunited them with their *primal* selves in other universes.

It was complete insanity, certainly. Young Victor often heard the story he'd lived through, as SeCan society repeated Samuel's delusions to deny them, thus burying them deeper in the culture's soil. Swear words like "shocks" became part of the nation's vocabulary—the way "laws" did during Reconstruction—and Samuel's beliefs became an underground mythology. Not true, of course. But maybe …

The universe is an explosion that never ceases. We coalesce in the cooling eddies of spacetime.

Victor sat in a classroom and could barely watch as the Carmichael story unfolded on a vidscreen on the Ludlum Middle School classroom wall. He ignored the voice that intruded on his thoughts as best he could.

A memory becoming a dream becoming history on the blank canvas of the mind.

Cody Sisco

The mayhem in Carmichael proved too widespread to be covered up, so an example had to be made. SeCa would not tolerate violence. Samuel Miller—schoolteacher, technology evangelist, and trusted citizen—betrayed the nation's ideals and thus became a monster. An embarrassment. A lesson.

After the attack, SeCan officials had to let go of self-driving cars, but they salvaged the Mesh. Europeans' pragmatic cultural-imperial infrastructure adapted everywhere it gained a foothold, and a terrorized population put up little resistance.

With the Mesh in place in every home and pocket, there was no forgetting. Ever. There was no healing. There was no letting go. There was only continual propaganda against an enemy boogeyman, casualties heaped on an altar of remembrance, and perpetual paranoia.

A new genetic disorder, mirror resonance syndrome, captivated the imagination of that particular class of people who are always looking for a neck on which to place a boot. The Classification Commission's testing and patient management system would control people with MRS and help everyone else stay safe.

Samuel may have been the first but not the last, and time is a slippery lie.

He would forget if he could, ship all his memories to blank-space until they were faded to porcelain-white invisibility and lost in the confused interface of background and foreground.

Every year on the anniversary of the incident, the documentary played in schools and public buildings throughout SeCa while the local Mesh became unusable for any other purpose than remembrance. By age twelve, Victor had become familiar with the cold terror that surged through his bones whenever he was forced to view it.

A woman with haunted eyes on the vidscreen was describing how she survived the massacre. Victor recognized her, of course: Mía Barrias, the woman who'd saved him from one of Samuel's booby traps. She described her encounter with the killer on the day of her honeymoon, how she'd watched him murder her fiancé with a quantum-triggered Dirac shockstick pulse to the head, and how she'd escaped floating downriver and got help from police in a nearby town. She led the initiative that resulted in the Classification Commission and the MRS edicts.

MIRROR RESONANCE SYNDROME:
A degenerative brain disorder associated with electrochemical imbalances within mirror-neuron networks. These structures enable individuals to understand and interpret others' intentions and emotions. Symptoms of mirror resonance syndrome (MRS) can be severe, vary widely, and usually include habitual aggression and violence. Many people with MRS experience extreme emotional transference. The syndrome is linked to a genetic variation in less than 1 percent of the population.

Emotional hyper-reactivity over an extended period, including these progressively worsening symptoms:

1. Abnormally strong physiological and emotional reactions to physical or mental stimuli, including synesthesia and hallucinations

2. Subjective experience of being controlled, lacking autonomy, following a predetermined course, or reliving events (e.g., episodes of déjà vu lasting hours or days)

3. Persistent, immersive fantasies to the exclusion of reality and maladaptive daydreaming

4. Depersonalization, loss of emotional vividness, motor-body disorientation, dissociative states, or extreme variability in self-image

5. Episodes of "brain blankness," i.e., dreamlike fugue states and sleepwalking

6. Addiction to resonant-class narcotics [new criterion]

—*Diagnostic Criteria for Mental Disorders,*
Semiautonomous California Health Board,
Third (Revised) Edition

Being classified was worse than being any of SeCa's other untouchables.

The Catholics—weakened, anemic, and banned from other nations in the American Union—were tolerated only on the outskirts of Oakland & Bayshore society, never in elite circles. The Asian Refugee Act had expelled desperate new arrivals, forcing them onto farms in way out in the Long Valley or the slums of Little Asia on the San Francisco peninsula.

Even lower, basest of all, were people with MRS. The enemies within: hidden, unpredictable, dangerous, and terrifying. Best to keep them surveilled, controlled, and isolated. No expense was spared except research into a cure, which was so onerously regulated as to be banned in practice. Only Jefferson Eastmore dared defy it, and he did so clandestinely.

If fate can change at any moment, how do we discern the branching points of history? What if the cumulative velocity of paths not taken lead toward dark corners and destruction?

Victor endured the vidfeed silently, every muscle tense with self-control. He wasn't a Broken Mirror. He hadn't ever taken the genetic test for MRS; they weren't mandatory until age thirteen. Yet, with his blood-soaked, strange, and prescient dreams, he had always felt completely out of step with the people of SeCa, who, from the days of the first Cathar settlers, had exalted in freedom from violence by infusing it in every story, every fable, every sermon. Their rituals made him sick to his stomach. But he didn't dare ask to be excused from watching the vidfeed. Earlier, two girls had passed him in the hallway talking loudly, saying they could spot a Broken Mirror without trying. Everyone could. It was how they looked at you—no, it was hard to say precisely what it was. But definitely, they were easy to spot.

There was another reason for Victor to stay quiet. He believed he had seen the massacre in his dreams weeks before it happened, a secret delusion he knew it was wise to keep to himself. The worst thing he could be was anything like Samuel Miller. As the man became the enemy for SeCa to rally against, so did he become the template that Victor would resist becoming.

After the vidfeed ended and the room cleared, Victor left the classroom and shuffled quietly down the hall and through the exit doors, only to find himself surrounded by a crowd led by Alik, a perpetually scowling and surly bully, and his sycophantic friends.

Alik called out, "Hey, freaky face. Why didn't you cry during the vidfeed?"

An electric charge gathered in his mind. They always picked on him. They made fun of him for the way he talked, or they teased him for staying silent. He couldn't win.

"Look at his hands. He's gonna rip your face off, Alik."

It was true. Victor's fingers were rigid and curled like talons.

"Maybe he's a Broken Mirror," Alik said.

"I am not!" Victor yelled.

Alik stepped closer. Sweat gathered under the boy's eyes. Heat radiated from his skin in shimmering waves. "Who's next on your list, Sicko Sam?"

Victor cringed and kept quiet. He couldn't be called anything worse.

Someone shoved Victor from behind, and he lurched forward right into Alik's perfectly timed punch. Pain exploded in his nose, and rage took hold. He launched himself at Alik. The two boys struggled and stumbled through the cheering kids. Victor twisted free, falling. Alik staggered past and slammed headfirst into the side of a dumpster.

Elena Morales helped Victor to his feet. She had meaty limbs, a broad face, and a loud voice when she wanted, which was most of the time. Her strength seemed to have increased since transitioning: Eli, the weak, was gone; Elena, the fighter, stood strong. Her silky brown hair had a luster that seemed to glow from within.

She said in his ear, "You held your own, alright. Let me mess him up for you."

Victor gripped his aching stomach and shook his head. He didn't want trouble. He wanted this to be over and forget about it.

Elena said, "You know you're bleeding, right?"

She gently touched the bridge of his nose, which flared in pain. He licked his swelling lip and tasted blood. Nearby, a girl screamed and pointed at the foot of a dumpster.

Victor turned and saw Alik lying limp, eyes closed.

An administrator appeared and asked, "What's going on?" He spotted Alik and yelled at the crowd to back away. Using a MeshBit, he summoned an ambulance.

"This is supposed to be a day for peace and healing. Who did this?" The administrator scanned the crowd of students.

Heads swiveled back and forth between Victor and Alik's body, and many pointed at Victor.

Soon, an ambulance arrived, and pink-uniformed paramedics burst out. Strong arms lifted Victor, and he found himself alongside Alik as the vehicle lurched forward.

When they arrived at Oak Knoll Hospital, Alik was whisked away, and Victor was led down a corridor, where a pair of Helios lightstrips burned and sizzled only for him. He was left alone in a small examination room.

He looked down at his hands. Dried blood hid under a thumbnail. He picked at the specks with another nail, but tiny red stains remained in the hard-to-reach crevice. He scratched again, deeper. New blood seeped from the worn-away skin. Pain flared as sparks and neon blobs. He watched them bloom with each painful dig:

Cody Sisco

beautiful, multicolored, ephemeral things, like confetti aflame. They were his secret magic tricks and worth the pain they cost.

He sat in the room, waiting for someone to come and tell him what a bad person he was for hurting Alik. He listened through the door. Maybe Granfa Jeff would come. It was his hospital, after all.

Several minutes later, footsteps tromped closer, and someone knocked. A scowling man came in wearing a starched canvas coat adorned with the snake-and-staff logo. His name tag identified him as Dr. Rularian. He held Victor's chin with a hand that reeked of bleach.

"Open your mouth," the doctor instructed and roughly swabbed the inside of Victor's cheek. Just as abruptly as he'd entered, he left the room, shutting the door behind him.

Victor was alone again.

He imagined the worst.

Alik was comatose, and legal charges would be brought. Victor would be locked up and forgotten, while Alik would get many visitors during his recuperation. Well-wishers would stream into the hospital with their flowers, cards, and packages. No one would visit Victor in a dark cell for the criminally unredeemable. The one time he won a fight would be worse than all the times he'd lost.

Dr. Rularian returned. "Come with me," he said.

Victor followed him to a room packed with electronics on wheeled stands and wires limply strung about. He'd always been comfortable at the hospital, but this was different. This time, he wasn't trailing after Granfa Jeff, marveling at the wonders of health policy and technology: he was a problem. Two technicians stood by wearing translucent gel surgical masks and canvas hats. The burlier of the two unbuttoned Victor's shirt, pushed him into a reclining synthleather seat, and stuck small sensors on his forehead, neck, chest, inner elbows, and wrists. The other technician had a flat face as if he had no nose beneath his mask, and his skin looked perfectly smooth, like plastic.

"I'm going to put this over your head," the flat-faced one said, holding a helmet made of what looked like heavy obsidian.

Victor started to tear off the sensors. The burly technician with unblinking, black, lizard-like eyes placed a firm hand on his chest. The flat-faced technician lowered the helmet. It was lighter than he'd expected and very dark. A strange buzz coursed through his skin.

From the darkness, an image of a snarling cheetah sprang to life. His heart pumped faster and louder in the silence. The cheetah vanished, replaced by a close-up shot of a beautiful woman's face. Streams of tears ran down her cheeks. The rawness of her emotion pulled at Victor. More images popped into view and disappeared: two men nuzzling each other, other couples and throuples across the gender spectrum, all staring at each other close-up and smiling. He began to smile, too. Then he remembered he was sitting half-naked in a cold hospital room, covered in sensors.

He tried to lift the heavy helmet off. He knew what the tests were about.

"I said hold still!" The doctor commanded through a sonofeed in the helmet.

The helmet's visor turned transparent.

"We got a clear reading," Lizard-Eyes said.

"Are you done?" Victor asked.

Dr. Rularian said, "When the genetic test comes back from Gene-Us, we'll have enough to verify your diagnosis."

"What diagnosis?" Victor asked, stalling for time. He'd had many nightmares of being classified, although they'd all felt more real than this.

"Mirror resonance syndrome."

Victor tried to leap from the chair. Flat-Face pinned him with one gloved hand. Victor shouted, "I'm not a Broken Mirror!"

"Don't be vulgar," Dr. Rularian said.

"Are you testing Alik? He started the fight."

"We're not concerned with determining fault. We're only concerned with the public good. MRS is a dangerous condition that must be properly managed."

The door swung open, nearly swiping Lizard-Eyes' backside as Granfa Jeff entered the room. Tall and wiry, he always looked like a purposeful instrument cutting through ignorant thickets. He flicked his gaze toward Victor, the sensors, and each technician. Thunderous anger gathered on his face like a storm about to break.

"I'd like a word with you, Doctor. Outside, please." The doctor left the room. Granfa Jeff glanced sideways at Victor. "Tidy yourself up."

Flat-Face objected, "Sir, we're in the middle—"

Granfa Jeff turned to him and glowered. "This is my hospital. You should have alerted me as soon as my granson arrived."

Victor dressed and left the room. His parents sat on a couch in an alcove, and he rushed over to them. Ma kept her hands clasped before her. "We were worried."

His parents were always worried, always startled like deer. In some ways, they had never left Carmichael and still lived inside the attack. They expected threats to jump out at every corner, dangers to lurk beneath a porch step, and vehicles to run them down. In innocuous messages on the Mesh, they saw hackers and malicious intent. They feared menace from their combustible son too, who—after they'd awoken from the gas attack and returned home—couldn't stop talking. Endless, nonsensical words spilled from his lips, saying he knew Samuel was bad and had planned Carmichael for months, that crossing over wasn't the end, tortured echoes of the villain's as-yet-unvoiced claims spilling from the mouth of a child, hours of traumatized verbal flotsam pouring out, talking, talking, talking nonsense, until finally medics decided on a sedative and Victor slept. Over the years, it went mostly unmentioned by the family, him included, and the meaning and ramifications of a four-year-old's horrific recitations were erased. Except not entirely because both his ma and fa often looked at him like he might again, at any moment, erupt. Sometimes, however, eruptions were necessary.

Victor's fa placed a hand roughly on his son's shoulder. "What happened? Another fight?"

Victor glanced back at his granfa, who was pacing in front of Dr. Rularian, dressing him down, and drawing the attention of nearby nurses with his raised voice.

Victor said, "Alik started it."

Finished with the doctor, Granfa Jeff walked slowly toward them. "I'm sorry. If I'd gotten here earlier, I might have held them off. But I think we all understand this was inevitable."

Victor looked at his parents. "Inevitable?"

"We suspected," his ma said. Her clasped hands were bloodless and white with strain. "We'll take care of you. Everything will be fine," she told Victor but without certainty or reassurance in her voice.

Victor's throat closed up. "But there's no cure," he whispered.

His granfa grimaced. "If I can cure cancer, I can cure anything. You can count on it."

The next day, when he told Elena the news, she only nodded.

At first, he was upset that she was pretending nothing had changed—she walked with him to the cafeteria, and they ate rice noodles with ginger gravy at a table by themselves as usual—until he realized that, from her perspective, nothing had. He was the same, their friendship was unbreakable, and they could always count on each other.

29

Victor leaned back. He didn't want to hear more of Ozie's theories for now. He was tired and worried about where Elena had gotten to. He said, "I'm risking a lot. For all I know, you're trying to hurt my family's company for no good reason."

"Do you have a choice? Are you going to go back to SeCa, back to your family, back to a rancho?" Ozie poked the table. "This is bigger than BioScan, bigger than your family, bigger than Jefferson's post-mortem plans. The conflict between SeCa and the OWS is about to blow open."

Victor felt a sinking in his gut, as much due to Ozie's diagnosis of his alternatives as to some new bombshell that was about to land and cloud the picture even further. "What conflict?"

"The fate of people with mirror resonance syndrome. Our freedom. Our future."

Victor sighed. "You and me, people like us, maybe we *are* a threat. It doesn't take much to get us talking conspiracies and making plans we shouldn't be making."

"You're wrong." Ozie's face bunched up like he was holding back tears. "We are the victims of medical malpractice. All those people taking Personil. The facilities. The ranches. It's a twisted system."

"To some extent, you're right. I know. I know I am not my diagnosis, too. I'm broken, but I'm still a person. I wish I were normal—sometimes I really do. But whether I've got a medical condition or I'm the victim of social stigma, it's the same thing. I have to live the life I was born to. You do, too. We're stuck with what we've got."

Ozie's eyes were wide, glistening, shining in the neon glare flickering around them. He grabbed Victor's hand across the table with both of his. "No. You're wrong. You're a beautiful, unique, unbroken person, *and* there is an alternative for us. It's what Pearl and I were working on together."

"What alternative?" Victor asked, pulling his hand loose.

"First, you need to shift your mindset. People like us, we are not broken. We are gifted."

"I wish I believed that."

"We are," Ozie said. "We are experts on our brains and, therefore, everyone else's." He pointed to people at the other tables, not seeming to care that he was attracting their attention. He pointed to his temple. "We're cognitive seers. We just need the right environment and the right tools. Pearl and I are making an alternative possible. I move her herbs to clients in the OWS, and she distributes my brainhacking equipment in SeCa. But we can't let the Classification Commission off the hook. We have to end it." Ozie massaged the back of his neck with both hands, his fingers digging under the collar of his shirt. "You did get the sequences from BioScan, right?" he asked. "We're not going through all this for nothing."

"Yeah, I have them." Victor removed the Boze-Drive from his bag and held it above the table.

Ozie reached out to take it.

Victor pulled the device back. "If you want this, you have to do something for me first."

"I saved your—"

"Look, I listened to your theories. Now listen to mine. Granfa Jeff gave me a data egg." Victor removed the black data egg and set it on the table. When it started to roll away, he put it on his dinner plate next to the remaining sandwich crusts.

Ozie took the egg into his hands. "It hasn't hatched yet?"

"Hatched?" Victor gritted his teeth. It was a device, nonorganic. They shouldn't talk about it like it was alive. What mattered was getting it open. "No. It hasn't *opened*. I have no idea what's inside. It could be this plan you're talking about. It could explain everything. I want you to open it."

Ozie looked at the data egg and frowned at Victor, shaking his head.

"Impossible," he said.

Victor pleaded, "Whatever Granfa Jeff wanted me to know is in there. If you open it, I'll give you the BioScan data."

Ozie handed back the egg. "I can't help you."

"Why?"

Ozie held up a fist. "Piezoelectrically powered." One finger rose. "The battery *is* the data storage matrix"—another finger—"quantum encrypted"—and another—"and locked by *your* biosignatures," Ozie said, holding up four fingers. "This is the best black box that can be made. I can't open it. It's too secure."

Victor took the egg in his hand. Did it feel cold? "You seem sure about that."

"You can be dense sometimes, Victor. *I* gave this to Jefferson. Modded it in a dozen ways that he asked for."

Victor flinched. Was Ozie pulling his leg? No, he looked serious with his pouty mouth and hang-dog eyes. He and Granfa Jeff had colluded to lock away the old man's secrets, and Ozie was only now revealing this. Why?

Victor had a sudden flash of fear. "Did you cover it with polonium as well?"

Ozie reared back. "What? No! Victor, I'm a good guy. Jefferson learned about what I do through Pearl, and he came to me after a trip to Las Vegas with a long list of things that he wanted tech-wise."

Victor chided himself for suspecting Ozie. He wasn't a murderer. But how far could he be trusted?

"The egg isn't just a storage device," Ozie continued. "Put it near your head."

Victor laughed, but Ozie was clearly not joking. Feeling foolish, he held the egg to his forehead.

"How do you feel?" Ozie asked.

"Trapped by fate."

"Humph."

After several seconds, Victor asked, "What should I be feeling?"

Ozie's eyes glistened as he spoke. "The data egg holds a copy of your brainwave schema, adaptive biofeedback software, and a bunch of Dirac diamond-foam transceivers. It's a brain hack, like mine, and it's been working on you for months."

Victor dropped the data egg. Ozie stopped it from rolling off the edge of the table.

He held out his hand in a calming gesture. "Just listen. It does three things. For one, it minimizes resonant episodes—you should find it harder to go blank now than before. If you're off Personil, the effect cancels out, though. Two, the egg fucks with scanners, specifically those used during the reclassification appointment. Three, it's a data repository. Jefferson had me walk him through how to record messages and load it up with files and set a trigger for it to open."

Ozie held up the data egg, and Victor took it back, asking, "What kind of trigger?"

"He wouldn't say. He seemed paranoid at the time, but then... Look, this model could respond to brain waves, audio cues, pressure patterns. DNA. Bodily fluids." Ozie put a finger in his mouth and pulled it out. His saliva glistened under the flickering multicolored lightstrips, and Victor felt his groin pulse, remembering some of the things they'd done to one another. "But there's no way of knowing what will trigger it aside from asking a dead man. Keep it with you. Sleep with it under your pillow. Hell, sing to it; that might work too."

"Could you try to hack it anyway?" Victor asked.

Ozie shrugged. "Sure. I like a challenge, though I reckon I'll be wasting my time. I'll try if you do something for me."

"You get the Boze-Drive, like I said."

"I want more," Ozie said in a voice that sounded deliberately sultry, resonant.

Victor crammed the data egg back into his pocket. Ozie had once tricked Victor into creating a science project for him. It won second place, and Ozie took all the credit. He knew how to push Victor's buttons to get what he wanted. But Victor had grown in the past few years, and he knew when someone was taking advantage of him. "I'm done running errands for you. Tosh was right."

Ozie glanced sideways. "Tosh doesn't know anything but blood and guts. Stay away from him."

Victor felt heat building in his face and had the urge to split his friend's lip with his fist. "He helped get me this far. He wants to find out what happened to my granfa almost as much as I do. And he'll beat you senseless if you screw us over."

"You've been running your mouth like a printing press. I saved your ass," Ozie hissed. "If you hadn't left SeCa like I told you to, you'd be in a facility by now. Or worse. Bargaining with Tosh is like lubing your own asshole—a great way to get fucked."

As usual, Victor realized, Ozie was getting a rise out of him, the manipulative bastard.

"You didn't do me any favors. My family could have saved me. I could have hired a bodyguard instead of exiling myself to rendezvous with a conspiracy-obsessed data troller."

Ozie pounded a fist on the table. "You were losing it!"

A few of the other patrons looked over. Victor's heart thumped in his chest, ready to erupt. "We're amping each other up," he said, feeling his hold on consciousness slipping toward blankspace. Same as always; whenever he and Ozie got to talking, they started yelling and pulling each other's triggers.

"I know that," Ozie snapped. "Do what you have to do. Use the egg." He tapped on the table, and a robot came over and delivered a brainhacking cap. It looked like a ceramic bowl with raised ridges and nodules dotting the surface. He grabbed the cap, looking like a stimhead desperate for a fix.

Victor dug in his bag, searching for a fumewort tincture. *Hello, Mr. Resonant Episode. I can't say I'm glad to see you again so soon. Why don't you piss off?* Victor found a vial, uncorked its forest-green cap, and swallowed. The liquid burned going down. He closed his eyes, focusing on the sensation. Warmth spread from his throat. An acid-green haze appeared behind his closed eyelids.

Victor lowered his head and brought the data egg to his ear. After a few moments, he felt calmer, his mind clearing. Whether it was the egg, the fumewort, both, or neither, he had no idea. When he opened his eyes, he saw Ozie wearing a ceramic cap on his head and moving his lips into silent words.

Victor laughed. "You look—"

"Don't," Ozie warned with his eyes still closed.

Ozie looked as if he were listening to music only he could hear. They stayed quiet for a few minutes. Finally, Ozie seemed to return to the present. Victor waited till Ozie removed the helmet before asking a question that had been worming its way through his brain: "Have you heard of a drug that mimics our condition? Aura? It's a kind of stim."

Ozie rubbed his eyes. "Maybe. Dark grid rumors. Where did *you* hear about them?"

"Elena. She said it felt like her senses were sharpened. Synesthesia. Euphoria, too, for a while."

Ozie smiled. "You have an uncanny knack for arriving at a destination without consulting a map."

"What are you talking about?" Victor replied.

"You're running way ahead of schedule. Jefferson's plan was due to unfold over *years*."

Victor shifted in his seat. "I hate not knowing what's going on. It makes me question everything."

"Your classification appointment shouldn't have been for a couple more months, right? You went too quickly."

"I got called up. The doctor used a new type of scanning chair. It made my symptoms worse, briefly. Almost like they were trying to destabilize me."

"See? You call me paranoid. But it's simply adaptive behavior in the face of overwhelming hostility. What you experienced was probably interference from the data egg. Brains like ours aren't paragons of stability anyway." The brainhacking cap sat on the table, its glossy white ceramic nobs reflecting the multicolored lights of the café. "You've never been in a Class One facility, right?"

The robot returned and placed on the table a small chocolate cake with a mirror finish, smooth and silky. He could almost see their reflections in the icing.

"I haven't, no," Victor said. "They're in the vidfeeds though."

"Don't trust those. I haven't been to one, either. How about a rancho?"

"Only the one my granfa set up in Carmichael, the good one, not the rest."

"Let me get you up to speed. Jefferson had the subversive idea that people with MRS could be rehabilitated. Truth is, we don't really know much about MRS. Did you know that the number of times someone has been upgraded from a Class One to a Class Two is exactly zero?"

"Of course. It's a degenerative disease."

Ozie perched on the edge of the booth seat. "Is it? Does it happen to everyone? How bad does it get? How quickly?"

"I don't know about any of that," Victor admitted.

"Exactly my point," Ozie said. "After Carmichael, everything happened so fast. Suddenly, there's a new neurological condition and a genetic test, but no one can access the data. Something's happening with the Commission and the SeCa Health Board, and your family's company is involved."

"We're going in circles, Ozie."

"Things were in stasis for a long time, but Jefferson kept pushing at the margins. He upset the status quo. I think he discovered something or did something. We need to find out what. That's why I asked you to steal from BioScan and to come here. I can't say more now. I'll dig through the Boze-Drive, the Health Board's files, their research on Samuel Miller, whatever they've got. And I want to unencrypt the MRS gene sequence in the Boze-Drive. You write the program, and I'll get you the processing power. We'll figure out the rest together."

"What use will the MRS gene sequence be?"

"Victor, this is what Jefferson wanted. We'll figure out who killed him, I swear. But that's not enough. He's gone, and we're still here. We have to live in this world, as bad as it gets, as much as we wish it were different, and we have a responsibility to honor his wishes."

Suspicion, curiosity, hope, and the thrill of companionship swirled in Victor's gut. He leaned forward. "If I help you, promise me you'll tell me everything. No secrets. No more misdirection."

Ozie nodded.

"Okay," Victor said. That was as good as he would get—a promise with a minuscule chance of being honored. Ozie would try to live up to it until some glittering prize forced a different choice. And Victor would go along with it, short on options, with no way of returning to his life before because time with Ozie was charged and dazzling, and their friendship, though challenging, was irreplaceable.

Ozie breathed deeply and smiled at Victor. "Excellent. We can get started tomorrow. Be patient. You realize, once we start down this path, we're painting targets on our backs."

Victor snorted. "Too late for that."

"Stick with me, Vic, and I guarantee we'll find the answer." Ozie pointed to the Boze-Drive. "Keep that safe. I'll want it tomorrow." He patted the mason jar. "I'll send this to a lab. And don't tell your friend about any of this. She's hiding something from you. I can tell." Ozie stood and walked into the bustle of Springboard Café.

If Elena was hiding something, Victor was pretty sure he knew what it was. He'd seen it in the way she moved. She hadn't given up stims after all. He crammed the Boze-Drive in his bag and stood to find her.

30

Elena didn't want any part of the little boys' club. She took her half-full beer stein into an airlock, was waved through by an animatronic coat stand, and emerged into a dim area with the sound of wind in the trees and rain pattering down. Almost lifelike. A cozy, soft foam chair in the corner held her gently as she cradled the beer against her chest. Each sip felt heavier and more bitter, but she set it down empty.

Her feelings were both familiar and foreign. She'd been excluded by Ozie and Victor's tight and tiny circle of mutual fuckery plenty of times. It had always stung like a nail scratching a festering sore. But she was a different person now. Stronger. The little things couldn't set her back. In a different place and at a different time, she'd have felt hurt. Now? Numbness, frustration, and anxiety battled it out in her brain. *Fuck those guys.*

She got up, went back through the airlock, and took an out-of-the-way route to avoid seeing them hunched over the table scattered with crumbs and smears of condensation, and to avoid being seen. In a place like Springboard Café—so many places like it, priding themselves on being different, edgy, hip—there would always be someone ready to help someone score. The bathroom was down the hall, a large, nauseatingly bright room that sectioned off into several smaller rooms and smaller cubicles, arranged like a nautilus, spiraling into ever greater privacy.

A muffled word and quick exchange got her what she needed from an odd pair of freaks. She smoked, retraced her steps in the seconds before the fireworks really got going, grabbed a beer, plopped down, took a long, desperate gulping swallow, and let the medicine take her away.

31

After Ozie left, Victor stood up. Immediately, the robot wearing a top hat returned and extended a towel for Victor to wipe his hands.

"Would you like your cake to go, sir?"

"Yes," Victor said. SeCa was missing out on these clever things.

"You shall find it at the host stand as you leave. Please authorize payment."

The amount appeared on a vidscreen on one of the robot's forearms. Victor realized he didn't have his MeshBit with him and said so.

"You have been authorized to use the house account. VIP status has been assigned to you as well."

Victor tapped the screen to confirm. At least Ozie wasn't being stingy.

"It has been a pleasure to serve you. Have a pleasant evening," it said, then rolled away.

Victor wondered what other privileges a VIP at the Springboard Café was entitled to. Whatever the perks were, they couldn't make up for living within such flimsy artificiality. A strong gust of wind could blow it away, like a tumbleweed. Or, more likely, an electrical fault would fry the patrons inside. But at least they had robots here and no Classification Commission—not yet, anyway.

He searched for Elena in the lounge, hunting through dim candle-lit recesses, ignoring curious eyes staring back at him. Velvet cushions lined a bench along the wall, and alcoves held poster beds draped in gauze where couples and throuples reclined. Cocktails ornamented the tables, held in every shape of glass imaginable: tumblers, flutes, jars, and cubes. Fashionable, social, and at ease—it was a scene he would never feel at home in.

Elena wasn't there. He decided to check the bathrooms. On his way down a narrow hallway, he passed retro music posters for space rock bands from the fifties: the Planetoids, Twisted Funburst, and the Boob-Head Dickies.

Beyond shredded tire-tread curtains, the restroom reeked of so much bleach that Victor's stomach climbed his ribs. A single stall flashed a red occupied symbol; the others were green. Next to a hole in the wall where the urinal should have been, a handwritten sign read, "Water conservation at work."

He noticed another smell, too, an unfamiliar bitter tang. He waited, trying to breathe as little as possible. Shuffling and whispers came from the locked stall.

"Elena?" he asked. The whispering stopped, but the shuffling continued, and he heard trilling feminine laughter. Victor banged on the door. "Elena, are you in there?"

The lock on the stall door clicked, and the light turned green. The door swung open, and the tallest person Victor had ever seen emerged.

Two bloodshot eyes floated inside thickly maroon-lined eyes, and a triangular beard pointed toward pale half-moon breasts hoisted by a sequined and feathered corset. Glittering midnight-blue platform shoes clicked on the concrete floor as she approached Victor.

A deep molasses voice emerged from her silver-lipped mouth. "You really ought not to interrupt. Sebastian, come."

A thin, awkward boy stepped out of the stall. He wore only a pair of lime-green shorts made of furry fabric. His protruding ribs tented the skin of his hairless chest. Looking at his face, Victor saw he had been wrong: not a boy. Sebastian could have been in his forties or fifties, but his lack of fat and musculature made him look very young. His eyes, crisscrossed with bloody capillaries, sat deep within bruised eyelids, signs of an acute stimsmoke addiction.

"Tell me what you see, Sebastian," the woman said.

Sebastian slinked a few steps forward and fixed a shattered stare on Victor. In a voice like a rake being dragged over asphalt, Sebastian said, "Can't. Too much noise in the signal."

Victor backed away from the freaky couple, but the tall one shifted to block his way and leaned closer. "We were having a lovely encounter," she said, taking the boy's hand and cupping it to her breast. Sebastian nuzzled her side. "I was teaching him the most wonderful things. You could learn too. How to avoid a certain type of trouble, for instance. We saw who you were with. Both of them."

Her teeth reflected the bright neon lightstrip encircling the bathroom's ceiling. She easily outweighed Victor three to one, not counting the waif. He wasn't looking for a fight, but he didn't want to be pushed around.

Victor said, "You should probably get back to whatever you were doing and stay out of my business."

The tall woman ran her fingernails through a frizzy fringe of hair. "You don't instruct Theodora Tamarindo."

"Biiirddeeeee!" Sebastian's long-wailed vowels echoed in the tiled bathroom.

"Victor?" Elena's voice called from outside. "Are you in there?"

Theodora chuckled.

Elena stepped into the room.

"Your name is Victor?" Sebastian asked. He gripped Victor's shoulders. "That's not a bird name."

"I'm not a bird," Victor said, shaking off the other's hands, "obviously."

"Either you both get pleasant real fast, or you get out faster," Theodora threatened.

Victor didn't understand. "Fine, we'll be friendly," he said.

Theodora smiled and straightened to an unnatural height.

"That's not what *friendly* means," Elena said. "Friendly means sharing—Never mind. Let's go. Now!" She pushed him toward the rubber curtain.

"Guard your sweet cheeks," Theodora said. She winked and put her arm around Sebastian. "There's plenty worse out there than us, including a certain untrustworthy brainhacker, and with that face, you're just begging to be violated."

Victor and Elena brushed past the heavy, filthy curtains into the hallway and hurried outside together.

He looked up. Thousands of stars filled the sky, and pulses of drums echoed across the dusky lot. A fetid odor floated through the air, probably from the café's water recycling plant. Elena took his hand, and they walked to the lodge next door, remembering halfway that they needed their bags. They crunched through the gravel parking lot and retrieved their bags from the lockers. When they entered the lodge room, his vision was flickering from exhaustion.

The room contained twin beds, a chair and desk, and a vidscreen and MeshLine—a nice perk of staying in a brainhacker lodge. A shower stall, toilet, and sink were crammed in an adjoining bathroom. Elena sent him to shower with such conviction that he didn't protest.

When Victor was done, he cataloged his possessions while Elena showered. The data egg, the herb book, his dreambook, one sachet of fumewort and one of bitter grass, a half-liter of alcohol, two liters of distilled water, twenty empty vials and corks, three shirts, one jacket, three pairs of pants, ten pairs each of socks and underwear, and one pair of shoes.

Elena emerged from the bathroom with a puff of steam that carried the scent of musk and berries. She wore a white towel, the top of which clung to her chest and the bottom barely covering her rump. Victor watched her dry her hair with a second towel. Her clean, moist skin glistened. He jumped up and shoved his belongings back into his bag.

Elena asked, "What did you find out from Ozie? Did he ask you for money?"

Victor rubbed his eyes. He felt like he'd had more questions than answers. "It's a long story. We can talk in the morning."

She dried her arms and chewed her lip. Then she disappeared into the bathroom.

Victor stripped off the bedspread and crawled under the sheet and blanket. A few minutes later, she returned, cut the lights, and lay on the other bed.

After an hour of tossing and turning, trying every exercise he could to calm his mind and empty it of thoughts, he fell asleep. He dreamed of eggs cracking open and releasing dragons who razed the OWS's far-flung cities with fiery breath.

It was after eight a.m. when Victor woke up. The sheets were drenched with stale sweat. He dressed and spent most of the morning making tinctures while Elena slept. He was glad for the break from her nervous twitching. He smiled to himself—he was keeping his anxiety at bay more skillfully than she was.

Around noon, with a rumbling stomach, he crunched across the gravel lot to Springboard Café. Elena claimed to have a headache, so he left her in the room. He found a booth and ordered food. A half-hour later, Elena joined him.

Ozie found them and eased himself into their booth. He jerked his head toward Elena. "What have you told her?"

"Nothing," Victor said.

Elena brushed her hair back. "It's true. I barely got a word out of him."

"Good," Ozie said. "We can't be too careful. Take this." He slid a silver device toward Victor. It was the size of two hands side by side. He slid another device, a standard MeshBit by the looks of it, over to Elena.

"What is this?" Victor asked.

"A MobileMesh unit, new model, with some of my own modifications to make it untraceable. I call it the Handy 1000. Most of these are limited to the common command interface, but I've done a little creative reorganization. This one also connects to the dark grid. I've got one too. We'll use them to communicate. Don't lose it."

Victor picked up the Handy 1000. He yelped when it folded itself into a spiraling cylindrical tube.

Ozie laughed. "You didn't break it. That's how I usually carry it around in my pocket. Be careful, though. People will think you're walking around with some extra girth down below."

Elena rolled her eyes. Victor didn't think Ozie's comment bothered her—she'd never been particularly opinionated about biological parts aligning with gender roles. But unartful crassness could set her off. She said, "We should be making plans. What are you going to do with the tongue, for instance? We shouldn't just sit here, playing with gadgets."

They both ignored her. Ozie said, "You can put it around your wrist, too."

Victor found a square icon that caused the Handy 1000 to unroll itself into a sheet. He pressed it again, and the flexible glass curled itself up.

"Neat," he said.

He unfolded it again and studied the screen. He saw several unfamiliar icons beside the standard set and pressed one showing nine squares arranged in a grid. A map appeared showing the area where SeCa met the OWS. A green dot pulsed where the Springboard Café was. Blue marks, like upside-down Vs, were also arranged in a hexagonal pattern over the map. He pressed his finger against one of the icons, and more information swam up:

MT_OWS_904567.10
39.459033, -119.780910
64kbps, 34% adl
firmware update: Semaphore-38

Victor stared at the statistics, puzzling them out, fascinated by his first glimpse into the Mesh's innards. The V's must be MeshTowers, and the first line must be the identifier for the one he'd selected. The second line showed its geographic coordinates. The last two might be bandwidth and operating system. He assumed "adl" stood for "average daily load."

None of this information was usually available to users. Ozie had somehow hacked the Mesh.

There was another icon labeled "Log." Victor pressed it, and a long page scrolled by. He found a time-stamped command for a MeshID handshake, a code passed between devices that set up a secure communications link. Each handshake passed through dozens of MeshTowers, some more than one hundred kilometers away, if he was calculating longitude and latitude correctly. Dozens of handshakes filled the log. The device created a new false MeshID every few seconds and randomly rerouted requests and data through nearby MeshTowers to mask its location and activity—a genius technique.

Although it contained the same core functions as any Mesh interfacing device—messaging, data retrieval, and scheduling—the extra features rendered it much more powerful and secure.

Victor felt an elbow in his side and looked up. Elena was staring at him. "Earth to Victor," she said. "Your friend here has been rocking in his chair like a nutcase—"

"I object to that term." Ozie glared at her, then turned his attention to Victor. "If you can make the other thing do what we discussed, I think I've solved the processing problem."

"Processing problem?" Victor asked, struggling to keep up. Then he remembered what Ozie had said about writing a program to decipher the encryption to reveal the MRS gene sequence.

"In the Mesh, processing happens in linked clusters of devices. The clusters are called nodes. Las Vegas is a node. Bayshore is a node. Thousands of nodes are all over Europe, connected by low-orbiters and sometimes by physical cables. In the American Union, the links are mostly low-bandwidth MeshTowers, so I can't send much traffic through them. But if I move the satellites ..."

A sudden fear gripped Victor. He pictured a thousand satellites crashing down and incinerating him at ground zero. "You've got to be kidding."

Ozie shrugged. "They're mobile and autonomous. It just takes a little reprogramming. They usually cluster over important population centers. With a simple bit of coding, they'll adjust their orbits, increasing coverage here so that we can link processing capacities across the AU's western nations. We'll churn through the data, and everything will return to normal."

"What are you doing with the data exactly?" Elena asked.

Ozie smirked and waggled a finger for Victor to stay silent.

Victor smiled apologetically at Elena and shrugged. "Ozie, we need to be realistic. The amount of processor time is gargantuan. It would take years on the fastest computer."

Ozie smiled. "How much processor time?"

Victor calculated hastily and told Ozie.

"That's enough to plot a round trip to Mars for an entire botfleet," Ozie said, his eye wide.

"What are you planning?" Elena's eyes searched Victor's face. Before he could answer, Ozie shushed him.

"Let me think." A slow grin spread across Ozie's face. His eyeglasses flashed, reflecting the bluish image from a vidscreen on the wall. "We could chain the low orbiters together and get global coverage."

Two people in ultra-pliable synthleather tracksuits passed slowly toward the back of the room. Victor flinched. He looked again. They weren't his pursuers.

"We need to talk about the people following me," Victor said.

Ozie nodded. "We'll get to that. Hear me out first. Chaining the nodes is possible but risky. This kind of stunt is uncomfortably public. The Mesh reports would cover it. Most governments would notice. Every cybersecurity firm in the world would know. Actually, I'm not sure I can do it, and I'm sure I can't do it alone. I'd need your help."

Here it comes, Victor thought. *I'll bet he wants money.* He leaned back and watched blobs of light in the ceiling chase each other. Dozens of blue, green, and red trails flared in their wake. One blob caught the other in a spectacular crash that lit the entire room in a flame-yellow glow. Ozie never had any qualms about asking Victor to pay for his tech schemes.

Ozie cleared his throat and pulled at his shirt collar. "It's going to take a lot of resources. I need a hundred thousand AU dollars."

Elena smirked. "Told you." She laughed bitterly. "He wants your money. That's the only reason he dragged you here. All this talk about your granfa and conspiracies is a lie."

Victor looked carefully at Elena. The tension under her eyes, the curl of her lip, the way her nostrils flared. She was starting to buckle under the strain of keeping whatever secret she continued to cover up. She shouldn't be too harsh a critic of Ozie—they were both manipulating him. But though Ozie was a conspiracy nut, he wasn't excessively greedy, and they had made a good team for a while. Maybe they could again.

Victor placed his hand gently on Elena's shoulder. "You said you wanted to help me. I trust Ozie. I admit we haven't told you everything that's going on. What we're planning could help overturn the Classification System or at least stop its expansion." Victor turned back to Ozie. "What exactly would the money be for?"

"Equipment. Code. A few favors. It's not cheap to move a fleet of satellites."

Victor began calculating how much he would earn annually on the investments his granfa had left him and his shares in BioScan. Was Ozie's help worth three years of that income? He'd pay anything, do anything, to learn what had really happened to Granfa Jeff. He paid no mind to what would come after.

"Agreed," Victor said.

Elena rolled her eyes and said, "This has nothing to do with finding out who killed him. You know that, right?"

Victor said, "It's all part of the same package: decoding the gene, figuring out what MRS is and what we are, why Granfa Jeff was killed, how people with MRS should be treated, opening the data egg—they're all related, I get that now." He looked at Ozie and said, with doubt creeping into his voice, "At least we think they're all related."

Ozie said, "About decoding the gene: your program takes care of the processing, but we're still going to need the Human Genome Initiative's libraries of sequences to compare with the BioScan data."

"The HGI?" Elena's eyes grew wide. "That would cost millions. No! Tell me you're not planning to steal from the Institute!"

Victor swept the room with his gaze. "I don't see them lying around here. We need the libraries to filter the MRS genomes to find the right sequence."

"This is a bad idea," Elena said.

"We do what we need to do," Victor said.

Ozie smiled. The café's lights reflected off his ivory teeth. "Victor, you've got the right attitude. All it'll take is a data leech on one of HGI's machines." Ozie's grin widened. "Think about it. What an opportunity! You're going to steal from the Diamond King."

32

Elena woke to the sound of a car door slamming. The room smelled sweet and floral—probably an automated morning wake-up air-spritz. These brainhacker types seemed to have no limits when it came to drugs ... Then she remembered. Stimsmoke, last night. It was only a puff, but it meant she'd fucked up again.

Victor entered with his bag and a wad of trash balled in his hand.

She sat up and blinked. "Spring cleaning?" she asked.

"Getting the car worked on. Now that we're out of SeCa, they can retrofit it for automation."

"How exciting," Elena deadpanned. She rubbed her eyes. Her throat felt scratchy. More stimsmoke would numb it if she had any, but she knew she must not succumb to the temptation again. "I still don't understand why you let that dweeb manipulate you."

Victor looked up from the vial he was filling with herb dust, alcohol, and water. "I don't have much choice. He wants me to find the mirror resonance sequence. I want the data egg opened. We both want Jefferson's murderer unmasked. We have a deal."

"How can you trust him? I remember when he left. You were crushed." *Like when I left, too.* She lay back on the pillows.

Victor capped the vial and put it in his bag. "He's not trying to hide his manipulations. He always dangles a carrot a little bit further. I know what he's doing. But I know he can help me discover what happened to Granfa Jeff. And if he can help other people like me, then I'm going to help him."

"He's going to bleed you dry." Elena squinted. The pain behind her eyes would fade, eventually. "I know you want to get your hands on the MRS gene sequence, but I don't understand why."

"It's not random curiosity if that's what you're suggesting." Victor dropped his bag on the carpeted floor with a heavy thud. "The tests are run in a black box. We run the test and get a result, but we never *see* the sequence. The reference file, the actual sequence of base pairs, is encrypted." Victor sighed. "From what I understand, even the commissioners don't have access to it. It was encrypted years ago. An act of greed, national security, and paranoia all in one. When I think of how much information is locked away in private databases ..." He shook his head. "So I reckon Ozie's right; it's a disgrace."

Elena snorted. "How else would it be? Free information for everybody? His ideas are screwing with your head."

"I'm not completely clueless. I won't give Ozie what he wants without getting something in return." He picked up his bag. "I'll be at the café after I take the car in."

"I'll come find you later," she said.

After she dressed, Elena stepped outside, trying not to think about stimsmoke. She still hadn't told Victor about Lucky and Bandit. Guilt was a knife jabbing her with each breath, especially after he'd been so understanding about the stims. Since she found herself friendless and desperate in the Republic of Texas, her life had become a sad series of mistakes. No matter how painful, keeping secrets always seemed easier than telling the truth. Why couldn't she ever do the right thing at the right time?

The new MeshBit she'd traded for some of her cash the night before chimed as she crossed the gravel parking lot, which was already cooking in the day's heat. She answered and heard Bandit's voice.

"Runaway girl," he said. "You should have been in touch yesterday."

Elena grimaced. His voice sounded like fingernails dragged over concrete. She said, "I've been busy. You got my message, obviously. And now you have my new number."

"Where are you?"

Elena walked back to stand in the shade of the building. "We crossed the border."

"I figured."

"Was that your van on the side of the road?"

Bandit grunted. "Maybe."

Elena scanned her surroundings: a vast dirt plain with mountains to the west and desert to the east. "How did you know we were in the mountains?"

"Just stay in one place long enough for us to catch up. The border is closed today. Something to do with a security breach."

Elena looked at the road leading to the café. So, Ozie's handiwork wasn't undetectable. That didn't bode well for Victor. "Who ran you off the road?"

"Didn't get a good look. Thought it might have been you."

"I'm not that great a driver," she said. *That's a lie I can stomach. He doesn't need to know about all my racing wins.*

Things were getting complicated. If Lucky and Bandit were working for the Eastmores, as they said, who else would run them off the road? And what did that mean for her and Victor?

"What will happen to Victor when you catch up with us?" Elena asked.

"We'll keep him safe. Take him back to SeCa."

"He can't go back if he's being reclassified. It's a dealbreaker for me."

Bandit's breath whooshed through the speaker. "I'll check on that." He terminated the feed.

Elena crossed the road and found Victor talking with two mechanics outside the garage. She watched the mechanics inspect the driver's console. One of them affixed a device to the steering panel. They got out of the car and moved out of the way. Victor's car rolled forward into a repair bay, driverless. The mechanics hooted, apparently excited for a new project. That technology would get him arrested if he used it in SeCa. It was pretty clear, then, that Victor didn't want to go back, which left them drifting into danger and the unknown.

"Is it ready?" Elena asked.

One of the mechanics heard her and laughed. "Not nearly," he said, running his hand along the car's rear left fin. "We got to restore the automation protocols, add transponders, update the driving algorithm, and a few mods. Special package per Ozie's request."

"They need twenty-four hours to do the work," Victor told her. "We'll leave for Las Vegas in the morning."

Elena turned toward Victor and grabbed his shoulder. "This plan you've cooked up is a horrible idea. We should stay a few more days at least. You need to rest up."

He shrugged out of her grip. "We leave when it's ready." He authorized payment for the work on his car and left the garage.

She followed, cleared a lump from her throat, and said, "We can't leave."

Victor paused, glancing back, suspicion written all over his face, and said, "We are. At least, I am. Stay here if you want." He turned and walked toward the café.

She trotted after him. "Ozie's using you. If you want to find out what happened to your granfa, your best chance is to go back to SeCa and show the evidence to the police."

Victor wheeled around. "I can't go back! And I'm not sure I want to. I'd be reclassified in a heartbeat. You know that."

"Maybe not," she said. "Your family could help. You're an Eastmore, after all."

"I'm going, Elena. Make up your mind before tomorrow."

She watched him enter the café. Was he spinning out of control or making the best of a bad situation? How long before he did something he'd regret? But there weren't any good options. Going back could get him locked up. Staying wasn't viable; Ozie was roping him into serious crimes and messing with the Diamond King—a very stupid idea. Everything she'd heard from the Puros suggested he was a bloody, irredeemable tyrant. She had helped get Victor into this mess; she had to find a way out. Finally, she admitted to herself: she needed help.

Elena called Linda Eastmore, who answered on the third tone. "It's Elena."

"Where is Victor?" Linda demanded. "What have you done with him?"

Elena bristled. Linda hadn't returned her calls for several days, and now she wanted answers? "He's fine. We're—we're seeing the sights in Long Valley."

"I hired you to keep him safe, not go for a joyride."

Elena straightened. She was doing her best to navigate rough waters. Linda should give her some credit. She kicked gravel and found a shattered stim vial, pieces of glass lodged in the dirt. She scraped rocks back with her shoe to cover it. "Believe me, it's hardly a joyride. Look, Ms. Eastmore, I need to talk to you about his reclassification."

"You know they found my father-in-law's grave desecrated? If Victor had something to do with this, I'm holding you responsible. I asked you to help him manage his condition, not send him off the rails. If you have—"

"Ma'am!" Elena interrupted. "I'm trying my best, but he doesn't want to go home. He's worried about his reclassification. We need to know whether he can return to his old life or not." A road train of trucks passed by, their engines whistling, dust trailing and whirling in the breeze.

"It's pending." Linda Eastmore sighed. "Apparently, the doctor he was assigned wants to rule him a Class Two, but we're fighting it. Something about the test results being corrupted. It would help if Victor were here. We can't keep dodging the Health Board's inquiries, and they could ask him to come in again any day now. What are we supposed to say? He took a long holiday?"

"I'm doing my best."

"If you're trying for redemption, you're running out of time to succeed." Linda ended the connection.

Elena watched the last of the trucks disappear over a rise in the road. "Sometimes we hope for the impossible."

Organized Western States
6 March 1991

Victor smiled to himself, leaning back in his chair. Ozie had set Victor up at a computer terminal in a private room at the café with large portraits on the wall of dogs dressed in ballgowns and suits. The Boze-Drive had already been copied to the computer's archives, including the patient records and the analytical engine Victor used daily.

Ozie was on the other side of the room, peering at vidscreens and tapping on his type-pad. They didn't speak much. The project's requirements pulled their attention deep into a cyber landscape of code loops, access handshakes, and data queries. They piped up when they encountered an obstacle and needed help or when they finally cleared a blockage. To the part of Victor's mind that remained aware of his surroundings, the room glowed with amber amiability—a comfortable state of flow, friendship, and reaching for a vital goal.

Everything was easier now that he'd decided to follow Ozie's plan. Someone else could call the shots, and he could focus on what he did best: computational genomic analysis. It helped that the tinctures were working. With Personil purged from his system, he knew that the herbs coursing through his body were spreading dozens of biological compounds throughout his cells, changing the neurochemistry in his brain, subtly and steadily coaxing him toward homeostasis. Knowing the data egg was constantly nudging him in the right direction also helped, as did meditating for an hour with the help of one of Ozie's brain caps.

Victor knew he should call his family and let them know he was okay. He should talk to Karine and ask her again about the expansion of the Classification system. Instead, he threw himself into his work, and the small rebellion felt like easing into a warm bath and letting the world's troubles dissolve.

Ozie, sitting quietly with a brain cap on, took it off, stretched, and yawned. He looked at Victor over the rims of his glasses. "Are you sure you want to bring her along? I think it's a bad idea."

"She's coming, end of story," he said with more confidence than he felt.

Victor returned to his algorithm. Every line of code mattered when dealing with such vast sums of data. Processing the data in batches meant he had to take special care of how the data was broken and reassembled. Hours flew by.

During a test run on a tiny sliver of the genome, Victor recorded a few messages to try out the untraceable messaging function on the Handy 1000 that Ozie had given him. He sent one message to Ma and Fa to let them know he was okay and traveling up the Pacific Coast, intending to visit the First Nations of Canada. He tried not to think about what they made of his granfa's defiled grave and his sudden absence. He sent another message to Auntie Circe, asking her to contact him.

Victor squirmed, thinking about how much further across the line of good behavior he would advance by stealing the gene libraries from the Institute for Applied Biological Sciences. Thus far, he'd vandalized a grave and stolen from his family's company, crimes that might not land on him. But this theft would be a different thing altogether—a monumental heist. Researchers had to be licensed and pay huge sums to access a subset of the Human Genome Initiative's data troves. Now Victor planned to siphon all of it. It would make him infamous throughout the American Union if he were caught.

He pushed those thoughts aside. He had more coding to do and needed to create a lock on the program that Ozie couldn't break, an insurance policy in case his friend was only using him to get what he wanted, as Elena had suggested. He worked late, stopping only for a brief snack brought in by the tuxedoed robot, and then he returned to their rented room and passed out next to Elena.

Organized Western States
7 March 1991

In the early morning, before the sun rose, Victor sat on a bench inside the garage and ran remote tests on the BioScan data using his Handy 1000. His program worked as planned, indexing the genomic data and running comparison protocols to highlight differences between people with and without the gene. Once he had the reference libraries and connected them to the dark grid, his program could pick out the MRS gene sequence, provided Ozie could reroute the satellites in orbit. What had become of his life? Victor sighed, rolled up the Handy 1000 and stuck it in his pocket next to the data egg.

Elena paced outside. She had packed the car while the mechanics were still working on it, so the two of them were almost ready to go. He retrieved his bag from the trunk and downed a fumewort tincture. He would save the bitter grass, only taking it before sleeping to help with the nightmares.

The mechanics walked him through the car's new features. It opened when he pressed his palm against the door. The steering disc now showed the outline of two hands, the trigger for auto-driving mode. He programmed a test drive over Elena's objections and left her behind. He rode in the self-driving car a kilometer up the road.

He exited the car and stretched, anticipating the long drive ahead. Elena's erratic behavior would make maintaining his equilibrium harder. He wondered again if he should let her come along. He was planning an enormous breach of faith against one of the most respected scientific achievements the world had seen. If Elena came along and he was caught, she'd be deemed his accomplice. He should tell her to stay for her own good.

Distant, jagged mountains withdrew their shadows from the Reno desert. The sun would rise comparatively late due to the North Nevada time zone exception, one of the idiosyncrasies in OWS's mountainous regions.

A crackle in the dirt behind a nearby group of eucalyptus trees caught Victor's attention. Brown pods littered the ground along with dried leaves. The astringent scent of eucalyptus wafted by on the morning breeze. He returned to the car. When he heard another crunch, he wished he had a weapon. If the people following him tried to grab him now ...

Hooting, that sounded human, came from behind the trees. Maybe it was their signal to grab him. Victor turned full circle, determined not to be surprised from any direction. His guts dropped as he saw a man stumbling from behind a tree. Every sinew in Victor's body became taut as the man advanced unsteadily toward Victor's car. He had scraggly whiskers and hair like a greasy bird's nest. His parted lips revealed yellow, grimy teeth.

"Morning, feller!" the man said. "Good day it is! Spare me a dollar? I'm making camp on the other side of the golf course. Don't pay me no more to cut their grass. Got them bots. Please, kiddo. Help a stim slug out."

The stink coming from man's emaciated frame suggested disease. He was disgusting but not dangerous.

"You're on stims?" Victor asked. "What are they like?"

"Out of this world!" the hobo yelled. "Everything makes sense, and everything happens for a reason. It's divine."

The man seemed to have forgotten about Victor and stared at the ground, probing at his belly button, which poked from his undersized shirt. Then he licked his finger.

Victor found some water bottles in his trunk and a few packaged snacks and placed them in an ordered pile on the ground. When the hobo lifted his head, his eyes glistened.

Victor held up another bottle, which caught the sun's light and sparkled like a precious gem. "Everything happens for a reason," he said. He put the bottle down, got in his car, and drove back to the garage.

On the driveway, Elena looked at him with red and teary eyes. No. He couldn't leave her. Not while she was in torment and succumbing to the pull of addiction. She needed him to keep a close watch and fend off more opportunities for stimsmoke and maybe give her a purpose, a reason not to use.

"Let's go," he shouted to Elena through a lowered window.

She jumped in. "Step on it," she said.

Victor programmed the car for Las Vegas, and it began driving them south.

33

From the future, a dark hand returned and guided me onto a single path, away from the other tracks my life might have taken.

—Victor Eastmore, *Apology to Resonant Earth*, (transmission date unknown)

Organized Western States
7 March 1991

The car pulled itself around a sweeping curve. Jagged cliffs of rust-colored rock, sandstone, and white-streaked sediment rose above. When the road straightened, Victor and Elena glimpsed Las Vegas in the distance; the polished, improbable immensity of a city in the middle of nowhere made it seem like a mirage. Outside the city limits, fields of mirrors sprawled toward the hills. Black solar thermal towers punctuated the terrain at regular intervals like giant nails hammered into the desert floor.

The city layout resembled a giant bull's eye scratched into the dusty valley floor. The meticulously planned clock-face city, comprised of arcing apartment blocks, airtram circuits, and commercial skyscrapers that were arranged in concentric rings around Grand Park, a vivid circle of green. Two strips of parkland extended from Grand Park, dividing the city into quadrants named after the seasons. Painted with a pastel-green palette was Spring, which occupied the wedge from noon to three on the city's clock-face layout, beyond which sat pink-adobe Summer from three to six. With its golden-russet tones, Autumn occupied the space between six and nine. Winter's white-washed buildings, to their right and rapidly approaching, glistened from nine to twelve.

The Handy 1000 chimed, and Victor unfurled it on top of the dash. A message from Ozie read: "People following you crossed the border to OWS this morning."

Victor dragged both his palms down his face.

"What is it?" Elena asked from the passenger seat where she'd been dozing.

"They're still coming after us, whoever they are. They crossed over from SeCa this morning," he explained.

She waved as if she could swat them like flies. "They can't know where we are now, right? Don't worry."

Victor wanted to believe she was right. But why bother crossing the border if they'd lost the trail completely? They should be chasing his digital ghost up and down Long Valley. He downed a fumewort tincture and told himself to stay calm. *Might as well command the wind not to blow. But I've got to try.*

Victor tapped the dashboard to give the autopilot program more specific orders, and the car navigated toward the Institute for Applied Biological Sciences near Grand Park. The vista disappeared when the road dipped into a tunnel beneath Twelve-Six Park.

Victor glanced at Elena. The blue-tinted glare of passing light-strips flashed across her face. She scratched the back of one hand, raking her nails across her skin so forcefully that Victor worried she might draw blood.

He reached over and grabbed her hand, squeezing. "Who's nervous now?" he asked.

"Being underground ..." Elena hugged her chest. "I can't stop thinking about earthquakes."

"You know we're hundreds of kilometers from any significant fault lines." Victor looked up at the tunnel ceiling's broad arch, reinforced with thick pillars. It looked solid, but appearances could be deceiving. "You should be more worried about faulty construction," Victor said.

She glared at him. "Thanks, now I'm worried about that too."

The car drove itself into a tunnel spur and up an exit chute. They emerged onto a narrow two-lane street flanked by apartment buildings and commercial towers. Wide sidewalks with parallel bicycle lanes took up twice as much room as the portion of road allotted for motorized vehicles.

The car proceeded slowly and stopped at a turnout in front of a building that looked like glass cubes hastily stacked on top of one another. Victor and Elena climbed out and stretched. He took his bag from the trunk and sent the car to a parking garage.

"This is the place," Victor said, looking up at the building.

Elena bit her cheek and glanced back. He followed her gaze. Throngs of people strolled across an intersection, shaded by an enormous piece of fabric stretched high above the street, secured to nearby buildings by thin, nearly invisible wires. The sunshade converted solar energy falling between buildings into electricity. The buildings also had solar-gathering windows to generate electricity to feed into the city's grid.

Solar power was interesting but didn't explain Elena's frantic, darting glances.

Victor grew tired of waiting. "Let's get this over with," he said, striding ahead.

They entered the Institute's large atrium, which rose several stories and was supported by a lattice of white, curving beams that looked like giant ribs. They seemed out of place next to the smooth, rigidly geometric planes of the building's transparent skin. The reception area was separated from the rest of the building by waist-high glass panels. The floor was a flatscreen filled with flowing light that directed guests to the right while staff veered to the left. A bright green path led to a separate area that served as the tour-group waiting area.

Victor led Elena to the Institute's gift shop and bought a disposable imager, a case for it, and tickets for a tour. He shoved the data leech into the case and held the imager in his hand like any other tourist. They walked to the waiting area. Other people stood nearby: children with their parents, a few university-age youths, and several pale-skinned bespectacled businesspeople who might have been from overseas. Victor grabbed Elena's hand and pulled her close. She resisted momentarily and then relaxed, leaning her head against his upper arm.

Victor said, "I need you to distract the docent when we reach the genome library."

"I guessed as much," she said. "If you were good at sneaking around, Victor, you would have told me in the car, where we couldn't be overheard. That's Thievery 101."

"I'm not good at this, I know. But as far as anyone else knows, we're having a tender moment." He inhaled and smelled her hair. It was clean but musty. He couldn't smell any stimsmoke. "Are you feeling okay? You were fidgeting in the car."

Elena pushed back and looked up at him. "That's why you keep staring at me? You think I'm using stims again?"

"You haven't seemed like yourself since we reached Springboard Café."

Her eyes flicked rapidly over his face. She set her jaw. "It was just a puff," she whispered. "Sebastian and Theodora gave it to me, said I looked like I needed it. I wasn't strong enough to hand it back."

He wasn't surprised. He'd been right about Granfa then, and he was right about Elena now. A chill swept through him. The gift of a super-freaky brain that could guess the truth before being told wasn't anything he'd asked for.

"It's okay," he said, shaking away the chill. "You can be honest with me, you know. You don't have to hide it."

She looked away. He'd made her ashamed, but that hadn't been his intention. He'd simply wanted them to be on firmer ground.

Victor embraced her, feeling guilty for almost leaving her at Springboard Café. They needed each other. If what they had wasn't love, it was a shared understanding and a mutual need for companionship. She was a piece of his life he clung to, even while everything else was being chipped away. He opened his mouth to say how he felt, but the words wouldn't come. He didn't know how to express it. Instead, he hugged her tighter.

34

The Corp's wafting hot-bodied scent, a rotten fruit and acetone stench, permeated the Amarillo Cattle Company's feed warehouse, a burnt-out husk on the outskirts of town. A single lightstrip hung limply from charred ceiling beams. The concrete floor was pocked and stained by decades of blood, filth, and meat.

Elena turned away, gagging, trying not to let her Puros compatriots see her weakness. She was still a provisional recruit with a lot to prove.

Synthleather straps stretched around the prisoner's bulging thighs and arms. He refused to talk. His swollen limbs and tank-like torso indicated massive steroid use, as did the acne spreading down his face and neck. He had sandy hair, buck teeth, narrow shoulders, a bulbous chest, and limbs that seemed tumorous on such a small frame. A smirking, over-muscled kid who hadn't yet realized how much trouble he was in.

Tonight, Xavi, the Amarillo Puro's chief, had ordered Elena to lead the interrogation. She had instructions to find out why the trade truce with the Corps, in effect since before Elena joined the Puros the first time, had been canceled and to do so by any means necessary.

Darkness gathered around Elena and her fellow Puros, Chico and Davinth, while they questioned the tied-up Corp. Folks who didn't know the Puros probably thought they were hick farmers with political leanings. If so, they knew shit. The Puros were a family dedicated to principles of loyalty, rootedness, and, above all, purity. The Corp should have feared them more.

She made a retching sound at the smell the Corp gave off and said, "He looks like an inflatable dummy."

Chico laughed. "He's a juicer. What did you expect?"

Davinth, the Puro's most junior confirmed member, asked, "Been ragin' for a while now, haven't ye, boyo?"

Davinth had made the journey from Cardiff in the Welsh Protectorate to the middle-of-nowhere Republic of Texas and had become a drug-free zealot like the rest of the Puros. He was a dim bulb, always ready to follow along mindlessly, but at least he'd never realized that Elena was still dosing. She worried about Chico, though. He was wild, always looking for ways to impress Xavi, and perceptive enough that Elena avoided him when she was using.

Elena cursed herself. She hadn't been strong enough to resist a few puffs. Hot saliva stung the back of her throat. She refused to cough. None of her Puro dickiemates could know that she'd snuck stimsmoke in the other room while they were busy binding the Corp. Addiction was a leash tugging her down a path to ruin, and she couldn't break free.

The Corp didn't respond to any of their taunts. He stared at the walls and ceiling, ignoring them. This would be a long, difficult night if he wouldn't talk.

"Let's get on with it," Elena said.

Chico shredded the Corp's shirt with a pop-out blade and started scraping a strip of sandpaper across the young man's nipple. The Corp, who was probably only a few years younger, didn't scream, wince, or speak. Elena wished he would. The silence only encouraged Chico to get more creative. Elena looked into the Corp's bloodshot eyes so she wouldn't have to watch what was happening lower down.

"Why did you call off the drop?" Elena asked.

She hated interrogations and the stupid and ineffectual cruelty of her dickiemates. There wasn't much she could do about it, though. The Puros wouldn't pay a Corp for information, since their principles forbade bribery, so they had to rely on other tactics.

The Corp's expression was sullen and bitter, and he started sweating. Unfortunately, he appeared neither scared nor in pain. Chico tried cutting, squeezing, and breaking, and nothing seemed to affect the Corp. It was like he was numb all over, like his pain receptors were broken.

"I got it!" Elena said as she grabbed Chico's shoulder. She spun him toward her and smiled into his confused face. "He doesn't feel anything. Look!" She tugged hard on the young man's ear for effect. His head snapped to the side, and his teeth almost caught her fingers.

"Try that again, gums," Chico warned. He casually knocked a baton against the Corps' lips hard enough to split them. The Corp spat blood and looked away sullenly.

"Pain's no good. We need to scare him." Elena unclasped, removed her belt, and handed it to Chico, miming how to use it to block airflow.

Chico nodded, wrapped the belt firmly around both fists, stepped behind the Corp, and started strangling him. The Corp's eyes bulged, and the muscles in his face seized. Elena walked into his field of view, but the panicked Corp didn't see her.

Elena grabbed his ears and pulled. "Hey! Listen up! He's going to strangle you until I tell him to stop."

Chico watched her, waiting for the signal.

Elena said, "Keep going. I've got time."

The Corp wheezed and strained unsuccessfully to draw a breath. His face turned purple and appeared to swell. Elena nodded to Chico, and he let up. Ragged breaths wheezed out of the Corp's throat, and he began to cough.

"Tell me why you called off the drop, or he'll squeeze again. And again. Your brain cells will start to die off, and you don't have many to spare, am I right? All your buddies' drugs won't help. He'll keep going until you're a drooling vegetable. What do you say?"

Chico looked at the Corp with an excited grin that turned Elena's stomach.

The belt touched the Corp's neck. His face caved, becoming just another scared dickie. "Wait!" he pleaded. Words spilled out of him alongside gobs of spit. His eyes were dark black pools of fear. "I don't know why. We got the word—no more deals with the Puros. Everyone knows now. You're off limits."

"Why? Who gave the order?" Elena leaned in, then gagged. He was giving off some sort of gross half-metabolized oily odor, a by-product of whatever substances he was taking. "Why?" she repeated, backing away and blocking her nose with her thumb and forefinger. She couldn't stand his stench.

Both Chico and Davinth were staring at her with heads cocked. Gooseflesh rose on her skin. Neither of the guys was plugging his nose. They acted as if the smell wasn't there.

And it *wasn't*, she realized, her heart pounding.

The smell was in her head.

Flashes from previous stimsmoke highs slammed into her, and she sunk to the ground and leaned against one of the metal struts holding up the ceiling. She should have realized it sooner. The smell was an artifact of synesthesia, a side effect of stimsmoke that no one had bothered to explain to her. Maybe other users didn't quite understand it. Not everyone had a friend with mirror resonance syndrome.

The Corp spilled his guts to Chico and Davinth, naming names and describing the hierarchy of a local Corps franchise—she barely heard what he said. Instead, she smelled his fear and desperation. Elena watched and said nothing. She didn't think she could stand up.

Chico looked over at Elena and mouthed, "You okay?"

She waved at him to keep going.

"It goes way up," the Corp was saying. "Maybe as far as the King. All we hear is, 'Push the stims! Push the stims!' And now, 'no arms for the Puros.' Anyone caught in a deal gets his head bashed in."

Chico asked, "Who else are you going to sell to?"

"No idea. But I can find out for you. Just don't kill me." He looked at Chico with pleading eyes. "Or choke me again."

Elena stood, grasping the metal beam to haul herself up. She beckoned to Chico and pulled him to the side of the room. She wanted to release the Corp, but he refused. He slipped the belt around the Corp's neck and tightened it.

Elena took a step forward on wobbly legs. The floor vibrated under her feet, and shadows crowded her vision. She took another step and stumbled to her knees, retching. The sounds of the Corp struggling washed over her. She couldn't stop Chico. In between heaving, Elena wished again that Victor would return her feed requests. If stimsmoke mirrored his condition, he might be able to talk her through getting clean.

35

A docent approached the waiting area, heels clicking as she walked across the atrium. Her dyed-blond hair was pulled from her face into thick braids that spiraled up and around her head.

"Welcome," she said, smiling broadly. The glare from her bright white teeth obscured her face. Victor's brain was acting up, but he'd left his fumewort in the car.

The docent paused as if the tourists needed time to digest the full import of that single word, and then she continued. "Welcome to the Institute for Applied Biological Sciences. We are the largest research facility in the Organized Western States focused solely on the medical sciences. Today, I'll take you through an exhibit showcasing the discoveries and developments pioneered over our fifty-year history. You'll see our genomics lab, where approximately 40 percent of the Human Genome Initiative's first-pass sequencing was carried out. And I'll take you to our world-famous cafeteria, which is exclusively provisioned by our genetically modified crops and livestock. Supplementary information will be available throughout the tour to those with Mesh devices. Follow me, please."

Elena whispered in Victor's ear, "Fake food. The Puros would be freaking out."

The tour group moved past a set of glass partitions and a pillar with a blue light on top. When Elena neared the pillar, it turned red. The receptionist sitting nearby spoke into a microphone. Within seconds, a security guard emerged from a doorway and approached Elena. Victor watched with a mixture of fear and surprise.

"You'll need to check your weapon with us during the tour," the guard said.

"Oh, okay. I forgot I was carrying." Elena smiled as she gave up her shockstick and received a numbered token in exchange, but Victor knew she resented letting it out of her grasp.

"Weapons don't seem to be a big deal here," Victor remarked. In SeCa, carrying a shockstick would get you a gene screening and some jail time.

Elena shrugged. "Here and in the ROT, as long as you don't disrupt commerce or get caught doing crimes, personal freedom reigns."

The docent began to explain the founding of the Institute, which came about during the Repartition. She described how American Union tax rebates poured into the OWS's urban centers—its capital, Salt Lake City; industrial Portland; mineral-exporting Boise; and East-Asian-trade-oriented Seattle. Research-focused Las Vegas exploded into a leading biotech and materials science hub, one of the most important academic centers of the AU outside the Eastern Seaboard and the last OWS city along the Cold Nile Miracle route to the Democratic Republic of Mexico. Las Vegas was governed by a techno-libertarian criminal with a fetish for city planning, according to Elena's hushed whispers.

"The Diamond King or the chief of the Corps?" Victor asked.

Elena answered, "They're one and the same. And everyone here is obsessed with their social rating system. Numbers that represent class, status, pecking order. It's wild."

They followed the docent and the tour group up a long hallway that curved in a gradual spiral incline around the building's central column of stairs and elevator banks. The atmosphere was one of calm reflection and deep focus, about as far from the Springboard Café as possible. Victor wanted to live in a house that looked like this. Why hadn't anyone ever told him how amazing Las Vegas was?

As they followed the ramp upward, years were marked on the floor in glowing numbers. When the docent reached 1934, the wall lit up with a vidfeed showing the DNA molecule and a picture of the four coauthors of the paper announcing its discovery, one of whom was a tall, wild-haired twenty-something named Jefferson Eastmore. Elena took a photo of Victor next to Granfa's picture. The resemblance was apparent on close examination but not overwhelming.

At 1975, the wall activated again. Multicolored lines radiated from a central point. White numbers and letters surrounded the wheel of color.

"The human genome," Victor whispered to Elena. "Every base pair in every chromosome sequenced and mapped. It's the baseline for all individual genetic comparisons."

The docent overheard and gave Victor a satisfied nod. Then, she launched into a more long-winded explanation for those on the tour

Cody Sisco

with less scientific literacy. Victor wrapped his arm around Elena, tipping his mouth toward her ear. "In the next room. Get ready."

"Love you too, sweetie pie," she said. "By the way, I know what the human genome map looks like. I'm not stupid." She poked him hard in the ribs.

Victor suppressed a yelp and held his hands up in apology.

Elena smiled, and years dropped off her face, almost like they were two teenagers again, goofing off in one of SeCa's stodgy museums.

The docent led the group into a cavernous space that made them look like they'd been miniaturized and dumped onto a circuit board. Boxy machines the size of construction vehicles dotted the vast room. Racks of smaller metal boxes were arranged in long rows, separated by aisles. The treacherous terrain was strewn with cables like the webs of giant, sloppy spiders.

The docent explained, "Watch your step. Flexible crystal nano-tubes are replacing the original optical cables. A thousandfold increase in bandwidth." She gestured to a tangle of cables on the floor. "Data protection takes creative wiring."

A few tour group members laughed politely while the rest gawked at the machines and took pictures.

The docent patted the nearest machine. "Each RTX sequencer was dedicated to a single chromosome. This Institute was responsible for half of the raw sequencing data; the other half came from a consortium of universities throughout the New England Commonwealth, the Greater Ohio Constitutional League, and the Southeastern Confederacy. We also performed data verification for the HGI as a whole. Some of you might recall the day of the announcement when President—"

"Are these still running?" Victor asked.

A slight frown tugged at the docent's mouth and then vanished. She said, "Not all of them. Miniaturization has come a long way in the past fifteen years. The sequencing and storage capability to recreate the work done in this room could fit within a small car today. We do utilize some of the machines from time to time for niche projects."

"And the libraries? The complete set—they're here too?"

"Yes, at the Institute, we provide the HGI libraries, current and historical, to other research institutions to assist them in their genomic analyses." She cocked her head as if eager to hear another question, but he could tell she wanted to move on. Now that he knew there were, in fact, libraries there, he was eager for her to move on, too.

"Neat. Thank you," Victor mumbled.

"Let's take a look inside one of the sequencers," the docent said, leading the group further into the room.

Victor remained behind while Elena went ahead. She glanced back at him, and he waved her on. He slipped behind one of the machines, listening for a hum, any sign that it was turned on and connected to the Institute's network. It was silent. The case hanging around his neck thumped against his chest, and he fought to remain calm as he fumbled with it and removed the data leech that Ozie had given him.

In the next row, Victor found a whirring machine, through the side of which, he saw flashing diodes. He found a data cable at the back, crouched, and affixed the data leech. It would ping the data traffic flowing through the line, testing to see if it could access the genome libraries and find a path to the Mesh. In addition, a computer virus in the leech would seek out surveillance vidfeeds at the Institute and disrupt them.

Seconds ticked by.

Victor heard the docent continue explaining the HGI and the accelerated development of research and medicines that the project made possible. Finally, the light on the data leech turned red. He removed the device and tried another. Fifteen seconds later, another red light. He moved to another machine. Red light, no connection.

Footsteps clicked behind him. Victor whirled.

Elena beckoned him. "I've run out of smart questions for her, and we're moving on," she said.

"I haven't found it yet." Victor removed the data leech and darted to the next machine. Its cables snaked under a floor panel, which he prized open and tossed aside. He put the clamp around a thick purple cable. "We can't leave without connecting this."

Elena looked up at the ceiling. "What if they have vidfeeds?"

"Ozie's got that taken care of. The data leech is a cyber-sabotage smart bomb. They won't find it unless they physically stumble over the device."

A voice rang out from behind a rack of machines. "Excuse me!"

A security guard rounded the corner and eyed them suspiciously. He had obsidian-black skin, broad shoulders, and no hint of softness in his voice. "I need you to keep moving with your group," he said.

Victor froze where he was crouching next to the data leech. Unless he could lie quickly and convincingly, he could look forward to years in jail and, after that, the rest of his life in a facility.

Elena hauled Victor to his feet. "Oh, perfect!" she squealed. "We were trying to get a picture together. Do you mind?" She took the imager from Victor and handed it to the guard. He looked dubiously at the device. Victor shifted so that his foot hid the data leech.

"Just press that contact," Elena instructed. "Give us a three count, please." She squeezed Victor's middle and kissed his cheek, which made his chest warm, like drinking warm cider.

The guard was watching them closely. Victor blinked and put on a rictus smile, petrified that the guard wasn't buying it.

"Thank you, sir," Elena said.

The guard grunted. "Not my idea of a romantic date, but I don't claim to understand kids these days." He held up the imager. "One, two, three." The guard pressed the contact. "I don't think anything happened."

Elena stepped forward and grabbed the imager from his hands. "No, that worked just fine. It's silent, so I don't look like a tourist." She made the faux-shutter sounds that most imagers used these days.

Victor regained the use of his voice. "Did you see which way the tour group went?"

The guard wore the barest smirk on his face. "You must have missed them while you were smooching. Out the door and to your left." He turned and pointed.

Victor glanced down. The light on the data leech had turned green. "Let's get some lunch," he said to Elena with bluster. "Show us the way, please, kind sir."

They rejoined the group with the guard in the lead. Elena made a show of fixing her hair and checking her makeup in a glass display cube holding an ancient microscope. Victor rubbed his lips. None of the group seemed to notice their re-entry performance, though the docent narrowed her eyes for a brief moment. The guard smiled, turned, and left.

"Good work," Victor said to Elena. "I couldn't get a word out."

"You got the job done. That's what counts." She squeezed his arm. "We make a good team."

That might have been true, but he couldn't keep running and putting himself in danger. He needed to find a place to be safe and secure and enjoy every moment of his life before MRS took over. And he wasn't sure Elena would fit into that new configuration.

When the tour group arrived at the Institute's restaurant, Victor and Elena asked to be pointed toward the exit.

"Won't you be joining us for lunch?" the docent asked.

Elena piped up first, "I don't eat doctored meat."

The docent's eyes widened, and her mouth gaped like a catfish. She straightened her shoulders and said, "Our produce is safe and delicious, I assure you."

"I'm sure it is," Victor said. "It's just that we're late for—"

"For a lunch date, where we'll eat all-natural food," Elena said, tugging at his shirt. "I need to get my shockstick back, and we'll go."

The docent eyed them suspiciously, but she called a security guard who returned Elena's shockstick and escorted them to the front door.

They wandered into the sunshine.

"All set?" she asked.

Victor smiled. "I think this is going to work."

"Great, let's get a room," Elena said. "I need a shower before we head back."

"I like it here. It feels civilized. We can stay overnight."

Victor summoned his car, and a minute later, it arrived at the turnout. They climbed inside, and he programmed the destination: a hotel in the Summer zone. The car drove for a few minutes and stopped in front of a multistory building that curved away from them. A huge awning above was strung with lightstrips like paper streamers. They got out and placed their bags on an autoporter, a low hexagonal dolly, which followed them inside.

The hotel lobby had a polished, cream-colored laminate floor that Victor was surprised he didn't slip on. Large potted ferns bordered a walkway to the registration area, where a young man stood behind an oiled rosewood desk.

Victor reached into his pocket to pull out his Handy 1000, but Elena touched his arm.

"In case they're following you," she whispered, "let's put this under a fake name. And pay cash."

"I'm sure Ozie will handle it."

"Let's not press our luck." Elena elbowed him out of the way.

The receptionist smiled and asked if they would like two separate beds. "Adjoining rooms," Elena said.

The receptionist replied, "Don't miss the history exhibit on the origins of Las Vegas just past the elevators to your left."

On the sixteenth floor, they found their rooms, showered separately, and met in Victor's room.

"Can you show me more of the dreambook?" Elena asked.

"Why?"

"I finally got Ozie to talk before we left. I understand the conspiracy about diagnosing MRS, but I don't understand how your dreams fit into this. Ozie said he doesn't remember his dreams. Recurring dreams are apparently not a common symptom. Plus, yours might be coming true."

Bile rose in Victor's stomach. "They don't. It's just coincidental."

"You had a gut feeling about your granfa, and that means it's not just your dreams. Something's up with your brain. Let me help you figure it out."

Reluctantly, Victor withdrew the leather-bound journal from his bag and handed it to her. "They started as early as I can remember," he said, "but I only began writing them down when I was eleven, after the family reunion in New Venice."

"I remember that," Elena said. "It was my first time in the Louisiana Territories. I always thought it was strange for my family to join your family's party."

Victor shrugged. "Granfa needed to show how buddy-buddy he was with a union official. He wanted the union's support."

Elena opened the book. Victor headed for the door.

She looked up and jumped to her feet. "Where are you going?"

He shrugged. "To walk around for a while. Find a Freshly or whichever juice chain they have here."

"You should stay here."

"What? You don't think it's safe?" Victor closed his eyes and sighed. That was only partly the reason. He knew why she was objecting. She was afraid he would get in trouble again. "I'm doing fine."

She grimaced. "I don't think you should chance it."

"You're being paranoid." *Or maybe she's worried about something else?* "You don't have any stims to use while I'm gone, do you?" he asked, watching her carefully.

"No! But maybe I'll come with you."

Her expression was mottled by a streak of fear, a wave of embarrassment, depths of friendly concern, and desperation. He couldn't make sense of it, and the vigilance was exhausting.

"No offense, but I need a break. We've been in that car for hours, and I'm ..." He bit back a laugh. "I'm a big fucking tuning fork, and I need some silence, a reset."

"Don't leave the hotel."

"I can't live in a box. Broken Mirrors aren't a thing here, remember? The Commission has no jurisdiction. Don't they say that Vegas is the most organized city in the Organized Western States? I'll be fine." Victor pointed at the dreambook. "There's nothing in there."

Elena bit her lip. "Let me be the judge."

Organized Western States
7 March 1991

"I don't understand why you haven't returned with him yet," Linda said.

A loud banging sound made Elena hold the MeshBit away from her ear. After she had transitioned, she'd felt confident, ready to take on the world, feet solidly planted, mapping out her path and letting no one stand in her way. In all her interactions with Victor, she was the rock he could cling to. At some point, later, she couldn't say precisely when, the map she was using didn't work anymore. The borders had shifted. The landmarks had vanished. She didn't know which way to turn. And the thing that had been the source of her strength—her conviction that she would be happier as Elena than Eli—hadn't gone away but just didn't matter anymore. Redundant, like a coal-fired power plant after the laws to roll back climate chaos. So, yeah, she was a bit directionless and grasping at straws, but she wasn't going to take shit from Linda Eastmore.

"You know he's an adult, right? I understand he's your precious boy, but some distance from the Eastmores might not be so bad for him right now."

Linda gasped and continued through the MeshBit, "I should have known better than to trust you. How could I have thought an addict would be a reliable companion for my son?"

"Is that why you hired those other two to watch him?" Elena asked.

"What other two?" Linda snapped.

"Lucky and Bandit. When Victor visited his herbalist, they took her—"

"What herbalist?"

Why would she pretend not to know what Elena was talking about? She chose her next words carefully. "Victor found a woman in Little Asia to help him. An alternative treatment, herbs. I don't know the names. Haven't they told you?"

"You're not making sense. Haven't who told me what? The woman?"

"No. Lucky and Bandit," Elena said.

"You say those words like they should mean something to me."

Elena felt her insides freeze. Linda hadn't hired them. They'd been watching Victor, following him, trying to get their hands on him. And Elena had been helping them.

246   Cody Sisco

"Elena, I expect you to return Victor to—"

Elena terminated the MeshBit feed. She put a fist to her forehead, tempted to bang some sense in. How could she have been so naive? She had to find Victor. They had to go.

Organized Western States
7 March 1991

Victor rode the elevator to the bottom floor. The hotel lobby was quiet, and only half a dozen people moved through its cavernous expanse. He wandered into a long gallery containing historical diorama and mineralogical exhibits depicting Las Vegas's growth from a small frontier settlement to a juggernaut of mining, finance, and industry during the early part of the twentieth century. According to the exhibit, the city was now the proud center of techno-optimism, advanced materials research, and the tech-production hub in the Arid Lands.

A huge drill bit hung from a metal scaffold. It was large enough that, if it were hollow, three adults could climb inside. The plaque on the wall next to it said it was the first to use an ultra-strong compressed diamond lattice coating that allowed tunneling and extraction to extreme depths.

Victor reached the exhibit's end and pinged Ozie, who answered immediately.

"It's done," Victor said.

"Of course it is," Ozie said. "I got the notification in my feed when you placed the data leech. I've already started the transfer." There was a pause. "Are you alone?"

Victor looked around. "Yes, I'm alone."

"Well, I don't want to get your anxiety level up, seeing as you might—"

"I'm fine, Ozie. Just tell me what it is. I'm not going to crack."

"Those people following you showed up here."

Victor steadied himself against the drill bit. "What happened?"

"It's not like we're defenseless. I knew when they crossed the border, and vidcams spotted them a mile from the café. I sent a few of our armored cars to head them off. They didn't stick around long. They headed down the road like scared dogs. Thing is, how did they know where to find you?"

"I don't know." Victor wiped his forehead.

"I'm rechecking my systems, but it's possible there's been a breach. I'm pretty sure there's no bug in your car. But there's something else. It's bad." Ozie had been blustery before, but now he sounded worried. "Victor, Tosh was here."

"He's trying to catch up. No problem there."

"He took Jefferson's tongue."

"He what?" Victor said. "Why?"

"He wouldn't say. But I wasn't going to brawl with a guy twice my size. Look, your job there is done. You should get back here. But in case they're headed your way—"

"When were they there?"

"They could be in Vegas now if they knew to look for you there. You might want to take the long way back so you don't meet them on the Cold Nile road. Leave now, I'd say. It's the safest bet."

Victor used the Handy 1000 to find an alternate route back, and it calculated the travel time. "That's a six-hour detour!"

Movement in the lobby caught Victor's attention. Two figures rushed in, headed toward the reception desk. The man behind the desk blinked and took a step back. Then he grabbed the phone, speaking urgently.

"I'll call you back," Victor said and terminated the feed with Ozie.

Victor squinted at the figures, a man and a woman, uncertain if he'd seen them before. Could the people following him have found him so quickly? He hid behind a sculpture. His breath came in quick little sips. He would wait to return to his room until they moved on. He had to warn Elena.

An elevator chimed. Victor peeked out, feeling a tightness in his throat. Elena emerged from the elevator and approached the reception desk. The man and woman turned and spoke to her.

Victor's lungs spasmed, and he felt a desperate urge to cough. He pressed himself against the sculpture, bringing his hand to his mouth. He'd been so stupid. He'd assumed Elena was acting odd because of stims; in fact, she'd been betraying him this whole time.

The couple swiveled their heads left and right, scanning the hotel lobby. The man jogged to the front entrance and stepped outside, donning a pair of round sun goggles. He paced along the façade. Were the front windows reflective or transparent? Victor turned away in case the man could see him.

Footsteps approached the gallery. There was nowhere else to hide. Victor stepped from behind the sculpture and ran. He glanced over his shoulder. The woman was already chasing him.

He fled toward the exit.

36

Victor raced along the exhibit hall and burst through a set of emergency exit doors. The high desert sun was blinding. The sidewalk was mostly empty, but the man had circled from the hotel entrance and was running toward him.

Victor darted across the street, causing two cars to halt when their collision detectors activated. He ran faster. The air in his lungs burned, and his pulse throbbed behind his eyes. He heard Elena yelling for him to keep running, which made no sense, given that she'd betrayed him.

He pulled the Handy 1000 from his pocket to summon his car and glanced back. The couple were catching up to him, with Elena further back. Victor put on another burst of speed and reached a street that led toward the center of Las Vegas's clockface. In two blocks, the street met Three O'Clock Park. He ignored the "Stay on the Trail" signs as he ran, dodging between sharp-pointed aloe bushes, his lungs burning. His legs gave out when he reached the park's far end, and he sank to his knees. He glanced back and saw he wasn't far ahead of his pursuers. They'd catch up within a minute.

His Handy 1000 chimed. Seconds later, his car pulled up. Victor jumped up and dove in through the open door, only realizing as the car sped off that someone was already sitting in the passenger seat.

Tosh looked oversized in the smallish vehicle. He said, "You look like you're running from something."

"How did you find me?" Victor asked between gasping breaths.

"Been following those two idiots." He jerked a thumb back toward Lucky and Bandit. "Spoke with your buddy, Ozie, too." Tosh reached over and tapped on the control console. "I know a place we can go."

Victor watched in the rearview mirror as they left his pursuers behind.

Tosh asked, "Do you know who they are?"

"No idea. I thought they were with the Classification Commission, but if so, then why would they get in touch with Elena?" Victor wiped the sweat off his forehead. He'd been so stupid, believing her lies. "She led them right to me."

Tosh smiled, and the skin around his eyes crinkled. "Girl problems?"

"Friend problems," he said. "Worse than usual. Maybe I *am* bad luck."

"Where's my granfa's tongue?" Victor asked.

"It's in a safe place. You still have the data egg? Has it opened?"

Victor shoved his hand in his pocket and cupped the data egg, cursing it for not opening. "I've got the data egg, but everything else is in the hotel room. My herbs. My dreambook."

"I think you can live without your spooky diary."

"I need to burn it. That book could get me reclassified; no tests required."

Victor dug into the outer pocket of his pants and removed his last vial of fumewort. He gulped it down and closed his eyes, then asked, "Why do you want the egg to open so much? What do you think is inside?"

Tosh cocked his head. "I don't like to gamble, but I'm betting Jeff knew who poisoned him and that the answer is in there. When I execute his murderer, I want to be sure I get the right person."

"Ozie says it's locked, and he doesn't know the trigger," Victor said.

"I've got some ideas about that."

The car was heading southwest along a radial avenue between the seven and eight o'clock boulevards. Behind them, commercial buildings were giving way to high-rise apartment blocks. They headed far outside the city, passing fields of mirrors, following a thin strip of asphalt. A brightly lit, two-story building appeared ahead. It was newly built to look like an old-timey Western saloon with balconies hanging over a wooden porch and a hitching post between the building and the gravel parking lot.

"What is this place?" Victor asked.

"Best brothel in Vegas," Tosh said. "It's taken a while for me to catch up with you, but now it's time to get down to business."

"I'm not interested in brothels," Victor said.

Tosh chuckled. "No shit."

"So why are we here?" Victor asked.

"You know how some places have all those cameras and connections to the Mesh?"

"Yeah, of course."

"Well, this place doesn't. Now you know why it's the best. C'mon," Tosh ordered.

They exited the car and walked alongside a wooden fence bordering a wasteland of scrub and dust-coated cacti. Inside the brothel, wood-paneled walls the color of wine-soaked corks were dimly illuminated by lightstrips. Artificial sounds of wind and rain billowed through the lobby, sonofeeds from someplace wet and lush. A crowd dressed in modern clothes looked out of place in the traditional-style lounge, filling it with loud chatter.

Tosh led Victor past the lounge and down a hallway that smelled of mildew. They reached a door that Tosh opened with a key-shaped piece of plastic. The room inside was filled with overstuffed synthleather couches and chairs, plush ottomans, and a bed covered with pillows. And a bunch of large duffel bags looking like a nest.

"How have you tried to open it?" Tosh asked, shutting the door. He pointed at Victor's pocket.

Victor pulled the data egg out and held it up. "Ozie says it's unhackable."

"Yeah, he told me the same thing, but something's got to open it. Jeff gave it to you for a reason."

"If you were so close to my granfa, why didn't he tell you? Why didn't he tell anyone?"

Tosh didn't answer.

"What should I do? Sing to it?"

"If the egg was waiting for your monotone grunts, it would have cracked long ago. Jeff wasn't much of a sentimentalist, so I don't think holding it to your heart is likely to open it. Ozie mentioned fluids. Jefferson had a lot of samples with your name on them. Have you tried spit?"

Victor raised his eyebrows and brought the egg to his mouth. He stuck out his tongue and dragged the egg down its length.

Tosh smirked. "Like an expert," he said.

Victor's face flushed. "I guess you would know."

They stared at the egg. Nothing.

"How about blood?" Tosh pulled a knife from his belt. "I'll be gentle."

Victor hesitated. But for once, Tosh sounded sincere. Victor said, "Don't go deep."

Tosh grinned wryly. "They say restraint is a virtue." He gripped Victor's arm with one hand and, with the other, scored a shallow cut into the skin. A drop of blood welled up. Victor took the data egg and held it to the cut, hoping the polonium had rubbed off by now—just another risk in a long series of them.

Nothing happened.

Tosh looked disappointed and resheathed his knife. "Try pissing on it."

Victor's mouth dropped open. "Are you kidding?"

"I guess they made you do it in a cup at some point?" Tosh said. "Go in the bathroom, and don't come out until you've pissed all over it. Have a wank, too, and see if your jizz will open it."

"I'm not going to—"

"Just get in there and do it!" Tosh grabbed hold of Victor's shoulders and pressed him into the bathroom. The door shutting and leaving him alone was a relief.

Victor unzipped his pants and stood, aiming his penis with one hand and holding the egg over the toilet bowl with the other. Ozie had said Victor's biological markers might open the data egg, but it felt absurd to stand with his pants around his ankles, waiting for his bladder to cooperate. He leaned forward, propping his elbow against the wall, trying to hold the egg low.

Tosh knocked on the door. "I don't hear the waterfall."

"It's a balancing act."

"You need help?"

"No!"

"Just sit down. No one's judging your masculinity."

"Oh. Yeah, that'll work." Victor sat and held the egg between his legs and released a stream of piss, wetting the egg and his hands. When he was done, he groped for toilet paper and wiped it up. He stood, pulled up his pants, and washed his hands and the egg, drying them with a hand towel. "That didn't do anything," he said.

"Get hard," Tosh said through the door.

Victor could have guessed that Tosh would insist on trying everything. The man was a leering beast of sexuality. But Victor had to try everything in his power to open the data egg because he didn't really think Ozie would be able to help.

He grabbed his crotch through his jeans, already realizing it was hopeless. His penis was as limp as a braid of silk.

"This isn't going to work," he said.

"You need help?" Tosh said. Victor could hear the smile in his voice. *I'd be better off with Elena and her thug friends.*

"It's a stupid idea," Victor said. "Why would he have coded the egg with my ejaculate?"

Although, the nurses at Oak Knoll *had* made him jerk off a couple of times. They said they were testing for something—he couldn't remember what. Probably whether he would pass the MRS gene to his descendants or some research study. Or maybe to give it to his granfa for the cure research. *Yuck!*

Tosh said, "Come on. Give your junk a few yanks, and let's move on."

"I'm not—there's no hope with you standing out there listening."

Tosh opened the door and pointed at Victor's crotch.

"No! Stay back."

"Relax, we'll order in."

Tosh waved him into the room, and Victor followed reluctantly, taking one step at a time, inching toward the exit. He'd take his car and go, maybe back to Springboard Café. He just had to get past Tosh first.

Tosh pointed at the vidscreen on the desk. "Pull up a chair," he said.

Victor stood a few steps away. "I can see from here."

"Suit yourself. Let's see. You don't seem like the discriminating type when it comes to gender. So, do you like them white, black, brown, yellow, or red?"

Victor felt like smacking Tosh on the back of the head, but he resisted. "They're not crayons. Skin is skin." He looked at the duffel bags. "What is this place really?"

"Don't worry about that. This'll take twenty minutes. We order, they come in, get you off, and maybe the egg opens."

"It's a ridiculous idea. And it's, well, exploitative."

"This is a brothel, dummy. They want to be here, okay? They're happy whores who've got a sweet setup. They get to choose their clients. They live in luxury. They get to spend their time not working however they want, and they fuck for a buck. What's not to love?"

"You don't believe that, do you?" Victor asked.

"How many whores do you know?" Tosh countered.

"None," he admitted.

Tosh shrugged. "So, let's take a look at what's on offer." He drew Victor over to a vidscreen and pulled up the day's menu of flesh. Victor looked at the selection numbly. He would find a way out of here before anything happened.

"Whatever. Them. Hadrian." Victor pointed to a picture on the screen. They had dark brown eyes and jet-black hair. They looked friendly.

"Doesn't that look a little too much like Ozie?" Tosh asked.

"Fuck you."

Tosh confirmed Victor's selection with a tap of his fingers. An automated voice chimed, "Pose for your photograph in three ... two ..." Tosh reached over and pulled Victor onto his lap. "one ..." A bright flash filled the room. To Victor's ears, it sounded like glass breaking. The photograph captured him with his mouth open, a surprised expression on his face.

Tosh laughed. "We might need to retake it."

A chat screen opened with a message from Hadrian. *Are you a jokester?* it read.

Inexperienced and nervous, Tosh typed.

The response came through quickly: *I love popping cherries. Be right there.*

Butterflies flitted in Victor's stomach. He had to nip this in the bud.

Tosh laughed at him. "Are you a virgin?"

"First time with a sex worker, yeah."

Someone knocked on the door.

"Our order's up." Tosh stepped to the door and opened it.

Hadrian stood at the door in a white silk nightgown that dipped in a sharp *V* to reveal a smooth, flat chest. Their hair was pinned up in a bun.

"Good evening." Their voice was soft, playful.

Tosh bowed. "Good evening."

"Hello," Victor said, plotting a route out the door and back to his car.

Hadrian breezed into the room and sat on the edge of the bed, one leg splayed to the side. The hem of their robe fell only to the tops of their thighs. Their fingers ran along one edge of the robe's lacy lining. They smiled, "How would you two like to proceed? Is this a group thing?"

Tosh lifted his hands and smiled. "I'm just a tourist. He's going to do all the work." Tosh nodded at Victor.

They turned to him, their smile deepened, their nostrils flared, and a subtle blush rose in their chest. Their arousal sparkled around the edges of Victor's vision. Electricity rose from his groin and turned into a warm flush when it reached his chest.

They turned their body to him. "This is a treat. I rarely get to work on men under thirty and so handsome."

"How did you, uh, choose this line of work?" Victor asked. He took a few wooden steps toward the door, conscious of pressure building in his pants.

Hadrian ran a hand down their smooth leg. "Who wouldn't want to do this? When I was eighteen, I got the Impulse implant. Love is my drug, as they say. You can come here now."

"See, it's already working," Tosh said, pointing toward Victor's tented pants.

"Now, now, tourist," they said. "No talking during the show."

Victor was startled to discover his feet had crossed the distance toward them. His fingers were reaching out, slipping off Hadrian's robe, and digging into their arms. Hadrian gasped and then growled in satisfaction. They pressed against Victor, paralyzing him with their physicality and warm breath. He sank to his knees. Their scent moved inside him, filling his sinuses. He pressed his mouth on smooth skin where wiry hairs grew below their belly button. He pressed against them, immersed in pleasure. Everything else fell away.

His lips and tongue traced a path down. They rocked back and bowed their legs as a sigh rushed out. Victor continued to explore between their legs, seeking combinations to arouse and surprise. The sounds they made felt like they were coming from his throat, through his mouth. Salt and musk enveloped him.

Hadrian pushed him away and commanded him to undress. Their eyes were haloed with deep-purple fireworks. Victor didn't care that Tosh sat watching them. He hoped Tosh was envious. Victor tore off his shirt as Hadrian worked to unclasp his pants. Victor moaned, his pulse and breath quickening. A buzzing sensation rose from his groin, spreading heat throughout his entire body.

Hadrian stood and pulled Victor close, ushering him in baby steps toward the bed and lowering down. They helped Victor to enter them. He started to undulate, pressing into them, feeling arousal in their breath on his neck. A wave grew as he kept thrusting, approaching orgasm.

"Not like that, sweetie," they instructed. "Not like a machine. Like rain. Here." They rolled 180 degrees, then sat up, pressing down on Victor. "Feel that?" They moved against him slowly, quickened, and changed again. Their body flushed, and he felt them shaking with an orgasm; their cry vibrated as it left their body.

"Now you," they told him breathily.

He rolled onto Hadrian again. He lifted and pressed forward, not following a preconceived rhythm, aiming for slow, sleek thrusts; each new sensation guided him. Sweat formed on his brow and dripped onto their neck. His entire body—his hands and feet, all along his pelvis—heated up and became sublimely sensitive. Ripples moved over him, traveling through his skin and nerves, signaling an incipient euphoria.

Happy, unreserved. Bestial. His hips rose and fell faster, urgently. He saw colors and patterns behind his eyelids—heard a strange, unhappy sound, ignored it—his hands pressed down, his pelvis redoubled its rhythm, pounding harder, coming closer, the wave building.

"Not so fast," Hadrian moaned, though Victor heard it faintly as if it traveled a long distance from their lips to his ears instead of mere centimeters, and he slowed, worried he might come before the wave built even higher. Blankness hovered close, but he ran from it; thrusting seemed to keep it away. He moved spasmodically, chasing the onrushing feeling like an electrical charge building before a thunderstorm.

"Stop!" They beat his chest with their fists. "Can't you hear me?"

"I'm coming," Victor yelled, hoping they felt how he did—bright, pure, hot.

Tosh gripped Victor's arms, pulling him off. He moaned and came suddenly but not pleasurably. His groin surged, and he splattered on the carpet, only he didn't feel the wave. The delicious tension had vanished. He felt only an empty pumping. They'd ruined it. Why?

Victor turned toward them and opened his mouth to ask, but something was wrong. Hadrian sat facing away from him, slouched.

But he didn't understand why. He stood there, not knowing what to say or do. It had been good, hadn't it?

"I don't know where you went, but it wasn't a good place," Hadrian said quietly. "You almost broke my wrists! Damn, I was going to let you come in me. Gets me twice as high."

He had done it again. Hurt somebody without realizing it.

Hadrian started toward the door.

"Wait!" Victor called. "I'm sorry. That was my first time doing it for real. I didn't mean to—"

They turned and stared at him. Victor's saliva had evaporated, leaving his throat sealed by glue.

"Please," he tried again, "I got carried away. I didn't know I was hurting you."

They crossed their arms and leaned against the doorway, scowling at him.

"I'm sorry," he said again, sitting on the bed, looking at the carpet, stained by his ejaculate.

"Pay double, and I won't report it," they said. From the corner of his eye, Victor saw Tosh hand Hadrian their robe. They left and shut the door behind them.

Victor searched for words on the dirty carpet near his naked feet, but he found none. Tosh didn't seem too perturbed by what he had seen, neither aroused or appalled. Why had he let Tosh put him in this position? Was it all a joke to him? Victor felt mortified.

"Well, mission accomplished." Tosh rubbed the data egg across the sticky carpet.

Nothing happened. The data egg stayed locked.

Victor turned away. He'd never felt so alone, but tears wouldn't come. He was as dry as the Arid Lands.

37

Victor lay on his back, immobile, while jets of fire scorched his body and roared in his ears. Heat seared his skin, muscles, and bone. They sloughed off like liquid, caramelized, crisped, and blackened, and finally vaporized and joined the surge of combustible gas flowing through the chamber surrounding him.

The painful dream of suffocating conflagration was familiar. Some details had changed—this time, he was in a small stone chamber, a kind of blast furnace—but the feeling of his body flaring like a match remained the same. In the fire dreams, sometimes he lay atop a pyre with the smell of fresh lumber accompanying the scents of charcoal, ash, scorched bone, and rendered flesh. Other times, he fell down the vast gravity well at the center of the solar system, until the sun's flares vaporized him. When his brain was hyperactive, his dreams repeated several times per night, like a second hand that ticked back and forth, repeating the exact moment over and over.

Tonight, as he lay on the smooth stone, every cell caught fire, chemical bonds ruptured, and electrons split from atomic nuclei. He turned to plasma and dissipated. Everything burned, atomized, and blew away.

Then the second hand ticked backward, and his body reformed.

That wasn't the only way that time behaved strangely in the fire dreams. Time moved forward at different speeds. Sometimes so slow that each electromagnetic pulse in his nerves lasted as long as a relaxed breath; sometimes so fast that the entire dream lasted for the blink of an eye. The fire dreams were a cycle of disintegration and reformation. His body vaporized, time reversed, the chemical bonds of his cells reassembled, and his body reformed. Then, time's arrow resumed its path forward, and he burned and died. Again and again. The infernal torture wasn't real, and he knew he would wake up unburned. But his real life seemed far away and as illusory as dreams seem during wakefulness.

The fire faded, darkness returned, and Victor shook, turning onto his side, legs juddering against the soaked blankets covering him. He smelled bitter grass oozing from his pores as he wiped sweat away from his brow. Turning onto his back, Victor stared at the ceiling, at nothing. He was useless. Worse, he was hurtful and out of control.

He shouldn't have let Tosh pressure him; therapy should have kept him from making such loony mistakes. He'd not, it seemed, come very far at all in managing his condition. All of Dr. Tammet's therapy amounted to gimmicks. All Granfa Jeff's lessons were lost on Victor's misbehaving brain.

On the other side of the darkened room, Tosh snored so loudly that Victor thought the man's skull might implode. Victor wanted to hold a pillow over his mouth. If he couldn't control himself, he could at least control the people he surrounded himself with. Tosh was bad through and through. He should have seen that earlier. He wouldn't trust him anymore.

And Elena. What should he do about Elena? She wanted to help him, she said, but that wasn't all. Something was driving her, some motivation she might not understand any more than he understood. And that imperfect knowledge might get him captured or killed.

Victor tossed and turned, fretting, unable to decide.

Semiautomous California
8 December 1984

On a foggy winter day when Victor was sixteen and in his final year of high school, Granfa Jeff brought him over to the hills of the San Francisco Peninsula. Moisture swirled over the bay. Eucalyptus trees swayed in the wind, dropping their seeds and acidic pungency. There were no crowds at the expansive private menagerie back then. In 1984, only members of the Zoological Society could visit.

Victor was grateful for the opportunity to get out of school. His parents didn't understand the strength of MRS stigma. How could they? It hadn't existed when they were his age. They believed he needed "exposure" and "socialization" and "the benefits of mingling with young people." The combination of Cathar good vs. evil values, European social engineering, the invisible influence of the Mesh, and good old-fashioned fear created conditions that were nearly unlivable for people with MRS. If he could ever find a way to explain what he put up with daily, it would horrify them.

He and Granfa Jeff went first to the Africa Zone and wandered between the lairs of rhinoceroses, elephants, giraffes, and other exotic species. Rich, funky, tangled smells wafted from the enclosures. Further on, Zoo Ranger Mikke, a tall man who had a slight limp and a dark beard that wrapped from ear to ear, met them at the penguin exhibit. He wore canvas shorts, despite the cold. In a thick Northern League accent of melodic vowels and soft glottal explosions, the ranger thanked Jefferson for a recent gift to the zoo for primate research. He said to Victor, "I bet you're wondering how one hundred chimpanzees from halfway around the world ended up here?"

The ranger smiled wide. It reminded Victor of a gluttonous cartoon bear known for scooping up rainbow trout by the handful and eating them whole. Victor nodded, flushed by the ranger's attention.

Ranger Mikke asked Jefferson, "Did you know Sir Louis Bradley?"

Granfa Jeff stopped walking. "Of course. A brilliant man. His accomplishments are astounding, especially considering that they happened behind the green line."

Victor knew Rhodesia was diplomatically isolated from the international community, even as it fed the global black market diamonds, platinum, gold, and, most importantly, rare earth minerals—the only alternative to the Organized Western States' near-monopoly.

"Why is there a green line?" Victor asked.

Granfa Jeff shook his head. "It's a long story that begins with the beheading of the king of Rhodesia. Another time." He turned to Ranger Mikke. "About my proposal ..."

Victor sensed a boring conversation about money looming, so he broke away and walked to an enclosure where a pride of lions lazed together, sharing their warmth. He wanted to squeeze through the bars and cuddle them, nuzzling into their fur. Too bad he couldn't feed them Personil to ensure they stayed calm.

Victor overheard Ranger Mikke saying something about chimpanzees. "Yes, we could do it here with enough resources and time to grow the population."

Victor turned around, curious to know if *that* was what this trip was about. *Was Granfa Jeff going to invest in the zoo's expansion?* The business of the Holistic Healing Network was always a kind of background noise to their conversations. He remained fuzzy on the details, but he didn't care, since he didn't expect to ever get deeply involved in the family business. One needed a solid background in finance or medicine. However, running a zoo might be fun before MRS and eventual catatonia did him in.

"We can discuss the details later," Granfa said. "I appreciate your discretion."

Victor had noticed Granfa's habit of withholding information, compartmentalizing, and sharing only the minimum necessary tidbits to get what he wanted in return, but Victor had assumed it was a natural inclination not to involve children, especially one as troubled as he was, in the business of adults. Looking back, after dealing with the fallout of secrets compounded with lies and misdirection, Victor wondered what else Granfa had been hiding, whether he traded in misinformation, and if the myth of the man whose brilliance bestowed gifts upon humanity was intended to cover up a darker, more complicated truth.

The ranger, Granfa, and Victor resumed walking and soon arrived at a blocky modernist building. Inside, beyond a small reception area crowded with potted plants, brightly colored carpets traced paths through a maze of desks and cubicles. The paintings and pictures on the walls resembled classic works of art but with monkeys and apes instead of humans. The one nearest to Victor showed a female bonobo reclining on a stone bench as a group of males fought over her. Tacky.

Victor and his granfa followed the ranger to a room with a few vidscreens, a MeshTerminal, and a large window. Beyond the glass, a chimpanzee—a muscular, hairy, and slack-breasted female—snacked on some grapes hanging in bunches from a padded scaffolding rig. The chimpanzee glanced up occasionally but never fixed her eyes on the observers—a one-way glass.

Ranger Mikke placed his hand on Victor's shoulder, a too-familiar gesture for someone he had just met for the first time, yet Victor felt heat moving into his shoulder and, surprisingly, didn't mind.

"That's Sofie," Range Mikke said, pointing through the glass at the chimpanzee. "You're going to go meet her in a moment. She's thirteen; a young person, like you. She loves puzzles. We give her the most complicated ones, and she always impresses us. We thought she would be a good first experience for you."

"Good experience? What am I supposed to do?"

Granfa Jeff said, "We're going to observe your interactions. We're only beginning to understand how great apes perceive and communicate. We also want to observe you. It may help us discover certain aspects of your cognitive process."

Victor bristled. He and the chimpanzee had something in common already. They were both being scrutinized.

"You mean you want to find out what's wrong with me. Do I have to wear one of those helmets?" Since his diagnosis, he had spent lots of time at Oak Knoll with a heavy bucket on his head to measure his brain activity.

"No, this is purely about observing behavior," Ranger Mikke said. "Let's introduce you."

Victor had second thoughts. "Is Dr. Tammet here?"

Granfa Jeff said, "No, Victor. We disagreed about the need for this particular experiment."

His granfa hadn't let him down yet, so Victor followed the ranger while his granfa stayed glued to the one-way glass. *Now I'm the show. Boy meets ape; merriment ensues.*

Victor stood inside the closed door as Ranger Mikke moved deeper into Sofie's enclosure. She met him halfway and gave him a humanlike hug, hooting and patting. She seemed to think she was friends with the ranger. *A massive case of Stockholm syndrome*, Victor thought. Although, if she was born inside, how would she ever know she lived in a prison?

Ranger Mikke took one of Sofie's hands and slowly led her closer. Unlike her caretaker's contained gait, hers rolled from side to side. "Sofie, this is Victor. I want you to say hello."

The sides of her mouth pulled apart, revealing giant teeth. She watched Victor with her nut-brown eyes and made a quick gesture with her fingers. Wrinkled skin piled around her face, rising in unfamiliar contours. Her gaze passed over him, and her mouth worked, compressing and extending. Victor half expected her to speak.

"Can you shake hands?" the ranger asked both of them. Victor thrust his hand out, nobly attempting to bridge the gap between species. Not that it would do any good. The intellectual gap between apes and people was too wide. The experiment was a joke.

Sofie's large eyes looked at Victor's hand and then his face. She hissed. Before Victor could pull his hand away, she slapped it to the side hard enough to make it sting. Her flat, worn teeth were visible in her dark mouth as she screamed at him. Victor stumbled back into the wall, plugging his ears, while echoes of her cries faded gradually. The ranger tried calming Sofie, but she shrugged off his attempts and hissed at him.

Victor bolted from the room. In the hallway, Granfa Jeff grabbed his arm. "We'll wait a few minutes and try again."

"I want to go. She doesn't like me." Humiliation churned in his stomach. Still, there was something comical about it. Rejected by a chimpanzee. He must be the least likable primate on the planet.

"You didn't give her the chance. Hers was a natural reaction to your hostility."

"I wasn't hostile."

"Come here."

His granfa led him to a set of vidscreens. He activated a spectrum relay, and an image of Victor's face expanded to fill the vidscreen.

"Look here." His granfa pointed, tracing Victor's brow, eyes, and lips. "I'll advance the feed slowly so you can see from when you entered the room until she slapped your hand. This expression—your lips are compressed, nose slightly scrunched, brow furrowed—is a blend of anger, contempt, and fear. When you offered your hand, she saw it in that context, arm thrusting out like so. To her, it was a challenge."

"So?"

"You were projecting negative emotions, and Sofie registered them."

"I wasn't thinking, 'Hey, chimp, let's fight,'" Victor said.

"It doesn't matter. You may not have been thinking about it consciously. What you were feeling was written all over your face."

Victor looked away. To not be aware of his own emotions and yet to succeed in broadcasting them to everyone in sight—it was like living in an inside-out body, wearing organs like clothes, and walking around oblivious to others' screams of horror. People called that "normal socializing." It gave him chills.

Victor said, "A chimpanzee with empathetic superpowers. What's next? Cats in space? Or are you saying she's a Broken Mirror, too?"

"I know you're upset, but think for a moment. What does this experience tell us?"

Victor bit back another remark about him being so monstrous he couldn't make friends with animals. His granfa was giving him a chance to use and demonstrate his intellect, so he shouldn't waste it, especially before his next dose of Personil returned his mind to dullsville.

"I need to control my expressions," he said, "so I don't get into trouble."

His granfa shook his head. "That comes later, and it's an imperfect skill. Even the most skilled, con men struggle to keep their true feelings from peeking through. The lesson is more fundamental than that."

Victor looked at the ceiling, replaying the encounter in his mind. He had walked in, following the zookeeper, observing Sofie. She had greeted the man, followed him, looked at Victor, at his hand and his face—*That's it!* She had *examined* him.

"She read me; she read my emotions."

His granfa nodded. "Precisely. And what does that mean?"

"It's a process, a procedure. Like taking a measurement."

"Go on."

"If she can read emotions like this, then I should be able to as well."

"You've almost got it. This process is automatic, almost unconscious. People pick up on these signs and interpret them without being aware of them. Your special challenge is that this input is not modulated. Your inhibitory circuits aren't up to the task, so you're living in the reverberations of other peoples' emotions and your own commingled. I believe you can moderate your responses. You don't have to surrender to them. It's a skill that can be learned. Moreover, I believe you can have influence. A soft hand, a warm gaze—your power could be tenfold."

Victor felt his eyes widen. After a moment, he asked, "I'll be able to read people without automatically, you know, *feeling* them?" He didn't say the corollary out loud—that maybe he could make people feel things. It felt too wild, too speculative, too much like a path toward retribution for how he'd been treated.

Granfa Jeff rubbed Victor's back. "Think of the insights you have access to, to be conscious of the emotional states and relationships among a group of people, which others intuit but don't necessarily understand. I believe a career in diplomacy could be quite fitting."

Victor looked again through the glass, and in Sofie's face, he now saw not a collection of hostile features but a forest of signs and signals that needed to be decoded.

"I want to learn how."

Organized Western States
8 March 1991

It was four a.m. Tosh was still snoring next to Victor in the adjacent bed.

Victor should never have come to the brothel. Tosh was a bad influence. Although Elena had deceived Victor, she'd also helped him stay sane. The incident with Hadrian would never have happened while Elena was looking after him. And, he admitted, he missed her. He couldn't just leave her and move on. He had to hear her side of the story.

Victor knew it was time to confront some hard truths. He squeezed the Handy 1000 and spoke Ozie's name, squeezing again to confirm the feed request. The device chimed.

"Ozie," he said. "You've been lying to me."

"No, I have—"

"Stop. When I asked you to open the data egg, you said it was impossible. Then, when you needed me to get the gene libraries, you promised to open it. But you can't do it, can you?"

There was a long pause. "I only said I would try," Ozie said. "I think it's keyed to open in response to your brain patterns."

Finally, the truth. "So, you can't help me?"

"Mapping a mountain is different from climbing it. We don't know which patterns will open it."

"You should have told me. Focusing on brain patterns helps avoid awkward situations."

"Such as?"

"Never mind. Now, Ozie, I've got some truth to share with you, too. How's that analysis program coming along?"

Ozie hesitated. "The libraries are here." Victor heard the sound of typing. "I'm, uh, I'm having trouble initializing your program."

Victor closed his eyes and allowed himself a prideful smile. "Yes, I know. It's locked."

"What?"

"Do as I say, or I won't unlock the program."

"For fuck's sake. We're on the same side, Victor!"

"There aren't any sides."

"Hang on." A low hum came through the sonofeed's speakers. Victor pictured Ozie wearing his brain cap with its ceramic knobs and penetrating magnets. "What do you want?" Ozie asked.

"Tell me everything you know about my granfa's murder."

"We've talked about this, Vic."

"No, you've talked *around* it. You're keeping things from me in case you need to use them against me down the line. What do you know?"

Ozie whistled, an eerie sound suggestive of the windy desert plains outside. Then he started talking. Most of it was the same information he'd disclosed in dribs and drabs: Jefferson Eastmore had come to Ozie for help programming the data egg and to learn about brainhacking. The SeCa Health Board's Classification Commission was to be the model for legislation elsewhere, yet Jefferson had stood in its way. Once he was gone, the Board's plan steamrolled ahead. Jefferson had put Ozie in touch with Pearl, and they exchanged secure messages to plan for an alternative system of care for SeCans with MRS. Ozie also paid attention to Jefferson's movements over the last few months of his life, noting where he went by the digital traces he left in the Mesh.

Victor's ears perked up when Ozie mentioned Oak Knoll.

Ozie explained, "I wish I'd gotten inside HHN before Oak Knoll closed. By the time I got your help, after the merger, it was too late. Here's the big news: you mentioned a compound to me before, a possible cure, remember?"

Victor thought for a moment. "It was XSCT-19900032."

"Right, well, there are no records of it within BioScan. We searched Oak Knoll, and there's nothing left. That's what Jefferson tasked Tosh with."

Victor looked at Tosh asleep on the bed beside him, reeking of sweat.

"I got to thinking about records," Ozie continued. "Usually, they have a converse duplicate."

"A what?"

"Let's say I issue an invoice to you. You've got to issue a purchase order or pay using a MeshCreditLine. A clever digital snoop can match the amounts, names, or some information tying them together. Or if you send me a feed request, it shows up in your sent queue and my incoming queue. Most communications are transactional and leave a converse duplicate. Send, receive; debit, credit. If the compound doesn't show up inside BioScan, maybe it'll show up somewhere else. Somewhere your pal couldn't reach during his purge."

Victor stared at the dark ceiling. "That's like sifting sand on a beach."

"I'm not sifting through years of data. I narrowed it to a few months before and after Jefferson closed the hospital. And because I knew about the compound, I knew what I was looking for."

"And?" Pulling information out of Ozie was next to impossible. Maybe Victor should try again when he was back at the Springboard Café, using a shockstick.

"I found something interesting," Ozie said.

"What?" he asked. Despite every way that Ozie was manipulating him, Victor still hoped something good might come from them working together.

"It might be nothing."

Victor put a hand on his brow. "What is it?"

"Of course, it also might be something."

"Just fucking tell me!"

Tosh sat up, quick as a spring, finally awake, and looked around. "Who is that?"

"Ozie," Victor said over his shoulder.

"I'm here. It seems Jefferson made a trip to Texas right after a cold storage shipment to the same place, two days after Oak Knoll closed. It looks to me like something was *moved* and had to be kept chilled, and he wanted to be there when it arrived."

"What was moved? To where?"

"According to the record, that Compound XSCT was delivered to the Lone Star Kennel & Spa in Amarillo, Republic of Texas. I looked into it, of course, and uncovered a few interesting facts. You want to hear them?"

Tosh stretched, got up, and stood next to Victor. "What's he going on about?"

Victor shushed him. "Yes," he said, huddling over the Handy 1000.

Ozie continued, "One: Jefferson owns the kennel, or he owned it. It was sold to a man named Mason Charter."

Victor nodded to himself. "I know Mason. He and my granfa were—well, I guess you'd say they were rivals and friends at the same time. But why would granfa have owned a kennel?"

Ozie said, "That's not all. Two: There's one name on the employee roster that can't fail to ring some alarm bells."

Victor gripped the rolled-up Handy 1000, trying to avoid squeezing it into fragments. "What name?"

"Hector Morales. Elena's father."

Organized Western States
8 March 1991

"Are you alone?" Victor asked.

"No." Elena's voice was tense over the Mesh connection.

"Can they hear me?"

"No." Less certainly, she said, "I don't think so. Their names are Lucky and Bandit. They won't say who they're working for."

"I want to understand why you lied to me. And I need your help. And my things."

"Anything you want." She sounded ready to burst into tears. He didn't think she was faking, but it was hard to tell without seeing her face. "Where can I meet you?"

"There's a clockface at the center of Grand Park. Can you get there alone?"

"Probably not. But I—I have the souvenir from the institute."

Souvenir? Victor thought she meant the data leech at first and worried that she'd sabotaged his plans yet again, but then he remembered her shockstick.

"Tell them to stay back while we talk, or I won't show up," he said.

"I didn't know, Victor. I thought I was helping."

"Midnight," Victor said and terminated the feed.

The rented room at the brothel had a back patio facing a tall mountain. Shadows smeared deep chalk-art hues of lavender and rust across the rocky heights.

Tosh grimaced at Victor. "Big risk," he said.

"I need to know the truth."

"Could have asked her right then."

Victor wanted to see her face, to know if she regretted lying to him. "If Elena's father is involved, we'll need her help to get him to talk."

"What's going to keep them from scooping you up?"

"You, if you're any good."

Tosh poked Victor's shoulder. "I'm not your personal bodyguard. My interest in you only goes as far as revenge for Jeff's murder."

Victor had no illusions about their relationship. He was a pawn in Tosh's game, helpless and easily manipulated. "I wonder. Seems like you're going to a lot of trouble for the sake of loyalty."

Tosh said, "You can think what you like. Nobody has pure motives. Not even you." Tosh pulled out an ArmorGuard SecondSkin and slipped it over his torso. Only his head and hands were exposed. "Gotta keep moving forward, Victor. That's the secret. When the egg opens, we'll know."

It seemed absurd that the data egg meant so much to him. Loyalty and friendship were currencies Victor didn't understand. He was sure Tosh had ulterior motives, but who could guess what they were?

Victor said, "If *we* discover anything, it'll be because of me."

Tosh stepped closer. He was five centimeters taller than Victor and tanklike, but Victor stood his ground. They were going to do this his way or not at all.

"You look anxious," Tosh said. "Are you keeping something from me?" One eye narrowed skeptically.

Ozie had unknowingly taught Victor the basics of manipulation: provide enough information to get what you want, but hold back the truth, let it slip in dribs and drabs, and string everyone along to get what you want. Elena had also taught him how to lie with half-truths. He'd need to use both to get what he wanted from Tosh.

"I'll tell you everything if you keep those thugs off me long enough to get my things back. We'll meet here afterward, and I swear to tell you the whole story."

A half smile spread over Tosh's face, but his eyes were hard. "You better."

Victor nodded. "How will you hold them off if they try to grab me?"

"That's my business. But if you see smoke, run away from it."

38

The model of Las Vegas was a city within a city within a city. At the center of Grand Park stood a large circular stone platform. The avenues, parks, and buildings of Las Vegas were depicted in miniature on its surface. At the center of the platform was a saucer-sized representation of Grand Park with a millimeter-diameter engraving of the stone platform. Within the engraving, it was said, was a nanoscale representation of the city, the park, and the stone platform.

From where Victor stood below, he saw knots of people strolling, laughing, and pointing at details in the miniature city. He spotted Elena scowling at tourists taking pictures in front of their favorite o'clock. He didn't see Lucky and Bandit, but he was sure they were nearby.

Victor stepped into Elena's path. She moved toward him as if to embrace him, but he held up a finger to ward her off.

"How long do you think before they try to grab me?" he asked.

"Five minutes, tops. I told them I could get you to come willingly."

"Tell me why you came to SeCa," he said.

She sighed and seemed to sink. "Your ma contacted me."

"What?" He hadn't expected that.

"She found me is more like it. I was using again, hard. The Puros had kicked me out. I was living in a shithole with some squatters. Linda called and told me you needed help. She said she'd help me if I helped you. I got clean at a clinic in New Venice. The Puros agreed to take me back. I was arranging everything, staying clean, mostly. Then your granfa died, and I flew west early."

"So you were spying on me from the start?"

"I was helping. Your ma said you'd been spiraling since Oak Knoll closed. Then Lucky and Bandit found me, called themselves freelancers. They said they were going to watch you when I couldn't. It all seemed legitimate. They said your family hired them. They knew all about you. But when you found the polonium, I started to have doubts. I stayed in touch with them only to learn more. Something didn't feel right. I tried to get them to back off. I don't know how they found us. I swear. It wasn't me."

"You met them at the hotel."

"They called me, so I came down. That's the truth. You have to believe me. I wanted to tell you, but I was afraid. I thought I could do it all myself."

Victor examined her face. Fuzzy peach honesty blended with sour yellow regrets. He did believe her. She made mistakes. Should have told him everything much sooner; keeping secrets to help him hurt instead. But he knew she wanted what was best for him. Besides, he wasn't going to give up on a friend. She was walking a tightrope as much as he was. Maybe they could steady each other and find the sanctuary of firm ground.

Dozens of people wandered across the stone platform. Lucky and Bandit, whoever they really were, wouldn't want to risk so public a kidnapping, but Victor and Elena couldn't stand around talking forever. "What do they want?" he asked Elena.

Tears formed in her eyes. "I don't know. When they took the herbalist, I assumed they were from the Health Board, but they aren't, are they? Do you think they killed Jefferson?"

"I don't know. Ozie doesn't think so. Do you have all my stuff?"

She patted a bag hanging from her shoulder. "Yes," she said. "I had to smoke with them to get them to trust me. I swear I didn't want to, though I guess another part of me did." Elena looked up at him, blinking. "What do we do now?"

"Get ready to run. My car is nearby."

"You want me to come with you?"

Victor nodded.

She hugged him fiercely. "I'm so sorry. No more secrets, I promise."

Victor took out his Handy 1000 and pressed two buttons. One activated a feed to Tosh, the other to his car.

"I'm taking you home," Victor said.

"Home?" she asked.

Three clattering metal balls rolled across the platform and spewed smoke, clouding the air. The crowd panicked, shouted, and scattered. Victor hauled Elena by the arm, following the five o'clock radian.

"Come on," he yelled. "Try not to breathe."

Screams echoed behind them as they ran past the stone platform and continued along gravel paths that crunched beneath their feet. Victor ran as fast as he could, counting on Elena to keep up. He didn't look back. He didn't want to know if Tosh or the two "freelancers" were gaining on them. He climbed a set of stairs, crossed a bridge over a dry flood-control channel, and descended to a street. He saw his car ahead.

A sharp pain in his back felt like a pulled muscle. He stumbled but stayed on his feet and kept moving forward. He reached around, and his hand encountered cool metal that fell away when he brushed it. His head grew foggy.

Elena caught up with him. "Almost there. Keep going," she said.

Haze descended, but he kept pumping his legs, letting her guide him forward. He felt himself tumble and was surprised to land in one of his car's clipped velour seats.

"Texas," he mumbled. "Get us to Texas."

The heavy weight of sleep pulled him down into blackness.

39

"Wake up," Elena said.

Victor opened his eyes. The road was uneven, making the vehicle rock and sway. "Where are we?"

The map put them only thirty kilometers from the border with the Republic of Texas. The autopilot was slowing their vehicle to avoid a collision. Blocking the road were two spidery vehicles with massive black struts connecting the passenger cabins to the axles and sitting on oversized wheels.

They came to a halt thirty meters from the roadblock, the autopilot giving them plenty of room.

"Are you okay?" Elena asked.

Victor shivered to wake himself. "I think so. We escaped?"

Elena nodded. "You took a sleep jabber to the back. We zigzagged through the city for hours to make sure they didn't know which way we left. Things were fine until ..." She jutted her chin toward the vehicles on the road. "This isn't good."

"Who do you think they are?" he asked.

"Doesn't matter. Who do *they* think they are?" She adjusted her seat from reclined to upright. "Probably Corps looking for some AU dollars."

Behind them, dusty hills. Ahead, the giant spider buggies blocked both lanes and shoulders of the road, beyond which a gradual decline led down to the flat tumbleweed-and-dirt desert.

"Maybe they just want to talk," he said.

Elena looked at him, and they both started laughing.

"If they're Corps," she said, "all they care about is money and drugs. Best-case scenario, they want a bribe. Worst case, they've been warned about us and want to take us prisoner. Worst, worst case is they're unaffiliated—they take everything and leave us to die."

"That's reassuring."

The doors on both sides of one of the vehicles in front of them swung upward; instead of spiders, the vehicles now resembled black wasps. A man and a woman used handholds and foot ledges to descend to the road. The woman's purple spiky hair and close-shaved sides of her head reminded Victor of a felt-tip pen. The man wore a wide-brimmed hat and a long coat that would be sweltering unless it had cooling packs sewn into the lining. He might be carrying live animals inside the coat, for all Victor knew. The pair walked toward them slowly. At least they weren't Lucky and Bandit.

Elena unclipped her seat belt and reached for the door handle.

"What are you doing?" Victor grabbed her knee.

She smiled crookedly as she detached his hand. "How sweetly protective. I'm going to talk to them. If I signal with my hands, come rescue me. Don't hesitate to run them over."

Elena got out of the car and turned back toward him. "You've got collision sensors on this thing?"

"Yes, of course, but—"

"Turn them off."

Elena stepped away and left the door open. Hot air seeped in. Victor turned the chiller off to save fuel, and the thin sweat coating on his body instantly turned into a flash flood. The couple had stopped about twenty meters away and waited for Elena to approach. She greeted them, placed her hands on her hips, and swiveled left and right, miming a sore back. The woman said something, but Victor couldn't hear. Elena pointed at the spider buggies and then back the way they had come. The three started to approach Victor. Victor dictated a quick message to Ozie, "Stopped at the ROT border."

Elena climbed into the passenger seat and whispered, "Get ready. I don't believe for a second what they're telling me."

The woman bent toward Victor's window and pointed at his device. "What's that?"

Victor said, "I'm trying to find—"

"It's like I said." Elena leaned toward the couple standing outside and affected a Texan accent. "We meant to head south after Las Vegas. Turns out this road heads nowhere we want to be."

The man bent over and placed his hands on his knees. His scruffy and oil-stained face scrunched. "Don't matter where you're headed. Noncitizens got to pay the exit fee. So says the Diamond King."

Elena said, "But if we're not leaving this way, we should pay another checkpoint, right? We'll just turn around."

"You'll pay us. Pay them too, most likely," the woman said. A silver nose ring glinted. Her ears carried at least twenty more pieces of polished jewelry.

Victor doubted they were enforcing a legitimate toll. An actual checkpoint would have signs. This was just a gang of thugs.

"How much is the fee?" Victor asked. The amount he was sweating made him look suspicious. He reached toward the steering disk's panel to turn on the chiller, but the man's arm shot into the car and pinned Victor to his seat.

"Just settle down for a sec," the man said. "The fee's three hundred. Make it two if you throw in that fancy thing in your lap."

Victor felt a surge in his gut. "That's not—"

"I got three hundred right here." Elena reached into her bag, which she had wedged protectively between her ankles.

The woman said, "Think you might have more than three in there. We'll take five and the Mesh thingy." She waved toward Victor's crotch.

A film of slick rage infiltrated his brain. He slipped his hand into his pocket and pulled out a vial of fumewort tincture, popping the cap with his thumb. He poured its contents straight down his throat. *Calm. Controlled. Breathe.*

"What's that? Drugs?" the man asked. "We'll take that too."

"It's medicine," Elena said.

Victor imagined bashing the roadblocker's skull against the hot desert road until his eyes popped from their sockets.

"Victor, calm down," Elena said. "Look at me. Look at me."

He turned. Her gaze flicked downward toward the curve of her thigh, behind which hid a Dirac shockstick. The kind Samuel had used in Carmichael, illegal in SeCa, a debilitating weapon in the hands of his friend. *Do I know her at all?*

"We'll just give them what they want"—her hand jiggled the weapon—"and then we'll *go*."

"Tell you what," the woman said, "we'll just take everything."

Victor's gut sank into his seat, but he wore a mask of calm resolve. He turned toward the pair and whispered, "You can try."

The two extorters bent forward to hear him better. Victor snapped his seat back. Elena fired the shockstick, hitting the man in his face. Dirac forces played on his nerves as he growled, drooled, and jerked.

Victor slammed his hands on the steering disk, and the car barreled forward, barely missing the woman. In the side mirror, Victor saw her dig in her pocket and launch what looked like a stone in the air after him.

He accelerated to maximum throttle.

A thunk hit the top of the car, denting the roof, and thunder exploded above them. Flames bloomed in every direction, followed by smoke, and suddenly, Victor couldn't see anything. A wave of heat overcame him, though he wasn't sure if it was the explosion or adrenaline.

They left the cloud of smoke in time to see the edge of the road approaching, and it passed underneath them as they bounced roughly downward through desert scrub, and their tires dug tracks into the dry dirt.

Victor looked at Elena, glad to see her conscious. She pointed toward a pair of giant cacti. He steered hard left, clipping them with his right mirror.

Back on the elevated road, one spider buggy turned to follow. Purple hair was climbing into the other. Victor sped faster. The vehicle bucked and rocked over the uneven desert floor. Ahead, a natural ramp rose to meet the road, and he accelerated toward it. They reached the road with a gut-wrenching leap and violent touchdown.

"Great job," Elena said. "But now they've got us."

The spider buggies were behind them, closing the gap.

"This is what Ozie warned us about. We're prepared," he said.

He reached down to the control panel the Springboard Café mechanics had installed and pressed all three buttons. In the rearview, he saw thick sludge spread across the road. Tiny flashes of metal glittered in the car's wake, and haze spewed from the tailpipe. Victor accelerated the car to the maximum.

One spider buggy broke through the cloud, speeding at an angle toward the side of the road. When it reached the shoulder, it dipped and wobbled, flipped, and spiraled end over end across the desert. They never saw the second vehicle emerge from the smoke.

Elena reached up to a fist-sized dent in the ceiling and ran her fingers across it. "Fire grenade," she said. "We're lucky the blast deflected upward. Are you okay?"

Victor realized he was hunched forward, straining every muscle. Checking the rearview and finding nothing, he restarted the autopilot and let the car take them onward. He started to feel the calming effects of fumewort.

"I guess that's where the saying comes from," Elena said.

"What?"

"No one leaves Vegas easy."

40

I used to feel ignored, stepped on, and brushed aside. I'd give anything to return to those days. Now, I feel an invisible force pushing me forward. Nothing I do or say can change its course. I'm not saying it's not my fault, but I couldn't have foreseen what would happen.

—Victor Eastmore, *Apology to Resonant Earth*, (transmission date unknown)

Republic of Texas
8 March 1991

When Victor and Elena drew close to Lone Star Kennel outside Amarillo, the sun had disappeared below the horizon before they pulled to the side of the road. Light towers blazed around the kennel, illuminating polished buildings that looked out of place in the midst of fallow fields. A dry creek bed lined by tall, wispy trees cut across the sparsely vegetated plain. Several black, insect-shaped vehicles were parked in front, and people clad in battle gear swarmed the building.

Elena placed a call on her MeshBit. "Mamá? It's me, yes. Is Papá all right? What's going on at his work?"

Victor heard Maria's high and tinny voice coming from the MeshBit. "Elena? What's wrong?"

"Where's Papá?"

"He's here, with me, at home. Are you—"

"Oh, thank the Laws."

"Elena—"

"I'll call you back." Elena terminated the feed.

Victor nodded at the men and women flanking the kennel doors. "Who do you think they are?"

"Corps, no question," Elena said. "We'll never get in. Are you sure Ozie isn't trying to trap you?"

"He wouldn't do that."

"I hate to say it, Victor, but you're not the best judge of character."

He blinked. It was hard to judge someone's character when they lied with every breath. But now wasn't the time to argue with her. "Ozie wants to find the truth as badly as I do."

Elena gestured at the scene in front of them. "We're not getting in there without help. I count Corps, armed, and there could be more inside."

"Maybe your papá can tell us what's going on."

"I don't want to involve him."

Victor gestured toward the kennel. "He's already involved. Let's just find out what he knows."

Elena took a breath. "Okay. But it's going to be awkward."

As she leaned over and programmed an address into the steering disk, he noticed that her hair smelled of sweat. He was pretty ripe, too, actually. The car turned around and headed back into town. They passed old ranch homes on large lots, entered a more compact subdivision, and soon arrived in front of a house with a porch wrapped around both sides. The car parked itself on the street, and they got out. Victor shuffled behind Elena and followed her inside the Morales family's house.

His shoulder caught on the frame as he passed through the front door.

Elena grabbed his arm to steady him. "Are you okay?"

"Yeah. I'm rationing my fumewort, and I'm starving," he said, not surprised that his body was starting to twist away from his control.

"Me too," Elena said.

The scents of garlic, ginger, and other spices filled the humid house. Elena's ma, Maria, bounced around the kitchen, preparing at least six dishes simultaneously. Her hair was tucked beneath a bright yellow knitted hat, and her face was heavily made up in brilliant streaks of color—reds, purples, and black—that reminded Victor of the canyon walls on the outskirts of Las Vegas.

"Mamá," Elena said, standing timidly in the doorway.

"*Dios mío*! Look who's back." Rather than doting on Elena, Maria pointed at her daughter. "We need to talk, Elena Martina Morales. First, take this outside á Papá y tu abuela." She acknowledged Victor with a nod and sent them to the back porch with a pitcher of iced tea and glasses.

"'We need to talk'?" Victor whispered.

Elena whispered back. "She doesn't want to show how much she's missed me. I stole money from my parents when I was stimming. They're still mad, I bet. And ashamed."

Beyond the porch, there were no fences. Rather, a large common area between houses had been turned into a community garden. Long shadows stretched across the yard, spreading like purple inkblots between loops of lightstrips. The shadows moved and curled like thick, dark tentacles. Victor rubbed his eyes and heard squeaking and rustling sounds. Great—he'd have to deal with Elena's family through a haze of synesthesia. He needed food, sleep, and a good dose of medicine, but with dwindling fumewort and bitter grass supplies, he would have to settle for two out of three.

Elena's pa, Hector, and her abuela, Julia, lounged on a wicker sofa. Hector had wild black hair, as if he'd never met a comb, and a slow-shifting gaze that made him appear perpetually lost. Julia, on the other hand, had a hard stare and a quick tongue that was always ready to give a verbal lashing. Her gray hair was gathered in a tight ponytail.

Hector jumped up when he saw Elena and rushed over, wrapping his arms around her tightly. "Where have you been?"

"*Hola*, Papá."

He held her at arm's length, and his gaze played over her face, inquiring. "We were worried."

"I'm fine. You remember Victor."

"Hello," Victor said. The sound of his voice alarmed him; it was hoarse and unsteady. The less he said, the better.

Hector shot a concerned glance in Victor's direction that felt like a gut punch. Julia, who was never a woman to waste words, even on politeness, nodded grimly to Victor. His skin chilled.

Victor started to lose his grip on the tray. "Elena, the glasses," he said, panicking. She steadied him, and, working together, they poured the iced tea and sat on the wicker couch in the gloom. The tea tasted strongly of cinnamon and something he couldn't place. The lightstrips buzzed, and the tentacle-shadows writhed.

"The police broke the ceasefire today," Julia announced. "Two Puros dead. But I guess they deserved it."

Victor expected Elena to shoot back something sarcastic like, "Nice to see you too, Abuela."

Instead, she looked out at the yard. Victor imagined he heard her teeth grinding together, and then, looking more closely, he realized that they were.

After a moment, Elena turned to Julia and said, "I'm sure they didn't deserve to be murdered."

"Good riddance," Julia said.

Hector and Elena both opened their mouths, shocked, but neither spoke.

Julia continued, "They are terrorists! No one feels safe anymore while they run about, doing as they please. They should be put down and—"

"Abuela!" Elena slammed her glass down and tea sloshed onto the table.

With quiet heat, Elena said, "It's a social justice movement, Abuela. They started farm collectives, joint savings banks, education funds, and anti-narcotics patrols. I mean, from what I've heard, there wasn't much of a government in ROT at the time, was there?"

"Still isn't one worth paying taxes to," Julia said. "I don't need your lecture about the past, Nieta. And you mind your manners. It's been months since you paid us a visit, and we know why. Don't make me regret allowing you back here."

"Mamá! That's enough," Hector pleaded.

Elena wiped her wet palm on her pants. "I'm just saying the Puros don't go looking for fights, so the police must be to blame. You don't see them arresting Corps, do you?"

Victor put a hand on her shoulder. She sounded ready to snap.

"Get rid of them all! Half your generation turns to drugs, thanks to the Corps, while the other half adopts that purity mumbo-jumbo. Kids should study, work, and start families like they used to. I assume that's why she dragged *you* here?" Julia looked at Victor, expecting a response. He almost laughed at how cruel she was being; it was absurd. He shook his head and fought back a wave of nausea. Of all the bad synesthetic effects he'd experienced, nausea was the least desirable. If he stayed perfectly still, the feeling might pass. Elena seemed to register his discomfort.

Hector cleared his throat. "I also overheard that the Puros found a new cause."

"What are you talking about?" Elena said, perhaps a bit too quickly.

He cocked his head. "The Human Life Movement," Hector said.

Elena said, "That's ridiculous."

"What's ridiculous?" Maria came onto the porch and sat down in a nearby rocking chair. "Just a few more minutes until dinner," she added.

"What's the Human Life movement?" Victor asked, trying to ignore the ways his body was misbehaving. Information was good.

Information was neutral. And it would distract him from the crone scowling at him.

Elena turned to Victor, "Seriously, you don't know?"

"A bunch of sociopathic nutjobs," Julia seethed.

Victor shrugged his shoulders. Dizziness rose and blotted out his vision. He said through his blindness, "No. Whatever it is, we don't have it in SeCa." His view of the porch returned, first in gray, then in color. Maybe he wouldn't pass out after all. *Hooray.*

Elena crossed her arms. "I guess it's only in ROT, or maybe it started here." She chose each word carefully. "It's a splinter group from the Puros. They believe human life is sacred and that we need to preserve our natural heritage."

"Chiquitita, what does that *really* mean?" Maria asked.

Elena sipped her tea. "It's on the papers they hand out in the plaza. They are preserving humanity against technological corruption. Anti-science paranoia, most of it, but some of what they argue makes sense, especially about food. Without natural food, we can't be natural humans."

"See?" Hector said. "A bunch of horseshit. Enhanced food is more nutritious and affordable. A perfect match for the Puros. They can be insane together."

Julia nodded. "And we'll suffer the consequences. The Puros used to be local boys fighting for independence from Washington. Now they've all lost their way."

Elena tensed. Victor bounced his knee against hers, and she smoothed her hair, apparently rethinking the wisdom of getting involved in a discussion of Puro ideology with her family. They exchanged a glance and a sly smile—both their families were eager and exhausting debaters.

"What you say is not true," Hector said. "The Corps were trying to keep the States together."

Julia tut-tutted. "That's what you were *taught!*" She wore a cruel smile. "Do you know the Corps are trying to pass a bill to investigate the invasion of Miami?"

Maria sighed, and her gaze wandered across the yard. "That again."

"But that was decades ago," Victor said.

Julia said, "It's never too late to fight over the past."

The scorn on her face hadn't gone away. Her disdain was static electricity on his skin. His own volcanic anger threatened to escape.

To calm himself, he imagined diving to the bottom of the ocean, trapping the heat in his core with cool, firm pressure.

Julia clucked and continued. "They say President Kennedy masterminded the invasion before he was impeached."

"What?" Hector yelled. "That's crazy!"

Julia said, "A lot of people benefited from the invasion. Federal monies went to Florida and Cuba for rebuilding. The president doubled the defense budget overnight and looks so *strong* in those propaganda reels. I guess the only losers were the people in Miami who died, but there are memorials for that sort of thing."

Hector said, "The death toll in Havana alone was many times worse than all of Florida."

Maria's smile at Julia was as sharp as a fistful of razors. "Your theory has a fatal flaw, Julia. Kennedy didn't want European troops on AU soil *again*."

"The law of unintended consequences," Julia said, sipping her tea. "Or maybe he was secretly German."

Elena cackled. "Okay," she said, "that's the funniest thing I've heard in weeks. Also, the most insane."

Julia said, "We can't pretend there's no world beyond our borders. The invasion derailed the American Union's plans to enter the Sino-Nippon Conflict. Millions of people were displaced."

Victor said, "I know. A lot of them came to SeCa."

Julia laughed, but it was closer to a bark. "And look what a mess that became. The Pacific Coast will slide into the ocean one day, and all those foreigners and fog-headed, sun-dazzled fruits and nuts will throw a party at the bottom of the ocean. And your family will be the boat that floats when all the others have sunk. It should be called the Permanent Entitlement for how it's benefited you Eastmores. How much are you Eastmores worth these days?" Julia asked with a mocking lilt in her voice.

Victor reddened. "If this is what floating feels like," Victor said, "then I'll take any alternative."

"Let me check on the food," Maria said and returned inside.

Victor's head swam with hunger. He could make it a few more minutes, if he could put the stomach pangs out of his mind. He turned to Hector and said, "Why there are so many Corps at the Lone Star Kennel?"

Hector froze. His slow-roving gaze became a frightened deer darting in every direction. Victor hesitated, puzzled. He'd expected

Hector to have seen or heard something but not be so scared that he couldn't speak. After a moment of quiet, Hector seemed to recover his composure, cleared his throat, and ignored Victor's question, asking instead, "Victor, are you and Elena together again?"

Victor choked on a sip of iced tea.

Elena patted him on the back. "Papá," she scolded.

Hector cocked his head, waiting.

"Excuse me," Victor said once he had recovered. "We haven't—"

"Are you an item, or aren't you?" Julia asked.

"Drop it," Elena said with such ferocity that Julia rocked back in her seat.

Hector pointed at his daughter. "Elena, you shouldn't talk to your—"

"Enough," Elena said. "We need to wash up before dinner. Come on, Victor."

Victor rose unsteadily and teetered past the table, following her inside.

"He didn't answer my question about the kennel," Victor said.

"I know. We'll ask again at dinner," Elena said. "Do you need help setting the table?" Elena asked Maria.

"Yes," Maria said, "but Victor can get started on that. I want to talk to you."

Victor collected plates, silverware, glasses, and napkins and began setting the table while eavesdropping on Elena and Maria in the kitchen. They seemed to be discussing Elena's behavior over the past few months. Victor arranged all the place settings twice to keep his mind off the mismatch between his empty stomach and the piles of food just a few steps away. He wondered if he could sneak any spoonfuls directly from the simmering pot. Under Maria's watchful eyes, probably not. Each second oozed along at a snail's pace. Finally, after what felt like an hour, Maria called them to eat.

The Morales family jumped into action. Serving dishes were transported to the dining table, drinks were retrieved from the second chiller in the basement, and seats were pushed in and out so each family member could take their place. Roast turkey parts landed on plates. Many plates of greens moved around the table, along with potatoes and rice. All the dishes were generously spiced with dried chili de arbol, epazote, and cumin, and garnished with lime wedges and accompanied by mole.

Victor controlled the urge to inhale the food all at once by methodically trying moderate bites of each dish and combining them to test the flavor combinations in his mouth. He couldn't keep his mouth full; every bite was instantly down his gullet, as if his stomach had suction powers.

The diners moaned with pleasure. Maria beamed and poured glasses full of maroon liquid that Victor initially thought was wine, but it was lightly carbonated and sweet, tasting like anise. The drink accentuated the taste of the food perfectly. He lifted his glass and chugged half of it down.

"What magic did you cast on this food, mi corazón?" Hector asked.

"My secret," Maria said and rested her chin on the backs of her hands. "Mustard seed, curry powder, and cinnamon. Not too much. Some secret sauce. You like it?"

"Delicioso!" Elena said.

Julia pushed a few forkfuls around. She said, "It's good, but it's not truly Mexican."

Victor took a bite of the green beans, tasting earth, chlorophyll, and umami. The browned parts added a smoky aftertaste. Crystals of curry powder and salt tingled on his tongue. The moment extended, the flavor developed and changed, becoming oily and bitter, the flesh of the green beans roiled in his mouth. He swallowed and closed his eyes. The tastes intensified, waves of soil and sprouts and spices—

"Victor!"

Elena was shaking him.

He opened his eyes. Everyone was staring at him. Elena looked concerned. Her parents traded confused and embarrassed glances. Julia reproached him with a disdainful look and said, "Such obscene sounds are not welcome in my house."

"What happened?" he asked. It had just been a moment. The food had tasted better than any in his life. Everything else had faded away.

Elena leaned over and whispered, "You were moaning for, like, twenty seconds."

"I'm sorry. I was so hungry, I got carried away," he said. This wasn't the right time to discuss his withdrawal from medication. Not in front of her parents.

Elena whispered, "No, I'm feeling it too. Like when I was on— like before. Supercharged senses."

Victor looked again at the wine glass. He took a drink. The aniseed splashed his tongue, and he was on a roiling journey of sensation. "Maria, what is this?"

"It's Pump. You like it?" She smiled tentatively.

"But where did you get it?" he asked.

"The mercado. Everyone's drinking Pump now. 'Tastemaker. Pump makes dinner an occasion.' The ads are everywhere."

"This wasn't here when I was here," Elena said. She took a small sip while Victor watched. She nodded. "Mmm. My tastebuds are *stim*ulated."

Stims. An amount so small no one drinking it would suspect. He gently put his hand on Elena's arm, a warning. She pushed the glass away, blushing, nodding.

"This is sold legally?" he asked.

Maria said, "What do you mean 'legally'? Of course. Pump is everywhere. They've been giving out samples for free at the market for the past few weeks. Drives the Puros crazy."

"I wonder why," Victor deadpanned.

Julia gave him an angry look. She hadn't touched her drink at all. She moved it to one side.

"It's just a drink," Maria said. "It's not even alcoholic, so I don't know why they care. Too much sugar, I guess." She sighed. "They don't want anyone to enjoy themselves."

Elena was silent, but Victor could tell she was having trouble staying quiet. His mind was racing through the implications. Illegal stims like Aura were only the tip of the iceberg. The ROT was being flooded with a product mimicking MRS. Victor wondered what Ozie would have to say about it. He'd call him tomorrow after food and rest.

Making a mental note to avoid Pump, Victor helped himself to a few more slabs of turkey and turned to Hector. "You worked with my granfa for a long time, right?"

"A dozen years. Maybe longer."

"We were so sorry to hear about Jefferson's passing," Maria said. "I wish we could have come to the funeral."

"And he helped you?" Victor asked Hector. "After the thing with the unions, he got you a job here in Amarillo?"

"That's right," Hector said, looking warily at Victor.

"He trusted you, so I'm going to trust you as well. I plan to visit the Lone Star Kennel in the morning."

Hector looked down and scraped together the few remaining food bits on his plate.

"Is it safe?" Victor asked. "I saw a bunch of Corps out front."

Hector stiffened.

"Papá?" Elena asked with a look of concern on her face.

Hector raised his head, and Victor saw fear swirling around his eyes. "The kennel was always jointly held by Mason and Jefferson. After Jefferson died, I heard about a lawsuit. The court ruled in favor of Mason yesterday. The Corps showed up today."

"They're working for Mason?" Victor asked.

"Who knows? The Corps are in charge now. That's all that matters. And no, I don't think it's safe for you there. Or for anyone. You should stay away."

Victor slumped and put down his fork. How would he get past a flock of Corps to search the kennel for the XSCT compound?

Maria said, "There's no sense in wasting your trip out here. You should stay longer. It's so nice to see you." She watched her daughter's reaction.

Elena smiled shyly, "We were hoping to stay here. At least for tonight."

"This isn't a hotel," Julia said. She was glaring at Victor. "You're trouble, and I want no part of it."

The other three Morales family members froze.

The spit in Victor's mouth dried up. What had he done to upset her?

Julia said, "We've had enough of you upstart Eastmores. You ought to go back to working the plantations where you belong."

Elena and Maria began speaking at once.

Victor cut them off. "I've been hated for a lot of things. This crosses the line. I'm not ashamed of my skin or heritage," he said, staring at Julia. The room fell silent. Julia raised her eyebrows in mock surprise. This set Victor's blood boiling. He opened his mouth to yell, but Elena kicked him under the table.

She leaned over and whispered, "Deep breaths. Don't let her rattle you."

The anger faded, crowded out by a fondness and a connection to Elena deeper than family. He picked up a turkey drumstick, found a succulent bite, and ate, working hard to ignore everything around him. He said, "I thought all racists had moved to Florida."

Elena put her hand on his forearm, though she meant it as a reassuring gesture; it landed like a molten brand frying his skin. He jerked away and sent a glass tumbling off the table. It landed with a soft thump on the rug.

"Well done, young sir," Julia said mockingly.

Victor flinched. "All you've done since I got here is berate me. I've had enough."

Julia turned to her son and said coolly, "I won't be spoken to like this in my own house."

"Then treat me with respect," he said.

The other family members were shocked, but Victor thought they all agreed with him, at least a bit. Julia, however, looked at him from underneath condescending eyelids; her mouth twisted in contempt. "I won't have you staying in my house."

"Mamá!" Hector complained.

"Please, Julia, don't be like that," Maria begged.

Elena lifted her hands above the table. "Everyone just calm down."

"No," Victor said. He was tired of people. All he wanted was to sleep. "I'd rather go."

"No!" Elena hissed. "You can't. It's not safe."

Hector and Maria looked at each other questioningly.

"I'll be fine," Victor said. Turning to Hector and Maria, he said, "Excuse me." He ignored Julia completely.

Elena followed him to the front door and said, "Victor, don't leave."

"I'll just set the car on autopilot to drive me around all night. That should be safe enough."

"If Lucky and Bandit are following us, what's to stop them from grabbing you on the road?"

"My cool head under pressure."

Elena's eyes bugged out. Then she laughed, but it soon turned into a groan. "If you go, I'm coming with you."

Victor sighed. His mind was shutting down. He leaned on the wall for support. "I can't stay awake any longer." He rested his head against the wall for a moment. His brain matter had collected at the bottom of his skull and solidified.

Elena bounced on her tiptoes. "I'll grab some blankets."

Victor dozed, standing, while he waited for her to return, aware that indistinct shapes lurked nearby, ready to come alive in his dreams.

She kissed him lightly on the cheek when she returned. "Let's go. Don't worry," Elena said. "In the morning, we'll find the Puros, and they'll help us—you'll see."

41

After driving throughout the night, rolling through darkened neighborhoods, and skirting the deserted downtown, the car took Victor and Elena to the outskirts of Amarillo, where, as the sun rose, they entered a neighborhood with closely packed houses. Elena had said they would find Puros to help them at the kennel, but first, she was making a detour. At the entrance to the neighborhood, a faded sign read "Paradise Gardens," though there wasn't much idyllic about the run-down houses and unkempt yards. The car pulled up to a vacant lot cluttered with charred debris.

"That was where my Puro pod lived." She put a hand to her forehead and lowered her head. Victor was pretty sure she was crying.

He looked at the abandoned, fire-gutted house. The blaze had consumed most of the roof and upper story. Charred black mounds dotted the dirt yard where flaming insulation and drywall had rained down. The nearest building, a sprawling ranch-style home, appeared untouched.

Victor leaned back, feeling strangely numb. The scene should have upset him—the house's wreckage was far too similar to what he'd seen in Carmichael—but he felt something close to serenity. He should have been bothered that he hadn't been able to search the kennel yet and that the Corps stood in his way. Instead, blankspace pervaded his sensations, dulling them and making everything seem inconsequential. Perhaps he was becoming inured to setbacks. It no longer seemed strange when something didn't go his way. It seemed normal, as if the universe had a plan for him, one that he was not party to yet. It didn't appear to require his cooperation and didn't care what he wanted. A marionette dragged by its strings into an uncertain future.

That didn't mean he would give up. He would keep fighting, even if the spirit wasn't in him. It was how life was now. He and Elena would figure out how to get inside the kennel, with or without her Puro pals. At this point, he didn't care how dangerous it was. He realized it was a foolish attitude, but with every other aspect of his life stripped away, what was left was a thirst for the truth.

Elena turned toward Victor and said, "You're not the only one who knows how to lose. ROT policy toward Puros falls somewhere between harassment and eradication. See?" She banged the dashboard. "I'm sure those drug-pushing bastard Corps didn't think twice about burning this place down."

"I get it. Elena, do you know anywhere else the Puros might be? Assuming there's any left—" Victor stopped himself. There was no reason to paint a worst-case scenario for her.

Elena wiped her tears with her thumbs. "We can try the main square. Call it a hunch. You're familiar with those. They usually set up a produce market there. The police always shut them down, but they always go back."

Victor drank a fumewort tincture and followed it up with a bitter grass. The chemical heat burning his throat didn't bother him anymore, either. In fact, he welcomed it. "Let's go see."

She programmed the destination into the car's system. It drove slowly while Victor peered around, watching his mirrors to check if they were being followed. Cars passed them. A few fretful pedestrians rushed across the wide streets, daring to cross mid-block, perhaps afraid to be seen waiting at intersections.

They passed warehouses and pinched their noses as a blood-and-shit reek invaded the car.

"Slaughterhouses," Elena explained.

Downtown, a few buildings reached as high as two stories. Most were low-rise and ramshackle. They parked in a half-empty lot, got out, and wandered past a few worn-down shops selling secondhand goods and cheap trinkets. Amarillo's central plaza lay ahead: a dusty, sunbaked slick of asphalt surrounded by a few restaurants, a post office, and a general store.

Elena pointed to the far side of the plaza, where catering tents shaded tables of produce from the harsh sun.

"The Puros will be there," she said. "But I need to talk to them alone. We didn't part on great terms."

She pointed Victor to a nearby café and insisted that he go there and wait, saying Puros didn't like strangers. More likely, she had some other rationale. She always seemed to have hidden motives, and—if Victor was honest with himself—part of him must have liked that about her. Why else would he have welcomed her back into his life as quickly as he did? Unpredictability and impulsiveness were the things he liked about her because he couldn't afford to be those things himself.

As he walked across the plaza, Victor examined the town more closely and realized it wasn't as bleak as he'd first assumed. The architecture was surprisingly contemporary. A fountain tucked into one corner of the square provided limited relief from the steadily building heat. He'd assumed the town would appear stuck in the Repartition era because only big cities seemed to thrive after the devolution of former-US federal powers to the nations of the American Union. Not so. Although Amarillo didn't appear to be wealthy, neither was it falling. The new was mixed with the old in a way that felt organic, nothing like the high-tech splendor of Las Vegas or the rigid formality of Oakland.

Tall, fluted trees lined a broad promenade stretching from the plaza to the central train station. He recognized the species. That type of elm had been genetically engineered to resist fungi that had caused massive tree die-offs in the early twentieth century. The ROT wasn't as backward as Elena had made it out to be.

However, beneath the patina of civilization, something menacing lurked among Amarillo's residents. They watched him when he wasn't looking, but they looked away when he turned his gaze to meet theirs. Fine. He was as eager to slip past them and do his business as they were.

Café Magyar, the place Elena suggested, had an outdoor area wrapped around the building's mirrored façade. A broad red-white-and-green-striped awning shaded the chairs and tables. Couples and a few loners sat at tables leisurely taking in Amarillo's best scenery: the almost featureless plaza.

A few young, fresh-faced wait staff dressed in Hungarian-peasant costume navigated between tables. One of them approached Victor and asked where he would like to sit. Her flashing smile gave him a brief taste of sweet, sparkling wine. He could almost hear her fizzing. He should probably double his dose of fumewort to get control over the sensations, but then he would run through his supplies too quickly, and besides, for the moment, it was a pleasant feeling.

The hostess tilted her head, waiting for a response. Victor smiled and nodded to a seat, to which she guided him. He sat and ordered a faux-café. There was no chance of finding real coffee in a town as small as Amarillo.

When the server left with his order, Victor rubbed the data egg in his pocket and wished it would open. Ozie had finally come clean and said Victor's brain patterns might be the key to unlocking it. He tried a sequence of prime numbers, repeating the owl mantra in his head, picturing his granfa's face. Nothing worked.

He needed a real plan, and time was short. Eventually, Lucky and Bandit would find them. Or maybe Tosh would catch up first and wouldn't be pleased by how he had been ditched. As much as it pained Victor to admit, he could use Tosh's help to break into the kennel.

The hostess returned with a steaming cup. He sipped the bitter drink and realized with a puzzled smile that he was actually in a pretty good mood. Despite the setbacks he'd faced and the feeling that worse things lurked just over the horizon, all the same, he was enjoying the drink, the solitude, and the novelty of his surroundings. For the moment, he was free, and it felt as good as a sunbeam through rainclouds.

Victor took out his Handy 1000, which told him via squiggles, sigils, and letters that Amarillo was blessed with fifteen Mesh towers, one of which he could see poking its silver-pronged crown above the multistory buildings by the train station. The computing capacity of the local node was negligible, especially compared to the bounty in Las Vegas. There couldn't be more than a couple hundred devices in total.

He wished Ozie had explained more of the features of his Handy 1000 before they left Springboard Café. The way Lucky and Bandit kept showing up meant they had some way of tracking him. The Handy 1000 might be able to disrupt it.

Playing with the analytics, Victor found a scatterplot showing the relative contribution of each device in the node. Aside from the towers themselves, the Handy 1000 topped the list. Ozie had assembled powerful hardware. Victor was grateful for whatever tricks were masking his presence from the Mesh operators, who would surely want to get their hands on it. A skull-and-crossbones icon near the bottom of the vidscreen caught his eye: alert settings.

Cody Sisco

Victor reviewed the options and set an alert for any connection to a device with "countermeasures"—whatever those were, they sounded problematic.

Elena emerged from the canopy of white tents on the other side of the plaza and half-jogged toward Victor. She was breathless when she sank into the seat across from him.

"They're not here. None of the big dogs. Just the farmers. Purely secular."

"When you say that—"

"I know it's not the right word." Elena rolled her eyes. "I mean the nonfighters, the ones who till the dirt. The guys I know, they were the enforcers, the protectors."

"The people who know how to handle a shockstick."

"Exactly. Shocksticks and more. They're not here."

"So, what next?"

"Word will get out that I'm looking for them. We should make contact in an hour. Maybe two. We stay put."

"We can wait with drinks, I guess."

"You done with that coffee? Want a beer?" she asked.

"Yeah, they'll come by."

"I'm not waiting."

"A dark one, then."

Elena walked to the bar.

Victor turned again to his Handy 1000. There was another alert option: "Proximity." He activated it at the default ten-meter option. The alarm immediately sounded. Someone in Amarillo had been tagged. He tapped on the blinking icon. The details were unrevealing:

```
MeshID: 8428-94988-223585
Model: BioLoc.32 v2x03
Power: 32w
Distance: 8m
```

Victor reset the distance threshold to five meters, which would include only the people sitting on the outside patio.

"Doneghy's is all they had," Elena said, gently lowering a dark pint onto the table. She sat and sipped from her golden brew with a full head of white foam.

Victor took a sip. The alarm sounded again. He looked down. The distance now read *<1m*.

He looked up.

"What's wrong?" Elena asked.

A sinking feeling dragged on his bowels. "A BioLoc alarm went off. It means there's a flesh-compatible MeshID nearby." He took three full gulps of his beer before saying in a carefully level voice, "I think you have a chip in you."

Elena reared up as if he'd struck her. "No way."

He swiveled the Handy 1000's screen so that she could see. "That's you. No other explanation. It showed when you walked back just now."

Elena's eyes pleaded for him to say he was joking.

"You know what this means, right?" Victor said. "They're tracking you. That's how they found us in Vegas."

She pushed against the table, and beer sloshed over. "I bet that fucking clinic did it! I went there to recover, not lose every shred of my privacy. Is chipping people without their consent legal in the Louisiana Territories?"

Victor kept his voice level even as his heart started racing. "Forget that. We need to be practical. Maybe Ozie can figure out a way to deactivate it or mask your signal. Until then, we have to keep moving." Victor stood up. "I think I need to go to the kennel alone. Maybe I can talk my way inside."

Elena stood up, too. "You're not thinking straight. Those Corps probably have the same orders as the ones who stopped us at the border. They're an *organization*. We need the Puros to—"

Revving engines interrupted her. Screams rose from the catering tents and market stalls, and people began to stream across the plaza.

"We should go," Victor warned.

Elena jumped up and made for the source of the commotion. "Let's see what it is," she said.

"Elena, wait!"

A crowd of young men wearing dark clothing and orange masks burst from the market and fled toward an alley. Three old roadsters pursued them. One sped around and cut off their escape, corralling them. People ran from the plaza, scooping up their children and hurrying into the alleyways. One man brushed past Victor, nearly knocking him over.

"What's going on?" Victor demanded.

"Not good," Elena said. "When Corps meet Puros, people die." She took a few steps toward them.

Victor grabbed her arm. "Where are you going?"

Elena dragged Victor forward, stopping fifty meters away from the dickies. "We came here to find the Puros. There they are."

The Puros were on the defensive, penned in by the Corps' cars and menaced by additional members arriving on foot. The two groups converged and fought, trying to slice each other with knives—machetes, stilettos, katanas, some so big they could have been cavalry swords. Victor tried to pull Elena away. The Corps might be too busy attacking to notice bystanders, but he didn't want to be there when their attention shifted. Except Elena wouldn't budge. She brought out her shockstick. The tip glowed red.

One Puro, wearing a bright orange shirt, backed away from the group. A purple-mohawked Corp, who seemed to be the leader, followed, flashing a foot-long knife. He hacked it down and up, lunging, grinning, and laughing. Victor had seen people like that in Oak Knoll, doped out of their minds, hallucinating voices and visitations from gods. Were all the Corps high?

The orange-shirted Puro, separated from his companions, glanced over his shoulder at the circling cars. Sensing victory, the Corp lunged forward. The Puro sidestepped, whirled, and jump-kicked the Corp in the back, who stumbled into the path of a black roadster. His hands flew up, knife abandoned, as he tried to lurch past the vehicle, but it was too late. The roadster was on him. His legs bent backward; he disappeared under the car. The Corp driver swerved hard but too late. Tires screeched, and the vehicle rolled, flinging two passengers to the ground. The other two roadsters slowed to a halt.

Victor felt tingling on his skin as he heard sirens. Two police vans barreled into the square. Officers jumped out and raised riot shields. Beyond the line of police, Victor spotted Lucky and Bandit scanning the plaza with viewfinders.

Victor hissed in Elena's ear, "They're here. Come on!"

An officer stepped forward with an air cannon strapped to his belly. A wave of shimmering light pushed forward. A thunderclap erupted, followed by a wall of dust. The confused dickies were blown to the ground. Windows from nearby buildings shattered, raining shrapnel.

Victor pulled Elena down and clutched her hand. The dust cloud blew across the plaza, sweeping over them like a tornado. It was no use talking; they wouldn't be able to hear until their ears stopped ringing. Through the clearing dust, he saw gas canisters launching from the police vans and spewing white fog across the plaza. Sleeping gas. But at least it masked them from Lucky and Bandit.

They got to their feet, carefully avoiding broken glass, and hustled from the plaza to an alley around the back of Café Magyar. He patted Elena in a few places to signal he was concerned she might be hurt. She did the same and signaled she was okay.

He patted his chest. "Me too," he mouthed.

Movement flickered in the corner of Victor's eye. The orange-shirt Puro took a few lurching steps around the corner of the café. He doubled over and took one more slow, tottering step forward, then fell, rolling onto the ground on his side. The front of his shirt glistened with blood. Elena approached him, leaving Victor yelling at her back. The Puro opened his eyes, locked them on Elena's, and pleaded silently for help.

Noting the orange-dyed scars that covered the young man's arms and legs, Victor felt his nerves were at full stretch. He and Elena should leave before the Corps found them, before Lucky and Bandit found them, before the police found them. Maybe he could get inside the kennel now, while the Corps were distracted.

He ran to the corner and looked toward the plaza. A gust of wind thinned the sleeping gas. Police officers in breathing masks had subdued some of the fighters and placed them in restraints. When Victor turned back, Elena was gone. He ran, panicking. The alley twisted around and met another alley, which led back to the plaza in one direction and a parking area in another.

Then a hand gripped his shoulder. He jumped and turned.

Elena was holding a med kit in her other hand. She led him back to the bloody Puro, where she knelt and gently lifted his blood-soaked shirt, revealing a curving slice deep in his gut. There was so much blood. Elena leaned over the young man and used pieces of gauze from the kit to wipe blood from his wound, making her way along the path the knife had taken. Victor felt as if every one of his nerves were ready to fire simultaneously, but she seemed calm and focused, her movements measured and confident.

"We need to get him to a hospital," she said. Her voice sounded far away. "Victor, call your car."

He started to respond with a disbelieving retort—*There's no way he's getting in my car!*—when the Puro grasped her arm and said, "No hospital. Please help me, Elena."

"You're hurt, dumbass." Elena tore a roll of gauze into strips. "You need a doctor."

The Puro was struggling to communicate. "Doctors fine. But hospital means police. Can't get caught. You can be my pretty doctor." The Puro's weak smile vanished when she applied more pressure to his wound. "Nice touch," he said through sharp and shallow breaths.

"How does he know your name?" Victor asked.

"This is Chico. We're acquainted," she said.

He saw her expression's evasiveness, stubbornness, and a purple hint of pride.

Chico looked at Victor. "I have money. If you can keep me alive and away from the police, I'll give you thousands."

"That's not going to work on him," Elena said. She turned to Victor sharply. "Call your car!"

"You're not serious!"

"Trust me," she said without looking up from the Puro.

He summoned the car but got no response. "There's no signal. I don't get it. There should be a signal. The tower is right over there."

"Forget it. Go to your car and bring it here. We'll load him in." She gave him her shockstick. "Watch out for Corps."

He'd never held one before. They conjured up too many memories of Carmichael. "But—"

"Go! Run!" she ordered.

Elena was begging for his help, and he couldn't say no. He took off without looking back, feeling light on his feet like he might float into blankspace.

42

"I'll pay you back for this," Chico said weakly. "Whatever you want. A million dollars."

"Bribery is bad manners. And Xavi would disapprove." Elena applied pressure to his wound. Returning to Amarillo had been the best choice of a set of bad options, but it was worse than she could have imagined. It shouldn't be a surprise. Things had been off the rails in ROT for a long time. Everyone was scratching for what they needed to survive, and there wasn't enough—no hope, except for what they found in each other. Like the deluded, idealistic fool she was trying to save.

Chico smiled at her through heavy lids. "You think I'm cute when I'm bleeding all over you."

"Shut up." The sight of blood didn't bother her, though it oozed in thick and heavy rivulets across his exposed stomach.

Despite the sweat coming off it and his painful grimace, Chico's face was nicely shaped. He had smooth skin and a surly mouth. She felt a sudden urge to kiss him. *Symptoms confirmed: I have a fetish for desperately helpless guys.*

"Do you like my scars?" he teased. "I got more that I can show you."

"Is that a circumcision joke? Stop kidding, or I'll punch you in the knife hole."

"You wouldn't punch a dying man."

"Dying?" She laughed, intending to reassure him, but it sounded like a bark. "I don't think so."

She shifted and pulled Chico's torso onto her lap, keeping pressure on his wound.

A siren whooped. Paramedics were somewhere nearby, not that they'd be any help. They would take one look at the orange scars on his arms and turn him over to the police. She would be charged as an accomplice to the murder of at least one Corp, maybe more. That was the best-case scenario. More likely, she could expect whichever policeman appeared to have a monster-sized grudge against the Puros. She'd heard of police killing dickies on sight and then covering up their crime.

Only Puros cared about other Puros. That was the first lesson they'd taught her when they'd pulled her from the path of an oncoming train.

"I saw the house," Elena said. "How bad was it?"

"We lost four," Chico said, grimacing.

Elena looked into his rich-brown eyes surrounded by long lashes. Chico was street-smart and emotionally normal for a Texan dickie. Plus, he knew about her transition and didn't care. Some Puros could be rigid about that stuff. He was a good catch—for her. But first, he would have to live.

Elena twisted her neck and watched the entrance to the alley. Before Victor had run off, she'd seen the resonance start to come back. Hopefully, he hadn't blankly wandered into the dickie war zone. She held her hands against Chico's wound. His eyes were closed now; he'd passed out.

Five minutes passed. Was Victor coming back? Maybe the Corps had found him ...

Oh, shit, the chip!

Gooseflesh rose on her arms. If Lucky and Bandit hadn't caught Victor yet, they would find *her* soon. That bitch Linda must have arranged to have her chipped. She would never set foot in an Eastmore-run hospital or clinic again.

Chico stirred in her arms. "Am I going to be okay?" he asked.

"You won't bleed out," she said, "but you'll still be dumb as a brick."

"Elena Morales, you can be a real ball crusher, you know that?" He found her arm and squeezed it. "Sorry. Thank you. Don't let me die, or I'll haunt you bad."

Her heart thudded. He couldn't die in her arms; she couldn't live with that memory. How badly she wanted stimsmoke. It had been two days since her last puff and more than a month clean before that. But it couldn't be helped. Call it the cost of minding Victor, which she'd screwed up royally. Now, this mess. She was the only person he could count on. That meant something. She had a responsibility to him just as he had one to her. The lyrics of a Twisted Funburst song popped into her head. *For love or money, I'll stick with you like glue.* The chorus, again and again, droning in her brain.

Where the hell *was* he? As much as she wanted to help Victor get his answers from the kennel, the Puros couldn't let an attack like this go unpunished. The carnage in the plaza was beyond anything they'd experienced. This wasn't about harassing Puros—this was about destroying them. Was it a coincidence, or did it have something to do with Victor? Could Lucky and Bandit have teamed up with the Corps?

Elena looked toward the end of the alley. How many Puros and Corps were out there, bleeding, dead, or captured? She'd seen four, maybe five. Whatever was so important about Victor to them surely wasn't worth all of *this*. The Puros would want to retaliate right away. They might even take her back if she helped them fight. But the Puros taking on the Corps was foolish. They would be crushed. It would make a good distraction, though, and might give Victor an opening to get inside the kennel. Which was worth more? Her surrogate family or Victor's truth?

She heard the crackling of wheels and an engine's purr. Victor's car turned the corner, rolled forward, and stopped before her. When he got out, she saw his expression wavering between anger, fear, and the terrible blankness of a resonant episode.

"Grab his feet," Elena said. She tried not to think about the trouble ahead. "We'll put him in the back, and I'll hold him while you drive." She gently patted Chico's face. "Chico, wake up. You need to tell us where to go."

His eyes didn't open, and fear froze her lungs. Was he dead?

43

Victor picked up the unconscious Chico by the torso while Elena grappled with his legs. His body was sagging and swaying as they took small steps forward, the car door refusing to open itself on Victor's grunted command until the third try. Elena dropped Chico's legs and ran around to the other side of the car so she could climb in and pull him through, and Victor lifted and shoved so Chico's head and shoulders finally rested on Elena's lap in the backseat. Blood streaked across the upholstery and splotched Victor's shirt.

Victor got in, put the car in gear, and drove down the alley to the main road, keeping it in manual mode. "Where to?" he asked.

Elena coaxed Chico to consciousness and asked for the safe house address. His eyes fluttered as he said, "Fifteen Baldwin Street."

Elena directed Victor. "Left here. A couple kilometers."

"You've been there before?" Victor asked.

"Never in my life."

Digging into his pocket, Victor took out a few leaves of fumewort and put them in his mouth. Sucking their sustenance was less effective than taking a tincture, but he didn't trust his coordination to single-handedly uncork a vial while driving, and the manual mode was faster. He mashed the leaves between his teeth to get saliva flowing. The leaves began to soften and give up their pungent bitterness.

"Wait, stop!" Elena yelled. "Back there. That drugstore." She rattled off a list of necessities.

Victor parked in front. "You want me to go in there looking like this?" He held up his bloody hands. Wiping them on the clean parts of his shirt only lightened the red hue.

"Yes. Just be quick."

Five minutes later, pulse racing from the awkward stare of the drugstore clerk, who had noticed the blood on Victor but hadn't mentioned it, he returned to the car with gauze, medical paste, and pills that might save Chico's life.

They arrived at the house on Baldwin Street, a small two-story building with a driveway shielded from its neighbors by tall hedges. Nothing from the outside would identify the house as a hideout for dangerous thugs. A wood-shingled roof sat tidily above slightly rusted rain gutters. White paint contrasted with dark red window frames. Another car was parked in the carport, so Victor pulled behind it.

Victor and Elena got out of the car. Gurgling sounds could be heard from small chiller units dotting the exterior windows of the house. A moment later, three men with clean-shaven heads emerged through the front door, followed by two women wearing odd, bell-shaped hats. The men approached and bookended Victor. When they recognized Elena, and she told them about Chico, they helped ease the wounded Puro out of the car.

Victor waited by his car, awkwardly avoiding the gazes of the two dickie women on the porch whispering to each other. He tried to wipe Chico's blood from his arms, succeeding only in spreading it around.

The leader, Xavi, issued orders to the others in a surprisingly melodious voice. He was tall and broad-chested, with an orange scar running from his temple toward his ear. His silver-blue eyes were set in a round, powerful head.

"What happened?" he asked.

Chico's eyes fluttered open as he was conveyed in the dickies' arms toward the front door. He said, "Ambush at the market. A dozen Corps. Police, too."

Xavi asked, "Where is everyone else?"

Chico shook his head and passed out.

Xavi looked at Elena. "You take care of Chico, and then you leave," he said, and went inside.

Elena pulled Victor toward the front door, saying, "Come on."

Victor resisted. "We should get out of here. The longer we stay in one place ..."

Elena grabbed his hand and said, "Victor, this is one of those situations that you could easily screw up. Play it cool, and Xavi might help us at the kennel."

Victor dug in his heels and stopped on the welcome mat. "We need to move on."

"We can't yet," she said. "Maybe we should split up."

"What?"

"Lucky and Bandit are looking for you, but they're tracking me. If we split up ..."

He saw the logic but couldn't help feeling that she was ready to get rid of him now that she was back with her group. "Where would I go?"

"Fine, stay here. We can talk after I help Chico." She turned to enter the house.

"Wait, I'm coming." Victor rushed to the car, grabbed his backpack, and hoisted it on his shoulders.

They went inside. The house looked like every surface had been worn away, nicked, or cracked. Dirt caked the hallway. The kitchen, by contrast, sparkled. Utensils were mounted on the wall, fitting cozily within their painted outlines. Pots and pans hung from the ceiling. The chrome stovetop gleamed. The Puros were slobs everywhere except in the kitchen.

Victor and Elena continued to a room with two couches, overstuffed bookshelves sagging against the walls, and a sliding glass door that led to the backyard.

"I have bandages, antibiotics, and some surgical tools, just in case," Elena announced.

Xavi gestured to her to get to work. He stood next to Victor, towering over him. He probably weighed as much as Victor and Elena combined. Large muscles prevented his arms from hanging straight. Victor stood as tall as he could while not seeming to try too hard and said, "I'm Vic."

"She told me."

Chico reclined on one of the couches, which had been draped with a plastic tarp to protect it from blood, a pointless effort since Victor was sure he could spot at least three, maybe four, dried stains on the filthy carpet.

Elena knelt beside Chico, who looked at her fearfully and said, "I don't think the bleeding stopped."

"I'm going to take a look, clean the cut, and seal it up," she said. "Then we'll get you some antibiotics and a sleeper pill—I assume that's okay," she said, looking pointedly at Xavi. He nodded. Elena brushed the hair from Chico's forehead. "In a minute, you can take the most luxurious nap you've had in a long time. Ready?"

Chico nodded, less visibly anxious.

"This shirt is not going to make it," she chirped as she clipped it away with scissors. "Xavi, Victor, bring me some warm, damp towels."

Victor followed Xavi to a closet to gather towels. They ran the warm water in the bathroom, wetted the towels, and returned them to the table next to Chico.

Elena cleaned around the wound with the towels. A trickle of blood oozed out, but the inside appeared to have mostly clotted. She pulled on a pair of gloves and opened a tin of antibiotic permapaste.

"This is going to hurt," she said. "I don't want you to twist, flex, or do anything to aggravate the wound." She smiled at Chico. "That's my job. Victor, take his hands. Not too hard, just to remind him not to move."

Victor took a few hesitant steps to the couch and clasped each Chico's hands, applying pressure to pin them deep into the soft cushions. Sensations moved through his arms, vibrations like bass notes in time with his pulse. A searing pain flared in his gut, and sweat broke out on his forehead. He was the last person that should be helping someone who was wounded.

Elena said, "Breathe calmly and concentrate on the feeling in your hands." She was talking to Chico, and Victor knew he should look away, only he couldn't help but watch as she scooped a generous portion of the permapaste goop over her fingers and inserted them into the fissure. Chico gasped. He squeezed Victor's hands, and Victor squeezed back. The room rotated as gravity did cartwheels around them. His lunch started to climb, and he gulped it down again.

Elena brushed the permapaste inside the wound, leaving a generous coating. Blood began to pool in the crevasse. She seemed to realize what she'd done because she soaked the blood with a dry towel, grabbed an aerosol can of a quick-clotting agent, and sprayed the tissue.

Victor noticed a change in her features. The anxious scowl she usually wore lightened. Her eyes brightened, her hands moved with competence, and her gaze flicked between Chico's wound, face, and body. Victor could tell she was watching every movement, every breath, every twitch of the man's face. Her hands—wiping away blood, dipping her fingers into the jar of ointment, spreading it in the wound—were swift and sure.

She was in her element, feeling how he felt when analyzing gene sequencing computations. Laying on hands and healing were the things that gave meaning to her life. Their troubled relationship started making sense, and the knowledge made Victor wince. She wanted to feel the same way by helping him, but his problems were too complex and intangible, so she was never satisfied.

Words left his mouth before he knew he intended to speak. "Is that what I am to you?"

She didn't seem to hear him. Her focus never wavered from helping Chico.

Victor spoke louder. "Elena, what am I to you?"

She looked up, puzzled.

"Tell me," he demanded.

"Not now, Victor," she said, looking down again at Chico.

"Am I a health-care project?" He couldn't stop himself. The words kept coming out, hurtful, rising from a pit of pain in his chest. "A salve to your bruised conscience? A way for you to keep going? What am I to you?"

"This isn't the time, Vic."

"Come on, man," Chico said, lifting his head. "Let her work."

Xavi raised an eyebrow, but he remained silent.

Victor wondered how many people she'd patched up during her time with the Puros and why it hadn't been enough, why she'd returned to stims even at the risk of being thrown out, and why she'd decided on helping Victor for her next attempt at self-salvation. He let go of Chico's hands, stood, and turned away, looking through the glass door at the back of the house. The yard glowed under the midday sun.

Victor glanced back and saw Elena wipe around each edge of the cut with gauze. She stuffed another wad of it into the wound and taped it up. Her voice was carefully neutral as she said, "The paste will slowly dissolve as the tissue starts to heal. We need to replace the gauze every day at first. It's going to make a great scar."

Chico told Xavi, "Make sure you've got enough ink for my next scartoo."

Victor saw Elena smile. She fished more pills from the med kit and helped Chico lift his head to swallow them. She stood, placed all the bloody articles into a plastic bag, washed her hands in the bathroom, and strode to the front entrance, not once making eye contact with Victor. He and Xavi followed her while the other Puros remained with Chico.

Elena told Xavi, "He'll be out for a few hours. He needs to take sedatives and antibiotics every few hours after that. It'll be a few weeks before he can get up and move. You guys can handle finding a catheter and a bedpan?"

Xavi nodded.

"Okay, there's something I need to ask you." She pulled Xavi into the dining room.

The other Puro, pacing up and down the hallway, approached Victor, eyeballing him cautiously. "I'm Davinth."

"Victor."

Davinth's short gray hair pointed in every direction like dandelion fluff. Though he was skinny and much thinner than Xavi, muscles stood out on his forearms. He said, "Elena's not exactly welcome around here. She's trouble."

Victor stayed silent.

"The kind of trouble that can't stay sober."

"That's how you recruit people, isn't it, by finding addicts? You must expect them to relapse sometimes."

"Yeah, it don't always stick, but we try. They fall down enough; we tell 'em we're better off without 'em."

Victor said, "She's been clean for months. You'd be lucky to have her back."

The Puro nodded toward Chico. "If he lives, I'd say she's earned another shot. Not up to me. You want to put in a good word for her; go talk to Xavi."

Victor turned toward the front of the house, where Elena and Xavi were having a shouting match that seemed to be gaining strength. The Handy 1000 vibrated in his pants. He took it out and looked at the display. It was a feed request from Ozie marked urgent. Victor walked to the glass backdoor, slid it open, stepped into the heat, and sat on the lip of a rickety, unshaded deck. He opened the feed.

"Victor, I have news." Ozie's face flickered, but through the static, Victor could tell he was smiling.

"What is it?" Victor asked.

"Pearl's here!"

"Hello, Victor," she said from somewhere off the feed.

"Pearl! Are you okay?"

"Fine. Fine. Not too badly bruised. And you? How are you feeling?"

"I'm running out of herbs," Victor said.

"We'll send some to you soon. Tell us where."

Relief washed over him.

Ozie said, "Vic, that's not all. The processing went off without a hitch. We have the mirror resonance syndrome gene sequence. There is a problem, though."

"What?"

"We've been hacked. I found tracker worms in the dark grid. Every time I take one out, five more pop up. They're going to find us eventually unless we go dark."

"Who?"

"The Diamond King."

It was starting to sound as if Ozie blamed all his problems on a mythical ruler, a fiendish opponent responsible for the ills of the world—although Victor didn't mind hearing Ozie's theories since it made him feel like the sane one of the pair.

Ozie continued, "He's sniffing me out. I've got to go."

"Wait, I need to ask a favor," Victor said. "Elena is chipped. I'll send you the ID. Is there any way to block people from tracking her?"

"I'll see what I can do." Ozie's face faded from the display. Victor sent him the ID.

The sun beat down from almost directly above. Victor's head felt full of steam, and his stomach flipped.

He was familiar enough with his symptoms to know they were rearing up again. It must be around noon or a bit later. He pulled a vial of the fumewort tincture from his pocket. Pearl would send more soon, thank the Laws. He would have to reserve a MeshLocker at the train station.

Tipping his head back, he poured the tincture down his throat. It was a game he played, trying to bypass his taste buds. Enough drops missed their mark, however, and the smoky, oily, and astringent taste flooded his mouth. The vapor stung his nose. Victor's stomach flipped again, this time urgently. No food cushioned the arrival of the tincture against his soft muscles. He should eat. He got up and stumbled inside.

In the hallway, Elena and Xavi were still discussing their plans. Elena looked at Victor quizzically. "What was all that about earlier? Are you okay?"

"Fine. Need food," Victor said, brushing past her. He opened the chiller door and almost cried out in delight. The cold box was filled with fresh vegetables and greenery. So much produce—a large bunch of carrots with their leafy tops, bags of lettuce, peppers, tomatoes, and plastic containers hiding more culinary delights. It was the last thing he had expected to find. His eyes were also drawn to a dark, dense, seedy bread on the bottom shelf that looked nourishing.

"We need to talk about what we're going to do," Elena said from the doorway.

"Do we?" Victor asked. A little voice inside his head told him not to listen to her, to forget the food, to leave right away, not to spend another minute in the Puros' stronghold.

"Victor, I think we should go," Elena said. "I don't want to lead them here."

"Oh, yeah? I mean, I agree, but I was going to make a salad. Ozie can help, I think. Do you—"

"Hold up there," Xavi said, pushing Victor away from the counter. "Lead who here? What's going on?"

"Hey, Xavi," Davinth called from upstairs. "There's a van parked outside. I think it's Corps."

44

Davinth burst into the kitchen, yelling, "Those Corps fuckers found us, and I want to know how!"

"Show me," Xavi said.

He and Davinth ran into the dining room and crouched by the windows. Elena was close behind.

Victor's gaze drifted to his hands, which held the salad precursors he desperately wanted to assemble into a meal. He raised a carrot to his mouth, took a large bite, and followed the others as he chewed. In the dining room, Elena stood while the Puros crouched at the window, their faces pressed close. Xavi peered through the slats of the blind.

"How long have they been there?" Xavi asked.

"Not more than ten minutes," Davinth answered.

Victor paced behind the two Puros, straining to see outside, but it was useless. The two men were huge, immobile stones blocking his view. The muscles on their necks flexed and tensed as they tried to get a better view outside. An artery that ran down the side of Xavi's face pulsed like something was trying to free itself of the flesh.

Victor returned to the lounge. Elena followed. "Are you alright?"

"It could be Lucky and Bandit. Staying here could get me killed."

"We're safe for now. Let's try to keep it that way."

Xavi entered the room. A black, wispy halo of suspicion surrounded his red eyes. Victor took a step sideways, searching for an escape route, but Xavi darted forward, wrenched him off his feet, and slammed him into the wall. Victor tried to squirm away, but Xavi pinned him in place.

Xavi said, "Did you lead them here? Who are they?"

Victor tried to shake himself free. "Who are who? I didn't see anything."

Elena tugged on Xavi's giant arm. "Let him go!"

Xavi hauled him upstairs. Victor stumbled into a room overlooking the front yard, and Xavi's massive paw returned to his neck, pressing his face into the window.

"Who are they?" Xavi asked.

A white van was parked outside, blocking Victor's car in the driveway. Several more cars were parked farther away. A few ROT flags flapped in front of neighboring homes. Reflections off the windshield blocked his view of the van's interior, but Victor thought he could see movement inside.

"Nobody knew about this house this morning, so how come they're here now?" Xavi said, spraying a cloud of moisture that came to rest on Victor's neck.

Victor shrugged. "I don't know. Maybe we were followed bringing your mate home."

Maybe they followed Elena, but that's not for me to say.

Pain screamed in Victor's wrist as Xavi squeezed the bones together.

"Stop it!" Elena yelled from the doorway.

"Your friend here brought us some unwelcome visitors."

"No, it's not his fault! It was—"

Victor let out a cry of pain to interrupt her. He couldn't let Elena confess that the bad guys were following her. It wasn't her fault she'd been fitted with a BioLoc MeshID. As much as he disliked the Puros and their brutality, and as much as her actions had frayed his trust, he couldn't let her ruin her chances to reconcile with them. She needed them if she was ever going to quit stims.

"Xavi! This isn't helping!" Elena wedged herself between them, and Xavi let go. Victor steadied himself against the wall while they faced each other, glowering.

A woman rushed onto the landing from a room down the hall. "Keep it down! Lila and I are doing the accounting." Another woman with glasses and frizzy red hair peeked out.

"Victor is rich, and he's got powerful friends," Elena said, pleading. "We need him."

"What's going on?" Lila asked.

Elena told her, "The Corps are worse than we thought. Did you know that Pump is spiked with stims? Who else would do that?

If we don't fight back—" She turned to Xavi. "Look, the Corps are outside, and you want to get even with them, right? Us too. You can name your price if we take care of the guys outside and help Victor. Think about it. More weapons." She turned to Victor. "Right?"

He nodded. Money-wise, it might clean him out, and he hated to owe these thugs anything, but he needed their help.

Xavi ran his hands over his bald head and stretched his shoulders and neck. He looked like a boxer about to enter the ring. *Such stupid, muscle-bound confidence*, Victor thought.

"Okay," Xavi said. "We need the bucks, no question." He turned to Elena. "Come on."

The two hurried down the hall into a bedroom, with the two women following. Victor stayed put and looked through the window again. A cloud had moved in front of the sun, and now he could see through the van's windshield: two people, a man and a woman, Bandit and Lucky. They were leaning forward in their seats, peering up at the house, looking directly at him. Bandit still wore a silly pair of round-eyed sun goggles that looked too stylish to be functional. They could follow Elena, but they couldn't follow *him*, not if he was careful.

Victor backed away from the window and started down the stairs, treading quietly on each step. He tiptoed to the back of the house, past Chico, who was still passed out on the couch, put on his backpack, and looked through the glass door.

The yard had no fence. He could run past a neighboring house to the next street—but then where? They were on the outskirts of the city. His car was blocked in, and anyway, Lucky and Bandit could follow it. He would have to run many kilometers to get anywhere worthwhile. Still, if he could escape unnoticed, that might give him enough time to get to a taxi, a bus, or the train terminal. He heard thuds upstairs and the sounds of large objects being shifted and dropped on the floor.

Davinth came into the room. His wiry frame and gray hair made him look about fifty years old, but he moved like a young person, fluid and quick. He watched as Victor dug into his pocket and pulled out his last fumewort tincture. He popped the cap and drank it in one gulp.

"What was that?" Davinth asked. The lilt that came into his voice set Victor on edge and triggered his memories and senses. Danger smelled like smoke in a forest.

"Herbs," Victor said. "To replace my medicine."

"Herbs," Davinth repeated. "Interesting. Those Corps outside, they're here for you? What did you do? Steal their drugs?"

The last thread of Victor's patience for his guardians snapped. "What is with the Corps and Puros and drugs?" Victor edged a few steps toward the glass door.

Davinth eyed him warily. "The Corps keep pushing them from Vegas. They control the border. The police are useless. No one to help us but ourselves."

"The drug the Corps are pushing. What is it?" asked Victor.

Davinth's face darkened. "Stimsmoke. Some people call it Aura. Makes people see shit that isn't there. Gives them epic déjà vu. Makes addicts out of them. It's a stain on the purity of our homeland. To be truly pure is to know yourself and your weaknesses and look to others to help you stand proudly and free. How are you going to do that with a body full of poison?"

Before Victor could answer, a long honk was followed by a short burst. Davinth grabbed him and pulled him down the hall to the window by the front door. Three massive insect-like vehicles, similar to the ones Victor had outmaneuvered in the desert, had pulled up beside the van. Bandit got out of the van, spoke briefly to one of the vehicle drivers, and then approached the Puros' front door, stopping several meters away with his arms raised, palms open.

Elena and Xavi dragged several bags down the hall. Shapes made of metal and plastic peeked out of the bags. Weapons.

"More Corps showed up," Davinth said. "This one outside looks like he wants to talk."

Elena put her hand on Victor's shoulder. "It's going to be okay."

Light thumps sounded at the door, too weak for knocking. Xavi pushed past them and opened the door to look outside. He held a shockstick at his side. Victor followed with the others. Small stones littered the front steps.

Bandit stood on the walkway at a distance, smiling, but his eyes were hidden behind his creepy goggles. Keeping his arms raised, he pointed one finger at Victor. "All we want is him. Give him up, and we go away."

Davinth jerked his head at Victor. "Let's give them what they want and be done with it."

"We're not going to do that," Elena said. "Right, Xavi?" Her eyes grew wider when he didn't answer.

"He's not a Puro," Davinth complained. "They outnumber us. Look at those tanks. Bet they've got better gear than us, too. I say kick him out and cut our losses."

Elena took a step toward Xavi and lowered her voice. "We can call the police."

"They'll arrest us and give those guys a bounty. We're fucked," Davinth whined.

"Then we fight." Elena ran back to the weapons. "Come get your gear," she called.

Victor turned, but before he could take a step, he hurtled backward through the open door, spinning from the force of Xavi's shove and skidding across the grass. He landed on his butt as the door slammed shut. He could hear Elena shouting behind it.

He scrambled to his hands and knees. His bag lay a meter away in the grass. Hurting from scratches and soon-to-be bruises, Victor wished he could tear Xavi to shreds. But there was no time. Bandit came at him.

Victor jumped to his feet and started to run, but there was nowhere to go. Bandit approached in three quick steps, and swung his arm at Victor's chest, shoving him to the ground. Victor was dragged to his feet and flung over Bandit's shoulder.

He struggled, but Bandit managed to rush him into the van. Victor's head grazed the ceiling as he was flung inside and pinned there by Bandit's solid and wiry arms.

The woman, Lucky, sat next to Victor. "Got you," she said. "Victor, up close, you're such a doll." A hood descended over his face. She pressed something cool onto his bare wrist. The blackness of the hood grew darker, and his head lolled back. Unconsciousness overtook him.

45

Victor woke up sitting on something hard. His head felt swollen, pounding as if about to burst. When he opened his eyes, he saw only blackness. His body couldn't move, bound to a chair by his chest, arms, and legs. His wrists, behind his back, chafed against restraints that bound them together. Shapes shifted in the dark. Artifacts of his starved vision, or synesthetic echoes of his hearing, he couldn't tell.

Where was he?

A little voice in his head answered, *You're in SeCa, imprisoned in a Class One facility.*

His pulse spiked. He threw himself to one side, feeling a moment of weightlessness until the chair legs thumped back to the ground.

"Hello?"

His voice crackled electric-blue in the dark. He was in a small room, judging by the echo. He smelled cheap plastic carpet, a subtle paint residue, and synthleather. This wasn't the treatment standard for Class Ones. No one cared about people with MRS once they were committed. Maybe he was doomed to whatever semicivilized tortures could be devised. He'd heard they could be shipped offshore, free from constitutional protections. Perhaps they'd let the syndrome's effects eat away at his mind until only a husk remained.

A just punishment. Alik had been a husk for a long time. More recently, Victor's behavior was deteriorating, becoming more antisocial and aggressive. He'd horrified his family with his accusations of murder. He'd left Granfa Jeff's body out in the open air. He'd hurt Hadrian by going blank. He might have killed the Corps who stopped him on the road from Las Vegas. There didn't seem to be a limit to how awful he could be.

Months ago, he could have pictured himself living a semi-normal life. Now, he had to doubt that he was still sane. What if a manic fantasy had taken hold? Granfa Jeff's murder, Victor's flight from SeCa, his pursuers, a mystery man named Tosh, Ozie's conspiracies—maybe his mind had finally fractured, and the darkness would never lift. But he was aware of the recent madness—the truly insane never doubted themselves, did they?

If it was all a delusion, how could his brain have constructed such elaborate memories of Pearl, Ozie, Tosh, the Corps and the Puros, Lucky and Bandit? He couldn't have dreamed up a Puro safe house if he'd never been to one. He'd never seen Las Vegas or Amarillo or shared the view of Lake Tahoe and the Sierras with Elena. He held memories of those places in his mind as clear as day. These were the facts; they were his link to sanity, and darkness couldn't erase them.

Victor blinked his eyes, willing his vision to find light, and found a tiny yellow sliver beyond his right shoulder. A door, an exit, maybe? Proof that he wasn't imprisoned in his imagination?

He inhaled. A Class One facility wouldn't smell so plain. It would reek of an institution: piss and bleach and worse. Maybe he was back in SeCa, and this was a room on a ranch for Class Twos, where he would have nothing but time to read, study, and engage in productive work. He would be blessed with free time but not freedom.

Perhaps he could tutor the other residents. He had undoubtedly gone further in his education than most Class Twos would have. *There might be animals—horses to ride and care for, maybe goats and sheep*, a part of him whispered. The speaker, his doubt personified, was a glittering obsidian shape winking and sparkling before his sightless eyes. *No more struggling. No more fear. Surrender.*

But a tiny flame burned in his chest. He wouldn't calmly accept his predicament. He wouldn't indulge in delusions of self-doubt. He would never stop searching, never stop demanding the truth.

His body tensed against the restraints and tested the bonds. He flexed and relaxed his legs, earning a few millimeters of wiggle room. He flexed harder and heard a ripping sound. The straps must have been fastened with scratch loops. Not terribly secure. His feet jerked hard and made a tearing sound. The straps ripped apart, and his feet and lower legs were free. He paused, now hoping no one could hear him struggle and pant.

Victor wriggled forward, moving his shoulders like a swimmer, back and forth, jerking upward, lifting the rear legs of the chair a few millimeters off the ground each time. The chest strap climbed his torso until it pulled painfully at his underarms. He leaned forward, lifting his shoulders and arms as high as possible behind him and pressing as hard as possible. The chest strap ripped free and slackened, falling to his waist.

Victor tugged his wrists, trying to raise them higher, but his back muscles cramped. He bent forward and pressed his forehead to his knees. He breathed, trying to direct oxygen to the spasming line of tissue, willing the muscles to relax. He would try again in a minute.

Victor raised his arms again, took a gasping breath, and pulled them higher, leaning forward, straining and stretching muscles that screamed for him to stop. A high-pitched whine escaped his mouth. Then his hands jerked forward. His face smacked into his knees. It hurt, but he didn't care. His nose throbbed. His hands rested on the seat behind him, free from the chair but still bound together.

He twisted, feeling with his fingers around the left side of the chair behind him, where the strap circled his thighs. His fingertip found an edge of the strap and traced the seam where hooks and loops joined. Twisting further, a back muscle strained. He ignored it, trying to make contact with more of his fingers. He managed to grasp the free end. Finally, with a grunt, he peeled off the strap and released his legs.

Victor stood up quickly. Too quickly. The blood rushed out of his head. Losing his balance, he fell to one side, but managed to keep his head from banging against the floor. Wriggling toward a wall, he hoisted himself to sitting.

One restraint remained, binding his wrists. He slithered in the darkness, finding the overturned chair. His shoulder bumped against the chair leg. He used the edge of the chair leg to pry one end of the wrist strap away from the other. He repeated the motion once, twice, three times, and the seal was broken, the strap flung to the side. Free.

Victor checked his pockets for his belongings, but they were empty. He crept in the darkness toward the strip of light under the door. People were talking outside. Holding his breath, he strained to listen. He could only pick out a few words: something about patience and money.

His hand hunted for the doorknob, and when he found it, he pulled himself up. A low hum filled his ears. All his muscles clenched. A lightning storm of pain shot through his hand and coursed through his body. He leapt back, electrocuted.

He howled, filling the small room with his cry. He felt wetness spreading across his crotch. The doorknob had shocked the piss out of him. He slammed his elbow against the door.

A man's voice, Bandit's, said, "I wouldn't touch that again. I just doubled the power setting."

Had he been there the whole time? Listening to Victor struggle, refusing to answer his calls? Watching him, perhaps? There could be an infrared camera somewhere.

Victor resisted the urge to pound the door and throw himself against it. He searched the wall and found a touch panel. Light rained down from the ceiling. The box-like room was unfurnished. Thin beige carpeting covered the floor. There were no windows, only a single closed door. Plain and calming, the room looked like the one Dr. Tammet had designed to help him during blankouts. The door looked solid, but there was no locking mechanism on his side of it.

"Where am I?" he asked. "Why did you bring me here?"

There was no answer.

He put his ear against the door, avoiding the knob, and listened for movement. Silence.

"Did the Classification Commission hire you? You can't extradite me without a trial, you know. Your jurisdiction ends at the SeCa border."

Bandit chuckled softly. He sounded relaxed. "I couldn't care less about jurisdiction. Don't worry. We're taking you back to SeCa as soon as we get paid."

Paid by whom?

Victor's forehead rested against the door. He said, "I'll pay you to let me go. Please, if you give me my things, I can make the transfer." As he spoke, his breath rebounded in his face, a sour stench smelling of acid and heat, metabolic byproducts of the sedative they'd given him.

"We've already got a buyer."

Victor slumped back against the door. He had trouble believing anyone—even his family—would care enough to pay.

He rechecked his pockets. Still empty. He didn't have much to work with. The chair sat overturned in the middle of the room, and the restraints lay nearby like snake skins ... or insulators! The synthleather straps might let him grip the knob without getting zapped.

But Bandit was on the other side, and he was strong, probably steroid-enhanced. Not the type that Victor could overpower. He would have to wait for a better opportunity.

Victor gathered up the straps. Minutes ticked by. Then shouting came from somewhere beyond the door.

"Hello?" Victor asked.

No answer, but he could hear strained voices.

It was now or never.

He stood and wrapped the restraints around both his hands. He gingerly tested the doorknob. A slight buzz tingled in his forearms; nothing like the sharp zap he had received before. He gripped the knob with both hands, but his fabric-wrapped hands rotated uselessly. He pressed harder to create friction, and felt the knob begin to turn, then accelerate on its own.

The door opened inward, and Victor stepped back.

An unfamiliar man dressed in black with glinting metal weapons strapped to each limb stepped into the room. A Corp. He was pointing a shockstick at Victor's heart.

Victor closed his eyes, cringing and bracing himself for a Dirac pulse that, at such close range, could leave him paralyzed for life. But it didn't come.

He opened his eyes and caught a glimpse of a crowd dressed in battle gear through the open door.

Standing in the doorway, behind the man with the shockstick, as proud and authoritative as a military commander, with crossed arms and a wispy corona of hair, was his BioScan supervisor, Karine.

"There you are, Victor," she said. "Don't worry. I brought some Personil. You'll be feeling fine soon enough."

46

Republic of Texas
9 March 1991

Victor staggered forward, covering the damp spot on his crotch with his hands. He followed Karine and her band of Corps into a large room packed with cubicle dividers, desks, and chairs. A thin layer of dust covered everything. He looked out dirt-streaked windows. The sun was setting, bathing the view toward Amarillo's train station in orange light.

Someone cursed nearby. Victor turned. Lucky and Bandit were on the ground, being tied up by the Corps and fuming. One of the Corps had taped their mouths shut. Karine whispered in another Corp's ear, then pulled Victor gently by the arm to a pair of office chairs. They sat facing each other.

Victor nodded to the people guarding Lucky and Bandit. "Who are they?"

"Corps, our security partners." She sounded genuine, yet queasiness churned his stomach. If Karine was working with the Corps, who were Lucky and Bandit working for?

Karine leaned forward, clasped her manicured hands in front of her mouth, grass-green painted nails glinting, and watched him closely. After a moment, she said, "We're taking you home."

"What if I don't want to go?"

Karine looked at him, surprised. "You may not be thinking clearly. We found strange herbs among your possessions."

"Do you have the data egg, too?"

She shook her head.

Victor lowered his head. He'd lost both the data egg and the Handy 1000. Not to mention his dreambook. Now Karine would drag him back to SeCa, where he'd spend the rest of his life in confinement.

"Listen, Victor," she said, "We're going to help you get past this. Circe has arranged a place for you in Carmichael."

His stomach flipped as he pictured a facility filled with vacant-eyed, piss-reeking invalids. But Carmichael was home to a facility for Class Ones and a ranch for Class Twos. He asked, "The ranch or the facility?"

"That's up to you," Karine said. "We need a full account of your activities over the past week to undo the damage you've caused. That includes the intrusion into our network. You can't possibly have accomplished that alone. If you tell us everything that happened and who helped you, then you'll go to a Class Two ranch. Otherwise, I'm afraid we'll have to take you to a Class One facility. It's your choice."

"You don't understand," Victor said. "There's a war over stims. They're flooding into the ROT, and *they* are part of it." He pointed at the Corps. "Stims are being added to drinks and sold in *supermarkets*. Everyone is becoming addicted. Wait—" Victor reared back in his chair. He remembered sitting in Karine's office as she described how MRS and addiction were at the center of the project she wanted him to lead. "BioScan is going to benefit from all this. The new project …"

"It's time to get back on your medication."

She wanted to silence him, didn't she? What did he really know about Karine LaTour? She was an old family friend who had worked with Circe in Madrid at the start of their careers. She was good at her job: fair, ruthless, and ambitious. She treated Victor as a project, a resource to be fixed and used. He'd always thought there was something more to her feelings than professional ties. A mysterious charge filled the air whenever she looked at him, though he'd never known whether it was attraction or repulsion. Despite all that, he suspected she wouldn't hesitate to lock him away.

Karine blinked at him, and he was surprised to see a pink glow of compassion in her expression. Maybe he could persuade her to help.

Victor said, "They're not fantasies. Jefferson died of radiation poisoning. I found proof."

"I'm not going to validate your delusions by discussing them."

"My mind is not the problem. There's something wrong with the way people with MRS are treated in SeCa. As far as I can tell, there's nothing *right* about it. I know about plans to put ranches and facilities everywhere. Europe's next, too, isn't it? You can't do that."

Karine crossed her arms. "We have a good system. A humane system. The rollout has been carefully planned."

"You don't even realize that what you're doing is wrong. How can you not see it? How can you go against what Jefferson Eastmore stood for? He didn't want the Classification System to expand. He was killed because of it. You have to see the logic in what I'm saying."

Karine sighed and reached inside her blazer pocket. She withdrew a pill case, which she opened, displaying two doses of Personil and three pills Victor didn't recognize. "You're making exactly the kind of illogical deductions that indicate mania." She was clinically cold and cruelly logical. She seemed to believe what she was saying. Laws, she was good at spinning the truth.

Except Victor knew that *he* was not the problem.

Karine held the pills out. "Last chance."

"I'm not taking those," he told her.

Karine signaled to one of the nearby Corps. Victor hadn't realized they were lurking so close. He started to turn, then felt a cool sensation on his neck. A medpatch. He reached to remove it, but the Corp clamped a hand on his neck to prevent him.

"That'll keep you docile for the ride to the airport," Karine said.

Usually, adrenaline would have flooded Victor's system at the mention of flying. The worst panic attack in his life had gripped him for hours during a flight from Oakland & Bayshore to Oklahoma City. But the medication that moved from the patch into his skin dulled his emotions and made him feel as if he were wrapped in cotton and rocked by gentle waves.

Then, gradually, Victor moved outside himself, hovering, barely connected to consciousness.

"I won't force you onto Personil for now," Karine said, "but remember that Class One facilities can do what they like, and Personil is a mild option compared to others. It's not too late to change your mind. Who helped you steal BioScan's data? Can you hear me?"

As she spoke, Victor felt himself drifting. He was only catching a word or two at a time. Karine leaned toward him, cupping his face in her hands, which helped pull him back into his body momentarily. He heard her say, "I won't have to deal with you anymore."

Then, like a string had been cut, he floated up to the ceiling, hovering, watching the Corps led Lucky and Bandit down the corridor. Karine gestured to Victor's docile body. Other Corps lifted him by the arms and escorted him to the elevators.

It was a strange sensation to watch himself, to feel as if he were split in two—*two* pieces!—body below and mind above. He didn't fight or struggle. It wouldn't make a difference if he did. Instead, he enjoyed floating, watching events unfold.

Karine, the Corps, and their three prisoners rode the elevator down to a subterranean parking garage. Two black vehicles awaited—*another two, always two; when would he know what two meant?* Karine, a male Corp, and mindless Victor climbed into one, while the remaining Corps maneuvered Lucky and Bandit into the other.

Soon, they were traveling through Amarillo at dusk. Victor's disembodied self trailed behind the vehicle, high above, tethered to his physical self by the thinnest thread imaginable. Most strangely, there was no hint of blankness, and its absence felt like a piece of himself was missing.

From his vantage point high above, he spotted another two vehicles in the road ahead and saw with eagle-sharp vision that Tosh and Elena sat in each, blocking the way. Victor watched with growing alarm as two projectiles shot from one of the blocking cars—a violation of the global arms control regime.

A missile hit the vehicle carrying Victor. Flames bloomed underneath, and tires melted onto the asphalt.

Rescue is here, he thought, as the tether connecting his mind and body snapped, and his consciousness whirled into the infinite sky.

47

Victor woke to find Elena leaning over him. He lay on a bed in a bleak room: dingy carpet, stains on the walls, sagging furniture.

"You're safe, Victor," Elena told him. "No panicking, okay?"

"I—Karine was here." He remembered being out of his body, but it was like a dream. He sat up, feeling aches and pains all over.

"She's next door, along with Lucky and Bandit. Tosh has them tied up. We took you on the road. Do you remember?"

Victor rubbed his eyes. "I wish I could make it through one day without being drugged, gassed, or knocked unconscious."

Elena said, "Understandable. I have good news and bad news. Good news, I'm a fantastic spy. When Tosh found me at the Baldwin Street House, we agreed to work together to get you back. I hid my MeshBit in his car and returned it without him noticing. Bad news, it recorded a conversation between him and the King."

Haze interfered with Victor's thoughts. Tosh was involved with the Corps? He shook his head and climbed out of bed. "The King is like the boogeyman. You're as bad as Ozie, blaming some shadowy figure for everything."

Victor said, "It doesn't make sense. Karine was working with the Corps. If Tosh was too, what the shocks is going on?"

"The Corps aren't a tight-knit organization. They're dickies for hire. They fight each other as much as they cooperate. But they all serve the King. He has them all chipped." Victor opened his mouth to question this, but she held up a hand. "I don't pretend to understand how they work. Don't think of them as a single organization. They're more of a loose franchise of assholes."

Victor laughed.

"Now that they've come into conflict, they're getting sorted out by a higher authority. Tosh. You know what this means," she said. "You can't trust him."

Victor groaned. The shifting allegiances and rivalries made his head ache. "You're sure it was the Diamond King?"

Elena nodded. She said, "If you ever get the egg open, whatever's inside, you can't let him have it."

Victor tried not to think about it. "I'll worry about that once I've got it back. I want to talk to Lucky, Bandit, and Karine," he said. "This is my chance to sort out the truth."

They walked outside into twilight. Ten identical lodge rooms faced him across an empty parking lot.

Elena said, "The cars are around the back." She laughed bitterly. "Tosh brought weapons. No surprise there. The Corps are lying in the road where we blasted them."

Elena led him to a door and keyed the code to unlock it. He stepped inside.

Someone lay on the floor—Bandit. He seemed to be breathing.

Tosh was tightening a set of ropes that bound Lucky face down to one of two beds. Karine, unconscious, chin lolling on her chest, sat on a chair by the bathroom door, secured by synthleather straps, much as Victor had been a few hours before.

A slim desk and a chest of drawers shared the small space. Through a doorway, Victor could see a tiny bathroom. The unit served only as a brief resting place for people on their way elsewhere. The lightstrips in the ceiling glowed dimly. Their biofuel reserves were running low. Elena entered behind him and deadbolted the door.

Tosh saw Victor and calmly tucked away a loose end of a strap. Then he lunged at Victor across the small room and poked a stiff finger into his chest. "You run from me again, and I'll kill you."

"Guys, calm down," Elena said. "No harm, no foul."

Victor crossed the room and sat on the bed, running his hands across the bedspread's gaudy pattern. "No, you won't," he said quietly. "You need me to open the data egg."

Tosh stared at him for a moment. Then he harrumphed.

"Speaking of the egg, where is it?" Victor asked.

"We looked but didn't find anything except this junk." Tosh waved at the bedside table, which held two sleep jabbers, a Dirac shockstick, and a pack of stimsmokes. There was no data egg and no Handy unit. His backpack and herbs weren't there either.

"You want your stuff?" Tosh asked.

Victor nodded.

"Let's ask this dickie," Tosh said and spat on the rug next to Bandit's face.

Victor helped Tosh lift Bandit onto the second bed.

"First things first," Victor said. He untied Bandit's shoes and wrestled them off. Reaching around the man's hips, he unfastened his pants and jerked them free as well. The most challenging step was slipping Bandit's floppy arms out of his shirt, which he accomplished as Tosh stood by and watched with a creepy leer. Soon, Bandit was only covered with a pair of briefs. Victor did the same with Lucky, stripping her down to her panties and bra.

"What's that all about?" Elena asked.

Victor tossed the clothing to the floor. "They'll be more eager to talk."

Tosh pulled coils of synthleather cords from a gear bag and twisted them around Bandit's body and limbs multiple times, trussing him.

Victor said, "Whatever happens, they brought it on themselves."

Tosh rummaged in his bag, then held up a cylinder and tossed it to Elena. "This'll do the trick."

She examined it. "Skinjector stimulant, wake-up juice."

"Do it," Victor said. "Him first."

Elena pressed the Skinjector into the soft skin behind Bandit's knee. Seconds later, his gasp echoed through the room, and he began to cough. Bandit strained against the synthleather and turned his head in Victor's direction. "Oh. Just the person I wanted to talk to. I have a question about Broken Mirrors. Why are they all such assholes?"

"Where's my stuff?" Victor asked Bandit.

Tosh sat on the bed and leaned an elbow on Bandit's back. Bandit groaned under the bigger man's weight.

"Tell him." Tosh pressed down harder. "If you don't answer our questions, we'll start working on your companion. Where's the data egg?"

Bandit became still.

Victor asked Tosh, "Can you make him talk, or can't you?"

Tosh pulled a cudgel from his black bag. "Most useful starting tool."

Victor looked into Tosh's eyes, and a pleasurable tingle started in his lips.

Tosh traced the curve of Bandit's cheek with the cudgel's tip. Then he pressed more strongly, smooshing and lifting, tilting his head back at a sharp angle. Victor thought he heard Bandit's vertebrae grind against each other and couldn't be sure if it was his synesthesia or a real sound.

Tosh said, "I can shatter the bones around your eyes, break your nose, and knock out your teeth. I can leave bruises that won't heal for a month. I've beaten men so badly that they died from kidney failure, and I barely broke a sweat. Now, where is Victor's stuff? The egg, in particular, I'm interested in."

Tosh pressed the cudgel into the man's gut and lifted, pressing against a rib.

Bandit's brow creased, and he let out a pained, angry moan.

Tosh said, "That was the easiest question I'll ask you. Might as well save your strength for the others."

"Forget him," Elena said. She turned to Lucky. "Let's see what she has to say."

Bandit strained against the straps. "Don't touch her!"

"Tell me where my medicine is," Victor commanded.

Bandit said with a sneer, "Or what? You'll cry?"

Victor jumped on the bed and snatched at Bandit's black, greasy hair, yanking as hard as possible. Bandit yelled incoherently.

Victor grabbed hold of his neck. "Tell me, or I'll squeeze until you pass out."

Tosh pulled Victor off Bandit. "Let me handle this." He leaned over Lucky, found a suitable place on her neck, and jabbed her with a wake-up Skinjector.

"Don't!" Bandit yelled.

Tosh jerked a thumb at Bandit. "Stuff a sock in his mouth."

Victor found a sock. Bandit tried to move his head away, so Victor pressed a finger against Bandit's eyelid. "Open up, or I'll blind you!"

Victor scraped his fingers against Bandit's teeth as he shoved the sock in his mouth. The excitement churning in his belly wasn't to be trusted. He leaned against the wall, closed his eyes, and watched patterns form and evolve behind his eyelids: triangles, stars, fractals growing, moving, and decaying inside one another. The flows and turbulent colors were beautiful, but he would eat fistfuls of fumewort for a moment of inner quiet.

Victor felt a hand squeeze his shoulder. He opened his eyes. Elena looked at him with concern. Beyond her, Lucky's body writhed on the bed, her eyes fluttering. She opened them and saw Bandit tied up, face down. She groaned.

Tosh sat on the edge of the bed next to Lucky. He lifted her into a sitting position and stroked her back. "Morning, sunshine. Your friend didn't want to tell me where the data egg is. You're going to tell me now, or I'm going to beat him within an inch of his life."

She strained to look at Tosh. "You psychopath. Unless you let us go right now"—she jerked her head around—"What the hell is this?"

Tosh smiled. "Old habits die hard."

Questions tumbled from Victor's mouth. "Where is my stuff? Did you poison my granfa? Who hired you?"

Tosh clucked at him. "All in good time, Vic. It's important to establish a rapport."

Lucky tried to peek at her partner. "Bandit, you okay?"

Bandit's mouth was still gagged. His eyes widened, and his head alternately nodded and shook.

"Okay, I'm bored," Tosh said. "Where is the data egg? Now!"

Lucky was silent.

Tosh flicked open a knife. He held it up so both captives could see it. "One more chance."

"Don't be insane," Lucky said.

Tosh walked to the end of the bed and sat heavily on Bandit's left foot. He gripped the right foot, pulled it upward against the restraints, and clamped it underneath his arm. Then he carved a slit across the arch of Bandit's foot. Bandit's screams leaked out of his gagged mouth. Victor watched, feeling hot, wet tingling in his own foot.

"Stop it!" Lucky screamed.

Elena grimaced and crossed her arms but said nothing.

Tosh cut Bandit again. As the blade traveled, he pressed the point in deeply while twisting. Blood streamed onto the bed covers.

The room flooded with shame that smelled to Victor like muddy riverbanks. He moved to the window and peeked out between a gap in the curtains. A hobo trudged along the dirt sidewalk across the street. Trash blew by. A scratchy place at the back of his throat wouldn't go away despite his attempts to clear it. He wasn't responsible for Tosh's actions. The shame surrounding Victor was illusory: it wasn't his; it wasn't what he deserved.

Tosh seemed to be forgetting that the point of the torture was to get answers to questions. Victor walked to Lucky and slapped her face. "Where are my things? Tell me before he does something worse."

"Bastards," Lucky groaned. "It's in our van. Secret compartment to the left of the passenger footwell."

"The van's out back," Elena said.

Victor bolted outside, running to the rear parking lot and the van. He tore open the door, jumped in, and found the hidden compartment. He took out his data egg and the Handy 1000, whooping and smiling, feeling complete again.

Victor breathed on the data egg, licked it, and tried rubbing it between his hands. The device stared back at him like an ominous black eyeball. He shoved it into his pocket. The Handy 1000 blinked, indicating received messages. He quickly unfurled it. One message from his parents questioned where he was and why he hadn't called them. His aunt asked the same questions. Another from Ozie read: "More bad news: systems hacked. Café raided by King. On the move. Good luck."

There was nothing Victor could do about that. He fished into the recesses of the secret compartment, searching for his medicine. There was no sign of the bitter grass and fumewort sachets. The empty vials and alcohol for making tinctures weren't there either.

His bowels squirmed. No more herbs, and with Pearl on the run with Ozie, no way to get more. Maybe the Puros could find some. Until then, what would he do? He was barely holding himself together.

He searched the van, checking the glove compartment and the cargo bay. He came up empty. He looked under the seats. Nothing. Lucky and Bandit must have put the sachets somewhere else, maybe back at their office hideout. He would have to ask them. Perhaps impolitely.

Victor climbed out of the van and returned to the lodge, holding the objects in each hand above his head. Faster than he could react, Tosh snatched the data egg, putting it in a pocket and zipping it shut. Victor opened his mouth to protest, but Tosh pointed the knife at him and shook his head in warning.

Victor asked, "Why do you care so much about the egg?"

Tosh said, "Jeff gave it to me, but at the last minute, he changed his mind. Said he should be the one to do it. He seemed particularly worried about what might happen to you. And, man, let me tell you, he was right. You're a magnet for trouble."

"What else do you know?" Victor asked. "Now is the time to tell me, Tosh. Before you torture them anymore, we should compare notes."

"Jeff didn't tell me anything. That was how he operated, but this time I keep kicking myself for not forcing the truth out of him. Not that I could have. Stubborn goat. All he said was to look after you."

That's not an answer. "What are you going to do when it opens? Are you going to run to the King?"

Tosh stiffened but didn't say anything.

There it is, the truth, finally, Victor thought.

Victor would deal with Tosh later. He walked to Lucky. "I couldn't find my medicine. Where is it?"

"What are you—"

"The herbs! Little glass vials!" Victor turned to Bandit. "Do you have them? Are they in that office building?" He removed the gag.

Bandit shook his head. "I don't know what you're talking about."

"The herbs. My medicine. We'll cut you again if you don't tell us."

Lucky groaned. "Oh, Laws! They're gone, okay? She got rid of them."

"Who did?" Victor asked.

"She said they were junk."

"Who?" Victor asked. He felt as if he was finally getting to the bottom of why these two had been following him.

"Karine, you dumb shit! Since you went to that herbalist, she's been complaining about your herbs. She told her Corps to flush them."

"*She's* been complaining? You knew her before Amarillo, before kidnapping me?"

Lucky laughed bitterly. "Who do you think hired us?"

48

Victor sat down on the bed, speechless.

Could Karine have killed Jefferson? Why?

Through her role at Gene-Us, she'd had access to the genetic sequence linked to mirror resonance syndrome. She could have used that knowledge to manufacture stims. As a business leader in SeCa, she could have obtained polonium from one of her many contacts overseas. She had close enough ties to the Eastmore family to administer the poison. After Jefferson Eastmore died, Karine maneuvered her way onto the Health Board, where she helped shape SeCa's policy on mirror resonance syndrome. She was perfectly placed to pull all the strings. And when Victor had started snooping around, she'd hired Lucky and Bandit.

Shocks, it was obvious now. The sight of her tied to the chair unconscious made his stomach heave. He ran to the bathroom and closed the door behind him. Shaking, he turned on the faucets in the sink and doused his head.

"Victor?" Elena called from the other side of the door.

"Leave me alone!"

"Why were you following him?" Victor heard Tosh say over the sound of the running water.

Victor slumped against the tub and shuddered, breathing hard. His heart raced. His mind was caught in the resonance again. Fear spiking. Losing control. Blankness loomed over him. Compared to his anger, the blankness was soothing, but he didn't want to go blank. He stood shakily and gripped the sink with both hands.

Bandit's scream, muffled through his gag, surged through the closed door.

"Tell me everything Karine told you," Elena said from the other room.

Karine's wrongdoing could be bigger than murder. She might be responsible for all the addiction and conflict ravaging the Republic of Texas. She could have killed his granfa, organized a drug cartel, and tracked him to this wasteland. He pictured his hands closing around her neck and the look on her face as he crushed her windpipe. He had to confront her, but he needed a fail-safe in case he couldn't control himself.

Water dripped along the curve of his scalp and down his face. Shivering, he focused on the sensation of the drops crawling on his skin. He had to remain calm, coherent, and sane, but he didn't have the bitter grass and fumewort to help him. Fine. It would be difficult, but he could do it.

Bandit was whining in the other room. Bile rose in Victor's throat, and his mouth watered. He tried not to picture Bandit lying down, restrained, at Tosh's mercy. How far would Tosh go to get answers? Maybe Victor should try to stop him. But he wanted answers as much as Tosh did. Maybe more.

Tosh asked Lucky, "Did she order you to kidnap Victor?"

Lucky gasped, "What are you doing? Stop it!"

"Answer the question."

Lucky said, "We did it to protect him. To keep him safe from the dickies."

Tosh laughed cruelly, a sickening sound from someone holding a knife.

No use letting Tosh have all the fun. I could carve up Lucky and Bandit and do the same to Karine. It was a terrible thought. He couldn't let himself walk that dark path. He needed a distraction. *The wise owl listens before he asks, "Who?"*

Victor pulled out the Handy 1000, pressing the first name he saw: Circe Eastmore.

The call connected right away.

"Auntie?"

"Victor! Are you all right? Karine said she was going to bring you home."

"No, I'm ... I'm in Amarillo. I—I think I know ..." Victor had trouble forming words. He took a breath. He had to tell her, to warn her about Karine.

"Amarillo? I'm not sure where that is. Did Elena drag you there?

Cody Sisco

Oh, Victor, I'm sorry we ever got her involved."

Victor blanched. "*You* got Elena involved? I thought Ma found her."

"I thought you might need a friend with everything you were going through, so I suggested it to your mother."

A hot flash of indignation seized Victor. He terminated the feed and threw the Handy 1000 to the floor. Everyone in his life was pulling his strings, lying to him, compounding his problems. "We didn't want to upset you. Trust us, we know what's best," they said, even as they lied, withheld, and manipulated.

What I don't know is leading me to ruin, and everyone is so satisfied with how well they're protecting me from myself. Look where it got me.

In the other room, Tosh asked, "Why did you kidnap him? Think carefully. This knife is getting cold."

Lucky answered, "I told you! We were working for Karine. He stole data from BioScan, and we were supposed to get it back."

"Uh huh," Tosh said, "and how long have you been following him?"

Victor's curiosity pulled at him. He opened the door and peeked out. Tosh was holding Bandit's ankle and waving his foot back and forth. Blood trickled down his leg. Karine hadn't moved and was still unconscious.

"Victor, are you all right?" Elena asked. "Do we need to get out of here?"

"How long?" Tosh asked.

Lucky craned her neck to see what Tosh was doing. "As soon as the data went missing—"

"Wrong answer," Tosh sneered. "I was there at the graveyard, and so were you, *before* he stole BioScan's data. This is going to hurt, buddy." He cut into Bandit's foot, a deep slice that ran from the ball to the heel. Bandit's entire body vibrated and jerked as he screamed in his gag.

Victor tasted metal in his mouth, probably from the water. He wiped his lips with the back of his hand, which came away streaked with blood. He pursed his lips and felt pain. He'd bitten them.

Tosh said, "You were following Victor for weeks before he left SeCa, way before he took the data."

Lucky said, "Okay! Okay! Stop it, you sicko. We started following him back in December."

"Why?" Tosh asked.

"We were watching him for Karine."

"Why?"

"Ask her!"

Tosh grinned. "I will, but I'm not done with you two yet." He put down the knife and took the cudgel in hand, adjusted his grip, stood, and pinned Bandit's ankle against the bed with his boot. He swung the cudgel hard against the bottom of Bandit's foot. It landed with a wet smacking sound that turned Victor's stomach. Blood splattered the sheets and carpet. Bandit screamed and moaned into his gag.

"Tosh! Enough!" Elena yelled. "Let's wake Karine."

Tosh pointed at the captives. "I'm not done. These two stimheads need a lesson. Maybe you should step outside. Take Victor with you."

Elena looked at the half-naked bodies tied up on the bed.

Victor said, "I'm not going anywhere." He walked to Bandit and removed his gag. "You recorded everything I did for weeks, didn't you?"

Bandit said, "We saved your butt in Little Asia."

"And kidnapping me? You have an excuse for that, too?"

"You got mixed up with the Puros. It was for your own safety."

"For my own safety." Victor wanted to rip Bandit's head off and toss it like a bowling ball.

Elena walked to Bandit and let a drop of saliva splat against his cheek. "You messed with the wrong people."

Bandit growled.

"Bandit!" Lucky yelled. "Stop antagonizing them."

Bandit whipped his head toward his partner. "I told you! This was a bad job from the start." He turned to look at Victor. "Karine wouldn't say. My guess is she wanted you reclassified."

Victor's vision filled with light. He didn't dare move, afraid he'd trip and fall. Could she hate him that much? Blankness threatened to return.

"I need to think," Victor said.

"Are you okay?" Elena asked.

Tosh watched him closely. Elena stared at him, eyes wide with concern. Victor didn't care. Only Karine held his attention. She sat in the chair, unconscious, and he felt a tide of hate surge within, threatening to carry him into blankness.

"Did you poison Jeff Eastmore?" Tosh asked Bandit, sitting on his back, suffocating him. He let up on the pressure, and Bandit took a gasping breath.

Bandit said, "That's *his* crazy fantasy."

"Turns out Victor was right about Jeff being murdered," Tosh said. "Did you poison him?"

"No!"

Victor said, "We need to wake Karine. Now."

Tosh nodded, and he and Elena moved over to Karine.

While their backs were turned, Victor snuck over to Tosh's black duffel bag, pulled out a small fist-sized metallic sphere—a gas bomb—and shoved it in his pocket. He took out a gas mask and hid it under the bed.

Elena said, "We'll need to turn the screws hard to get answers. Agreed?"

"Don't worry about it, princess," Tosh said. "I can take care of this."

Elena took a menacing step toward Tosh. "If you're saying I don't need to get my hands dirty because I'm a woman, you're going to see them soaked in *your* blood."

Tosh chuckled and raised his hands in surrender. "All right, you convinced me. You've got the biggest balls in the room."

Elena scowled as she tested the straps around Karine, the way someone might handle fruits at the market to test their ripeness. She gave Karine the wake-up shot.

Karine raised her head, blinked, and looked around. When she saw Victor, she rolled her eyes, saying, "I hope you haven't completely lost your mind."

49

Victor felt his eyes boiling in their sockets as he looked at Karine. He tried to speak, but words failed him. He held out his hand for the cudgel, which Tosh supplied.

Karine's fiery hair-frizz quivered when she laughed. "I was too lenient. You should have been locked up long before now." Her confidence almost convinced Victor that she still had the upper hand. But she didn't know how desperate he'd become.

"You murdered my granfa," Victor said.

"You've gone over the edge," Karine said.

Elena added, "She's a cold-blooded maniac."

Karine stared at Victor, ignoring Elena. Disdain hovered around her eyes, irrepressible, butting up against a sliver of black fear. She covered the truth well, though. He admired her composure.

Karine said, "It's my fault, in a way. I shouldn't have hired amateurs. They were young and cheap, and I liked them. Well, her anyway." Karine glanced at Lucky's mostly naked body. "Victor, you can still come back, you know."

Elena leaned close to Karine. "You are one nasty bitch."

Karine spat in Elena's face. Elena wiped it, then threw a punch that whipped Karine's head around. Victor heard something crack. He didn't know if it was Elena's hand or Karine's cheekbone. Karine sobbed and moaned, then stopped. She looked at Victor, her face the color of naked embers. Her rage flowed into him and met its twin.

He wanted to kill her.

A tickling sensation danced on the back of Victor's neck; it was a moment before he realized Bandit was calling his name. "Victor! She's not going anywhere. How about you cut us free so we can put our pants back on?"

"No," Victor growled.

"I never meant for them to hurt you," Karine said. "They were only supposed to watch you."

Victor felt himself twitching, rage crackling just under the surface of his skin. "Is that supposed to make me feel better? That they were only *watching* me?"

Karine's tongue flicked against her lips. "To make sure you didn't slip up. Circe was adamant."

Breath caught in Victor's throat. Auntie Circe had known?

Karine seemed to read his mind. "Of course, she knew. She wanted you followed—for your protection. Then you hacked our network and disappeared."

"Why are you *here*?" Elena asked.

"These two called me when they saved you from the Puros," Karine said.

"I wouldn't call it 'saving,'" Victor said.

Ignoring him, she shot a withering look at Lucky and Bandit. "Unfortunately, they got it in their heads to ask for a ransom. Rather than pay it, I hired the Corps to get you back."

"Are those your Corps at the kennel?" Victor asked.

"Yes. Mason Charter filed a lawsuit, claiming it belonged to him rather than your family. The Corps are a hedge against the lawsuit's outcome. Possession is nine-tenths of the law, after all. Why are you so interested in it?"

Bandit pleaded, "Look, this is all just a big misunderstanding."

"You were going to *sell* me," Victor said, swinging the cudgel into Bandit's thigh. Bandit's yell sounded more surprised than pained. Victor reached down, found the sock, and stuffed it in his mouth again.

"I know you're upset."

Karine spoke softly and measuredly, but Victor felt her voice burrowing into his skin like a tick. "Be quiet!" he snapped.

He paced the room, watching Karine. He would smack the truth out of her one blow at a time.

Lucky said, "We got greedy. Just let us go, and we'll disappear. We've got nothing against you."

Victor's ears were buzzing. It was too loud to think. Perhaps the universe had dark plans for him after all.

"Not one mistake," he mumbled aloud. "A lifetime of them." He put a hand on Karine's shoulder and looked into her eyes, light blue like a clear SeCa sky. "You hired them to watch me?"

Karine nodded vigorously. "That's the truth."

"For what it's worth, Victor," Tosh said, "people only say that when they're lying."

"You can still get out of this," Karine said. She looked at Victor intently. Her lips curved slightly as if she were enjoying the circus. She was undoubtedly clever enough to poison his grandfather and get away with it.

"You were playing with my life." Victor smacked her in the face. She was still. He paced in the small space between the beds, not sure what he would do next. Whom could he trust? Everyone seemed to have their singular version of the truth. His uncertainty was tearing him apart. He fingered the Handy 1000 in his pocket, then gripped the gas bomb.

Karine said, "Untie me and let them go. We'll forget this happened. A little slip-up. Completely understandable, but if I have to press charges, they'll put you in a Class One facility."

She was threatening *him*?

"Or I could kill you," Victor said. The calm, measured tone of his own words surprised him.

Karine laughed. "You'd never do that," she said.

Victor pulled Karine's hair—hard—jerking her head back. "You don't know what I'm capable of."

Karine's laugh was a rusty, coughing cackle. "You can't kill us. You wouldn't put your family through that."

Victor looked at the two freelancers bound and gagged on the bed, at Karine sitting in the chair, trussed like a turkey. It wouldn't take much. A blow or two to the head for each of them. They could drive the bodies to some remote piece of land and dump them. It would be easy.

Elena stepped forward and said to Karine, "It'll look like you got caught in a turf war. Victims of dickie violence in the ROT, simple as that. An investigation could take years."

Elena shoved Karine's head down. Her hair had lost its lift; red strands hung in her face like copper wire.

Victor remembered the incident in the juice shop. His hands had wanted to transform into claws and rip out that young woman's heart. It was the same feeling he had now: a pounding thunderous anger. And why not feel that way? He had a right. But he'd been wrong about the woman in the juice shop, hadn't he? Ric had wondered if she had MRS, too. Maybe she did. She might have simply wanted to talk to Victor. Everyone had a different truth.

Lucky's sobs grew louder. Bandit tried to say something through his gag.

"Victor?" Elena put her hand on his shoulder. "I think we have to get rid of them."

"Agreed," Tosh said, "Nothing personal, of course."

"Everybody shut up!" Victor yelled. He felt his heart racing. He said in a lower voice directed at Tosh and Elena, "I'm going to decide what's next. No one else."

Karine's voice pierced the dim room. "Victor, don't."

Elena whispered in Victor's ear. "She was going to lock you up and throw away the key! I'll do it, so you don't have to." Elena nodded toward Tosh. "We'll do it for you."

Victor looked at the bodies writhing on the bed, at Karine's hard, desperate face. They deserved to be punished. Tosh cocked his head to the side. He wore a know-it-all smirk under scheming eyes. Elena stood tall.

"Not yet," Victor said. "I need to know if she murdered my—if she assassinated Jefferson Eastmore."

"That fantasy again," Karine said. "I don't know *anything* about that."

Victor peered at her face. "You knew him. You poisoned him. You took his place on the Health Board. You got your fingers in his company."

A mix of emotions passed over her face: annoyance, incredulity, fury. But not guilt. She said, "You have a disturbing ability to ignore the facts when it suits you."

Victor said, "Radiation killed him. That's a fact. Tosh saw the evidence."

Tosh nodded.

Karine pursed her lips. "That's why the body was exhumed, wasn't it? What makes you think it wasn't an accident? Or suicide!"

Victor said, "He didn't want to see any of this happen—what's happened to people with MRS. Stims showing up everywhere—he would have hated that."

"More conspiracy nonsense."

"It's not nonsense. Stims mimic my condition."

"Of course they do. That's an open secret. You know about stims? Hooray for you. Pretty much anyone paying attention to the epidemic knows that. Why do you think we've been adjusting the diagnostic protocols?"

Elena sucked in her breath. "You want to treat addicts the same way you treat people with MRS?"

"Why not? The Classification System is comprehensive and humane. If Jefferson hadn't closed Oak Knoll, we'd have better treatments by now." She pulsed against her restraints. "The bigger problem is that we're constantly being hacked. That's what started this whole mess."

Victor leaned forward and smelled her perfume: lavender and sandalwood, hints of the ocean. He heard waves on the shore and tasted salt spray. "What do you mean?"

"Stims are based on a first-generation XSCT compound stolen from the Holistic Healing Network. Mind you, I was told all this secondhand after the merger." Karine's voice took on the monotone she used when dispensing updates at company meetings. "It wasn't just your family's company that got hit. Last year, there was an intrusion at Gene-Us, too. The accessed data included the MRS gene sequence. Someone used the stolen information to design and manufacture stims."

XSCT was the compound that had been shipped to the Lone Star Kennel. Victor had to find a way around the Corps guarding it. Maybe Karine wasn't completely useless.

Victor said, "But even my hacker buddy couldn't decrypt the sequence without ... drastic measures."

"Maybe your buddy is lying. Maybe *he's* the thief," Karine said.

Victor narrowed his eyes.

Karine continued, "We assumed the person who stole the sequence had a decryption key. There aren't many, but every member of the Health Board has one. Victor, are you sure Jefferson wasn't—"

"Wasn't what?" he asked.

"Now, don't get upset. But what if he was responsible for the stim epidemic? Maybe he meant for it to be an unsanctioned clinical trial. He could have manufactured the drugs at Oak Knoll and then hidden everything."

"That's ... He wouldn't ..."

Karine said, "Perhaps Jefferson couldn't live with what he'd done. You said he died of radiation poisoning? He certainly had the means to obtain polonium."

Tosh stepped forward. His hands were balled into fists at his sides. "Jeff Eastmore was a great man. He would never kill himself. Never."

Karine said, "I always thought so, too, but how else do you explain this? The other Health Board members are all policy wonks. They don't have the skills to pull this off."

"How do we know it's not you?" Elena asked.

Karine turned to Victor. Her eyes were large, open, hard. "I didn't poison him. You're creating a scandal, saying the most unbelievable things at the worst possible time. Are you trying to ruin your family's company? I know it's not a coincidence the intrusions started the day you disappeared. You stole, Victor. I hired these flackies to look after you, to protect you, and to protect your family's company. Ask your aunt. She knew. Yes, I made the mistake of not looking closely enough into their backgrounds. And maybe I should have had them on a tighter leash. Do you know the work involved in merging two companies? It's unrelenting. Things didn't go as planned, but it wasn't my fault. If you're looking for a culprit, you have to look further. Who benefits from stims?" Karine nodded at Elena. "Addicts get their fix and the drug pushers profit. The underworld wins. Not me. We're trying to bring order and healing to the world."

Victor looked from Karine to Elena and back again. "You're trying to distract me."

"Nothing of the sort. We all share some blame for the mess we're in. Her included. I arranged things with the clinic in New Venice as a favor to Circe. We were trying to help you. I suppose we should have ensured she could stay clean for longer than a few days."

Elena squared her shoulders. "Your clinics profit off treating addicts."

Karine said, "If I could wish away your addiction, I would. We tried to help you."

Elena said, "You put a chip in me!"

"A precaution. Which paid off, I might add." Karine smiled.

Elena got in Victor's face. "Let me kill her. If you let her go, she'll get you locked up. Victor, it's the only option."

Victor closed his eyes and pictured a solitary island, waves crashing on the shore. Wind shaking palm trees. Sand shifting in the dunes. Chaotic sounds and motion, blissfully meaningless. Soothing.

He'd come all this way for nothing. He had only a rough idea of what was really behind the stim market. He had no proof that Karine killed Jefferson. He barely knew who he was or what he was capable of anymore.

Victor opened his eyes. They were all looking at him.

Elena crossed her arms. He was numb with disbelief. The one person he cared about more than himself wanted to turn him into a murderer, a monster. She knew how much he feared this fate, how hard he'd tried to avoid it. But her need, the thing that drove her, whatever it was, the rage at an unfair world, the need to rectify it, came first for her. It was swallowing up his friend. Maybe it already had.

"I need to think," he said.

The room buzzed and hissed. Karine was either innocent or a crafty killer. Which was it? Victor fingered the gas bomb in his pocket again.

Tosh strode to the bathroom door, saying, "Let's talk in here."

"It's okay," Victor said. "Elena, will you—can I talk to you outside?"

Elena nodded, moved past Karine, and stepped around Victor. She opened the front door, cleared the threshold, and looked at him expectantly.

Victor slammed the door and flipped the deadbolt.

"Hey!" she yelled from the other side.

In a fluid motion, Victor triggered the gas bomb and threw it at Tosh's feet. White smoke jetted into the room, billowing across the floor. Victor dove to the bed's edge, grabbed the gas mask, and pulled it over his head. He belly-crawled back to the front door and curled into a ball, blocking it.

Tosh tried to pull him away to get outside. Victor tensed, his arms pinning the mask to his face. Tosh tried to pry it off, but coughs wracked his body. Victor squirmed, twisted, and kicked his foot up. It connected with Tosh's belly, and he sucked in a breath.

Smoke filled the room to the ceiling. The freelancers coughed. Karine screamed, perhaps not realizing it hastened her unconsciousness. She quieted, and her head drooped.

The two figures on the bed writhed. Then they, too, succumbed to the gas.

Tosh dropped to his knees. His hands latched onto Victor's gas mask. He coughed and pulled more lungfuls of smoke through his mouth. Victor held onto the mask. Tosh cursed, slumped down, and passed out.

The room was quiet. Victor was on his own. It was time for murder. Or perhaps something else.

50

Fog-white sleeping-gas particles filled the room like Mesh static. The filter on Victor's gas mask made it difficult to breathe, like trying to suck a juicebulb through a too-thin straw.

Victor wondered how long he could hide in this room. Elena was banging on the door. He couldn't sit there indefinitely, but he wasn't ready to confront her. He tried to open a vidfeed to Ozie and was surprised when the feed request was approved.

Ozie asked, "Laws, Victor, why are you wearing a gas mask?"

"Long story. Did you—"

"Look, can't talk long. I don't trust my programs to secure the feed. The Diamond King didn't like me messing with his MeshSats, and he traced me back to the café. Pearl and I are on the move."

"Ozie, did you steal the MRS gene sequence from Gene-Us last year?"

Ozie laughed. It sounded genuine to Victor. "Of course not," Ozie said. "If I had it already, why would I have had you steal it from BioScan?"

Victor said, "Someone broke into Gene-Us. Someone also stole an early version of the XSCT formula from Oak Knoll. That's what Karine told me, at least."

"And you believe her?" Ozie asked.

"I don't know what to think."

Ozie stroked his chin. "If she didn't do it, I'll give you one guess who else might be involved."

"The King?" Victor said.

Ozie said, "Correct. You asked me about that drone, remember? The one that followed you in the mountains? I found it. I tracked the operator back to Las Vegas. He's onto you, the Diamond King, onto us, and it started *before* you stole from him. I'm spooked. Pearl and I are going to set up somewhere quiet. Private. What are you going to do?"

"Search the kennel."

"Let me know what you find. And let us know where you'll be. Pearl's got some herbs for you." Ozie terminated the feed.

Victor watched the sleeping-gas eddies curl gently in the lodge room's still air. He had to find out what had happened to the XSCT compound, and the kennel was the key. Without Karine's help, though, it would be tough to get past the Corps.

Victor got up, leaned over Tosh's unconscious body, unzipped his pocket, and took back the data egg. Then he opened the door and stepped outside, leaving a crack open. He removed the bulky mask from his face and threw it on the ground.

Elena tried to peek inside, but Victor blocked her view. "What the shocks did you do?" she asked.

Victor brushed his sleeves and wondered how much of the sleeping substance had accumulated there. "I bought us some time. I couldn't think with everyone yelling at me."

She grabbed his arm. "Did you—"

"No." Victor shrugged her off. "If I didn't shut them up, though, I might have killed them."

Elena looked relieved.

"They'll be fine," he said.

She nodded, biting back whatever she wanted to say. Her eyes appeared to him a sickly green; even in the fading light, he could see how hard this day had been for her. He could blame stimsmoke's effects for running her down or her own bad judgment. He probably looked awful, too. His gaze flicked toward the motel window, but he turned away quickly. He didn't want to see his reflection.

In the parking lot, he stopped, and looked up at the stars. Only a few dozen peeked through the evening's dusty veil: Sirius, Betelgeuse, and the more prominent nodes of familiar constellations. Mars and Jupiter bracketed the moon, deceptively equidistant from each other in the sky but so far apart. Time and distance obscured the rest of the universe.

He turned to Elena. "You wanted me to kill them."

She flinched as if he'd slapped her. "I didn't—"

"How could you even suggest it? Ever since I was little, people that hate who I am have attacked me and treated me like I'm a bomb about to explode. You tried to light the fuse."

She shook her head and backed away. Only a car width separated them, but it could have been a wall of radiation. "I can't imagine what that's like. I know you're a good person, I do," she said, "but sometimes we have to do a wrong thing for the right reason."

Victor hung his head. He couldn't believe what she was saying. "What happened to you?" he asked. "When you joined the Puros, it's like you gave up the good part of yourself."

Tears streaked down her cheeks, catching the light pole's glare and sparkling. Her voice was ragged. "I lost that a long time ago." She wiped her cheeks with her sleeve. "They saved me. They gave me a reason to keep going."

Could the Puros and their cause have replaced him in her heart? They were something for her to take care of: a reason to put her needs and problems second. He saw her clearly now and kept his mouth shut. There were so many things he might say. He loved her, but they weren't good for each other. She had to feel complete without him, be happy by herself.

Victor peered inside the lodge room. They would probably be unconscious for hours. He nudged the door open to allow the remaining gas to escape. A breeze kicked up, and the air chilled his skin.

"I have to let them go," Victor said.

Elena said, "But that means they *win*."

He sighed. He hated that she argued when his choice had been made. "No, if I kill them, that's when I lose. There's no other option."

"She killed him!"

"She very well could have. But nothing I can do will bring him back, Elena. I refuse to become a killer."

"I don't think I could be so forgiving."

"I'm not forgiving. I'm going to find out the truth, and if she did kill him, I'm going to make her life a living hell. Or who knows? Maybe I'll learn to let the past go." Victor raised a hand in priest-like benevolence and met Elena's gaze. "Someday, I may pardon her sins."

One sole laugh escaped Elena's lips. Then she wrapped her arms around her chest, looking young, like her life clock had wound backward. He moved toward her and hugged her.

After a few moments in his embrace, she pulled away and looked at him with narrowed eyes. "You're not thinking about returning to SeCa, are you?"

Every minute of his life in SeCa depended on the mercy of people who didn't understand him. His family had formed an oasis of support beyond which only suspicion, hostility, and contempt existed. And then they'd hired thugs to keep him under surveillance. No, he would never go back to SeCa, even if he wasn't to be reclassified. Life for him there would always be confined by the radius of his family's wealth, power, and ability to carve out a safe place for him, which would be another kind of prison.

"No. I need to go someplace safe and civilized. SeCa's off limits, and it's too dangerous here." He smiled at her. "Maybe I'll move to an island in the Mediterranean."

She gaped, then laughed. "Stop joking around."

Insects began singing all around them, although they might have been buzzing the whole time and Victor hadn't been aware of them until he had summoned the idea of the Mediterranean from somewhere.

Winds buffeted Victor and Elena with dust and shards of gravel. Elena said, "Stay here. Please. You'd never have to worry about the Carmichael stuff again." She looked as if she wanted to reach out and touch him but wasn't sure of herself.

What to do? The few clothes and supplies he had brought could all fit in a small sack. He hadn't prepared for a journey longer than a week or so. He'd have to find a new source of herbs, a new regime for managing his condition. It would be like starting over again. But would that be so bad? The thrill of a clean slate began to take hold of him.

All he was sure of was Amarillo couldn't be his final destination. It wouldn't hurt as a stopover, though, while he sorted out where to go next.

Elena cocked her head. "Why the goofy smile?"

"It's nothing. I just—I'll stay. For a little while, at least."

Inside the motel room, the haze had dissipated. Victor untied Karine and gently slipped her body down to the floor. Elena brandished Tosh's bloody knife and cut the ropes that tied Bandit and Lucky to the bed. Searching around the room, she and Victor found the freelancers' clothes and confiscated belongings and placed them on the beds.

Cody Sisco

Elena pulled out a wad of cash and placed it next to Bandit.

"What's that for?" Victor asked.

"He needs to get his foot sewn up."

"Keep the cash. It's not enough." Victor transferred ten thousand AU dollars to Bandit's paystick with a note: "For your troubles. Let's hope this is the last time we meet." He did the same for Lucky.

"Now for Tosh." Victor started the Handy 1000's sonorecorder. "Tosh, no hard feelings, I hope. When the data egg opens, I'm willing to make a trade. Information for Jeff's tongue. That seems fair to me."

He sent the message to Tosh's feed queue.

"What about her?" Elena nodded to Karine.

"Now I make a devil's bargain. Any more wake-up juice in Tosh's bag?" Victor asked.

51

In his dream, Victor wandered along a riverside promenade, aware that he was dreaming and expecting to wake at any moment. Usually, his dreams faded once he became aware of them—especially without a bitter grass supplement—but somehow, this dream continued.

A fog rose, encasing him in a cool, gray void. The suspicion that he had forgotten a vital clue to his grandfather's murder crept over him. He needed to act but couldn't remember what he was supposed to do.

Waves lapped nearby, invisible in the mist, lulling him into a trance. This was a peaceful place. Victor sank to his knees, sitting on his heels, content. He pressed his hands on the promenade's smooth, cool cobblestones, and a little joy sparked in his chest. The wind played in his hair, and the mist receded, its tatters blown into thin filaments. The sky cleared. The waterfront was suddenly bright, though the sun still hid behind a rocky hill covered in elm trees.

Marshes and low hills extended to the horizon on the other side of the water, and an earthen levee upstream walled off his view. The locale seemed familiar but altered. He couldn't place it at first, but then he knew. *This is New Venice.* In the distance, he spotted the town's tightly clustered buildings lining the paths of the canals.

A figure scrambled onto a boulder ahead. Cloaked in shadow, the light around the figure vanished. The figure bounded toward him like an enraged bear, moving impossibly fast and flickering.

Closer now, the figure evolved into a naked man-monster with bloodshot eyes. He leaped on top of Victor, pressing him against the promenade. Jagged teeth descended and pierced Victor's neck, tearing flesh and tendons. The creature's fists slammed into Victor's chest. He opened his mouth to scream, but his lungs no longer worked—they were held aloft, oozing through the beast's claws. The monster-man's fists smashed down again, crushing Victor's nose and blinding him. Wet warmth flowed across his face. A final slam shattered his skull, the pieces rammed into his brain, and he died, his spirit propelled out of the world into the void.

Victor jerked awake. His heart thumped in his chest, yet his limbs were cold and almost numb. The predawn world was bathed in violet light. He must have fallen asleep in his car outside the kennel.

Negotiations with Karine had taken a few hours. Eventually, she'd agreed to his terms. She ordered the Corps guarding the kennel to allow him inside. She provided him with classified research on MRS, which he'd been reading when he fell asleep. And she'd agreed to intercede with the Health Board on his behalf and try to keep him a Class Three. In exchange, he'd untied her and agreed to her demands: to give up his "fantasy" that Jefferson Eastmore had been murdered and to tell her who was supplying him with tech. He planned to double-cross her, of course. For now, though, his path was fixed. Nothing save a meteor strike could keep him from searching the kennel.

A tap on the window made Victor jump. Hector rapped on the glass again.

Victor opened the car door, swung his legs around, and hoisted himself out.

Hector held out a steaming mug. Victor accepted it silently, trying not to shake. His neck ached where the dream monster had torn into it.

Hector took another cup from its temporary perch on the car's roof. They stood a few steps apart, taking tentative sips of the faux-café—a particularly unconvincing brand. A few Corps stood guard in front of the kennel.

"I could have convinced Mamá to let you sleep at our house," Hector said.

"I was fine," he said. The words sounded hoarse in his mouth.

Hector took another sip. "I won't have time to show you around today."

"That's okay. I just need to speak with the logistics manager. If you introduce me—"

"We don't have one of those."

Victor's gaze followed Hector's as it shifted to the stubby bushes fronting the kennel. They looked dead, but then, so did most of the vegetation Texans had imported to the semi-arid desert. In parts of SeCa, people adapted to the changing climate with succulents and other drought-resistant plants. Here, they tried and failed to nurture the iconic garden varieties of the East.

Victor waved his cup toward Hector to get his attention. "Someone in charge of the records then."

Hector rubbed his nose and sniffled. "Maybe Leroy, our sort-of accountant. Usually, he's the one who unloads the trucks and oversees the warehouse. But what are you looking for?"

Victor said, "It's something my grandfather asked me to take care of a while ago." He felt Hector's scrutiny as a tingling on his face. He had to get more fumewort. It had been about eighteen hours since his last dose. Hopefully, Pearl could send some soon from wherever she'd ended up. If she could come out of hiding long enough. Messages to her and Ozie went unanswered.

"Do you know why he came here in September?"

Hector flinched and took another sip from his chipped cup.

"What's wrong?" Victor asked.

"Nothing. Hot coffee," Hector said, but it was an obvious lie. His look askance, quavering voice, and a false boldness in his stature gave him away. "I didn't work that day."

"Please, Hector, it's important to me."

Hector looked at him for a long moment. Then he shrugged. "Better get going."

As they walked to the entrance, Hector summarized the layout of the kennel complex for Victor: cotton fields on one side and a golf course on the other. An administrative building welcomed new arrivals. Nearby, another large building housed the animals. A service road led beyond an automated gate around the back of the complex to smaller buildings, where supplies were stored and the on-staff veterinarian worked.

"Is the vet here today?" Victor asked.

"No, she isn't."

Hector led Victor past the guards and inside the administrative building, a low-ceilinged, flimsy, unimpressive aluminum shell not much more solid than a trailer. A conference room was tucked into one corner. A polished wooden bar ran at waist level below the front windows. A sign said, "Hitch Your Puppies Here," in loopy, hand-painted letters.

Drab brown curtains separated the entrance area from the remainder of the building. A female receptionist greeted them with a thick and happy drawl. Hector made introductions. The minutes stretched. She didn't know the complicated legal history of the kennel's ownership—"I was wondering why those rough guys were hanging around," she said—requiring Hector to explain Jefferson Eastmore, Mason Charter, and the Eastmore family foundation.

Victor's feet itched, but he forced himself to stand still.

Hector excused himself to clock into his shift.

"It might be a minute," the receptionist said, happily oblivious to Victor's stomach flipping and twisting.

A smile remained frozen on his face. He would say nothing to jeopardize his search.

"You can wait in the conference room. We have a MeshLine." Her eyes lit up with pride.

Victor entered the conference room and sat down, running his hands along the table's surface to calm himself. The vidscreen on the wall pinged that it had a live MeshLink. Victor entered his MeshID to access his message queue and entered his parents' IDs into the recipient field.

"I arrived in Amarillo the day before yesterday," he said—had it really only been that long? "I'm safe. I'll be in touch soon." The words displayed on the vidscreen as he spoke them. His parents would want to talk with him directly, and he wanted to hear their voices, but that could wait until later. He paused momentarily to appreciate the deep well of patience that had filled him recently.

Victor found a new message from Karine. *You've been reclassified in absentia—Class Two. We'll work on the appeal.*

She was backing out on that part of their agreement. Fine. He'd never expected her to follow through, and he wasn't returning to SeCa anyway.

He looked at the previous message she'd sent him last night. *The studies are not part of the official record. DON'T SHARE THEM!*

Residual sleepiness and the lack of juices and tinctures clouded his thoughts. How much had he read before he fell asleep? The prospect of digging into the research was like hitting a mother lode of endorphins and oxytocin. His brain revved up. The memory of the man-beast chewing his neck bones sent a shiver up his spine. He ignored the sensation and focused on the Health Board's research.

He skimmed the first paper's abstract. Two years after Carmichael, a genetic study had identified a mutation in the Lee-Lambda chromosome pair. The mutation was a single nucleotide polymorphism, meaning it was one slight difference in the sequence of nucleic acids that coded for a neurologically essential protein. Complex conditions were usually the result of many genes' interactions with the environment, and mirror resonance syndrome followed that pattern. Still, there was a marker for the condition that could be tested for.

Decades ago, they'd found a genetic fingerprint for mirror resonance syndrome. But *how* they found it was odd. They made brain scans of study participants and compared them to a single unnamed reference case. The study's subjects were "volunteers" from the unions in SeCa, some of whom were subsequently found to have MRS. This had been a sore point between Jefferson Eastmore and the unions for years. Why focus on that specific pattern of brain waves? What was the reference case?

It must have been a neural excitation wave from someone unequivocally diagnosed with mirror resonance syndrome.

Who?

Oh, of course!

Samuel Miller. It had to be.

The Health Board had studied Samuel: his genes, his brain. Through him, they'd found the first clues into mirror resonance syndrome.

Victor cursed. Everything seemed to trace back to Samuel Miller. He'd ruined so many people's lives! It wasn't just the Carmichael dead and their surviving loved ones. His crimes had also led to a draconian response: the Classification Commission. Samuel Miller was responsible for every misery suffered by every person with MRS. If Victor ever met the man, somehow, he would avenge the life he *should* have been living.

Victor turned to the next document. Researchers had studied neural networks grown from stem cell cultures. The mirror resonance genes changed how electrical impulses traveled through the brain, making the neurons easier to excite and harder to suppress—in effect, relaxing the brain's natural brakes.

Okay, fine, so in the second study, researchers found a link between genetics and MRS people's neurological function. Good for them. As Victor had always thought, and as the SeCa Health Board maintained, mirror resonance syndrome was a real, serious condition with a genetic basis, albeit one with a more complex origin than was generally understood: a constellation of genes rather than a single one.

There was one more study to review, but a visual hallucination of sparks erupting in time with dogs barking blocked Victor's view of the vidscreen. He repeated the owl mantra ten times, which caused the tiny fireworks to fade.

He pulled up the third document, a longitudinal study of the disease's progression. The conclusions in the abstract were all he needed to read. The mirror resonance genes created an unmodulated cognitive resonance, which manifested as symptoms of blankness, susceptibility to suggestion, and heightened flight or fight response, among others. However, the syndrome's effects were not deterministic with regard to mania, aggression, and delusional thinking, and deterioration wasn't assured. In other words, the paper explained, not everyone with mirror resonance syndrome was doomed to psychosis, violence, and catatonia.

People with MRS weren't inherently dangerous.

Breath caught in Victor's throat, choking him.

People with MRS aren't inherently dangerous.

People with MRS aren't inherently dangerous.

The SeCa Health Board had exaggerated the threat. Perhaps they'd even *increased* the likelihood of MRS people becoming violent by treating them as dangerous. Their cognitive function was steadily diminished by medication that did nothing but make them docile, malleable, and controllable.

It was a monstrous injustice. Thousands of people had their lives cut short, sequestered, diminished. Of course, people with MRS ended up catatonic. When everything is taken away, what does a person have left?

Sparks flared all around Victor. The world turned white, burning. His entire life had veered off track long ago, and he was only now realizing how bad it had become.

The receptionist knocked on the glass conference room wall. Victor jumped in his chair.

"Sorry to spook you, hon!"

The blankness ebbed and left Victor numb. He terminated his connection to the Mesh and followed the receptionist to an area cluttered with desks. They navigated through the disarray and arrived at a desk where a young man sat. He had slick hair, polished to a midnight black and pasted to his skull. All his clothes were black or near-black: jeans, a collared shirt, and a slim-fit jacket. He even wore a black pair of thick, square-rimmed glasses. Only his face, hands, and glinting silver jewelry hanging from his wrists, neck, and ears offset his dark clothing. The young man continued tapping, swiping, and clicking on various input devices while Victor and the receptionist hovered nearby.

Eventually, the woman interrupted gently. "Leroy, this is Victor Eastmore. He's the grandson—"

"I know. Give me a minute, okay? I'm lost in something," he said, continuing his frantic movements. "Victor, sit down. Thanks. One second. Okay. Done!" Leroy wiped a hand down his cheek and shivered. "What brings you here, Victor? Do you want a coffee? I've got a stash of the real stuff."

Without waiting for an answer, he got up and headed deeper into the building. Victor followed a few steps behind and watched as Leroy pulled cups and an unlabeled canister from a cabinet in the kitchen, placing them in the maw of an autobrew machine. While Leroy waited for the cups to fill, his fist hammered a rhythm on the top of the device. Victor watched him, unamused. Caffeine was a mild drug compared to whatever else Leroy was taking, judging by his motions. Stims probably.

"Sorry to hear about your grandfather," Leroy said. "What brings you here?"

"I'm looking after a few of his investments."

Victor struggled to keep any sense of urgency out of his voice. If he showed too much interest, Leroy might get defensive. Leroy nodded and then led Victor toward the back door, holding both cups in his hands, maneuvering the door open, and continuing into the yard.

Outside was a large, fenced area with lush grass, trees, and manicured bushes. A group of dogs were running and nipping at each other. Leroy chose a bench outside the fence and sat down with Victor. Only then did he relinquish Victor's cup.

"Do you like dogs?" Leroy asked.

The thought of chitchat wore through Victor's last nerve, but he tried to sound nonchalant. "Yes, of course."

"Hey, no need for the heavy sarcasm. I'm not much of a fan either."

Victor gulped the too-hot coffee and choked it down.

Leroy raised an eyebrow and then turned his attention to the three dogs running around the yard. "I used to like them. But now I *hear* them all the time—yapping, hysterical monsters. My tolerance for them is gone, gone, gone."

After Victor coughed and got his voice back, he said, "Jefferson arranged a shipment in September last year. Supplies in cold storage from a hospital in Oakland & Bayshore. Can you help me find them?"

Leroy sipped his coffee. His gaze bounced quickly between the snarling animals. He hiccuped and tapped his chest like he had tapped the coffee machine. "Excuse me."

"Can you help me track down what happened to them?"

"We can look through the records, but if you know the category, a shipment date, or the sender's name, it will help."

"I know the name of the compound. XSCT-19900032."

"Let's give it a shot. Can I enjoy my coffee first?"

Several agonizing minutes passed while Leroy lingered over the coffee, talking manically. Then Leroy led Victor back into the building and to his desk. He pulled up the warehouse records, quickly finding a log noting the supplies in question. He showed it to Victor. "See? Easy. The shipment arrived on the twenty-fifth of September last year. Nothing here to indicate what was done with it." He tapped a few commands, and pages rose and sank in response. "Huh, that's strange. It's not tied to any other records. Usually, we would have a receiving bill or something like that. No reference in the Mesh either. Chances are we put whatever it was in our chiller. Do you want to go see if it's still there?"

Victor wanted to scream, "*Of course!*" Instead, he merely choked out a quiet, "Yes."

Leroy took Victor past the kennel cells. Clouds of aerosolized dog dander, urine, and feces wafted through the space despite the loud rumbling and churning of an air chiller and filtration system hanging from the ceiling. Shiny ductwork snaked out the windows. Vibrations in the room were visible to Victor as a shimmer in the air.

The dogs ate and slept on two floors of rooms lining the sides of the long and narrow building. Their barks and whines followed Victor, jangling his nerves so much that his legs grew wobbly. Even Leroy picked up his pace. The dogs sounded murderous.

"I hate them when they get like that," Leroy shouted over the noise. "It's like they want to rip us apart. 'Man's best friend,' right?"

"Maybe they don't like being locked up," Victor yelled.

They exited the opposite end of the building. Victor breathed fresh air and listened with relief to the muffled cacophony of the kennel.

They took a footpath to a nearby warehouse. Inside, Leroy showed Victor two rooms holding chilled supplies, one freezing and one a few degrees colder than room temperature. They donned spare jackets and gloves when they entered the freezing one.

Leroy explained the contents, his breath emerging in frosted puffs. Specialty foods in large plastic tubs filled most of the shelves. These were for the high-end doggy guests with specific dietary requirements. Veterinary supplies sat in a chiller cube.

Victor picked up each bottle or package in turn, scanned the label, and moved on to the next, shifting them to reach the back of shelves, forming piles on the floor when necessary. He touched and examined every article in the room.

He looked everywhere. Leroy followed his lead and reported finding nothing. Victor double-checked everything Leroy did anyway. They didn't find anything labeled HHN, Oak Knoll, or XSCT.

In the other chilled room, Victor searched just as thoroughly, examining each vial and container and a small self-contained chiller, but he didn't find anything labeled for humans.

"I guess it's not here," Leroy said.

"We keep looking. Everywhere."

Leroy helped him search the rest of the warehouse. They looked through the records in the small warehouse management area. They looked inside boxes and plastic containers.

One question repeated over and over in Victor's mind. *Where's my cure?*

They examined all the labels. Could the labels have been switched? It would take Victor days to check.

They found nothing. Nothing to indicate anything. A dead end.

Victor couldn't move, couldn't think. There was nothing to do. He had failed.

"I'm sorry, Victor," Leroy said. "We clean out supplies every three months, so if we weren't sure what it was, it would have been disposed of. I can ask the other employees if they remember anything, but it will take some time. I can contact you if I find anything."

Victor looked carefully at Leroy's face. There was no sign of the compound nor what Jefferson Eastmore had done with it while he was here. But one thing was certain: Leroy was lying. He was keeping a secret and was nervous that Victor would discover it.

"You okay?" Leroy asked.

Thickly, through a congealing morass of anger, Victor gave Leroy his MeshID, and they walked to the administration building. Whatever was hidden in the kennel was deep; he'd need to return with a solid plan to uncover it. Victor was resolved but weary: his knees threatened to collapse with each step.

Softly, as if through tightly packed cotton earplugs, Victor heard noises from the dog pen growing louder and more alarming. They rounded a corner and saw a worker frantically attempting to drag two dogs apart—*why two?*—a boxer and a black lab. Vicious growling and barks pierced Victor's eardrums. The dogs lunged and strained against their collars, trying to tear each other to pieces.

"Oh, Laws," Leroy said. He ran inside the building and returned immediately. Yelling at the man beyond the fence to get his attention, Leroy passed a sleep jabber to him. The dogs bared their fangs. They fought, a whirling ball of growls, teeth, and injured yelps. Within seconds, one had gone limp. The other continued to attack. Blood covered its snout.

The man inside the fence hesitated, afraid to get too close. He had already been scratched on his hands and arms.

Victor's heart raced. The last time he'd seen dogs acting like this was when the terriers attacked Granma Cynthia. She'd said they'd been acting strangely for months—the trouble must have started around the time Oak Knoll was shut. Around the same time that the compound XSCT made its way to Texas, Jefferson had visited the kennel.

Hector had lied to him. Leroy was lying now. Jefferson had been here with the compound. *Did it have something to do with the dogs?* Victor looked at the dogs again. There were two in the yard and dozens within the kennel—a good sample size for an experiment.

Perhaps the compound was still there, only it was hidden within the animals, waiting for someone to extract it.

Victor shook. He couldn't take any more lies and secrets. If Jefferson had trusted Victor, he would have told him about this months ago. He wouldn't have hidden the cure. Victor was a big mess that everyone tried to work around. No one trusted him.

He fled through the administrative building. The office furniture flowed around him, and then he stood in the front parking lot, staring at his reflection in the glass wall. Shell-shocked eyes. Sagging skin. Wild hair. He looked haunted.

He stumbled away and crossed the parking lot into a weedy meadow. The blankness invaded. All he had to do was surrender. Like dust and gas hurtling around a protostar on the verge of fusion ignition, he would soon be trapped in a scorching orbit or swept away to the cold loneliness of space. And there was nothing he could do. Might as well try to break the laws of physics. He was on a path from which he couldn't escape.

His grandfather's words returned. *Never surrender*. The Eastmore motto. No matter how bad it got. *Never surrender*.

"Fuck you, Granfa!" Victor yelled across the meadow.

He imagined he could hear Jefferson's voice in response, a patronizing monotone saying, "You have a value and strength, a decent core at the heart of your brokenness." He remembered Jefferson giving him the data egg. "Listen. Hear my words. Never surrender." *Never surrender*. Despite the challenges, despite withholding critical information, knowing his life would be cut short, Jefferson had urged Victor to keep going, no matter how bleak his future appeared.

The blankness converged. Unlike hundreds of times when he was on the brink of a blankout and succumbed, this time, he faced it and fought back. Nebulous blurs at the edge of his vision expanded; everything went white as if thick clouds had descended. Forms swirled in the mist. He felt a presence, a sense of place.

Victor steeled himself, refusing to be moved, and watched the blankness evolve into something charged and dynamic, fractal patterns and kaleidoscopic colors. He couldn't make sense of what he was seeing, but he couldn't deny an overwhelming feeling of fullness. Blank space wasn't empty—it was a full world calling to him, demanding he cross over. He felt pulled toward it, yet he resisted.

The data egg buzzed in his pocket. At first, Victor thought he was imagining the sensation. The data egg buzzed again. He snapped back, heard grass rustling, and saw clouds high above, motionless. He stood utterly still, and the data egg buzzed again, vibrating against his thigh. He removed the egg with one hand and cupped it in his palm. A red circle ran around its circumference. The egg was hatching.

A hologram appeared and hovered in the air. Jefferson Eastmore—only his head, but big as life—meeting Victor's gaze. He sank down onto the dry grass and the face descended with him. He reached out his fingers to caress the face but the action distorted the image, so Victor withdrew his hand. The dead man began to speak.

"Victor, I made this recording because things must be said, and I'm afraid that time is not on our side."

Victor watched and listened, mouth open, scared to make a sound and interrupt the voice he'd loved hearing, the voice that had always made him feel safe and worthy, but now was also the voice that had lied.

Jefferson continued, "The data egg opened now because you've gained control over your episodes, as I knew you would. I'm very proud of you. Also, by now, you've passed at least one reclassification with a little help from this data egg. It's a remarkable technology, and I hope it continues to serve you well."

Victor's mind reeled. *So, that's what had opened the data egg—my newfound ability to stave off the blankness!*

"There's no delicate way to say this, and I wish I could save you from the shock, but I had best just come out with it: if you're seeing me, I've been murdered. I was exposed to many small doses of radioactive polonium, which have collected in my tissues and are killing me. It took me far too long to figure out what was happening, and now it's too late."

Victor clenched his jaw. He'd been right all along. Jefferson had known about the poison. Why hadn't he said anything?

"I know my murderer, and I know why I was poisoned. I can't tell you who it is yet. I'm sorry. The truth is far more dangerous than ignorance."

"No, no, Granfa, you have to tell me!" Victor felt sick to his stomach. He reached out to the hologram, and his fingers sliced through it uselessly.

"There are competing views about the future for people with MRS: some believe they can be cured, some believe they are gateways to other planes of existence, and some believe they can be fashioned into weapons. I believed you could be cured. I still believe that. Please believe me. You must fight against anyone who disagrees with my vision."

Victor asked, "Who did it? Why tell me all this and not who killed you?" A horrible thought occurred to him: perhaps Granfa Jeff didn't know.

Jefferson's recording said, "A cure is possible. However, the compound we were working on had unpredictable effects. I couldn't allow it to be used to turn others into mindless, ruthless soldiers or crazed, cultist sycophants. I could not let that happen. I may be dead, but I am not defeated. Through you, I hope to change how people with MRS are treated."

Victor's eyes shone. Granfa Jeff hadn't gone quietly to the grave. He'd died as he'd lived with big dreams and the capacity to take on the world. "Tell me, Granfa. What do I need to do?"

"My top priority is to keep you safe. Just as it wouldn't have been responsible to announce the true cause of my death publicly, it wouldn't be responsible of me to tell you who killed me before you're ready, before what I've set in motion bears fruit. In some ways, my murderer is more deeply disturbed than even Samuel Miller."

At the mention of that name, Victor's skin prickled.

"I need to warn you," Jefferson continued. "People may try to tell you there are spirits and demons in congress with humanity, that you are chosen to be a bridge between worlds, to lead an army. These are all devious dreams and deluded fantasies. The only solution, the solution you must pioneer, is to change the political climate. To gain acceptance and integrate people with MRS into society. This is your responsibility, your future. To be a leader. To change the world."

Victor felt his gut chill. *No, no, what are you thinking? No one will listen to a Broken Mirror. I'm an untouchable.*

"You can't do it alone. You'll be contacted by people. There's Ming Pearl, who is an expert on atypical medicinal compounds; Ozie, your friend from school; and a close associate of mine named Tosh. When the time comes, they'll reach out to you. Listen to their advice. Learn how they are making progress happen. But remember, the only person you can truly trust is yourself."

When the time comes, they'll reach out to you. But that's not what happened. Victor had found them: in Little Asia, beneath Oak Knoll, in the OWS wilderness. He'd gone in search of them *before* they'd come to him, thus changing the arc of Granfa Jeff's plans.

Jefferson said, "I want you to return to Carmichael."

Something inside Victor crumbled; he couldn't do that, not for a cure, not for anything in the world.

"I realize that might be difficult," Jefferson continued, "but I want you to work as a member of the staff at the Class Two ranch there. I hired them myself; they're open-minded and believe in my vision. Spend time with Samuel Miller. The data egg will help him, too. You must prove that alternative treatments are effective."

Victor swallowed thickly. Go back to Carmichael? Hang out with Samuel Miller? That was Granfa Jeff's plan? It was lunacy.

Jefferson seemed to hesitate. He looked away, and his next words were tentative and haltingly spoken. "Victor, don't tell anyone what I've told you. Nobody. Not your parents. Not Circe. Not even Cynthia. No one. You have to do this on your own. The data egg will open again; there's much more I have to say when you're ready. I love you. Goodbye."

The hologram ended abruptly and disappeared. The egg returned to its solid black color, except for a thin slice of red ringing it.

52

Dry grass crunched behind Victor. He turned to find Hector approaching. In the distance, Corps, standing in front of the kennel, watched them.

"Are you okay, Victor?"

No, he wasn't. His mind was still reeling. Granfa Jeff had said a lot yet left so much unsaid. "I got a message from my grandfather."

Hector frowned and narrowed his eyes. "I know about your delusions."

How much should he say? "Trust only yourself," Granfa Jeff had told him. But Hector knew something. "I know he came here. What aren't you telling me?"

"You must be imagining—"

"Stop. I've had enough. I can tell when someone is lying. Is it the dogs?" Victor asked.

Hector wiped his brow with a handkerchief. "You're supposed to tell me what to do. But Jefferson said you'd be here a year from now." He tugged on his ear. "You don't know, do you? Not the whole story."

Victor's face heated up. "What are you hiding?"

Hector glanced back at the Corps. "Those guys let you wander around today, but they've got no loyalty. They weren't part of the deal. They're *new*. I've got to work with them watching me every day. I have to look out for my family and their safety. Don't return until you can guarantee that." Hector stalked away, leaving Victor alone with the waving grass.

Victor stared at the data egg in his hand. The truth was never a revelation. It was a sliver lodged in his skin, evading his efforts to pluck it out.

No matter, he'd keep searching.

Victor's Handy 1000 blinked with a vidfeed request from Auntie Circe. He opened it as a sonofeed.

"What's going on? Victor, are you all right?" Circe asked.

"You got my message about Karine?"

"Yes, I spoke with her. I'm glad she found you."

His auntie seemed actually to believe the story he and Karine had made up: he'd gone hundreds of kilometers on a joyride with Elena, got caught up in gang warfare, and Karine had swooped in to save the day. It was astonishing how much she trusted Karine.

Circe said, "You realize your parents, all of us, are still worried sick about you."

"Yeah, I do. Sick enough to have me watched by Elena and two thugs."

"Why do you call them thugs? Karine assures me—"

"I'm not going to get into it with you. I'm just trying to find somewhere I can breathe. There's no such thing as a Broken Mirror here."

Auntie Circe clucked. "I hate that term. It's a horrible misnomer. You're not broken, Victor. You hold up a mirror to the people around you. If we see you as broken, it's because we don't like what we see in ourselves. Still, I think you'll be better cared for by us. The Class Two ranch in Carmichael is a model community. Not like the others."

Jefferson wanted me to work there, and Circe wanted me to become a patient. "I'm not coming back."

"Victor, don't you—"

"Do you believe people with MRS are dangerous?"

It was a moment before Auntie Circe spoke. "Maybe not all of them. Maybe they weren't before, but the situation now is clear. Some may be dangerous, but all of them are in danger. Without the Classification System to reassure the public, there would have been riots and lynchings. You see that, surely. For their protection, they must be separated."

"You believe that?"

"Of course! I may just be Auntie Circe to you, Victor, but I'm the chief of BioScan. I've seen the world beyond SeCa, beyond Europe—there are thousands of different cultures. I've learned from them. And one lesson is clear above all."

Her voice grew strangely harmonic, as if every word she spoke carried multiple meanings, resonances that he sensed but couldn't quite grasp.

"Every culture yearns for the good old days. They want to return to their roots, to find the good in them that has somehow dissipated with time. But they cannot go back. As much as my views differed from Fa's, we agreed on that point. The wheel of progress, he said, pushes us all forward. He was thinking too mechanically when he needed to think biologically, but the principle is correct. Cultures evolve. Organisms evolve. Our minds evolve. We develop new traits, new abilities, new norms, and one thing is certain: we cannot go back."

Victor gulped down a hint of sour bile and wondered at his strange reaction to her words. He said, "Granfa Jeff said something like that to me at Oak Knoll the day it closed."

"You've been tested," she said. "That's how I see it. You know ..."

"What?"

"Well, if you don't want to return to SeCa, and if we want to jump-start the research again, New Venice would be the perfect location. The Louisiana Territories are booming. The authorities are desperate to attract business. We could expand the clinic and create a full-fledged research center. Would you like that?"

"I—I'd have to think about it. Maybe," he said. He couldn't tell her that he'd just dreamed about New Venice. "But what about Europe? I could work from the office in Cologne."

"Maybe," she said. "You better brush up on your German first. Let's talk about it again in a few months. But what about New Venice, hmm? It's quiet and sophisticated. I'm sure your great-granma Florence would let you stay with her."

He hadn't seen Florence in years. "She must be ninety years old," he said.

"Exactly. I'll tell you, Victor, family connections grow more important with age. I'm sure she'd love to see you. Let me know soon, and I'll start the paperwork for Samuel's transfer."

Flames and smoke danced around the edge of Victor's vision. "What?"

"I know how you must feel about him. But he is essential to the project. We can limit your contact with him."

Victor remembered Granfa Jeff's message urging him to study Samuel. A queasy feeling turned his stomach. Jefferson had surely roped Circe into his plans as well. The suspicion that everything in Victor's life had been predetermined felt like a heavy weight smothering him. He had trouble forming words. "I never said ... I can't ... The chance to study Samuel might, I think, help us study the connection between mirror resonance syndrome and dreams."

"Dreams?" she said in a quavering voice.

He asked, "What's wrong?"

"Nothing. We'll need to discuss this later. We'll have a nice long chat about your treatment and our plans for the clinic. I've got to go. Take care, Victor."

She terminated the feed.

Victor walked to his car. The blankness had been *full*. What did that mean?

A single phrase from Granfa Jeff's message repeated in Victor's head. It was the one he'd been warned to disbelieve: "Chosen to be a bridge between worlds." That was the psychosis that had broken Samuel Miller.

The blankness was gone for now, but it would surely return. One day, Victor feared he would dare to invite it in and cross over.

53

I didn't know that moving to New Venice would expose me to people with such twisted minds. I thought Samuel Miller would be the worst. But it was bound to happen—I am an Eastmore. We attract the insane like gravity.

—Victor Eastmore, *Apology to Resonant Earth*, (transmission date unknown)

Republic of Texas
15 April 1991

Some wicked, parasitic vine had sent its tendrils into Elena's skull. Nothing else could explain the pain and pressure in her head. It might crack at any moment.

The agony pushed out all words, and Elena waited, willing the tide to recede, but as minutes passed, she remained submerged, silent, and suffering. She couldn't wait. She needed relief. Flinging the covers off, she opened her eyes.

The clock on the nightstand blared its message: seven a.m. Sunlight coming through the glass doors to the balcony seared the room. More drapes. They needed more drapes. The word repeated in her head. *Drapes, drapes, drapes.* The next item on the list, the next step in the cohabitation process. Always something to add to their nest.

The throbbing in her head threatened to blossom into a full-blown migraine unless she did something. The solution was obvious. Stimsmoke. Unfortunately, it would also worsen the problem. Just a single puff. She could inhale the precise amount needed—just a puff.

Congratulations, you're still addicted!

She hadn't taken Aura yesterday, opting for the cheap stuff instead. Big mistake. Half the high and twice the hangover. Never again.

Elena rolled over and pulled an arm across her face, covering her eyes and temporarily masking the headache. She needed relief.

It was a stark choice: either start her day with a pick-me-up or suffer through withdrawal for hours, likely days. Even the best pharmaceutical pain relievers were largely ineffective.

She had brought this on herself—no one else to blame.

Except maybe Victor.

Pearl was shipping him herbs again, so he ingested a different substance every night. There were no rules for self-medication, he'd said. Whatever worked. Anyone could do it.

His side of the bed was neatly tucked in. Had he slept in it at all? She thought she remembered him snoring next to her, but that could be a memory from any time over the past few weeks. Usually, he was a loud-growling, dream-tortured sleep-monster. But last night, she'd been pretty much dead to the world, stim-crashed beyond the ability to form any memories.

Why couldn't she smoke stims? Living with a person with MRS should be classified as a medical condition meriting the most potent prescription available. His moods, the whiplash of being emotionally tuned to someone on the edge—that's what had pushed her to stims again.

She rolled to the edge of the bed and sat up. Her headache spiked. She pulled on a clean pair of pants, put on a silk button-up, and stepped into a pair of dull gray flats. She was slimming down again, fast. Too much stimsmoke. If she didn't stop the upward trajectory of her usage, she would be emaciated and knocked down sick within a week or so. Typical seesaw: healthy-sick, sick-sick, healthy-sick, sick-sick. It's never normal once you've been addicted. You can never go back to who you were.

"Victor?" she called out.

The house sounded empty, but that didn't mean anything. He couldn't hear her from his hideout downstairs, and vice versa. If he had gone somewhere, she could step out onto the balcony. A quick puff and be done. Her luck, though, being what it was, meant that if she ever took the easy route, he would catch her in the act, which was definitely against the rules: his rules, the Puros' rules, and her own, until recently.

She had become skilled at breaking the rules in secret. Victor seemed more perceptive lately, but her denials thus far had kept him in check. That meant no smoking indoors or on the balcony when he was home and no smoking outside in public places—it was too likely one of her fellow Puros would spot her. They would punish her brutally; it puckered the skin on her arms to think about getting caught. No, she would only smoke when she was sure no one could spot her. Lockable one-person restrooms in sparsely trafficked establishments were the best places. Or in a car at night, far away from any streetlights. It would be so much easier to be a Corp and relax with your mates, doing whatever drugs you wanted, and never worrying about it.

Maybe she could get away with a quick puff on the balcony. Just this once.

Elena hunted around the bedroom for her purse. It wasn't on the dresser, by the bed, or hanging from the doorknob—all her usual places. The headache surged as she moved faster, but she powered through, looking high and low, determined to end it as quickly as possible.

There was nothing, no bag in the bedroom. Had she left it downstairs? She must have. Elena pulled a scarf from the peg in the closet. It was never warm enough now that she'd shed so much weight. She trudged downstairs and hunted in the living room and the dining room but still couldn't find her purse. A ragged growl escaped from her throat.

Her bag must be in her car. A muffled shuffling sound came from Victor's hideout. So, he was home. She would just pop by his cave to say a quick goodbye.

When she pulled back the curtain, she found him hunched over his Handy 1000.

"Morning," she said, half expecting him to ignore her, which he did at first, and then he raised his head and met her eyes. She patted his shoulder. "I'm going to the store."

He blinked at her but said nothing.

"Do you need anything?" she asked.

Victor didn't respond. His lips were pressed together, almost covered by his mustache experiment. He hadn't shaved his upper lip in two weeks, and she could barely stand it, but this wasn't the time to pick a fight.

Elena said, "As soon as I find my purse, I'm out of here."

Victor reached behind his chair and pulled up her bag. He held it at arm's length toward her, bunching its synthleather material. His eyes narrowed.

"Give that to me," she said. "What do you think—"

"I found your stims," he said.

His voice grated on her ears. Elena snatched her purse and plunged her hands into it, digging underneath cosmetics, tissues, keys—she found it. The tension drained out of her when her hands closed over the small cartridge of doses and the fireglobe.

"You need to stop," he said.

"Hush," she commanded.

Victor scratched his cheek rhythmically. "It's changing you."

She wanted to pull and tear at his face.

"Elena—"

"I know. I'm trying. It's just a little bit." Her hands vibrated, eager to begin the ritual.

He looked down at her feet as he spoke: "I have to go."

Elena carefully maneuvered the bag's strap onto her shoulder and tucked her paraphernalia inside. She couldn't do it with him watching. "No, it's fine. I'll go to the store. Tell me what you need."

He looked up and cocked his head. "No, I mean, I have to leave Amarillo."

"What are you talking about?"

"Listen. It's time. I know what I need to do."

"Vic, I've got a bad headache this morning."

"They're moving Samuel Miller to the clinic at New Venice. I'm going to start working on a cure there."

"What does he have to do with a cure?"

"It's complicated. I have to go to find out."

"No. No, you don't." He shouldn't put his life, his stability, at risk again. "Please say you're kidding," Elena said.

He shook his head slowly.

Hot tears started to swell her eyelids. She wanted to shake the stupid notion out of him.

He watched her, his eyes cold, his mouth firm.

Her words finally found their freedom in a whisper. "I'll stop using stims. I'm done. Starting now."

"Elena—"

"I promise. From now on." She threw the bag off her shoulder, and it landed on the ground with a thump.

He pressed his hands together and lifted them to his lips. "I'm going to do this. I have to. Come with me."

She ran a hand through her hair. It snagged, and she yanked free more than a few strands. She looked away toward the home they'd not yet finished making. "No way."

"The clinic there—"

"This is crazy. They chipped me!" She pointed to the cuff around her calf that blocked MeshTowers from tracking the signal.

"I might find some answers, and you might finally beat your addiction. They could deactivate the chip."

She screamed at him. It felt good, like pieces of her lungs were ejecting from her mouth and splattering him with her anger. It was his family's fault she had that thing in her. Who was he to speak to her so sanctimoniously? She wanted to get clean—of course, she did. Yet here she was, screaming at him, willing to do anything to take another puff.

He got up and hugged her. "I've been in touch with Ozie and Pearl. They're going to help you. They've got more brain-fixing tricks than any doctor in the world. Between them and the clinic staff, we'll make you better."

Shock him. Shock them. Shock everyone to hell. She had wasted months on him, fantasizing that they could be friends again, and now that she had him, she'd ruined it. But she still had her Puros. She would get by without him.

Republic of Texas
15 April 1991

Victor placed his bags in the trunk and pushed the lid closed. It clicked pleasantly. He felt the urge to open it so that he could close it and hear the sound again.

Elena stood by, watching him sleepily. Her fight for sobriety used every bit of her strength. He wished it were easier for her. They'd fought for an hour before he finally convinced her to accompany him. "I know what it's like," he'd said, "and the best thing is to start someplace new."

Standing by the car, he said, "We're ready."

"Is that everything?" she asked. "Did you pack all my clothes too?"

"I think so," he said. He smiled at her. "Are you sure you're ready for the Louisiana Territories? Can you manage to live somewhere stunsticks are illegal?"

A smile flickered on her face but left a moment later. "I'm going to be fine."

"The Louisiana Territories are civilized, especially New Venice," Victor said. "We'll be safer there than here, that's for sure."

"Tosh is going to find you eventually," Elena said.

Victor had used the Handy 1000 to turn off the tracking device Tosh had put on Victor's car. "I know. I'm counting on it. He's got Granfa Jeff's tongue. I'll have to deal with him someday."

Victor opened the car door, glanced at her, and nodded. She climbed in. He started the car, and they drove away.

The squat, dust-caked houses of Amarillo spread across the plain. The car rumbled across train tracks and crossed a bridge over a dry arroyo. At the edge of town, the street came to a *T*. Left would take him to the OWS and SeCa, and to the right was New Venice in the Louisiana Territories. He turned right.

They passed a turn-off that would have taken them through a subdivision and to the kennel.

Good riddance, Victor thought.

Two minutes later, without thinking, he turned the car around, bumping across the dirt median, and took the turnoff. Soon, the façade of the Lone Star Kennel appeared, and he pulled into the parking lot.

"Why are we stopping?" Elena asked.

Victor said, "Give me a minute."

He got out of the car. No other vehicles were in the lot, only pavement, grass, and sky, covered by high clouds—big, remote, and unhelpful. The wind brought an acrid, stinking tang of animal waste. He tapped the car with his fingertips in three-second intervals.

If Jefferson had done something to the dogs, getting proof wouldn't be easy—he'd need a laboratory. Victor could be patient but not endlessly so. He'd be back soon.

Grasses rustled in the breeze. A flock of birds flew in from the north, descending on scrubby trees at the edge of the parking lot and twittering loudly to each other. Victor imagined the dogs in the kennel rolling over in their sleep, twitching.

Circe's words returned to him: he was a mirror to others. He was the world's reflection. What is a person, if not a consciousness that makes meaning by relating to others? Why not be happy with that?

His mind wasn't the problem; it was his surroundings. What might he become if free to make his way far from negative influences? Independent? Stable? Like a noble gas in the atmosphere—present but nonreactive? He wanted to lead a life of his choosing. He wanted to trust the people around him. He wanted

Jefferson Eastmore to be avenged. He wanted to stop wanting everything so fiercely.

Most of all, he wanted to *not want* a cure so badly. If he could accept himself now, he wouldn't need a cure. A cure would change how he saw the world and how it smelled and felt. His neural currents would trace new courses through his brain. A cure would be a mental reboot, a factory reset of his brain back to an as-designed, normal-functioning mind that should have been his from birth. He'd be someone new. Yet, strangely, for the first time, he didn't want to become a different person.

Birds chirped, oblivious to his musings. It wasn't just flight that gave them freedom. They never had to ask themselves why they sang.

Victor strode to the wire mesh fence surrounding the kennel and looked at the automated gate. It didn't open for him, of course. He paced back and forth on a small strip of landscaped grass, straining to hear sounds from within the kennel, but instead hearing only the rush of wind and the chirruping of excitable birds.

He returned to his car, leaned against it, and felt the sun's warmth. Despite being low in the sky, its fusion-born photons felt marvelous, like warm rain on his skin.

Victor climbed back in the car, squeezed Elena's shoulder, then sat back and stared at the dry plains and a big, gray, hazy sky.

New Venice or bust.

TO BE CONTINUED

Afterword (2016)

Thank you for reading *Broken Mirror*. Please share what you thought of the book with your friends, or head on over to Goodreads or the retailer's page online to leave a review.

When I began writing this story in 2012, I envisioned a series of books that would follow Victor Eastmore's adventures on Resonant Earth. However, the scope of the tale I wanted to tell was far grander and the world much more sophisticated than my storytelling skills. I finished the first draft in 2013 and realized that I'd written an opening trilogy to a series that would have at least six and possibly more installments.

As I write these words, ending the first book of many, I'm looking forward to taking up the rough drafts of the second and third books in the series, which are mostly complete yet still in need of restructuring and editing—and good titles.

I mention all this because I know how it feels to read "To Be Continued" and not be able to immediately move on to the next installment. As a teenager, back when the internet was new and giant chain bookstores were ubiquitous, I would routinely browse the science fiction section, head to the R authors, and check to see if next installments of Kim Stanley Robinson's Mars Trilogy had been published yet. It was a long wait, but well worth it.

All that said, I promise to be diligent, to be open, and to be focused. I promise the sequels to *Broken Mirror* are coming soon.

Cody Sisco

Afterword (2024)

Well, that didn't go as planned.

The sequel to *Broken Mirror*, titled *Tortured Echoes*, was published one year after *Broken Mirror*. That's fast. *Tortured Echoes* tells the story of what happens when Victor Eastmore and his nemesis Samuel Miller converge in New Venice. I'm immensely proud of it. I tell people it's the superior novel. I began work on the third book shortly thereafter with plenty of confidence, copious notes, and big ambitions.

So, what happened was I built a couple of distinct pathways into the publishing industry at the same time. I co-founded the Made in L.A. Writers indie author co-op. We publish short-fiction anthologies and organize events at local bookstores and libraries. Simultaneously, I started a literary events and media company called BookSwell that connects readers and writers and celebrates authors from communities that the publishing industry has historically overlooked. And I began freelance editing, which I enjoy immensely.

All of which is to say that I did not prioritize my writing as much as I should have. I fooled around with a couple of other novel and novella manuscripts and started an urban fantasy series of short stories. And I slowly accreted words, sentences, and scenes for the third book. The pandemic saw six months of absolutely nothing from me and then a spurt of creativity to finish the manuscript, which then sat on my hard drive, neglected for a year.

Which brings me to this second edition. I suspected when *Broken Mirror* was published that someday I would revisit it. Decades ago, I remember reading that Stephen King had published *The Gunslinger* in 1982, the first in his Dark Tower series, and then edited and released a revised and expanded second edition in 2003. It fired up my imagination. What had he changed? Why?

Over the last few years, I found my storytelling and narrative skills growing and evolving, and I realized that soon my talents would be up to the task of revision. I made the time. I churned through the chapters. My aims were to smooth readers' entry into the Resonant Earth world, amp up the queerness of the characters, and ensure consistency with the books that follow in the series. I hope I've accomplished all three. Thank you for going on this journey with me.

Acknowledgments (2016)

This section could also be titled, "A Litany of Thanking."

I am deeply grateful to my family, friends, colleagues, and strangers who encouraged, critiqued, supported, and spurred me on during the three years it took to write, edit, and publish Broken Mirror.

The editors who helped shape this novel also deserve thanks. They are very talented professionals without whom my novel would, frankly, suck. My thanks to Lindsey Alexander, Stephanie Mitchell, Justin Taylor, and Beth Wright. I'm also deeply in debt to my Beta Readers. They have seen this novel evolve and improve thanks to their insightful feedback. Thank you to Cynthia Cason, Derek Jentzsch, Jessica Barnett, Jason Groves, Luke Klipp, Stuart Kochmer, Jeffrey Lais, Kristin Larson, Holly McHugh, Richard Merrill, Cecile Oger, Jack Small, and Katie Vigil. A special shout out and thanks to three other members of a "group of four" who diligently shared their writing and insightful critiques over the past year: Nick Duretta, Cristina Stuart, and Suki Yamashita. And my thanks to the members of the Northeast Los Angeles Writers Group, especially Margaret Mayo McGlynn, Stephen Brown, Mike Radice, Gabi Lorino, Peggy Gregerson, and Jodi Lampert.

Dan "Thomas" Small: thank you for years of friendship and mind-shattering discussions, and for all your help making this story live up to your standards and mine.

Most of all, I want to thank my husband, Jay Fennelly, for believing in my dream, loving and supporting me, and being there for me throughout cycles of confidence and doubt, satisfaction and despair, and the mundane day-to-day process of getting the words out.

Finally, "thanks" doesn't do justice to the impact my family has had on my writing—thank you all. Grandma Lois, your signed copy is on its way. Tom and Sue, thank you for raising me amidst books, libraries, and stories, and always encouraging me to try new things and rise to any occasion. And to Jess, Abi, Marcel, and Luca: you mean so much to me—I'm so grateful to be part of your lives.

Acknowledgments (2024)

Well, here we are again. It's been a decade since I first started working on this book, and now I can finally say it's finished ... again. Lol. I've learned so much about publishing over the last several years, and the most important lesson is that no one is alone; in other words, no writer succeeds without community. I am so very grateful to Sara Chisolm, Gabi Lorino, and Allison Rose for your comradery, inspiration, and dedication to our Made in L.A. collaborations, including your feedback on the Resonant Earth series. To Xochitl-Julisa Bermejo, Shonda Buchanan, Mike Che, Jen Cheng, Nicholas George, Ryane Nicole Granados, Katy Grenfell, Reuben "Tihi" Hayslett, Lisa Kastner, Matthew Kressel, Janice Rhoshalle Littlejohn, PJ Manney, Noriko Nakada, Tisha Marie Reichle-Aguilera, Brian Sonia-Wallace, Alexander Vidal, and Désirée Zamorano: thank you for being in community, for your work as outstanding literary citizens, and for just being awesome all the time. To Frank Castellucio, David Fitzpatrick, Manuel Igrejas, Cynthia Zhang, Ira Logan Earl, and Sherri L. Smith: thank you for your feedback and encouragement. To my editors for this second edition, Molly Thornton, Kate Maruyama, Andy Hodges, and Lorna Partington Walsh: you've been a joy to work with, and I greatly value your editing suggestions.

I had a few goals for this second edition. I wanted a smoother, faster-paced onramp to the series. I wanted to look again at queer inclusion in the story and to examine and amend some of my biases. I wanted to showcase the central dilemma of the story, as I saw it: the tension between truth-telling and secrets among family, friends, and acquaintances. And I wanted to flex some of the storytelling skills I'd accumulated over years of working as an editor and helping other authors sharpen their manuscripts. I hope you enjoyed this first installment of the Resonant Earth series and that you'll keep traveling with me on this epic journey.

About the Author

Cody Sisco is an author, editor, publisher, and literary community organizer. His LGBT psychological science fiction series includes two novels thus far, Broken Mirror and Tortured Echoes. He is a freelance editor specializing in developmental editing of fiction and an acquisitions editor for RIZE Press, an imprint of Running Wild Publishing. In 2017, he co-founded Made in L.A. Writers, an indie-author co-op dedicated to the support and appreciation of independent authors. His startup, BookSwell, is a literary events and media production company dedicated to lifting up marginalized voices and connecting readers and writers in Southern California and beyond. He serves as a co-executive on the Board of Governors for the Editorial Freelancers Association, as the treasurer for the LGBTQ+ Editors Association, and as a board member at APLA Health.

Connect

You can read more about the events that set Victor's journey in motion in "Believe and Live," a short story set during the Carmichael massacre. Subscribe to my newsletter for a free copy at codysisco.com/contact/.

Indie authors depend on word of mouth. Please consider leaving a review at the retailer where you purchased *Broken Mirror*, Goodreads, or other platforms. You can find links on my website at codysisco.com/books/#Broken-Mirror.

The story that began in *Broken Mirror* continues in *Tortured Echoes*. Read more at codysisco.com/books/#Tortured-Echoes. The first chapter follows.

Excerpt from *Tortured Echoes*

Two Classification nurses in blue coveralls brought Samuel Miller onstage. He moved in a kind of lurching hobble, his wrists and ankles shackled with carbon fiber cables. His eyes gazed forward, witless. The Personil had had the intended effect.

A quiet murmur threaded through the crowd that had assembled in the National Theater as the nurses led Samuel into a steel-barred cage.

Mía Barrias stood offstage next to the folds of a gold-and-blue striped curtain, watching the nurses affix a biometric lock joining the cable to an eye bolt protruding from the stage. They checked his restraints again.

"You don't need to be gentle," Mía said into the small voicecap pinned to her collar. "He can't feel a thing."

The nurses' sonobulbs relayed her comments to their ears. One of the nurses glanced her way and nodded.

Samuel Miller's arms hung limply at his sides. To a casual observer, he would have resembled a wax figure in a museum of the macabre. *Come look at the madman of SeCa. Gaze in astonishment and revile him.*

The nurses left the cage and locked the door. A loud clang resounded though the theater. The crowd was silent for a moment, seemed to draw a collective breath, and then erupted in shouts, shrieks, and catcalls of obscenities.

Their howling wasn't a surprise, but its strength startled Mía. Thirty years after the Carmichael Massacre and the people of Semiautonomous California still picked at their scabs. She didn't blame them. Samuel had been the source of so much of her own anguish that even now, decades later, her mouth filled with venom on seeing him. He was older and wrinkled now, blank eyes reflecting a blank mind, but the monster who'd killed her husband on their honeymoon, and hundreds of others, was still in there somewhere. She knew it.

The ruckus went on for some time, survivors and victims' families making themselves heard with force and energy. Mía waited for them to calm down before giving her remarks. This was their good-bye, a final send-off, and it shouldn't be rushed. Samuel Miller's custody was being remanded from SeCa's Classification Commission to BioScan. Soon he would be moved to a facility in the Louisiana Territories, where the research into mirror resonance syndrome that had been on hold for two decades could begin again. Everyone would benefit.

She checked that no one was looking and pulled a tiny pliable flask like a jellyfish from her boot. Bourbon. If there was one consolation prize for moving to the LTs to supervise Samuel's care, it was being closer to the source of her favorite medication. She swigged what was left, wiped her mouth, tucked the flask back in her boot, and walked onstage.

Like a switch had been flipped, the crowd's jeers transformed into cheers and applause. She waved to the audience as she approached the cage, then turned to stare into Samuel's dark brown eyes from a few paces away. Nothing going on in there, thanks to a quadruple dose of Personil. He looked younger than his fifty-something years close up. Though his eyes were open and he blinked every few seconds, she didn't see a single spark of consciousness, exactly as the Commission board had agreed—they weren't putting him in front of a SeCa audience with anything less than total cognitive suspension.

Still, she knew this wasn't entirely true. Somewhere, deep in his brain, sensations were registering, although they would most likely fade without becoming memories. Maybe later he would wonder why his wrists hurt. Not now.

She turned to face the crowd. The cheers intensified. She was their hero. The woman who'd escaped Carmichael—and returned with help. No. The terrified woman who'd run away. She'd tried to correct them countless times, but no one would hear of it. She'd made investigating Samuel Miller and others with mirror resonance syndrome her life's work, created the Classification Commission, and put a stop to the bloodshed. She was their hero.

Mía stood at the podium and spoke. The lines were the same as always, her canned speech that for decades had functioned like a healing ritual. *What happened to me in Carmichael. How I escaped. What I vowed to do*. Men and women in the audience were crying, faces upturned.

Now she came to the pivot point, a new line. An untested one.

"Today marks a new era for SeCa. We are ready to move on."

Lately she'd been wondering if, after all that had happened, she'd led SeCa down the wrong path. The Classification Commission had been designed to protect the populace, to make them feel secure, and to return them to a society free from violence. But if the people's pain persisted after so much time, perhaps they hadn't been healing. Perhaps instead their rituals normalized victimhood and fetishized the stigmatization of Broken Mirrors.

"The people of SeCa are unfortunately familiar with the dangers of mirror resonance syndrome," Mía said, "and they have worked diligently to create a society free from fear. I'm here to tell you today: we no longer need to carry our burden alone. Samuel Miller and a portion of our MRS patients will be transferred to the Louisiana Territories, where they will remain in the custody of BioScan. For this, we are grateful."

As Mía wrapped up her remarks, she noticed that the survivors and victims' families were lining up on a wooden ramp that led from the hall to the stage. The first five in line were in wheelchairs.

She had gotten to know all of them over the years. The woman whose sister had died in the gazebo. The mother of the boy whose house had been obliterated in front of Mía's eyes. The brother and sister who'd lost their parents to rampaging autocabs.

As Mía watched, the first several groups approached the cage and leered at Samuel. A few even spat through the bars. Broken Mirrors in SeCa had always created a spectacle—providing people with an outlet for their fear and anger served a specific purpose after Carmichael. Now she wondered whether the people of SeCa could move on. Was today helping? The Classification Commission couldn't just whisk Samuel away. They'd decided that the people needed closure. One last ritual.

Mía wished Jefferson Eastmore was here to assuage her doubts. He would have cleared his calendar to attend if he were still alive. Oddly, today there were no Eastmores in the audience, but then, they would have added a gloss to the event that wouldn't have entirely been welcome. The Eastmores somehow always attracted attention, even when they didn't seek it out.

A commotion in the audience drew her gaze. Security officers in black-and-green uniforms surrounded someone in the queue. The stage manager's voice whispered through the sonobulb in her ear, "They confiscated a stunstick. The man is demanding they let him continue anyway."

"Fine, let him approach—but with an escort," she said.

Are our enemies our own creations? was a question Mía hadn't thought to ask until it was too late. Worse, what if your enemies were powerless—guiltless even—and yet you punished them all the same?

Samuel deserved every insult heaped on him. But what about the rest? They needed a fresh start. That's what she was working toward, why today mattered so much. A fresh start for her and for people with MRS everywhere.

"Murderer!" The shout came from a woman standing in front of the cage, her hands gripping the bars, shaking so hard, Mía was surprised the whole apparatus didn't rattle.

Samuel stood there, shackled, medicated. His mouth opened, and a low moan escaped.

Mía hurried to the cage, leaned into the steel bars, and looked closely. Samuel's gaze met hers as another moan, a long rolling O, came out. He was coming to.

"Get him offstage," Mía said into her voicecap.

The people in line started to bunch up, rushing the cage, reaching through the bars.

"He's awake!" someone cried. "The bastard can hear us!"

"Ghosts," Samuel said, his voice ragged and gurgling.

"Sicko Samuel," a woman yelled, and the crowd took up the chant. "Sicko Samuel! Sicko Samuel!"

"Ghosts! You're all ghosts!" Samuel shouted. He lunged forward and fell, pulled up short by the restraints.

Security officers were pouring onstage from the wings, holding back the crowd so the nurses could remove Samuel from the cage. The stage manager bounded over to Mía, pony tail bucking, and escorted her offstage. She resisted. "Turn up my volume," she said. He did.

"Please remain calm," she pleaded.

No one seemed to hear her. People started pelting Samuel, the nurses, the security officers with objects: MeshBits, bottles of nail polish, keys, whatever they could pull from their pockets.

"Shut the whole thing down," she told the stage manager. But he was no longer in charge. Security officers were trying to push people back down the ramp. Trinkets and trash flew onto the stage. Mía ripped off her sonobulb and voicecap, found a door marked "Emergency Exit," and hustled down a hallway to another door.

Then she was outside, catching her breath.

The fog had already rolled in, and the air was filled with the sounds of engines, people shouting. She rounded the corner and stopped, dumbstruck.

Thousands of people were assembled at the steps to the National Theater, their disparate chants rising and falling. Police in riot gear were struggling to establish a barricade. She checked—this was not getting Mesh coverage. Sirens came from the direction of City Lake, echoing through the canyons of skyscrapers. The sea of people in front of the theater surged against the barricades. Mía walked closer, approaching the battle lines from an odd angle.

A policewoman stopped her.

"What do they want?" Mía asked.

"Blood."

The officer pointed to a statue of Jefferson Eastmore at the center of a plaza across the street. The statue's hands held a DNA molecule styled to resemble Hermes's serpent-entwined Rod of Caduceus. At its base was a platform of wooden pallets. A noose swung from the rod several meters over the pavement.

The policewoman's mouth twisted in derision. "Can't say I blame them." She looked at Mía and seemed to recognize her. She blanched, opened her mouth: "Excuse me, I'm so sorry. I didn't realize who you—I'm so sorry."

Mía thought to ask if the crowd would be a problem, if she should do something to secure Samuel's passage out of the city. Had they gotten him offstage?

The crowd's plaintive cries washed over her.

"Don't let the murderer escape!"

"Justice before mercy!"

"Death to Broken Mirrors!"

Mía's throat burned. Tear gas somewhere nearby.

Her MeshBit vibrated. *Prisoner secured*, the message read.

She shook her head, turned away. She'd done enough to make SeCa what it was. She could do no more. It was time to start over somewhere else. She would do better this time.

Want to read Tortured Echoes?

Visit codysisco.com/books/#Tortured-Echoes

Printed in the USA
CPSIA information can be obtained
at www.ICGtesting.com
CBHW030701180624
10244CB00004B/6

9 781953 954077